TO LEAVE A MEMORY

A Warm Coming Together

PAT DUNLAP EVANS

PUBLISHER'S NOTES

Copyright © 2015 Pat Dunlap Evans
Revised June 8, 2025 (minor text corrections and bio update)
Published in the United States of America by A.M. Chai Literary

Cover Assistance: Pam Boyd Roberts
Cover Photo: © Zurijeta/Shutterstock

ISBN: 978-0-9968822-0-0 (Paperback)
ISBN: 978-0-9968822-1-7 (Kindle)
ISBN: 978-0-9968822-4-8 (E-Pub)

DEDICATION

In memory of James C. McKinley
University of Missouri at Kansas City
A fine teacher, author, and drinking pal.
You started this.

PROLOGUE

"The bitterest tears shed over graves are for words left unsaid and deeds left undone."

— **Harriet Beecher Stowe**, from *Little Foxes: Or, the Insignificant Little Habits Which Mar Domestic Happiness*

Chapter One

NOVEMBER 5

S omething to read might silence the memories. Especially in the wee hours, as El Niño pounds the roof Andrew has shared with Lizzy for fifty-plus years.

He shuffles about the dark living room in his untied red terry robe and worn leather slippers. Here and there, he points a penlight to light his way.

Through a picture window, lightning cracks an iridescent web across foreboding clouds. Andrew counts one-one-thousand, two-one-thousand, then three and four, until a distant rumble punctuates the rain's drumming.

Andrew nods in agreement. *A good four miles away.*

In the bookcase, a fat, ragged yearbook catches his eye. His fingers scan embossed letters that spell out, "Campus, Emory University." He flips through to a black-and-white photo.

What a fair-haired young man, so confident of his future. He would marry Elizabeth Montague — he calls her Lizzy — a lovely Kappa pledge, and they would have a big house with long porches in front and back so the couple could watch their children play. And Andrew would be an academic star whose history books headline the *New York Times* bestseller lists.

He whispers with a smirk. "That was the plan, anyway."

He turns to Lizzy's page in the sophomore section and caresses her cheeks with his aged fingers. To him, she looks like Joanne Woodward, a Georgia-born film star of that era, although Andrew's collegiate photo of Lizzy is too prim and proper to be a sexy pin-up.

A smile flutters as Andrew remembers kissing Lizzy's lips, touching her hair, and taking her hand. As he pats her photo in fond recollection, a yellowed invitation falls from the yearbook's back cover. Andrew strains to pick it up.

"Atlanta Country Club Spring Dance," the faded script heralds in a drawl.

His lips curl into a smile. "Ah, the dance. Such youthful passions."

He fondly strokes the embossed letters and slips the invitation back, but discovers an ancient sheath of tissue pressed over a flattened corsage.

He lifts the fragile tissue and pats the crinkled petals. The faded ribbons are colorless in the penlight, but Andrew knows they once were aqua. His eyes mist.

"In spite of everything, she's kept it all these years."

Chapter Two

TURN AROUND

A young mother caresses her baby's peach fuzz hair and rocks him to a drowsy lullaby.

"Too-ra-loo-ra-loo-ral, Too-ra-loo-ra-li, Too-ra-loo-ra-loo-ral, Hush now — "

Her sweet song drifts into a murmur as her eyelids flutter. On the border of sleep, a vision transports her to a mystical highway, where rain falls in dark rivers, lightning forks across the clouds, and thunderclaps shake the earth.

Suddenly, a sedan roars by in a blur. Through its rear window, the young mother sees a navy blue and white letter jacket on the hardtop's back deck. As the car speeds around a turn, lightning strikes the highway centerline. Tires slide on wet pavement. In REM state, the young mother hears a sickening crunch as the car rolls into a ditch. Debris clangs on the asphalt and thuds as it hits the soggy ground. The letter jacket lands on the pavement. Rain pelts a white leather sleeve.

The young mother jolts awake and strains to escape the vision. Fearfully, she holds her baby so tightly, he wakes and cries.

Too many years later, a melancholy Lizzy turns and gathers the bed covers more tightly.

Andrew is wandering the house again.

She feels the same deep ache. There seems no way to right the terrible wrong.

Through the blinds, she sees a flash. She waits until God's thunder confirms what she knows to be true.

"You're right," Lizzy whispers. "Time to turn my life around."

Chapter Three

NOVEMBER 6

R ain or shine, Lizzy zealously reserved Saturday mornings for
visits from her three grandchildren and daughter Jane, who
live several streets over in Atlanta's Druid Hills. This Saturday, Lizzy
wielded a broad cast-iron skillet as she fried thick bacon over gas
flames. Just turned seventy-one, she was in much better health than
Andrew and had kept her figure, in a curvy, senior-citizen way.

"I'm so glad the rain stopped. That soggy, old gravel driveway —
" Lizzy said, loud enough for Andrew to hear.

There she goes again about the gravel driveway.

Andrew scowled as he pretended to read the *Atlanta Journal-
Constitution* at a round breakfast table, nestled in the curve of wide
bay windows. Even if he found Lizzy's culinary hubbub annoying, he
admired her determination. Good luck to anyone who got in the
way of preparing Saturday breakfast for Jane and the grandkids.

He stole a glance to watch Lizzy's hips as she turned the bacon
strips. Years had passed since he'd followed through on any romantic
notions, but Lizzy's shapeliness still stirred his desire. He felt a tingle
rise under his red terry robe and grinned.

Lizzy turned the burner to its lowest setting. "These thick slices
take forever to get crisp, but the kids don't like bacon when it's even

a bit too brown. Now, let's see, I need eggs, milk, and cheese for the strata."

Andrew rarely replied to her one-sided murmur. He knew it got her goat. Besides, he had no desire to endure the morning's breakfast of bothersome grandchildren and gossipy women. His manuscript and his aging red setter Walter awaited him out back. When Lizzy went to the refrigerator, he took advantage of her distraction and snagged two powdered cake doughnuts from a box on the table. He slid each into a robe pocket.

With a woman's intuition that bordered on psychic vision, Lizzy whirled, carton of eggs in one hand, quart of milk, and cheese in the other, then froze Andrew with a glare.

"Those are for the grandkids. You know you're supposed to watch your fat and sugar intake. And now that you've got my attention, you'll need to get dressed before Jane and the kids get here. Just stick that filthy robe in the laundry bin. You both are overdue for a good bath."

With a huff, Andrew put the doughnuts back. Irritated that Lizzy had caught him, he silently feigned interest in something out the back window.

She sighed, exasperated, hoping to get a word back.

Instead, Andrew peered outside at nothing until even he could not keep up the silence. He tapped on the window. Within seconds, Walter plopped two muddy paws on the center pane.

Andrew called loudly, "Walter, I'll be out in a few." Then, to Lizzy, he muttered, "The old boy is a mess after El Niño's fury last night. If you'd let him stay inside instead of having to cower in his doghouse — "

"You bought that doghouse so Walter could stay dry when it storms. He's a dog, and that's his house."

"But when he comes out to do his business, he gets muddy. So, now I have to clean the window."

"The dog jumped on the window because you tapped it."

Andrew hated when Lizzy had him in a corner.

"Please, Andrew, can't you at least say hello to your daughter and grandchildren before you use some excuse to vanish?"

Andrew tapped the window again.

Walter obliged with another pair of muddy paws.

Andrew heard Lizzy sigh in frustration, but he ignored her. Just like he avoided most issues, especially the one that had remained between them for years, ever since —

Oh, there it was again. The pain.

The divide between them was hers to endure and his to bridge.

TIRES CRUNCHED on gravel as Jane's hybrid minivan pulled in. Out piled three squabbling kids bundled in jackets, hats, boots, and gloves, since the weather was illogically cold for early November.

Age twelve, Billy Jay was first out, followed by his younger brother David, age ten, and little Elizabeth, eight.

"David, you can't call shotgun for the ride home. You rode shotgun last night."

"Naw, I didn't. Elizabeth rode shotgun, didn't she, Mom?" David whined.

Elizabeth screeched toward the driver's side. "Mommy, David's lying again."

Abruptly, the minivan door opened, and a frowning, frazzle-haired Jane slid out. Mid-forty but lean and athletic from frequent jogging with her husband Alan, she slammed her door for emphasis. "Billy Jay, David, Elizabeth, hush. Gizzy will be irritated."

Billy Jay shook his head and laughed. "Gizzy's always irritated."

Jane could not resist a smile as she shooed the kids to the porch.

SET back from the street in the affluent area of Druid Hills, Andrew and Lizzy's house was a sprawling, beige-brick ranch with long covered porches across the front and back. All around, generations of yuppies had refurbished similar-era houses, some of which were featured on annual benefit tours. But too much around Lizzy and Andrew's property had been new long ago. The vibrant robin's egg-colored trim had faded to gray. The primrose jasmine Lizzy planted to brighten the front yard with yellow flowers was now so overgrown, she could not see her neighbors' home across the street. The gravel driveway had never been converted to the brick Lizzy always asked Andrew to have installed. And out back, leaves from another autumn rested in soggy layers.

Like most elderly couples, Andrew and Lizzy had their territories set out. For her, that was the spacious kitchen where she whipped up meals with a passion, or her "sunroom," as she called it, one of the original back bedrooms that was now used as Lizzy's office. Both the kitchen and sunroom overlooked the expansive, overgrown backyard.

Andrew's territory was his workshop, an aluminum-sided building he erected decades ago to escape the chaos of their two toddlers. Then an associate history professor at nearby Emory University, he had come home one evening with a lecture to prepare but found every room cluttered with primary-colored toys and two hysterical children who wanted something *other* than their toys.

Andrew cowered in the hall bathroom to finish his work. Then, the next morning, he drove to a dealer on Route 403, and before Lizzy could say, "Bacon," the biggest aluminum-sided, steel-framed building Andrew could find had landed on a concrete pad in Lizzy's backyard.

She absolutely hated the sight of "that rocket barn," as she came to call it. The afternoon sun glanced off its aluminum siding in a beam "as bright as a rocket launch." Indeed, each afternoon a blinding ray shot through the windows of Lizzy's sunroom and glanced in a flash off the large oval mirror above her desk.

Following Andrew out to the backyard, Lizzy pleaded, "Why not paint the workshop a robin's egg blue like our trim? That would coordinate things a bit."

Andrew countered that a pale color might reflect as much light as the aluminum, so he suggested a dark brown.

"Not some doo-doo brown."

"How about black?" Andrew chuckled, knowing Lizzy would not like that, either.

"You've got to be kidding," she fumed, then went back inside.

And so, the workshop remained Andrew's reflective fortress.

ANDREW HEARD Jane's car door slam and looked to see if Lizzy heard it too, but she was beating eggs in a big aqua bowl while keeping a stern eye on the bacon. As quietly as he could, Andrew slid back his creaky chair to escape. But, *darn those kids*, the doorbell rang and rang.

"Oh dear, they're here so early! Can you get the door?"

Andrew flashed open his robe, smiling in a dare. "I'm still in my robe and not much else."

Lizzy shot him a look. "Not much else is right."

Andrew did not counter. He had planned his next move.

ON THE FRONT PORCH, the kids jostled to see whose fingers could press the doorbell the most times to make it ding, a-ding, a-ding.

"Enough, kids. I said, enough!" Jane shouted above the din, but the kids giggled louder. With a resigned smile, Jane let them play on. This was the only contest Elizabeth usually won. Smaller, she could weasel between her brothers to ding, a-ding, a-ding.

IN THE KITCHEN, Lizzy's glare aimed to penetrate Andrew's persistent wall of inaction. He felt her stare but only leaned nearer the window, as if the glass were his shield.

"Oh, I give up. You go do what you want out in that rocket barn." She wiped her hands and bustled toward the living room.

Andrew habitually craned to catch sight of her hips as she sashayed down the hall in her patio dress. As her footsteps quieted on the living room carpet, Andrew imagined her walking by the baby grand piano, where she would gently pat one or two of the many treasured photos in elaborate frames. Here, each grandchild posed with an angelic smile. Billy Jay, David, and Elizabeth. And their mother Jane, a frizzy-haired college graduate in one pose, and a lovely bride with ironed hair in another.

Just beyond stood Lizzy's wedding portrait, alongside a high school photo of Billy. Not the oldest grandson, Billy Jay, but William Montague Ward, Andrew, and Lizzy's son. Blue-eyed and golden-haired, his big smile shone above his navy blue and white letter jacket.

FROM THE KITCHEN, Andrew heard Lizzy open the front door. He strained to hear the tenor of the visitors' voices, mostly the high notes of the children and women, except for Billy Jay's hoarse baritone that too-often squeaked to boy's soprano. A wee part of Andrew wanted to join this morning's fun, but the greater part compelled him to flee.

Andrew heard Lizzy croon the same tune she sang every Saturday.

"Hellooooo. How are my favorite grandkids? And how's my favorite daughter?"

"I'm your only daughter, Momma," Jane dutifully replied, followed by little Elizabeth's recitation, "And we're your only grandkids, Gizzy!"

"And we're your only grandkids, Gizzy," Andrew whispered to himself in the kitchen. "Those skunks will be here within sixty seconds. I gotta get moving." He grabbed two fat, powdered doughnuts, stuffed them in his pockets, and scooted out the back door. His red robe flapped in the breeze.

Soggy from the rain, Walter barked ecstatically and jumped on Andrew's exposed chest. He raised an arm to keep the muddy dog in check. "Down, boy. You might snag my dick with those paws. 'Lizzy make you stay out last night? Let's head to my doghouse. I'll crank up the heater and dry you off."

Walter bounded ahead on the stone path, then up the steps, where he panted and paced until Andrew unlocked the workshop's glass-paned door.

Once inside, Andrew exhaled in relief. This was his lair. All around were remnants of his career. Stacks of thick history textbooks, ten of which he had written, albeit not one on the *Times* bestseller list, and beside them stacked boxes of students' term papers and racks of magazines in which Andrew had published articles. Along one wall, a battered sofa sagged from decades of naps, and the coffee table was littered with empty Cracker Jack boxes. Throughout the room, balls of crushed paper had landed on boxes and lampshades.

Clearly, Andrew's den had never felt the touch of Lizzy's feather duster. He rarely attempted to organize the files on his massive pine desk, although he occasionally cleaned his red 1961 IBM Selectric typewriter, a remnant from Emory. He loved that machine, a marvel in its day. The first model that used a type ball to imprint letters to strike the page. He loved to watch the ball jump and turn, snap a letter onto the page, then poise to await Andrew's next keystroke. And the Selectric had a return key instead of a metal handle.

By the time Andrew retired, everyone else was using computers, so no one even noticed when he took his red typewriter home. Although Jane had bought him an iMac last Christmas, the white box sat unopened on a dusty credenza behind Andrew's frayed leather chair.

"We made it, boy! The harem cannot take what the harem cannot see." Andrew held a doughnut high for Walter. The old dog hesitated. "Come on, Walter. We can still get it up!"

As if the dog got the joke, he gleefully sprang and chomped the powdery treat.

Andrew got a kick out of that. "Sweet revenge. None of that diet talk in here." He mimicked Lizzy, "You've got to watch your fat and sugar intake."

Andrew bit into his doughnut with a glint of vengeance. Sugar dusted his gray muzzle as the old man and aged dog relished their doughnuts in peace.

~

In a flurry, Lizzy helped Jane and the kids stow their jackets, hats, and gloves.

Little Elizabeth snuggled close to her grandmother's hip. "I'm freezing, Gizzy."

"You're a weenie, Elizabeth!" Billy Jay scoffed. With coffee-colored hair and ginger snap eyes, he did not look one bit like the portrait of his namesake Uncle Billy on the piano.

"Be kind to your sister. Treasure each other. You never know when — " Lizzy trailed off as she realized where her thoughts were headed. She changed the subject. "Come see what Gizzy's cooking. I found a recipe for a new dish called a 'strata'." She sniffed the air, and her face fell in distress. "Oh dear, Janey, I left the bacon on the burner!"

A black fog spewed from the skillet as Lizzy and Jane flew into the kitchen. While Jane pulled a cord to turn on the overhead fan, Lizzy grabbed hot pads and yanked the pan off the stove. Then she poured spewing black grease into an empty coffee can she kept at the back of the stove. "Darn. I'll have to start all over."

"We've got all morning, Momma. Like always, every F-ing Saturday." Jane smiled to soften what had sounded more biting than she intended.

Lizzy gave Jane a stern look, then pushed open the windows above the sink. "I know it's chilly, but we've got to get this smoke out of here."

"Not to worry, Momma. Just turn on the exhaust."

As the smoke cleared, Lizzy got out the makings for virgin mimosas for the kids and champagne mimosas in tall flutes for Jane and herself. Lizzy poured a bit more in her glass than her daughter's and, with a silent toast, Lizzy took a deep sip before she restarted breakfast with a fresh pack of bacon.

At the round table, the kids squabbled over which piece to place for the Giant Panda jigsaw puzzle Jane had brought, since Lizzy and Andrew's house did not have the Internet. Although the kids could still use their smartphones, Jane had issued an edict for Saturday breakfasts. Solve puzzles the way Jane learned long ago at that same table before computers took over her life.

As the kids settled in, Jane took a seat on a stool next to the range. She knew better than to ask if she could help. This was Lizzy's show. Besides, she found her mother's fluster amusing.

"Where's Poppa this morning?" Jane baited.

Lizzy's eyes flitted toward the back door, but she tried to mask her dismay. "That rascal escaped to work on his manuscript again. You know, the novel I told you about. He's dredged up all sorts of records. Says his ancestors were gold miners up near Dahlonega. He's the history professor. I suppose we have to believe him."

"There's a wealth of genealogy online if you would just get connected. Is he at least using the iMac to write?"

"What's an iMac?"

"A computer, Momma. The one I gave Poppa last year."

"How would I know? I haven't been inside that horrid rocket barn since it landed."

"You should go out there. See what he's written."

"That's his cave. I read that book about Mars and Venus."

"You and Poppa still not getting along?"

"Not getting it is more like it." Lizzy shook her head before she took another long sip.

"Momma! The kids."

"Oh, better the kids learn about life now than have reality kick 'em in the head when they're forty."

"Momma — " Jane caught herself. She did not want to go down this road. It always led to her big brother Billy dying.

The mimosa had lowered Lizzy's inhibitions, but she did not say more. Not about Billy. Still, she wondered if now was the right time to tell her daughter her news. She sighed at the weight of it. There was so much to plan and consider.

Lizzy had decided to leave Andrew. She had saved for years, ever since he stopped holding her at night. Ever since his weary eyes continually avoided hers. Ever since his guilt became impenetrable silence or sarcastic retorts. But to announce her decision would mean that Lizzy would have to go through with it. Leave her husband and home, not just fantasize about the idea. With a modest IRA and minimum Social Security, she could afford a small place. Maybe a room in a home near Jane and the kids. But she could not afford anything as spacious as this home she had roamed for fifty years. Still, sacrifices would be needed for her to escape the void of marriage to a man whose sullenness she could no longer endure.

She took a breath to tell her daughter, but nothing came out. Maybe this was not the best time. As Jane had cautioned earlier, "Mom. The kids."

Well into mid-morning, Andrew sat in his untied robe and chattered aloud in a practiced patter to Walter, although the dog had drifted into a deep snore as Andrew researched copies of records in a folder labeled "Georgia Family Tree." The file rested beside several typed pages of a manuscript titled, "*To Leave A Memory, a Novel and Apologia,*" by Andrew Comstock Ward."

When Andrew took a break and leaned back in his chair, his head bumped the dusty iMac box behind him on the credenza.

"Jane and her contraptions. Walter, how could a systems analyst like my daughter appreciate the relationship an author shares with his writing instrument? Long before the typewriter, marvelous works flowed from rudimentary implements, even chisels on stone, paint on fingers, and plant juice on bird feathers. Did Proust need a computer to write *Remembrance of Things Past* or, as they now call it, *In Search of Lost Time?*"

At the sound of Walter's name, the dog exhaled in apparent agreement and curled more tightly around Andrew's ankles.

After giving the dog a loving stroke, Andrew loaded a page into his red Selectric.

"Mind you, I'm not trying to rewrite history. Life is made of decisions, good, bad, or ineffectual. What concerns me is how to leave a memory, one that will be precisely as I saw it. All Lizzy can see are reflections on that two-sided mirror between us. But how can I show her what has passed through my separate eyes?"

Andrew's reverie transported him to the long-ago dance when Lizzy was twenty-one, dolled up in an aqua taffeta sundress, adorned with a white orchid corsage with matching aqua ribbons. Andrew was in graduate school while Lizzy was a junior English major with a minor in education.

On the bandstand, a singer in a blue tuxedo crooned a Pat Boone song, "April Love," one of Lizzy's favorite oldies. Andrew and Lizzy slow-danced until he twirled her away, like he had seen dancers do on *American Bandstand.* Just before he guided her back into his embrace, she blushed, breathless. Somewhere within Andrew's brain, a synapse captured that image of Lizzy. Forever after, that was how he remembered her.

"The way she looked when we were young." Andrew recalled the bounce of her blond bob and the glow of her gold-green eyes. Passionate promise. But this image suddenly vanished, replaced by a recalcitrant vision, perhaps because Billy's birthday had been that past Wednesday, a day that passed without comment between Andrew and Lizzy, although each had remembered it and retreated further from the other.

"Or how it was the night our Billy died," he murmured aloud. "Stormed all day, remember, Lizzy? Black-green sky. Day dark as night. The lights went out, and bolts of blue-white lightning were our only illumination, except for the candles you lit here and there.

The flames reflected gold on the walls as our shadows followed us to the living room."

In Andrew's memory, Billy had donned his letter jacket, his name proudly embroidered in gold on a white sleeve. A senior football star, he and his buddies were heading to see their basketball team play in Marietta, up the highway from Atlanta.

Lizzy had fretted all afternoon. As Billy got ready to leave, she timidly reminded Andrew of the premonition she'd had when Billy was a baby. "I know you think it was just a nightmare, but we'd be foolish to tempt fate in such a storm." As she spoke, she put her arm around young "Janey," whose eyes brimmed with fearful tears. "Please don't let Billy go."

Andrew dismissed Lizzy's concerns with a fond pat. "Storm's headed east. No worries. It'll be long gone by the time the boys get to Marietta."

Billy hugged his mother and promised he would be fine. He shook his dad's hand as the two males dismissed the fears of a woman whose gut screamed she was right, although she silently prayed she was wrong.

Andrew's voice echoed off the workshop's metal walls. "Billy pulled on his jacket. You pleaded again not to let him go. But I got angry and said, 'Phooey to your woman's intuition, don't be such a mother hen,' remember?"

"Billy hesitated at the door. Patted his pockets. No keys. I fumbled through mine and lifted them like a prize. Billy and I laughed. Your fingers pressed to your lips. What else could you do? My male mind was made up. And Billy wasn't about to tell his pals that Mommy wouldn't let him go. When he waved goodbye, just like that — " Andrew snapped his fingers.

Walter startled from his snooze, expecting it was time to go out.

Andrew calmed the dog as he recited his daily memory to his wife, to himself. "He was gone, Lizzy. Just like that. Our boy. Even in that dim light, I remember him in colors. That navy blue-and-white jacket he was so proud of. Golden hair, cheeks rosy with excitement, eyes bright as opals above his starched white shirt and black jeans. How brilliant the colors of his life swirled into that black-green night, while you, Janey, and I watched him vanish."

Andrew silently recollected how a police officer had stood in the living room that night as Andrew and Lizzy held one another and sobbed, their anguish so intense he thought he might disintegrate, and wished he could have erased himself but for his duty to Lizzy and Jane.

Yes, he had been wrong, but he never said, "I'm sorry." And forever after came the wall between them. Oh, if they could turn back the clock. What would each have said then?

Andrew pressed back tears and leaned to touch Walter, who arched to accept the caress and licked his master on his bare thigh.

LIZZY DID NOT HAVE time to make the fancy strata, so she served bacon, cheesy scrambled eggs, and the box of assorted doughnuts, minus two powdered ones, along with another mimosa for herself and Jane. To Lizzy's relief, her grandchildren gobbled their eggs, scarfed down one doughnut apiece, and went back to their puzzle. But perhaps things were too comfortable for Jane.

"So, how long will the civil war with Poppa last? Until death do you part?"

"Civil war?" Lizzy snapped back.

"Momma, you know."

"Well, Dear Abby, how should one behave if, God forbid, death takes one of your children?" Lizzy turned to empty plates and hoped Jane would let that go unanswered.

"I wouldn't let it ruin my marriage."

"Darn it, Janey. Stop pressing. Andrew's and my marriage is our business, not yours."

Jane softened. "But where did Poppa go? After Billy died, it was as though I didn't even have a father. Still don't. He's always behind that aluminum wall in the backyard."

"I'm not the one who put that up."

"You might be the one who has to open the door."

Lizzy grew exasperated. "Every year, when Billy's birthday rolls around to remind us that Andrew let him go, you peck, peck, peck. Why don't you say these things to your father? He'd let you go on, say something sarcastic, and you'd feel like a fool. The way I feel almost every day."

"Momma — "

ANDREW BLEW his nose on stray newspapers, then rummaged through his "Georgia Family Tree" folder. He pulled out a deed from his great-grandfather's parcel near Dahlonega, Georgia, the family gold mine, or at least that was the tale told through several generations. The year of purchase was 1889, more than sixty years after North America's first gold rush had stormed through Dahlonega and the nearby town of Auraria.

"Walter, long before Spaniard Hernando De Soto arrived to search for gold in the 1540s, the local Cherokee tribe had mined gold in the surrounding hills. In fact, 'Dahlonega' was a Cherokee word for 'yellow' or 'gold.'

"English colonists also mined gold in the area during the early 1810s. But in 1828, a white hunter named Benjamin Parks tipped over a rock on the Cherokee reservation and found the prized stone full of gold. He told other miners, and thousands of white miners and settlers soon flooded the area. Within a few years, the Georgia legislature pressured the federal government to confiscate all Cherokee lands, and by 1838, the Cherokees were driven out on what later was called the 'Trail of Tears.'

"Wouldn't you know it, but the federal government opened a mint in Dahlonega that same year.

"A decade later, word arrived that gold had been discovered in California. In a flash, most miners headed west, but in 1880, hydraulic mining made the industry profitable again in Georgia.

"So, Walter, that's how the Cherokees got screwed, but there was still gold in 'them thar hills.' Or at least that's what the Dahlonega Mint assayer promised. And my great-grandfather took the bait."

Andrew put down his papers and typed, hunt and peck, as he struggled to bring his main character Ward Comstock to life, a retired U.S. Cavalry lieutenant with pale hair, bright blue eyes, lean frame, angular features, and high cheekbones. This description was based on a tintype Andrew discovered in a dusty box reclaimed from Grandmother Ward's attic. Her father — Andrew's great-grandfather — was Andrew's spitting image.

Next in Andrew's tale, a blond barmaid named Charlotte Gerard made her debut, described in his literary imagination exactly the way Lizzy looked when she was twenty-one. There was no genetic possibility that Andrew's great-grandmother and Lizzy could look alike, but he dismissed that detail.

"A writer needs a bit of license," he murmured to Walter.

Andrew had decided that his first chapter should begin with action to entice the reader, so he furiously hunt-pecked scenes of a bar fight between Ward and a menacing rail yard worker. After Ward won the tussle, he bragged about his mine to the frivolous Charlotte, who Ward persuaded to cash in her savings and leave for the North Georgia Mountains with him.

Andrew leaned back and stretched his hands around his neck. "Walter, is a fool born or made? If Ward Comstock and Charlotte Girard represent my great-grandparents, I might be trying to say that I inherited my foolishness genetically."

At the front door, Lizzy hugged her grandchildren and kissed each three times, with "Muhh-wahh" at the end of each smack. Then she gave Jane a light hug and a peck. Each knew better than to say what was on their minds, especially after several mimosas.

"Thanks for breakfast. I love you, Momma." Jane's tone was more a reminder, not an expression of emotion.

"See you next Saturday, dear."

As Jane and the kids drove off, Lizzy's practiced smile and wave pretended all was well, but her stomach churned. Could she do this? Leave Andrew, leave her home, and divide the family, not that the family was not divided already.

Where Lizzy would live remained the question, a small room she envisioned somewhere. She wanted windows so she could see outside. But there would be no expansive kitchen for her to host her grandchildren, no space for a piano to display her many photos, no bookcases for her cherished scrapbooks and yearbooks. In exchange, there would be no meals to cook, no laundry to do, no husband to ignore her. In many ways, her life would change for the better, but would such a limited existence be the right move?

Back in the kitchen, she poured a glass of champagne — to heck with the orange juice — and wiped the skillet dry.

OVER THE REMAINS of a Saturday evening spaghetti dinner, Jane and her husband Alan sat at a sleek metallic dining table, surrounded by tall leather and nail-head chairs. Breakfast, lunch, or dinner, the family dined in this expansive room because Jane's latest puzzle was usually stretched across the breakfast table near the kitchen.

Besides, Alan enjoyed looking at their groomed front lawn. Darkly attractive, he was a tax attorney, consulting to some of Atlanta's major corporations. To befit his stature, he had renovated their two-story mansion several years before. He wanted a house that made a statement, but Jane had been so busy with her career and the kids' schedules, Alan called a top-rated architect and interior designer, gave each deep pockets and said, "Make it happen." Not long after, the house was selected for the socially prestigious Druid Hills Home Tour.

Saturday dinners were Jane's rare chance to reconnect with Alan after a busy week, so she scooted the kids off for TV and poured them both a second glass of the Oregon pinot noir Alan had brought up from the basement cellar.

He took a whiff. "Oregon pinots have certainly moved beyond the barnyard bouquet."

"I bet even Momma might like this one. It's a rung above her Columbia Crest Merlot."

Alan nodded, then absentmindedly asked, "How did your visit go this morning?"

"Same song and verse. Poppa hid in his workshop. Momma was defensive."

Alan quickly realized he should change the subject. "So, how about jogging the park trail Sunday morning? No work."

Jane ignored his diversion. "I just wonder how things get so polarized? My parents have been this way since I was in junior high."

Alan kicked the table leg in regret for having brought up the subject. "Jane, stop driving down the long road to tragedy. You obsess about it. I've always thought you should name one era 'B.B.D.' for 'Before Billy Died,' a second era 'A.B.D.' for 'After Billy Died,' and a third era 'A.B.B.' for 'After Billy's Birthday.' It was last Wednesday, right? I put it on my calendar, along with your menstrual cycle, so I'll know when I shouldn't press your sensitive female buttons."

"You wouldn't be so sarcastic if you had lost a brother. Just like that — " Jane snapped her fingers. Her eyes glistened. Then she picked up Alan's dishes with a telltale, angry clank.

Alan tensed. "Honey, I want to be supportive, but sometimes, you don't even need an 'era' day to get into a funk." Alan puffed in frustration. How could he regroup to the delightful moments before he'd opened his mouth? "Dare I hope time heals all wounds?"

"This kind of wound is hard to heal."

"Jane, you keep reopening it. All this stuff about your parents' relationship, Billy's death. What about our lives now?"

"Please argue with yourself. I'll do the dishes." Jane headed toward the kitchen.

"I guess that means you're not in for a 'B.S.' night?" Alan called out as she disappeared. He heard the dishes hit a counter, then Jane's footsteps as she returned to the dining room.

"'What do you mean, a 'bullshit' night?" She whispered so the kids would not hear.

"I meant a 'beasty sex' night. You be the girl beast and I'll be the boy."

"Oh, Alan, for God's sake."

"Maybe I should have said a 'capital S' night. You know, it's spelled 'S-E-X'? That thing your parents don't do anymore, but we sometimes do when you're not pissed at me. By the way, you look quite lovely tonight. Very sensual."

Jane shook her head. "No, you don't."

"What did I do now?"

"Elizabeth is having a friend sleep over."

Alan whispered, "We'll lock the door. I promise to be quiet."

"If you recall, Elizabeth was conceived the night you promised to pull out." Jane gathered more dishes and headed to the kitchen.

"I don't have to pull out anymore. We're in a whole new era. 'P.V.' Post-vasectomy."

Jane tried to ignore him, but remembered Alan's earlier comment. "How do you know my parents don't do it?"

"They're old. It's a valid assumption."

"Momma hinted at something today. I think she would like to have sex, but Poppa won't."

"Old guys have problems. That may happen to me. That's why we need to take advantage of the time we have."

"This is not about your erections."

Alan positioned a table knife like a cigar. "Enjoy one while you got it, Schweetheart."

Jane managed a resigned sigh. Annoying as Alan was, he was right. She did succumb to a blue mood about Billy's death each time a reminder came. She leaned over Alan's shoulder and took a noodle from a bowl. She configured the pasta into the shape of an "S."

Alan did his best Groucho leer. "Ah! So, we're in for a beasty sex night, after all?"

~

A MILE AWAY, Lizzy warbled a chorus of "April Love" at the piano, the old Pat Boone song she and Andrew had danced to long ago. She remembered how she later hummed that tune in her dorm room and twirled as if still dancing. As she took off her corsage, she sniffed its sweetness one last time, then gently wrapped the flowers with a tissue from the corsage box. She pressed the treasure back inside her yearbook, along with the dance invitation.

Lizzy went to the bookcase and peeked inside the yearbook. Yes, the corsage was in its honored place, although the waxed paper had loosened, and she wondered why. She gingerly lifted the frail floral to her shoulder and hummed "April Love" in a wavering contralto. As she circled the living room, she did not realize Andrew had walked in.

He chose sarcasm as a way out. "May I have the next dance?"

Lizzy's cheeks reddened. "I guess you caught me being silly. This is my old corsage, you know, from the yearbook."

"What corsage?"

"The one from the spring dance, remember?"

"That brain cell must have shriveled long ago."

She displayed the dried flowers. "Well, the corsage is still here. So am I, at least for now." Lizzy hoped Andrew might question what she meant. If he suspected she might leave, would that break through his emotional wall?

Andrew slid toward the kitchen. "Anything left of the doughnuts?"

With a resigned sigh, Lizzy refused to nag him about sugar, fat, and salt. Back when Andrew turned sixty, his cholesterol levels and blood pressure shot through the roof. So, every meal Lizzy cooked over the past fourteen years was from scratch. Low-cholesterol, no-sodium, forget the fat or cheese, much less bacon, which she loved. She dutifully prepared each meal with her husband's health in mind, but resented that growing older meant loss. Loss of beauty, sex, love, friends, eggs, cheese, whipping cream, and brie. That's why she loved to cook for her grandchildren. No food boundaries there, except Andrew always went for the leftovers.

In the living room mirror, Lizzy caught sight of her reflection. My goodness, she looked sad, even angry. She took a breath and tried to focus on her future. If she left Andrew, she could eat bacon whenever she wanted. Even brie. But despite those delights, her spirits remained dark. She felt out of synch. Something else was wrong, other than her impending separation. What she did not know. Just one of those feelings. The ache of a premonition, the inkling of fear. She tried to shake it off by giving her corsage a light kiss before placing it in its honored space inside the yearbook.

Later that night, as she and Andrew got into bed, he reached for his latest *National Geographic*. Lizzy turned out her light and curled under the floral spread. It was a remnant from her hunter-green and burgundy decorating period. With her back near Andrew but not touching, she hoped he would reach out. Stop her before she follows through with her plan.

From her position, she could not see that he was surveying her curves. He wondered if she would be interested. That is, if his equipment would cooperate. Darn thing had not held a stiffy in years, but something between them was brewing. For him, it was a yearning. Lizzy's mention of the dance and his own memories during last night's storm had sent his mind and body where even stubborn fools rush in.

Gazing down his torso, he felt the shimmer of erotic tingling but feared his blood pressure medicine would stymie any effort born of a wisp of memory. Besides, the attempt might lead to embarrassment for him and disappointment for her, something neither of them needed this week of all weeks. He sighed and settled in to read.

Lizzy heard his sigh and gave up, too. She silently recited her prayers and finished with the same line as the night before.

Dear God, please send a sign whether I should leave or stay.

∼

Across town, in a California king bed that belonged in an ad for *Interior Design* magazine, Jane and Alan made love like a couple who knew one another's needs very well.

With a satisfied smile and a throaty sigh, Alan rolled on his back, his dark furry chest damp with the sweat of exertion. "You've still got it, Schweetheart."

"For God's sake, enough with the Groucho act." Jane swatted him with her pillow but gave him a lover's smile.

T he soothing voice of a host on Lizzy's classical radio station woke her for church. "Another unseasonably cold and misty November day, thanks to our pal El Niño."

Andrew sleepily rose, grabbed his clean red robe Lizzy had insisted on laundering, and plodded out under an umbrella to get the Sunday paper.

Still in the bedroom, Lizzy got dressed in front of a stand-alone mirror that had been her grandmother's. She tugged a royal blue jacket over a black skirt that hugged her hips too tightly and peered to survey her gray-blond hair and deep wrinkles that were the image of her grandmother staring back. She reached for tweezers to pluck out a stray chin hair. She had an old-lady beard, couldn't deny it, or turn back the clock. But wouldn't it be wonderful — just for one moment — to have another twirl around the dance floor?

Now in the living room, Lizzy reached for her purse on the burgundy wingback chair, reupholstered after a long-ago fire. At that time, it was harvest gold. Billy's senior year. That was the fall Billy came home with his —

She brought herself back from the perpetual precipice.

"Oh dear, I cannot waft down that same lane. If I don't get going, I'll be late." Lizzy patted the wingback chair and Billy's photo, trying to put sad memories to rest. As she opened her umbrella and headed to the garage, she and Andrew crossed paths like characters on the lawn of a Seurat painting.

~

MOMENTS LATER, from the kitchen, Andrew heard Lizzy roar away in her vintage Jaguar. He grabbed two more of the leftover doughnuts and went out back, where Walter greeted him with barks and muddy paws on Andrew's red robe.

"Down, boy, Lizzy just washed this thing. Let's get out of this damn drizzle."

Inside the workshop, Andrew turned on the space heater, then tossed both doughnuts high. The dog caught one while the other rolled under the sofa. Walter looked puzzled. Should he enjoy the pastry in his mouth, or try to retrieve the doughnut under the sofa? He dropped the first, then rooted with his long nose and tongue to snag the second doughnut, which he downed in two bites.

"What about this one?" Andrew pointed to the first doughnut Walter had dropped.

The red setter took a few seconds to process that question, then gleefully gulped down the second pastry. He barked for more but received only a pat and grin from Andrew, who then settled at his desk. As soon as Andrew made those click-click sounds with the typewriter keys, Walter curled under the kneehole opening, surrounded Andrew's legs with his warm body, and fell to sleep with a sigh.

In the next scenes of Andrew's novel, he described the deep green and violet-crowned ridges of Northern Georgia that rose like shadowy fortresses in the eyes of his hero Ward Comstock, as he rode along a primitive road outside Atlanta, accompanied by the bar wench Charlotte Gerard.

~

To Ward's dismay, *Charlotte complained constantly about her steed and begged to rest, but Ward refused to stop until the impending dusk and cold forced the issue. He watered the animals at a nearby stream, tethered them in a grassy spot, then retrieved biscuits and jerky, which Charlotte choked down as she shivered by a small fire Ward had managed to start.*

After her meager meal, she headed over to the horses.

Ward heard Charlotte rustling about, but he could not see what she was up to until she reappeared at the fireside, dressed in her mother's lace wedding dress.

"I've no way to bind us legally as a couple," Ward protested. But Charlotte looked so lovely in that dress, and her dollar-sized nipples beckoned him through the lace. Ward froze in desire as her delicious silhouette glowed in the fire's golden flickers. He hesitated but, compelled by indefatigable lust, he vowed to Charlotte, "I, Ward Comstock, take thee Charlotte Girard as my common-law wife."

With that, Ward fell prey to the wiles of a wanton woman, then rolled on his back, spent. That distance from Atlanta, more stars than he could count were sparkling in the night. He stared at the shimmer.

'Remember this night,' Ward whispered to himself. 'Memories are like gold dust, sprinkled on a velvet sky.'

~

Andrew leaned back from his work. "That's a pretty good line, eh, Walter? And, after saying, 'I do,' my great-grandfather's goose was cooked. I guess that sounds grim, but my great-grandmother really was a bar wench, according to family lore. So, Ward got what he asked for. We all do."

He patted his "Georgia Family Tree" folder again and tried to figure out his next scene.

~

LIZZY TOOK her customary place in the third row at the Druid Hills Unitarian Universalist Church beside her lifelong best friend, Mary Louise Joseph, a Black woman everyone called "Ouisie" — an old-fashioned southern name. Stuffed inside a bright pink wool suit, Ouisie was about fifty pounds heavier than she wanted to be, with bleached and dyed short frizzy hair that was a rainbow of black, blond, and strawberry highlights.

Next to her, Ouisie's husband Guy Joseph had been óne of Andrew's colleagues at Emory. Short and slight, with salt and pepper hair, scraggly, graying goatee, and widely set dark eyes, Guy had taught African American history from the time it was first introduced until it was renamed Black history. In conversations with Lizzy, Ouisie often complained about Guy being limited by his race, while Andrew's golden-haired academic star rose to full professor, department chair, and *emeritus* status.

Privately, Ouisie nagged Guy to publish more often and press for broader responsibilities and course assignments, but Guy would reply, "My dear, even though my family's ancestors immigrated to the States from French Guiana, the current powers at Emory see me only as an African American man who should teach only Black history. Even if I published the world's greatest textbook on South America, or even ancient France, I would remain stereotyped."

Despite the men's differing races and ranks, the women had been best friends since childhood. The two couples socialized often early in their careers until Billy died. After that, social life ceased for Lizzy and Andrew, who rarely went out beyond Lizzy's Sunday church and her brunches with Ouisie, which Andrew did not attend.

A few months before this morning's service, the congregation had hired a new minister, a cherubic, balding, and bespectacled man of about fifty, who, from the remarks in his sermon, did not sound to Lizzy as if he had any spiritual faith.

"Only when we move beyond traditional beliefs in God as a supernatural being can we explore religion as mature thinkers."

Lizzy wondered if this fellow was a UU atheist, a new trend that dismayed her greatly. She couldn't understand why anyone would want to be a minister — even in a doctrine-free church — if he had no belief in some sort of "spirit of life" beyond the earthly domain.

The new minister grinned. "But these theological questions are why I work on Sundays."

During the offering, as the pianist played a Bach interlude, Lizzy's eyes centered on a bas-relief sculpture embossed on a curved white wall behind the minister's podium. Within the graceful artwork, twin circles surrounded a chalice, the symbol of the Unitarian Universalist faith. This sculpture became a point of solace after Billy's death. When Lizzy focused on the chalice's symbolism — the cyclical nature of life and the eternal flame of human faith — she felt a respite of peace.

After a rousing hymn, a layperson snuffed out a lighted flame on a brass chalice, and the congregation recited, "We extinguish this flame, but not the light of truth, the warmth of community, or the fire of commitment. These we keep in our hearts until we are together again."

Tears came to Lizzy's eyes each time she recounted those words. They were the essence of her faith, although her spiritual beliefs were far more God centered than the bulk of other Unitarian Universalists who attended that day. Some wore buttons that branded themselves as a "Jewish UU," "Atheist UU," "Humanist UU," "Wiccan UU," "Baptist UU," or another. If Lizzy had worn a button, it might have said, "Theist UU," but Lizzy would never wear a button.

At the end of the service, the black-robed minister stretched out his hands and boomed, "For those who seek God, may your God go with you. For those who embrace life, may life return your affection. And for those who seek a better path, may you find it, and the courage to take it, step by step, by step. Amen."

Lizzy felt uplifted by this new minister's benediction, but she wondered why his sermon discouraged her from seeking a spiritual God. She'd have to ask Ouisie about this later.

The service concluded with Hymn #121, "We'll Build a Land" from *Singing the Living Tradition*. The congregation sang with fervor. "We'll build a land where we bind up the broken. We'll build a land where the captives go free, where the oil of gladness dissolves all mourning. Oh, we'll build a promised land that can be. Come build a land where sisters and brothers, anointed by God, may then create peace: where justice shall roll down like waters, and peace like an ever-flowing stream."

As Lizzy sang, she concentrated anew on the bas-relief sculpture, until she remembered.

Oh dear. I'm going to leave Andrew.

~

ANDREW STARED at his still-blank page. Although he had published academic critiques and university history textbooks, admittedly with extensive research support from graduate students, not to mention the red pens of meticulous editors, he wondered if he could write a novel with the metaphorical impact, characterizations, and story line to convey his decades-overdue apology to his wife and describe to her his life's memories?

Andrew blew out a frustrated sigh.

Walter exhaled too.

"Walter, all this gold-rush paraphernalia won't amount to a row of beans unless I can craft a tale that survives my passing. People are born, live their lives, dream their dreams — despite life's disappointments — then leave behind deeds, dance invitations, and crinkled corsages. But can I spin a tale that's good enough for Lizzy to see the vivid colors of my memories?"

~

IN JANE'S EXPANSIVE BEDROOM, she pulled on faded jeans, black boots, and a chartreuse cashmere sweater for the office. She had taken on a major project to show her boss she could do it, and Monday was showtime.

Jane's competitive nature often exasperated Alan, especially when he was left to parent the kids. "You really have to go in on a Sunday?

I figured we'd go for a run and let the kids bike. I can't handle all three without you, especially Elizabeth and her wobbly training wheels."

"Honey, I've got a presentation tomorrow morning for the guy who pays my salary and the client who pays his. Meryl next door can keep an eye on the kids while you run."

"What'll she do with her other eye?"

Jane grimaced at Alan's annoying pun and started to leave, but turned to give him a flirtatious smile. "Thanks for being such a dedicated lover and a wonderful father, too."

Alan returned her smile, and his dark eyes glistened in remembrance of their beasty sex night. "Even when you're pretending, it revs my motor." Yes, he still had it. All her talk about her father had not gotten him down. He smiled at his silent pun about getting down. What he'd gotten was laid.

GUY STAYED after the service for a board meeting, so Lizzy gave Ouisie a ride to a nearby omelet cafe. Brunch after church was a tradition the two women had practiced for decades, even as far back as the late '70s, when people would stare at the black-and-white pair of females when they walked into a restaurant together.

After the server poured coffee, Ouisie eagerly started whispering so loudly that anybody could hear. "Guy says the board is upset about this new minister. The first thing he did was hire a red-headed bimbo to run the office. Her name is Margaret, and she has the biggest bosoms I've ever seen on a human being. We suspect the two were lovers before he came here."

Lizzy put a finger to her lips. "Having big boobs does not mean she's a bad person."

"One of the board members drove by the minister's apartment last week and saw this Margaret woman walking out his front door!"

"The board is spying on the minister's personal life?"

Ouisie nodded. "I went by the office to check her out. She talked on and on about her new eye shadow she can smear on in six colors."

"Eye shadow. Boobs. Surely there's more to this woman than church gossip."

"I suppose even ministers have their desires. As do I," Ouisie sighed, fanning herself with a napkin.

"I had hoped this new minister would be a spiritual leader, but his sermon and benediction were contradictory. I couldn't figure out whether he even believes in a God."

"He's a Humanist, he says. Has Andrew heard him preach?"

"You know Andrew has not been to church since — "

"Oh, I get so wound up in my world, I forget about yours."

"Well, my world is getting complicated. I want to tell you something, but you must keep it secret, not even tell Guy."

Ouisie's eyes widened. Not only did she thrive on gossip, but also, she also loved secrets, although keeping them was not one of her best traits.

"You know you can tell me anything," Ouisie promised, but Lizzy hesitated in sudden avoidance. If she said this thing aloud, that meant she had to do it. She decided to temper her announcement.

"Ouisie, you and I have talked about my problems with Andrew. He is so stubborn that nothing can change. But time is passing, and when I look in the mirror, I see my sad grandmother staring back."

"Are you seeing a ghost? Another premonition?"

"No. I see my grandmother's eyes in my own. I'm pulling gray chin hairs now, and I realize I don't have much time left."

"Talkin' to the choir. I look like my Auntie Vemba, droopy eye lids and all."

"I didn't tell you before now because I'm afraid to say it. I'm trying to decide whether to leave Andrew."

Ouisie's irises grew wide as peach pits. "What? Why?"

"Ouisie, you know why. Certainly not to have another man, not at my age. Who'd have me, anyway? More than that, who is there to have? But day in, day out, Andrew hides out in his rocket barn to write who knows what, some family history, or so he says. He hasn't seen his daughter or grandchildren in months, even though they come for breakfast every Saturday."

"Guy and I haven't seen Andrew in years, and we live a half mile from you."

"I'm at wits' end with the isolation. So, I thought I could leave. Rent a room. I've been saving, and I have an inheritance I put into an IRA. And there's Social Security and Medicare."

"Give up your home? Why don't you have Andrew live in the rocket barn? For gosh sakes, he spends day and night out there while you shop, cook, wash, and clean. You've made his life all too convenient."

"Janey tells me I need to push for a resolution, but I'm weary. Our marriage has been this way so long, I don't think I've got the desire to break through."

"Please consult someone — definitely not our lascivious new minister — but a marriage counselor. You shouldn't leave your home. Andrew is the problem."

"I can't send *him* packing because I'm not happy. He's paid for everything."

"You paid for everything. If only he had listened." Ouisie's cheeks flushed with anger beneath her almond-hued skin.

"Now, Ouisie, don't get angry with Andrew. That's my job."

Ouisie patted Lizzy's hand. "I don't want to encourage you to leave, but you can stay at our house if push comes to shove."

"Guy would feel invaded. He'd have to wear a bathrobe all the time, instead of wandering around in his shorts, or whatever he wears over his, well, you know."

"You certainly wouldn't inhibit any great sex life, although I wish. Where there's desire, there's hope." Ouisie's napkin fluttered to her cheeks, which flushed deeply red under her dark skin.

"Me too. I wonder if there's time for another roll in the hay."

"My latest fantasy lover, after I say my prayers, of course, is that French actor, Omar Sy. Have you seen him on Netflix in 'Lupin'?"

"We don't have cable. Or the Internet. Andrew refuses to pay for what he calls 'the ruination of the American intellect.' Maybe in my new place I'll get both."

Ouisie took Lizzy's hands. "You could find someone on a senior dating site."

"Oh, Ouisie."

"Who'd have thought that we'd wind up a pair of seventy-year-olds on the make?"

The two girlfriends giggled like sisters, but Lizzy grew quiet when she remembered the next steps. She had to tell Andrew and, even more daunting, Jane.

∽

ANDREW'S next scene described Ward and Charlotte's ride up a rocky road toward Dahlonega, forty-five miles north of Atlanta.

∽

THE INCLINE GREW STEEPER, and the road narrowed to a wisp of a trail. Ward took the point while his newly bedded Charlotte bumbled behind. To his ear, her round rump plop-plopped in a syncopated jiggle with the clip-clop of the horse's hooves.

Despite the chill, the day was resplendent with sunshine that sparkled on the dew still clinging to the leaves. Ward stopped for a moment to survey the glistening spectacle of the violet-crowned mountains ahead. As he surveyed the horizon, his internal cerebral camera recorded visions of the clear, light skies above and the glimmering trail that seemed to point the way like a golden beam from the heavens above. In fact, the light put Ward in such a dream state, he did not realize that behind him, Charlotte was looking fretfully back toward Atlanta.

She missed her Pa Pa's saloon, her bordello girlfriends, even the rail workers, bankers, and drunks she had serviced in bed. Pitiful tears streamed as she recalled the imagined glory of her former life, compared

*to life now on the back of a horse, even if promised riches awaited her on
the bumpy path ahead.*

～

"Hey, Walter, did you know I speak a little French? Here's where
Charlotte whispers, '*Mère de Dieu! Qu'ai-je fait?*' as tears stain her
pretty cheeks."

～

Inside the black-mirrored office building of Georgia Software
Solutions, a five-foot-tall jigsaw puzzle dominated one wall of Jane's
office. The puzzle had been a challenge from a co-worker named
Dale, who told Jane he could design a puzzle she could not solve.
One Christmas, he presented her with a whopper he'd had made of
3,000 pieces, just black colons and forward slashes on a white
background. She took six months, but she glued it together and
framed it.

Dale appeared to be so miffed he didn't say a word.

"Not a word? Not one word of praise?" Jane had chided, which
pissed Dale off even more.

Now at her desk, she went to work on a fulfillment solution for a
major retailer. Frowning, she riveted her attention on this, her tenth
time analyzing each facet. Her fingers flew on the keyboard.

Compared with her parents' liberal arts degrees, Jane's
fascination with technology was an aberration. She had excelled at
math in school, while her brother had almost failed algebra. In fact,
Billy's teacher gave Billy a failing grade in his junior year, but the
principal changed it to a "C" so Billy would stay eligible for
football.

Andrew and Lizzy never knew about the grade change. Jane's
secret to this day.

She remembered how Billy's sky-blue eyes had implored her
never to tell. "Poppa would make me quit the team. And Momma

would march up to school and give the principal fits. You cannot tell, Janey. Promise?"

"I promise," young Janey had said.

Jane stopped her edits. Why did this memory fly in today, of all days?

Alan simply does not understand. Forgetting is impossible.

ANDREW ENJOYED rare solitude in Lizzy's kitchen domain as he made a sandwich out of Saturday's breakfast — a heap of the forbidden cheesy eggs and bacon, smashed between two leftover chocolate glazed doughnuts, gleefully slathered in Durkee sauce, and garnished with sliced tomatoes, onion, lettuce, and four pieces of salty pickled okra.

At the round kitchen table, he again scanned the paper, drained two beers from Lizzy's stash that she kept for Alan, and relished the silence. Oh, he loved his wife deeply, but ever since so long ago, he found it easier to be alone than in the same room with his family, or pretty much anybody other than Walter.

Down the hall, Andrew swallowed two antacids from the bathroom cabinet, brushed his teeth, and gargled to erase the telltale odors of beer. He leaned into the mirror and massaged his beard, then decided to shave and get dressed for the day. "Even I know when I'm a bit too funky," he joked to himself.

Spiffed up, he headed out under his umbrella and made sure to dispose of the beer bottles in the outside recycling can. He looked down at Walter. "Now she won't give me heck."

Walter barked with glee.

"You do your business?"

Walter as much as said, "Yes" when he barked again in reply.

Just then, Andrew heard Lizzy's car pull into the drive. Reluctantly, he strode toward the garage. "Need any help?"

"There's just this. I can handle it. You had lunch yet?"

"I fixed a salad." Although this was a lie, the sinful doughnut sandwich had lettuce, onions, and tomatoes. "I figured you and Ouisie were at brunch. Was Guy there?"

"He had a board meeting after service. Ouisie said he was going to play cards after that."

"You'd think he was Episcopalian."

"Ouisie mentioned that the new minister hired his girlfriend to run the office."

"Got the Unitarians all stirred up? They'll start calling 'em Shakers again."

Lizzy was not amused. "Are you coming in?"

"I'm working on my first chapter. Not sure how to turn history into fiction."

"Guess it's not as easy as you thought?"

"History is what happens. Fiction is what you create."

"Dinner's at six-thirty. Pot roast."

"I thought I wasn't allowed to have pot roast."

"New recipe. Roast simmered in beer. Guaranteed zero fat."

"The beer part sounds tasty. You go obliterate fat while I write the Great American Novel."

"Speaking of that, Janey asked me yesterday why I hadn't come out to see what you've written." As soon as she said this, Lizzy wondered why she would mention it, but she had noticed Andrew's confession that he was struggling with his writing. Was that a sign she should keep trying?

"Six-thirty. I heard you." With that, Andrew rushed to the workshop, let Walter inside, and locked the door with a loud click, fearful that Lizzy might invade his space.

"Guess that's my answer," Lizzy muttered as she headed inside.

BACK IN THE KITCHEN, Lizzy trimmed fat from the beef and browned it in a porcelain-coated Dutch oven. Then she got out four beers and noticed her supply was now short by two. "I'll have to buy more beer for Alan. But at least booze thins out Andrew's cholesterol."

She poured four beers into the pot and added no-salt, no-fat beef consommé.

"One of these days, I'll cook the final roast for Andrew." As her words echoed, she imagined living alone. "I'll get a cat. Andrew can have Walter."

She poured a glass of merlot. Good old Columbia Crest usually took away the blues.

～

INSIDE GEORGIA SOFTWARE SOLUTIONS, Jane glanced at the puzzle on her wall. At the bottom was a blue Post-it with a scribbled note from Alan. "Never let the bastards defeat you."

"I needed that today, Schweetheart."

～

ANDREW AND A DAMP Walter resumed positions at his desk. When Andrew hunched over his typewriter, Walter snuggled as far under the desk as his red setter body would fit.

"Atta boy, Walter. You're kind of stinky, but you don't ask a lot of questions."

As Andrew typed, instead of his determined writer's glint, he suddenly stared blankly at nothing, not the page, not Walter, not at his left forefinger that punched the same two keys over and over, while the type ball on his red Selectric bounced and hit the paper, bounced and hit the paper, bounced and hit the paper, until the repeated imprints made a hole at the end of the line.

In his mind's glimmer, he was eight years old, one summer morning at Lake Blackshear.

Chapter Five

ANDY

Flickers of sunlight feel like hot, white lights dancing on my eyelids as the window blind rocks back and forth in the humid breeze. The glimmers fade each time the blind flutters closed with a *clack*. I drift to sleep again until a whiff of air beams another white-hot flicker onto my cheek. I reach to wipe it away, but with each puff of air and click-clack of the blind, the summer sunshine sings, "Come on, boy, wake up, wake up."

Drawn out of my dreams, I open both eyes. In my big boy's white jockey briefs and tank t-shirt like Daddy's, I stretch my arms and legs as far as they can reach. Then I remember. Yes, school is out for the summer. I'm at Grandpa and Grandma Ward's cottage on Lake Blackshear, a long drive from home. Momma, my sister Sarah Little Shit, my stinkin' brother Tommy, and our aunts, uncles, and cousins are here to swim, fish, and canoe in the lake's cool water.

There aren't many powerboats on this lake, but as soon as I sit up, darn if I don't hear the far hum of a boat motor. I lift the blind and peer out, too full of awe to express what I see, a mirror of water reflecting the blue sky, jus' waiting for me to jump in. High above, gulls circle in figure eights and seem to call, *Andy, Andy, Andy*, while the distant, familiar buzz of that motorboat lures me outside to see if it's the most wonderful thing I can imagine, a wooden Chris Craft. That means big waves will soon roll to shore.

I tiptoe past my stinkin' brother Tommy, Sarah Little Shit, and six sleeping cousins, sprawled on cots lined up like inside an army barracks. Once I move beyond the doorway, I stop to listen. I hear Daddy's deep snore behind a bedroom door. Then I sneak out front and run barefoot to where twenty-two shallow steps lead down a gentle hill to a one-lane gravel road that divides the lakeshore from the houses. Nobody ever drives on the road because it's easier to park uphill, near the wooden fence that separates the cottages from the railroad tracks that carry passengers and freight three times a day between Cordele, Americus, and beyond.

As I rush down the steps, I cannot move my legs fast enough to get to the lawn, where I hop over ruts in the road and bound across tree-shaded grass. I dodge the squishy patch of dark green that oozes something smelly from Mr. Ground's septic tank next door. Then I run to the base of the wooden dock and see the first waves roll in, white-tipped. As I race toward the end of the dock, my bare feet *thump-thump-thump* on the planks. Tucked into a cannonball, I catapult into the breakers.

"Bonsaaaaiiiiiiiii, Chris Craft!"

Chapter Six

NOVEMBER 7, AFTERNOON

I n Andrew's workshop, one key hammered the paper under the line he had written.

"Not paying one bit of attention to the unhappy concubine who bumped along behind him,"

After those words, a word began with the letter "W" but continued in a repetitive line of "A" and then "W," "Wawawawawawawaw," until it reached the right margin. There, a hole widened as Andrew stared ahead, and his left forefinger rhythmically alternated between the "W" key and the "A" key, the "W" then the "A."

Walter did not budge. After all, his master was still making those click-clicks.

LIZZY LEFT the roast to simmer and went to her sunroom. From there, the windows overlooked the backyard and Andrew's workshop. She often sat at her desk and peered into the oval mirror to spy on the workshop. She could not see inside it, just the light that reflected on its siding as daylight arched toward the west. She had not placed the mirror initially to spy on her husband, but she surely had re-hung it at a more advantageous angle after the rocket barn was in place.

Lizzy flipped through the week's stack of mail, including a bank statement, IRA statement, Medicare statement, mailers for health insurance, life annuities, long-term-care insurance, walk-in bathtubs, medical alerts, and other attempts to scam seniors. She laboriously wrote "Please remove from list!" on reply cards. Then she stacked them on the piano before returning to the roast.

"Darn roast will shrivel to nothing in this beer sauce. And where is Andrew? He doesn't usually stay past sunset. Will he miss the final roast prepared by his devoted wife? That is, if I drink enough courage in merlot to tell him tonight?"

She went back to the sunroom and peered into its oval mirror. No sign of Andrew.

"Lacking any husband to dine with or divorce, would you like more wine? Why yes, I believe I would. Might be lonely on my own, but not much different from being married."

STILL AT HIS TYPEWRITER, Andrew stared blankly. His hands now quivered above the keys as vital sections of his brain ceased to function from lack of oxygen, although other brain cells transported him to his childhood summer days.

Chapter Seven

ANDY

We walk into the shadows of the garage, tiptoeing around the junk. Daddy wants to oil up the Sears chain saw to clear a cypress tree in front of the cottage. There's a lot of mossy trees and stumps still in the lake, even though the water rose back in the 1930s, before I was born.

"One tree a summer makes 'em go away," Daddy says as he gets the oil can and hefts the chain saw. He nods my way, which means, "Open the door."

In the sunlight outside, his blue eyes shine. Momma calls them "her precious opals."

I walk behind with Uncle Luke. He's a skinny, redheaded guy who married Daddy's sister, Sally. We meet up with our neighbor Otto Kaak. He's big and round, with a snaggle-toothed grin. He's from Germany. Daddy says Otto got out just in time. He's carrying two pairs of green rubber waders. Otto and Daddy pull 'em on, while I walk out to the end of the dock. Tommy watches from the shore.

Daddy holds the chain saw shoulder high. All three men wade in waist-deep. After much talk, Daddy picks a big, creepy cypress about twenty feet out. Uncle Luke doesn't wear waders because he's the climber. He swims out to the tree and shinnies between the thick lower branches, then works his way like a redheaded woodpecker up the trunk as high as he can go near the top.

He hollers down, "Line droppin'."

Down splashes a rope. Daddy and Otto tie the chain saw to it. Then Uncle Luke pulls the machine up and issues cusswords in a stream, since the chain saw darn near outweighs him. He struggles to pull it to the top, unties it, and lets the rope go. He fires up the motor and holds on like it's a bucking bronco. Stinky smoke and steam spew so thick you can't see Uncle Luke at all. But one by one, I hear the cut branches crack onto the lower ones before they fall and go whoosh into the murky water.

At the end of the dock, I crouch in the path of the oily exhaust. The fumes burn my eyes, and tears stream down my face. But I want to watch, so I stand my ground as Uncle Luke fells branch after branch, and Daddy and Otto drag each one to shore.

I ask Daddy if I can help.

"You're too little," Tommy hollers from shore.

"Andy, you've gotta be taller to handle this. But Tommy, why don't you wade in and see if you're tall enough to help."

"I'll help if my crybaby brother stays on the dock."

"I'm not crying. The smoke's in my eyes."

"Well, stupid, move away from the smoke."

"Tommy, quit fussing at your little brother. That boy's still on his Momma's sugar tit," Daddy says, mostly to Otto, who chuckles in a *ho, ho* that even sounds German.

Tommy puffs out his bony version of Daddy's barrel chest and strides in fully clothed to help the men in their conquest of the tree. I stand on the dock and wipe away my smoky tears.

Uncle Luke cuts his way down the tree to the point there's only one limb left above the waterline that he can stand on. From that branch, he hands down the chain saw to Daddy. Then Uncle Luke shouts, "Bonsai!" He does a belly flop into the water. When he surfaces, he shakes and shudders to wash away the cypress needles and wet wood chips.

"Shee-ut!" Uncle Luke hee-haws with a grin. His red hair looks like copper in the sun.

Daddy laughs in his deep voice. His wet, brown comb-over is floppy, and I can see his bald spot. He wades close to the last branch, holds the chain saw tight, and hollers, "Tommy, get back. No telling which way this branch will fall."

Daddy attacks that last branch while Tommy joins me on the dock. After it goes "thunk" into the water, Uncle Luke and Otto drag the branch ashore, then wade back out. The two steady Daddy by the waist as he plunges the running chain saw blade into the water up to the motor housing. Tommy and I watch in amazement as Daddy presses the roaring chain saw to the tree trunk. It's a good two feet wide. The chain saw jerks and thrashes into the trunk.

After about an hour of this, with Daddy takin' turns with Otto, the trunk tilts, and the three men push it into the water. Only thing left is a submerged stump that's so thick, it'll take a thousand years to disintegrate.

It takes all three men to lug the trunk ashore. With big smiles, they throw themselves on the grass and laugh a lot before they cut the soggy wood into logs and stack them to dry.

"Whew-ee! That was some shee-ut," Uncle Luke shouts after they're finished.

Daddy laughs deeply again and calls in his big voice uphill toward the cottage, "Ladies, it's bath time for the gentlemen."

That's the signal for Momma, Grandma Ward, my aunts, and female cousins to stay inside and close the blinds, so the men can peel off their clothes and wash naked at the outdoor pump. This time, Tommy joins the ritual while I glower in a crouch. My eyes still sting from the smoke, salty sweat, and angry tears.

I point at Tommy and laugh. "Tommy's got a pink prick. He's got a pink prick."

Daddy's growl echoes. "Andy, quit your girlie talk and run inside before I take my belt."

I cry out, "Daddy, you always say I'm on Momma's sugar tit, but then you send me to be with the sugar tits!"

But suddenly I remember when Momma and my aunts secretly peeked out the sunroom's side windows to watch the men get naked and soapy. So, I get the same idea and bolt across the lawn and march up the twenty-two steps. I can hear the women in the kitchen, my girl cousins playing the pump organ in the living room, and Grandpa Ward listening to the ballgame on the radio.

I have the sunroom to myself. I peek over the windowsill as the ceremony begins on the lawn. First, Daddy soaps Tommy to the point he's completely covered. Tommy gathers some bubbles from his scrawny body and throws globs at Uncle Luke, who soaps his bony self and tries to throw suds back at Tommy. Otto Kaak is the soapiest of all, covered in white over his thick, black body fur that even covers his German dick. Then Uncle Luke and Daddy grab handfuls of Otto's lather and throw the globs at Tommy until he's completely covered and squawks in laughter.

"I hate you, Tommy Ward," I say under my breath as I watch my brother have a soap fight with the grown-up men.

Chapter Eight

NOVEMBER 7, EVENING

The sky had faded to blue gray when Lizzy finished her wine. Time to make the sauce. She poured the braising liquid into her separator and chilled it for ten minutes, so the fat rose to the top. At this stage, she expected to see no fat rise, but to her amazement, there was still a quarter inch of grease coagulated at the top.

"Makes me think we should be vegans."

She whisked flour into fat-free, no-salt beef consommé and added that to the broth, along with eight no-salt seasonings. She turned up the heat and stirred until her sauce thickened.

Again, she checked the clock. Six o'clock and dark outside. She peered through the window and did not care if Andrew saw her this time, did not care whether he would be affronted. She was hungry, wanted dinner over, wanted a long bath and a good night's sleep. Tomorrow morning, she would tell him of her decision. She would make a nice breakfast. The final breakfast. Then she would pack and leave. For where, she did not know. But Ouisie's offer of a place to stay seemed like a good idea.

~

ACROSS TOWN, Jane closed her laptop, hoping that her analysis was in perfect shape. She would pick up dinner at Whole Foods, something healthy since Alan had jogged that day and would be on a fitness kick.

~

LIZZY LOOKED OUT BACK and noticed a red glow through the workshop front door. Suddenly, she realized what was wrong with her mind's picture. "There's no light on, but he left the space heater on. He's not even in there. That rascal."

Now and then, Andrew would sneak out to the Sonic Drive-In with Walter and come home smelling like a double bacon cheeseburger and chili-cheese Tater-Tots. Lizzy was incensed that he might do that tonight. She stormed outside and peered in the garage window. Andrew's beloved Mini-Cooper wagon was in its usual spot.

Suddenly, she heard Walter's bark from the workshop.

"Andrew! Dinner's ready," Lizzy called out.

Walter's bark echoed back from down the stone path.

Lizzy hesitated. She was afraid to barge in. Still, no light was on, and Walter was barking. Lizzy headed up the path. Walter scratched from inside. Lizzy crept up the steps and knocked.

"Andrew? Are you in there?"

Walter barked and scratched frantically.

"What's going on, boy?" Lizzy knocked again, louder. She tried the knob. "Andrew, why is this door locked?" She jiggled the knob again. "Are you in there? Andrew!"

Walter whimpered and whined. Lizzy did not know where a key might be, but she figured Andrew must have hidden one. She looked under the mat and beneath a dead potted plant, then reached on tiptoes to feel along the top of the doorjamb. There it was. Her fingers touched metal, but the key fell to the porch and bounced off onto wet leaves. Lizzy thought she might have to get a flashlight, but she rummaged through the leaves until her fingers felt metal.

When she unlocked the door, Walter jumped and whined.

"Walter, get down. What's the matter?" Her eyes strained to see inside the dark space. When her vision adjusted, she saw a human form behind the desk.

"Andrew? Did you fall asleep?"

There was no reply.

"Andrew! Wake up. It's past time for dinner."

Walter barked urgently.

"Hush, Walter. Oh, where is that light?" Lizzy's fingers fumbled until they located the switch. In the stark fluorescent glow, she saw Andrew staring blankly ahead.

"Andrew! Are you awake?" Lizzy rushed behind the desk and noticed his left hand quivering above the keyboard. His right arm hung slack at his side. His eyes were wide and glassy. Tears streamed. His mouth was agape. Saliva ran down onto his shirt collar.

"Andrew! Can you hear me?" She leaned close to listen. Yes, she could hear him breathe. "Andrew! What's the matter?"

His eyes glared vacantly.

"Just stay there. I'll call Janey."

Walter barked excitedly.

"Yes, Walter, I know. You're a good boy." Lizzy's voice cracked.

She ran to the house as Walter barked from the steps where he stayed to guard his master.

Lizzy dialed Jane's number from the kitchen phone.

JUST HOME WITH dinner in bags, Jane heard Lizzy's name sound on the Caller ID. Jane sighed loudly, determined not to answer. She had three hungry kids to feed and wanted everything to be perfect for Alan, her self-imposed penance for her decision to work that day.

When the landline rolled to voicemail, Jane sighed in relief. Then her cell phone rang. She fumbled for her purse and saw "Momma." *Give me a break*, Jane thought, but her impatient "Hello" turned to urgent commands as she heard Lizzy quaver the details about Andrew.

"I'll call EMS and be right over." Jane reached for the landline and punched in 911.

ANDREW LAY on a padded platform in the Emory University Hospital radiology department. He did not react to the blaring lights, the straps that held him, or the hums, buzzes, and clicks as a computed tomography machine scanned his brain. Simultaneously, his interior mind was busily projecting visions far away from this cold and sterile place.

Chapter Nine

ANDY

The noon train out of Americus roars by as my buddy Danny Kaak, my stinkin' brother Tommy, and me slip between two broken fence boards behind the cottage. We run down the tracks to chase the caboose and holler, "Toot, toot, toot," as we reach to pull pretend whistles. We wait to get a signal back as the caboose jockeys around the bend like an orange mirage shimmering in the heat.

Danny's pissed. "He tooted at us yesterday."

We balance single file on the iron rails, one foot in front of the other, until Tommy steps on the wooden ties and hops, a game he calls "1-2-3." He's older than me by four years and makes up most games and all the rules. He changes them whenever he wants and serves as the head referee too.

I hate Tommy.

Each of us younger boys takes turns on one of the ties. They are spaced twenty-one inches apart, or so Tommy says. He knows a lot of stuff like that. We leap the distance of one rail tie, then two rail ties, then try for three, downright impossible for us younger boys, but not for Tommy when he gets a good run.

'Course, Tommy always wins since he's the only one who can leap to the third board. That pisses me off.

"I don't wanna play your stupid game. You only win 'cause your legs are longer."

"Daddy always says, 'Life isn't fair.'"

"Daddy's not fair."

"I'm gonna tell him what you said." Tommy gives me a look that sends me to sulk.

Danny tries to fix things. "Tommy, how 'bout you jump two more rail ties than Andy and me before you win? That'd make it fair."

"Okay, you babies. I'll spot you two ties, but just for today."

So, we hop, skip, and jump up and down the rail ties — nobody wins — until we are a half-mile west of the cottage. I try hard to keep up, but Danny's almost a year older and two years taller. After a half hour, our faces are watermelon red and dripping with sweat. Danny and I make it the distance of two rail ties, but we miss when we try to jump three. Tommy misses when he tries to reach the fourth board. Grown-ups couldn't jump that far, either.

"Now, nobody's gonna win," Tommy says.

"That's more fair than you winnin' all the time."

"Is not."

"Is too!"

Spittin' in each other's faces, Tommy and I holler until I get so worked up, I lunge and swing my fists in a fury. Always younger, always shorter, always weaker, always behind, not to mention Daddy's least favorite. That game I never win. But since Tommy is a head taller, he holds me off with two stiff arms. Furious, I swing right and left, but I only connect with air.

Danny's a year older and strong enough to pull me back. "Y'all stop it. Let's do what we came out here to do."

I take another run at Tommy, but he bolts, so I only land a weak brush on his back.

"Chicken poop!" I scream and kick rocks so hard I hurt my big toe. "Tommy Ward, I hate your chicken-poop guts."

"Andy, calm down," Danny says. "You two drive me nuts."

I stare at the railroad ties and mull whether to take another run at Tommy.

To distract me, Danny pulls out a bright penny. Loud enough for Tommy to hear, he says, "Here's the penny. We gonna smash it or what?"

Tommy saunters our way, but not within my reach. I glare at him, then take the bright copper coin out of Danny's hand and turn it over in my palm. The penny is newly minted and reflects gold in the sun. I ceremoniously place the coin on a railroad track.

Danny doesn't think this will work.

"Flat as a pancake," I say. "All stretched out like that fancy penny Daddy brought us from the state fair. Ain't that right, jerk?"

Even then, Tommy's a tycoon. "Once the train smashes the penny, maybe we can sell it to Danny's cousin for bait money."

"Momma says you can use bacon for bait."

"Andy, that's girl stuff. You'd just catch a crappie. You gotta use minnows for bass."

"So, let's use two pennies to make even more." Danny is proud of his financial wizardry, but then he realizes that he's gotta cough up the second penny. He doesn't want to, since five pennies buy an extra scoop of bittersweet hot fudge at Matt's soda fountain in Cordele.

I grab Danny's second penny and set it on the other sun-hot rail. There they lie across the ties, two bright pennies the same color as the Georgia clay. We watch as if those coins will stretch out right before our eyes. We stare until the sun roasts our heads as hot as the iron rails.

Suddenly, Tommy bolts down the ties toward the opening in the back fence. "I'm hot. Last one in the lake is chicken poop."

Danny and I run after. For the rest of the afternoon, we play World War II submarine under an upside-down aluminum canoe, still wearing our t-shirts, cut-off jeans, and Keds to protect our feet and legs from the long reach of the submerged cypress tree roots. Each of us fits in one section, and we hold on by the crossbars. Then we lower the rim so the canoe's top skims the surface.

That night, I share a bed with Danny, 'cause his rich cousin

Normie from Chicago is visiting next door. My bedroom is at the back of the house, so the wall beyond the bed is just a few feet from the fence. And beyond that, the tracks.

To stay awake, I tell myself war stories until I hear the train signal and hear the engine draw near. This is one of my favorite sounds, the midnight train out of Cordele, especially if there's a rainstorm like there is tonight. While thunder rumbles and raindrops drum the cottage's metal roof, I stand on the bed to feel the locomotive's roar shake the walls, even the bed itself. In the dark, I feel a sense of oneness with the engineer and brakeman who pass so close. Do they ever think that beyond the walls of this summerhouse, a boy like me listens to their engine roar, the *clackity-clack* of their wheels, and the lonely call of their whistles?

This night is even more exciting, as I imagine Danny's two pennies on the rails. I can see the wheels roll in slow motion to mash the coins so thin, his rich cousin will pay us a whole dollar. I want to sneak out, but I can hear Daddy's deep laugh through the walls, Uncle Luke's loud cackle, and Aunt Sally's giggles. I'll have to wait until morning. With my eyes alight, I can't fall asleep. So, I lie still and listen to Danny's allergic wheeze.

Chapter Ten

NOVEMBER 7, LATE EVENING

Lizzy waited for news in the hospital's crowded waiting room, along with Jane, Alan, and the kids. Wracked with guilt, Lizzy felt nauseous about her earlier determination to leave Andrew. When the two were married, she had said, "For better or worse," but now she wanted to bolt because she got worse. Although Unitarian Universalist doctrine touted a loving spirit, Lizzy feared the fundamentalists had it right. God would punish her if she broke her marriage vows.

God should strike me instead of Andrew. Why should he pay for my failing?

Lizzy's internal torment was interrupted when a young woman about thirty strode in. Her lab coat monogram spelled, "N. Fitzgerald, M.D."

"Mrs. Ward, I'm Dr. Fitzgerald. The CT and MRI scans confirmed what we suspected. Mr. Ward has had an acute ischemic stroke. You might call it a 'brain attack.' This happens when a clot blocks an artery and interrupts blood flow to the brain. As a result, brain cells die, and damage occurs."

Lizzy's frown deepened with denial. This woman looked like she hadn't yet graduated from college, much less medical school. "He's a professor, my dear."

"Momma, titles don't matter now. Dr. Fitzgerald, how much damage does Poppa have?"

"Time will tell, primarily because we don't know how much time passed between the stroke and when Professor Ward arrived at the hospital. Clot-dissolving drugs can reduce long-term disability, but only if administered within three hours."

"Three hours. Do you know how long it was, Momma?"

"How could I? I was in the house and, like always, he was out back in that — "

"Now, don't blame yourself, Mrs. Ward."

But I had planned to leave him, Lizzy reminded herself.

"Of course, it's better if we can intervene quickly, but long-term effects depend on the location where the stroke occurs, and the severity of the blockage."

"Oh, dear."

"Certain abilities controlled by one area may be lost, like speech, movement, or memory. Someone who has slight damage might experience weakness in an arm, one side of the face, or one leg. Patients who have severe damage may be paralyzed completely on one side or lose their ability to speak or comprehend. We'll know more as we do more tests. In the meantime, we'll continue to administer drugs that can reduce acute damage and lessen the risk of more clots. So, for now, you can see him, but don't expect any response. This is a situation that only time will tell."

IN HIS ROOM, Andrew lay motionless. His eyes appeared to stare at the ceiling, but he did not see the white tiles or overhead lights. His mind's eye vacillated between the blackness of nothing — no thoughts, no dreams, no memories, no sounds — and vivid scenes punctuated by rapid eye movement. Both arms and legs were strapped to the bed rails to keep him still. Tubes led from his hands and wrists to clear plastic bags that dripped various solutions. All about him, monitors with digital readouts whirred and beeped to keep electronic tabs as though he also were a machine that could be analyzed by the nurse's computer down the hall.

Little did Andrew realize that a real, live nurse fussed about and double-checked sensors. A buxom Black woman, her name tag displayed "R. McMahan, R.N., Emory University Hospital."

Cautiously, the door opened. Lizzy, Jane, Alan, and the kids squeezed inside and jockeyed for positions. Lizzy and Jane took opposite sides of the bed, where they patted Andrew's shoulders, the only parts of his torso that did not protrude with a needle or tube.

Jane spoke as if she had launched a meeting at work. "Poppa, it's Janey. I'm here with Momma, Alan, Billy Jay, David, and Elizabeth."

Andrew's eyes remained frozen.

Little Elizabeth stared at Andrew from the foot of his bed. "Is Grand Pop dead?"

"Elizabeth Jane, hush. Grand Pop is not dead. He's asleep with his eyes open," Alan said.

Jane had not wanted the children in the room, but had relented to their pleas. "Alan, I think you should take the kids to the waiting room."

"I'm twelve, so I'm big enough to stay."

"Me too."

"You're ten, David. I'm twelve."

"I'm older than Elizabeth."

Billy Jay smirked. "Everybody's older than Elizabeth."

"I saw a dead dog that got hit by a car. His eyes looked like Grand Pop's, only the dog's eyes were black."

Jane gave Alan a look that asked him to take Elizabeth away.

"Come with me, young lady. Nurse McMahan has been kind to let you see your Grand Pop, but it's against the rules for someone your age to be here. We've got to go down the hall."

"Aw, Daddy!" Elizabeth scowled at the nurse.

Nurse McMahan stifled a bemused smile, so Alan gave her an exaggerated wink as he walked Elizabeth out. Nurse McMahan winked back. She was used to being the bad guy.

The two boys gathered at the foot of Andrew's bed and patted his blanketed toes.

Billy Jay shouted, as though a loud voice could penetrate Andrew's apparent state of unconsciousness. "Hi, Grand Pop! How you doin'?"

"Billy Jay, he can't answer you, so there's no need to shout." Jane gestured at Andrew's open eyes. "Nurse, he doesn't seem to blink. Should we close his eyes?"

"Not to worry. He'll blink. Just less often. He's in what's called 'a near-vegetative state,' not a coma. I'll close his lids when it's time for sleep. But it's best to enable visual stimulation."

"So, he is awake. Andrew? Can you hear me? See me?" Lizzy asked softly.

"He probably can't understand you, so it's better if you just talk to him about your day. General things. The less stressful, the better."

"I don't really know what to say."

"Momma, just say anything. Let's see, Poppa, I had to work again today. On a Sunday, if you can believe that."

"Momma, that work talk is stressful. And every time you go to the office on Sundays, David acts up the minute you leave."

"I do not! Billy J. starts acting like he's the boss."

Jane glared. "That's it, boys. Go find your father."

David and Billy Jay resisted, but Jane shooed them out. "I'm sorry, Momma. I thought the boys were old enough." She stood quietly and patted Andrew's shoulders. "Say something, Momma. You've never been a shy violet. Where's that acerbic wit?"

"I'm not feeling very witty. My mind is in a blur. When I found Andrew, his eyes were so glassy. He just stared. Didn't seem to know it was me."

"I meant for you to talk to Poppa. Talk about your day."

"Janey, I feel like I'm on a stage with no lines to say. Oh dear, about today. This morning I went to church and had brunch with Ouisie. She and I had a long talk. Oh dear, I've got to call Ouisie. She and Guy will want to know. And I need to call Andrew's brother and sister, not that any of them give a hoot. Andrew hasn't seen his

brother since — " Lizzy stopped in her patented pause. "So, after
brunch, I went to buy groceries and got into a parking lot war with a
French-twisted Druid Hills trophy wife. I must admit, I was pretty
crafty, and my Jag beat her Lexus for a space. She was so angry, she
flipped me off. Can you believe it? On a Sunday! Then later, I ran
into that same woman in the gourmet cheese section. She looked
like a supermodel in her Michael Kors and Prada as she did
something so common as picking out a cheese. Of course, it had to
be a brie, a darn brie. As you know, Andrew and I cannot enjoy
cheese anymore. Oh dear, no stress. So, then I bought a roast, which
I told Andrew about. I used a recipe that is guaranteed to remove all
fat and does not require salt. You simmer the beef in beer and fat-
free, no-salt consommé, then pour the liquid into a gravy separator,
let the fat rise to the top, skim it off, then pour the defatted liquid
back and add more consommé, potatoes, onions, carrots, roasted red
peppers, thyme, a bay leaf, marjoram, black pepper, paprika, and
garlic, of course, you can't make good a good sauce without garlic —
"

Lizzy suddenly remembered, "Oh, Janey. The roast is still on the
stove. And the sauce!"

"Momma!" Jane exhaled in a deep sigh. But after seeing defeat
appear in Lizzy's weary green eyes that usually shone with dogged
determination, Jane tempered her tone. Just solve the puzzle. "I'll get
Alan to take care of it. Is the house locked?"

Lizzy fumbled through her purse and handed over her keys. "I
left the roast on simmer. It should be okay, but that beer sauce may
have boiled down to nothing."

"Momma, nobody cares about the damn sauce." Jane headed to
find Alan. Out in the hallway, she dreaded the encounter. Alan could
be a real pill, always had to be right, and he usually ground it in
when someone else made a mistake. Still, he had mellowed a bit after
age forty, as Jane had mellowed too. But she often wished she could
simply ask him a favor that he would not use as an opportunity to
rebut opposition counsel.

After Jane rushed out, Lizzy whispered timidly, "Nurse, will he be all right?"

"Only time will tell, Mrs. Ward."

"Oh, Andrew, please be all right." Silently, she bowed her head and prayed.

Please meet Andrew at his point of need in the area of his health, and please forgive me for my earlier plans and guide me to the right decision for our marriage.

Chapter Eleven

ANDY
....

D anny turns fifteen today. I'm jealous 'cause I'm a year behind. Cousin Normie is sixteen, and Tommy turned eighteen last week. I'm always the baby.

All four of us are tan as Tonto by the end of August. Danny's and my hair is sun-bleached white, but he has a shock of white-blond eyebrows above his brown, wide-set eyes. He's the only "rounder" in our cove. That means he lives at the lake all year round.

Danny's father owns a bakery in Cordele. Calls it "Kaak Bakery," pronounced "cake," a name we think is funny for a baker. Even more funny, Danny's mother's name is "Anna," and his sister's name is "Elle," spelled E.L.L.E. So, like Momma says, "No matter if you spell 'Otto Kaak' or 'Anna Kaak' or 'Elle Kaak' forward or backward, each spells the same."

That's a joke Momma tells every summer.

Otto is a great bass fisher. Every Sunday at sunrise, I wake to hear his five-horsepower, outboard engine putt-putt off to prime spots by the railroad tracks that cross the lake. "There goes Otto," I whisper as I peer at the silhouette of his aluminum boat in the gray light. I can't wait to see his baker's dozen of bass that afternoon.

We boys are chest-deep under the canoe when we hear Otto's motor hum in the distance. So, we flip the canoe upright, push it to shore, and run to the end of the dock until we see his boat rounding the point of land far left of our cove. We call that point "the rocks," but it's just a finger of land lined with rocks to protect the railroad tracks against the waves and currents. We wave and shout until Otto slows. Then he reaches down and pulls up a stringer of about a dozen green bass. He grins when we give him a big cheer.

"Fried fish for everybody," Danny shouts with pride, since Otto's fish will feed the entire cove. We city boys may seem ritzy to Danny, but Momma says we're not ritzy, even if Daddy's a banker.

Late Sunday afternoon, Otto builds a fire on the gravel road and hangs a deep iron kettle filled with Crisco blocks that melt like icebergs over the flames. Anna guts and fillets the bass under the outdoor pump, then soaks the fish in buttermilk and secret spices. Just before dinner, she dips each fillet in her flour and meal mix, then drops the fish into the hot fat until the kettle sizzles so full the oil spills over. Flames soar, and everybody worries that the whole kettle of Crisco will catch fire. So, Anna sprinkles the flames with flour, and the flares snuff out.

"Whew! Just three minutes to heaven." Anna wipes her hands on a checkered towel. When the fish is done, she scoops each piece with a big net ladle and puts the fish on Sunday newspapers to absorb grease. Some pieces absorb colored ink from the cartoons, but I don't like the inky ones.

Ready to eat, all four families in our cove — the Kaaks, the Kennedys, the Wards, and the Carletons — gather at long tables covered with checkered cloths and bowls of potato salad, coleslaw, brown-sugar beans, sliced red tomatoes, onions, sweet pickle chips, Aunt Sally's okra, Uncle Luke's recipe for tartar sauce he brags about every time he makes it. And for Danny's birthday, we lap up Grandma Ward's peach ice cream and a huge white cake Otto baked with lemon filling and red airplane decorations.

I eat so much my belly's about to bust. But we've still got two hours of daylight, so Danny, Normie, Tommy, and I head back to our World War II battles. With the silver canoe tipped over our heads, we push along, chest-deep in the sunset-tipped waters. Here and there, we change course to dodge stumps or the outstretched roots of moss-draped cypress trees that still await Daddy's chain saw.

We know the position of each stump and name them after enemy ships, aircraft carriers, or U-boats, the *Shōhō*, the *Bismarck*, the *U-101*.

Our voices echo inside. Normie makes loud "ping" sounds. He's the best at noises.

"U-boat off starboard bow," I say in my deepest voice.

Tommy appoints himself Captain every day. "Turn forty-five degrees to port and run alongside her."

"Surface, surface. I gotta get some air!" Danny hollers.

I figure his belly is about to bust, like mine.

Tommy's pissed. "Danny, we can't surface. *U-101* is coming."

Normie's a suck up. "Captain's right. We just got going, Danny."

Danny makes a bunch of choking sounds. "But I can't breathe."

I try to raise the canoe, but the older boys hold it down. "Danny will have a heebie-jeebie. Surface, surface."

"Only the Captain gives orders, and I'm the Captain."

"Tommy, quit being so bossy," I holler so loud, the echo hurts my ears.

Danny frantically yanks his crossbar. "I can't breathe, Tommy. I mean it."

"Com'on, Tommy. Help Danny out."

"Andy, you gotta call me 'Captain.'"

Normie chimes in. "Captain, you don't want Danny to have a heebie-jeebie. I've heard one, and it's pretty scary."

Tommy growls as if he can't stand us all any longer.

Seconds later, Danny grunts in a throaty roar that rises up his throat and comes out his nose and mouth like a wolf howl. I mean, this noise is creepy. Danny keeps it up forever and alternates between low growls and woo-wooooooooos that echo so loud inside the canoe, even Tommy wants them to stop.

"Goddamn it, Danny. All you pussies. Surface, surface," Tommy commands.

We lift the canoe above our heads.

Danny stops howling and gasps for air.

I am also glad for a fresh breath and the warmth of the sunset. My mind takes a picture of the golden glint on the green lake's ripples. The light reflects so much brilliance, I let go one side of the canoe and reach to touch the gold, only to see the glimmers disappear the moment my fingers touch the water.

Scrawny Normie forgets the rules and shouts, "My arms are tired. Dive. Dive."

"Normie, I give the orders."

"Tommy, being a captain doesn't mean you have to be a jerk." That's pretty brave for Danny. Even if he says it so quiet, I'm the only one who hears.

"Wait until I give the command, you creeps."

Tommy takes his darn time until suddenly that beautiful Chris Craft appears, droning right down the middle of the lake. This means a set of waves will soon roll our way. Far off, I see the first crest, a big one, white-capped with gleams of sunlight as it rolls.

"Waves! Waves!" I cry.

Normie hollers so loud his voice squeaks. "I can't hold up my arms anymore!"

"You cream puffs. First, you want air. Then you want waves." Tommy waits another minute until his own arms tire. "On my command. Dive. Dive. Dive!"

"Aw, Tommy. Waves," I holler, but we lower the canoe onto the surface. There's so little light inside, we can barely make out each other's silhouettes.

"Up periscope," Tommy says.

Danny makes his periscope sound.

I laugh. "That was good, Danny, even if you are a maniac."

Tommy tilts the nose of the canoe so he can see what's ahead.

Normie hollers, "U-boat, fifteen degrees to starboard."

"Maintain heading. We'll take 'em before they know we're here."

I remember the waves. "Let's surface. Waves are inbound."

"The U-boat will see us."

"But we'll miss the waves, Tommy. I mean, 'Captain.'"

I don't know whether Tommy also wants to see the waves, or he gives in because I call him "Captain," but at his command, we flip the canoe, push it ashore, and challenge the first breaker with our chests. As the rolling surf passes, I turn to watch the sunlit whitecaps meet the shoreline, and I hear the rushing waves break onto red clay.

Chapter Twelve

NOVEMBER 7, LATE EVENING

Andrew writhed as his one good arm fought the restraints. Lizzy patted his left shoulder to quiet him while he stared at something she could not see. A nurse busily checked tubes and punched buttons on the monitors, then left for her station.

Moments later, Jane rushed in with an exasperated sigh. "Momma, after enduring Alan's dismay about rescuing your roast in beer sauce and describing exactly what he must do to turn it off, he is on his way. Is there anything else that needs tending? I might as well call him before he builds steam for a rebuttal."

"I can't think of anything except, oh dear, Walter is outside. He's got a doghouse, but if this horrid rain doesn't let up, maybe he should stay in the utility room. I don't know about food. Andrew is in charge of that."

Jane shuddered. "We can take care of the dog when we get back to your house in a bit."

"I'm not going anywhere 'in a bit.'"

Jane realized she was in for a long night and pulled out her phone. "I'll call Alan about Walter. In fact, I'll put you on the phone and you can deal with my delightful husband."

~

ALAN and the kids nibbled at Lizzy's guaranteed fat-free roast. The kids pronounced the dish "yucky," but Alan found the small roast so delectable, he gobbled more than half.

The kids were still hungry, so Alan fixed cereal and milk to quiet their stomachs. With no high-speed wireless for their smartphones, the boys whined that they had nothing to do.

"Be creative," Alan said as he led them to the living room.

Billy Jay sat at the piano, where he pretended to be a virtuoso and pounded out a concerto. His hands rose and fell with the flair of a young André Watts, but the cacophony sounded like a cymbal crash to Alan's ears. He did his best not to say anything and hoped Billy Jay would wear down, eventually.

The noise did not seem to bother Elizabeth, who curled under a quilt Lizzy's grandmother had made.

While Billy Jay bashed the keyboards, David studied the array of framed photos on the piano. He picked up the picture of his Uncle Billy and then shouted above Billy Jay's din. "This guy doesn't look like a 'Billy' to me."

"Are you saying he doesn't look like your brother?" Alan shouted back.

"Yeah. They've got the same names, but Billy Jay doesn't look a bit like this dude."

"Billy Jay, will you please stop so I can hear your brother?"

Billy Jay held up his hands. "Well, you wanted me to be creative."

"I'm trying to discuss something with David. You can play when we're through, but more softly, please." Alan gathered his thoughts. "Son, bring the picture here."

Both boys grew quiet. Something was up. First, Alan had called David "son," something he did only when the topic was serious. This was rare, since Jane handled most of the discipline. Alan parented by rote. Eat your breakfast, take your backpacks, do your homework.

"David, your mom wanted to name her first son after her brother, Billy. He is the 'Billy' in this picture, your Uncle Billy. The one who died in a car wreck when he was eighteen. Your mom was only fourteen, and she was very sad to lose her big brother. So, naming you 'Billy' was her way to honor him."

David shrugged. "That's like trying to make somebody come back to life."

Alan pursed his lips in an ironic smile. "Knowing your mom, I'd say that's some of what she tried to do. She is not a woman who can endure missing pieces."

"I'm glad I'm not named after the dead person."

Billy Jay heard David's jibe. "Yeah, but you *look* like the dead person."

"I don't look like him, do I, Dad?"

"Do too, David. Doesn't he, Dad?"

"No, I don't. Do I, Dad?" David grew red with frustrated anger.

Alan got up and retrieved a scrapbook from the bookcase. He flipped through until he found pictures of Billy as a young boy. "See? David, you look a lot like your Uncle Billy when he was your age. In fact, you also look like your Grand Pop when he was a boy. See this? That's Grand Pop with a fishing pole down at Lake Blackshear. He was a good-looking boy in his day, blond and blue-eyed like you."

"David looks like a geezer!" Elizabeth chimed sleepily from the couch.

"My dear daughter, I thought you were asleep."

"I'm not a geezer. Make her take it back, Dad!"

"I don't think you should be upset, David. Someday, girls will be gaga over those baby-blue eyes you inherited."

"How come David gets all the good stuff? I got brown hair and eyes, and some dead guy's name I didn't even know."

"Billy Jay, your name should inspire you to do great things to honor your mother, her brother, and your grandparents."

"I think I'd rather have blue eyes and the girls."

"I told ya. Billy likes girls!" Elizabeth chimed in.

Alan tried to quiet the children's shouts of "did not, did too," but the yammering irritated the hell out of him. So, he gave up on his quest to be the world's most patient father and went to the kitchen. Maybe there was a beer Lizzy hadn't used to cook that roast. He couldn't find a bottle in the main fridge, so he went to the utility room and discovered Lizzy's stash of merlot.

"God bless you, Lizzy. You'd have to drink in order to tolerate that cantankerous recluse who looks like my youngest son."

~

BY THE WEE HOURS, Lizzy and Jane had bowed to exhaustion. The nurse injected Andrew's IV with golden fluid and lightly closed his eyelids, as if to say, "Goodnight" to him and his visitors. Unlike Andrew's previous agitation, he seemed to be in a deep sleep.

"Momma, don't you think you should get some rest now?"

"How can I sleep?"

"Poppa will be fine. He doesn't know we're here, so he can't know we've left."

"What if he comes out of it and I'm not here?"

"We've got to be patient. Strokes are not like the flu. Dr. Fitzgerald said his recovery will take time."

"Time. Time. That's all we've got in this world. In a lightning bolt, our life, my plans changed. Again. And Andrew drifted farther away, somewhere I can't reach."

"Probably to the workshop of his dreams."

"Dear Abby, I realize you don't think much of my marriage. Truth be told, neither do I, not lately. But despite our troubles, we love each other deeply. It's just been so darn long since — I'm afraid he'll want to tell me, but I won't be here."

"Momma, you know Poppa loves you. No words need to be said."

"God forbid if he dies before I hear them."

"Aha. So, you're the one who needs to hear 'I love you.' Like when a tree falls in the forest? Does it really make a sound?"

"Yes, like the darn tree."

"It makes a sound. That's been scientifically proven."

"Janey, I don't care about the tree. I just want to hear my

husband say, 'I love you.' Out loud. To me." Lizzy's eyes filled with tears. "Otherwise, there's just no point — "

Jane had pushed too far and knew it. "Come to think of it, I don't remember if Poppa ever told me he loves me."

"Of course, your father loves you."

"But if I've never heard him say it?" Jane gave Lizzy a wry smile.

"Ah, Dear Abby. Who's asking the existential questions now?"

"Not me. After a day of chart-busting stress, I need to rest. You do too. Time to leave. I'll keep you company at the house tonight." Jane patted her father, kissed him on his cheek, and headed out.

Lizzy waited until the door closed, then kissed Andrew lightly on his lips. She whispered, "If you wake up but don't see me, I'm still with you. For better or for worse."

Chapter Thirteen

NOVEMBER 8

Andrew's eyelids fluttered. He could tell he was not in the lake with his buddies, but he didn't know where else he was. Deep shadows and lights surrounded him, and there was a bank of dark windows. Through blurred vision, he made out a rectangle of fluorescent light from an open door. He lifted his head and peered into the haze. A woman in green scrubs passed in the blare of light. Andrew tried to call out, but no sound came. He tried to signal, but he could not raise his right hand. He yelled in frustration, but again, no sound came out. He stared into the rectangle of light, but the figure did not return. He tried to shout, "Help! Help!" and felt adrenaline shoot through his left side.

"Luuuuuzzzzzzy!" he mustered on his fourth try. He was startled to hear his croak, more a wheeze than a word. "Luuuuuzzzzzzy!" he called again. The noise made no sense to him. He tried to scream, "Help!" but only a growl came out.

Moments before, he had held a canoe above his head and felt the waves buffet his chest and rush past. Then things went black, and now he was in a shadowy room with lights that flashed and machines that beeped. In his mind, he had just felt sunlight and waves, but now he was shivering.

He tried to reach for a cover, but his right hand would not move. He reached with his left hand, but it was tethered.

"I can't move! Where am I?" Only guttural sounds came out. He strained against the tethers and again felt adrenaline zing throughout the left side of his body. "Luuuuuzzzzzzy!" He felt another zing as panic raced through his left armpit to the tips of his left fingers. "Luuuuuzzzzzzy!"

A dark-skinned woman in pink scrubs appeared through the blurry rectangle of light. She flipped on the overhead lights. They glared into Andrew's hypersensitive eyes. "Hello, Sugar. Nice to see you awake. My monitor told me you were agitated. Are you cold? It's like ice in here."

Andrew tried to slug her. "You goddamn bitch. Wan' Luuuuuzzzzzzy!"

The nurse patted him with a chuckle. "Now, calm down. You are in Emory University Hospital, and I'm a nurse here. I know that's confusing. Your wife brought you here last night. Looks like sunrise is a few hours away, if we see a sunrise. I cannot believe this rainy weather. So, you just relax, and I bet your wife and daughter will be back first thing."

Andrew looked about wildly and struggled as if in a straitjacket. "You goddamn bitch!" He desperately yanked the straps that held his left arm.

"Now, Mr. Ward, I'm not really a bitch, although my husband might have a word to share with you. You rest easy. I'll stay with you a while." The nurse patted Andrew's left shoulder the same way Lizzy had done hours before.

Trouble was, Andrew could not understand the nurse's words or his own words, and he had developed a proclivity to call her a "bitch" or any other foul insult he knew. In an uncharacteristic tirade, he let loose with a string that ranged from "goddamn bitch" to the unmentionable "C" word and the "F" word. At the same time, he fought his restraints with what strength his left side could muster. "Goddamn bitch. Wan' Luuuuuzzzzzzy!" Andrew collapsed, exasperated to tears.

"Now, now, I'll get another dose to help you sleep." The nurse headed out, returned minutes later, and injected more golden fluid into Andrew's IV.

He was high immediately. "Luuuuuzzzzzzy." He gave the nurse a lopsided grin.

She smiled back. "Feeling woozy, Sugar?"

"Shit, you bitch, wan' Luuuuuzzzzzzy!" Andrew again fought to loosen his tethers but could not escape. He dissolved in a sob that melted into a drug-induced void.

WHEN THE ALARM went off at eight, Lizzy jumped out of bed and let Walter out back. Because of the rain, she had allowed him to spend the night in the utility room. With Andrew gone, that somehow seemed okay.

She made coffee for Jane, who had spent the night, then grabbed a cup for herself and went to the living room to draw back the drapes. She had hoped to see at least a peek of sunshine, but saw only thick clouds of yet another wet-weather day.

"Will the rain ever stop?"

She hated bad weather because it always reminded her of Billy, always did. She sat in the burgundy wingback chair and tried to stop, but oh, like lightning, the memory reappeared.

After school, Billy had walked in with a grin. He stretched out his arms and spun slowly with a toothy smile that was still boy, almost man. He was showing off his navy blue and white letter jacket. "Well, Mom, how do you like it?"

His mother's gasp was not the admiration that the very confident Billy had expected.

Lizzy silently stared. She knew Billy wanted her to say, *Oh, how wonderful, oh, how handsome you look*, but she couldn't overcome the shock. And she certainly couldn't tell him she had seen the same letter jacket in her vision from long ago.

"Mom? You're not pregnant again, are you?"

Lizzy shook her head. Tears spilled against her will. Was there a way to stop the future?

"Gosh, Mom. It's my senior letter jacket. I thought you'd say it was cool."

Lizzy nodded silently but could not say a word.

Billy tried to comfort her, but gave up and headed to his room.

"Must be one of those female-trouble days," he mumbled.

Lizzy raised her head and deliberately watched her son walk down the hall, her eyes focused on the jacket as she searched for a sign that it differed from her vision. But her heart was impaled by the truth. This was the same jacket. Her vision had been more than a dream, something Lizzy knew in her heart, since she had descended from a long line of Southern women who claimed to have premonitions. Although the family's male counterparts dismissed them as "hysterics," Lizzy knew of one portent that had come true. She feared hers would follow the same path.

Her mother's mother, the grandmother who willed Lizzy the upright mirror in her bedroom, was known as "Little Grandma" because she was a tiny woman in a sea of tall offspring. Little Grandma was well known for her midnight visions.

Now and then, when young Lizzy and her family visited, Little Grandma would bolt from her bedroom in the middle of the night and shout, "Everybody get up. I've got to count heads." The children groused at such episodes, until one night over a Thanksgiving holiday, Little Grandma caused a tremendous commotion about a vision she'd had of her widowed sister Claire, who lived up north near Chatsworth. Claire had been at Little Grandma's that day for dinner, but left in the late afternoon.

Little Grandma shuddered. "I saw Claire's face so clearly. And she was tearful. Crying. Alone. I hope she didn't have an accident."

She was so convinced something had happened, she called Claire's house at two in the morning. There was no answer, so all the women knew they were in for a long night. Little Grandma fretted and fussed through the next morning's breakfast and lunch until the state police appeared that afternoon to announce that

Claire had driven her station wagon deep into Chattahoochee National Forest. As the story was told, Claire had stopped at her house to pick up her two cocker spaniels and a shotgun. She killed the dogs, then put the gun to her mouth. Forest rangers found her.

After that, everybody showed more respect when Little Grandma had a vision.

Still, Lizzy knew of only two premonitions from her side of the family that had come true. Little Grandma's. And Lizzy's prediction about Billy. "Then again, Andrew's mother Noreen had a premonition about Tommy's bike accident. And that's why Andrew — " Lizzy caught herself mid-sentence. "Stop. Stop. You must not go there today. Focus."

She went to the sunroom and sat at her desk. She got out her address book and called Andrew's sister Sarah in Boston, but got voicemail. Confused by the voice message system, Lizzy stammered in a discombobulated ramble until the system beeped and a stern voice gave her thirty seconds to finish. Lizzy did not know if she should continue, so the system said, "Your message has been left. Goodbye."

"Oh dear, I didn't leave a message Sarah could understand." She fumbled with the buttons to start over, but gave up. "She'll think I'm inebriated."

Lizzy habitually glanced at the mirror above her desk and saw Andrew's workshop looming like a haunted house across the misty backyard. A dark fog filtered over Lizzy's mind. *All this happened because I was going to leave him.* With a sigh, she paged through her address book to find Andrew's brother's number. But she thought better of calling the West Coast so early. Instead, Lizzy called her brother Yates, who was still managing partner of his Chicago law firm. Yates' time zone was an hour behind Lizzy's.

"What's the matter, Lizzy? The last time you called so early, Billy had died."

"What a way to answer the phone. Should I hang up?"

"Of course, I want to talk to you, but I've got an eight o'clock meeting. Let me call you from my car. You can ride to work with me vicariously."

Lizzy sighed and hung up, muttering. "Mr. Big Cigars and Motor Cars."

Her brother was older by four years and her least favorite because he patronized her, or so it seemed. Of her family's three children, Lizzy was the only female and, like Andrew, the only child who had remained in Atlanta. Also, unlike her two brothers, Lizzy did not have a stellar career beyond teaching elementary school before Billy and Janey were born. A woman of her era, she had married Andrew, supported them both until he finished graduate school, then quit after he got a job to raise their children. That was all the profession Lizzy expected.

The phone rang back, which startled Lizzy because she received so few calls. Sarah was calling back.

About that time, Jane shuffled in, wearing Andrew's red robe. She noticed her mother on the phone, so Jane went to the kitchen. As she blew on her coffee to cool it, she stared out at the gloomy morning. She had slept — rather, tossed — in a twin bed in her childhood room, still adorned with a pink taffeta spread and white French provincial furnishings. The décor did not keep her awake, but her struggle to move beyond her baby-girl rank in this home did.

Jane reached for her cell phone and called Alan. "Sleeping in that twin bed was surreal. I had to overcome the urge to ask Momma to tuck me in."

"She didn't, did she?"

"I imagine she would have, but I think she was so exhausted, she actually slept. At least I heard her snoring before I drifted off, if I drifted off. I'd feel myself drift into a REM state, then I'd jump for fear I'd miss something. Momma was up first thing, calling family."

"Lizzy is in her element when there is considerable drama."

"Not one she planned, but she's now a woman with a mission."

"That apple doesn't fall far from the tree."

Jane let that one go. After she gave Alan a quick "I love you," she dressed, then ventured into Lizzy's sunroom. "I'll take my car and see you at the hospital."

Lizzy's landline rang again. She waved a silent "okay" to Jane and nervously answered.

Thomas was on the other end. "Why didn't you call? I found out from Sarah."

"I didn't want to call that early."

"I'd already run three miles by five-thirty."

"I'm exhausted thinking about that. As I told your sister, Andrew is in Emory University Hospital. They are doing tests. I will call you after I speak with the doctor."

"What do they think hit him?"

"A stroke. An acute icky something. A stroke."

Thomas sighed. "Ischemic. Defective circuitry."

Lizzy counted to ten. "I'll keep you posted, Thomas." Then she hung up. "You will not nail your brother into any coffin."

Immediately, Sarah called back to say she would fly down the next day.

"Sarah, of course, you will stay at our house. You're Andrew's family. Thomas, too." Lizzy wondered if she meant that.

Next on Lizzy's list was Ouisie, who screamed for thirty seconds, then dropped the phone. Guy abruptly took over the call.

"Give Andrew our best and please let us know — "

Ouisie came back on the line. "Girl, are you all right? Do you need to talk? I know you were ready to, well, but now there's this, and so, what are you going to do?"

"All is on hold. I must focus on Andrew."

"But that's always been the problem."

Suddenly, Lizzy regretted telling her friend about her plans. "Ouisie, Guy might hear you."

"I understand. The good thing is, Andrew is at the hospital, so you can practice being, you know, see if you enjoy being on your own. We can even have a girls' night out!"

"Ouisie, enough."

"Mum's the word. Don't worry. You can count on me."

"What have I started?" Lizzy murmured after she hung up.

Immediately, the phone rang again. Thomas called to say that he would fly out the next day. "I would appreciate the accommodations offered through Sarah. I'm sure your home has fewer bed bugs than most Atlanta hotels."

Lizzy kept a determined smile in her voice, trying to joke. "Is that your idea of a compliment?" But she worried Andrew would be furious to know Thomas was staying at their home. She decided not to mention it.

Before she left for the hospital, Lizzy called Walter inside and fed him in the kitchen, muddy paws and all. Then she scooted him to his doghouse on the covered back porch. She felt guilty that the old guy would have to spend another day outside in the muck, but she could not leave him inside all day after a full meal.

With a damp mop, she freed the linoleum of Walter's prints. After that, she dashed to the bedroom and dressed. In Little Grandma's upright mirror, she leaned to pluck another annoying chin hair. Next, she retrieved a suitcase and packed Andrew's pajamas, slippers, underwear, t-shirts, toothbrush, toothpaste, comb, razor, aftershave, and his robe. Then Lizzy donned her ancient raincoat, took two boxes of Cracker Jack from the pantry, and rushed to her Jag. She floored it back to the hospital.

When Lizzy arrived in Andrew's room, Jane was in a side chair. Andrew was asleep, or appeared to be.

"Is he still in the coma?" Lizzy's tone sounded desperate, despite her determination to be matter-of-fact.

In response to Lizzy's voice, Andrew's eyes fluttered open. Although his vision communicated a confused array of images to his brain, he recognized the shape and sound of his wife. In fact, he was overcome to see the only person he could identify in this world of chaotic lights, dreams, memories, strangers, and blackness. His eyes filled with relieved tears.

"Luuuuuzzzzzzy!"

Again, his voice sounded like a wheeze, but Lizzy understood.

"It's you! The nurse said you woke up last night. I'm sorry I wasn't here. Janey made me go home to get some sleep."

"Momma would have stood beside your bed all night if I'd let her. But I can't have both of you collapse on me."

Andrew had not understood a word. "Luuuuuzzzzzzy!"

"I'm right here. I'll stay with you all night if they'll let me."

"Momma, you need your rest. How are you feeling, Poppa?"

"Luuuuuzzzzzzy!" The one word he could say. Nothing else made sense. Nothing seemed familiar. And who was that other woman? Andrew's left arm and leg strained at their tethers as he tried to get up. *Why is my left arm tied? Why can't I move?* His questions came out in growls.

"The nurse said you might not speak for a while, but that'll clear up."

"Momma, you shouldn't make promises."

Oh, Janey, give it a rest, Lizzy thought, but counted to ten.

Andrew stared in Jane's direction. "Who the hell are you?" he shouted. Although his words did not come out in a way Lizzy or Jane could fully understand, both women could tell that he did not recognize his daughter.

Lizzy patted his silver hair and saw that his opalescent eyes truly recognized her. "The nurse told me it's a good sign you're awake so soon. Sometimes it takes longer. She said the doctor will talk to us soon. You've had a stroke, but you'll be good as new."

"Momma, they said time will tell." Jane had emphasized the word "Momma" to educate Andrew.

"Time will tell what time will tell, but I know in my soul that Andrew will get better."

"I guess you have your orders, Poppa." This time, Jane emphasized "Poppa" and hoped for a glint of recognition.

Andrew stared at her in confusion. He tried to say, "*Why does that woman call me 'Poppa'?*" But instead he grunted, "Fuck that bitch. Wan' Luuuuuzzzzzzy!"

Lizzy understood the "F" and "B" words. "Oh my, Andrew. Why are you swearing?"

"He doesn't know who in the hell I am, that's why." Jane exhaled, on the verge of tears. "I think I'll go downstairs to the cafe. Give you two a moment." Her eyes brimmed as she walked out.

Andrew grinned in satisfaction. "Bitch damn 'way!"

"Andrew, that's Janey. Our daughter. Don't you recognize her?"

As Jane waited impatiently for an elevator, her tears fell like the storm that had begun outside. Nurses and visitors stared in alarm as they rushed past. She wanted to shout, "My father doesn't know me. He never did. He only saw his precious son and football star Billy." She jabbed the elevator call button five times. After what seemed like an hour, she found herself on a crowded elevator, surrounded by green-scrubbed gawkers. She sniffled into a tissue and internally chastised herself in the same tone Alan would have used. *Jane, you're being irrational. You cannot blame your father for his damaged memory.*

Lizzy was relieved that Jane's wounded ego was gone. "Our Janey needs reassurances. Our daughter. I can tell you don't remember who she is, but who could remember a thing with a clog in your brain, these incessant machines, and strangers running in and out. How do you sleep? Oh dear, I keep asking questions. Nurse McMahan said I shouldn't ask questions. Doctor Fitzgerald said that when people have strokes, connections shut down. But she's going to fix that. She's young but seems bright. You'll be home in no time. And things will be different this time. I'll try harder if you will."

Lizzy stopped for a breath. "Your sister Sarah is coming. So is your brother Thomas. I hope that's good news. And I called my brother Yates. He sends his best. I didn't call my brother Jeff yet because he's in Taiwan, last I heard. My baby brother, the world traveler. Oh, Guy and Ouisie will be here this afternoon. Ouisie screamed like a little girl, and Guy had to take the call until Ouisie recovered. I hope you will remember them, but if you don't, just say nothing about their being Black. Actually, Guy is from French Guiana. Born there, anyway. That's why his name is Guy. He had a very long African first name when the family immigrated to America, so his elementary school teacher shortened it to Guy to stand for Guiana. You'll remember all this when you get your memory back. Oh, let's see, I brought some Cracker Jack, even if they're not healthy, but maybe they'll help you remember home. I also brought your robe and slippers so you can stay warm in this frigid place. And I took care of Walter this morning. Outside it's — Oh, look at that lightning bolt. It shot across the sky like fingers on fire. They say it's an El Niño year. Our backyard is a river. I put Walter in his doghouse so he can stay dry. Poor guy doesn't know what to do without you. I guess that's where you'd rather be. Oh, not in Walter's doghouse, but in your workshop. But that's the problem, and I wish we could — " Lizzy's eyes welled with tears.

Frustrated by what he'd heard as indecipherable, Andrew did not understand why Lizzy was crying. "Shit, Luuuuuzzzzzzy!" he cried through his own streaming tears.

"Shhhhhh, Andrew. Why do you keep swearing?"

"Goddamn, Luuuuuzzzzzzy, bullshit!" Andrew pulled mightily at the straps that held him, but half his body seemed disconnected. He could only feel his left side.

Lizzy crooned as if calming a baby. "Now, now. Everything will be all right. I'll make sure of it."

Dr. Fitzgerald met Lizzy, Jane, Alan, and the kids in the waiting room. "As I mentioned before, Professor Ward has had an acute ischemic stroke, the result of an obstruction within an artery that supplies blood to the brain. A stroke usually occurs on one side of the brain or the other. Each side controls movement and sensations for the opposite side of the body. Our tests show that in Professor Ward's case, his stroke was on his brain's left side. That caused impairments on the right side of his body. As you can see, he can't move anything on his right side. With intensive rehabilitation, we can train other parts of the brain to do what the damaged part originally did."

Lizzy sighed. "Oh, I hope so."

"Another problem is called 'aphasia.' This condition makes it difficult for him to understand speech, or to speak, read, write, or even think of words. He may swear inappropriately now and then. In fact, the nurses tell me he's quite a foul-mouthed sailor."

"So, that's why he let go at me. Andrew has never been one to swear. He always said that profanity was the emotional crutch of the uneducated."

"Mrs. Ward, even the most educated may let loose with a tirade after a stroke. As your husband said, it's an emotional crutch. Their memories are damaged. They don't know where they are, who people are, what's happened to them. They're frustrated, confused, angry, desperate, so they might take a swing at you or me, or try to speak, but only cusswords come out."

"Janey, you should keep the children out of Andrew's room for a time."

"Momma, the kids hear worse on Netflix."

"Hopefully, his swearing will diminish over time. Also, Professor Ward may develop another problem called 'verbal dyspraxia.' This is when he knows the right words but has trouble forming them or putting the sounds together. For example, 'cup of coffee' may come out backwards and distorted, like, 'foppie of bup.'"

"Foppie of bup!" Elizabeth shouted in a giggle.

Dr. Fitzgerald gave Elizabeth a pat. "I know that sounds funny, but it's important not to laugh at your grandfather. If he uses bad words, just plug your ears. He doesn't want to be mean or nasty. With your love and help, plus some new medicines and therapy, he really can get better."

Chapter Fourteen

NOVEMBER 9 - 12

A ndrew's brother Thomas flew in from Silicon Valley and
stayed for three nights with Lizzy at the house. The more
enterprising of the two brothers, Thomas was an engineer before
most people knew what an engineer did. By age twenty-eight, he was
a stellar inventor at Bell Labs in Murray Hill, New Jersey, where he
designed and patented integrated circuits for silicon wafers. By age
forty, he grabbed the brass ring on the cusp of the Information Age
and formed a semiconductor company in Sunnyvale, California.
Intel bought him out when Thomas was sixty, a deal that made him
a gazillionaire.

"Rich as horse manure," Andrew muttered each time Lizzy
mentioned his brother, which was twice a year when greeting cards
arrived in time for Andrew's birthday and Christmas. They were
signed in Thomas's wife's hand.

As kids, the two boys had been at each other's throats and grew
further apart after high school. Their father, Comstock, often
bragged about his oldest son. "Tommy whizzed through MIT on
scholarships and got his master's in physics. I don't think I even took
physics in school. Didn't know what it was. For sure, my lovely
Noreen didn't take any physics class. I think Thomas's smarts must

have come from the milkman." Comstock would laugh after that, while his wife Noreen would glare.

When it was Andy's turn for college, he went to Emory University, where his family could afford the tuition, and he could live at home. Andrew was smart enough to receive a full scholarship, but they were not offered in Andy's passion, history. To make money on the side, Andrew — as he called himself after he received his bachelor's in liberal arts — taught history as a graduate assistant. After four more years, he earned his doctorate in U.S. history.

Thomas often chided his brother. "History, Andy? Engineering is the 'steel' of our generation. Being an intellectual and being rich are not mutually exclusive." Thomas's nasal tone agitated Andrew like squeaky blackboard chalk.

Over the years, the brothers saw one another as little as possible, usually at weddings or funerals. The two were so distant that Andrew did not call Thomas to tell him about Billy's death. Their mother, Noreen, had that sad duty.

"Andy's too distraught to tell you what happened. There was a terrible accident," she had said.

"What did Andy do?"

"A terrible storm was headed their way, but Billy wanted to drive his friends to a basketball game in Marietta. Lizzy didn't want him to go — she had a feeling, a vision from long ago — but Andy insisted it was okay. The road was slick. Billy skidded around a turn. The car flipped, and Billy died," Noreen sobbed.

"Andy has no common sense."

"Knowing Andy, he's taking full blame. Lizzy took it hard, of course, losing her firstborn. Although she's only my daughter-in-law, I love her like my own and feel her pain. If I ever lost my Andy — " Noreen dissolved into sobs.

"I was your firstborn, Mother."

"Well, of course, dear. What I meant to say was — "

"Oh, that Andy. Always first in your heart. But now that he's killed a son, doesn't that show you?"

"Now, Tommy. Don't blame your brother! How could Andy have known?"

"Lizzy had a feeling, like you used to get them. Remember my bike accident?"

"Tommy, do not darken your heart by blaming your brother."

"Andy was a stubborn, angry little boy, and now he's a stubborn, angry man. How could any father let a boy go out on a stormy night? Lizzy had a gut feeling. Couldn't Andy let Lizzy be right? Of course, if Billy had stayed home, he'd be alive, and no one would know that Lizzy's premonition came true. So, in a way, Billy's death serves some purpose. Proves she was right, not that Andy will ever admit it."

Thomas continued his engineer's analysis, while his mother wept on the other end of the line.

At the memorial service for Billy, the two brothers barely spoke. Thomas had flown in with his slip-thin wife Rhonda, a Smith College alumna with a frosted bob and country-club tan.

"I'd have thought the Ku Klux Klan would have burned the Unitarian church by now," she whispered to Lizzy in a poor attempt to lighten the mood after the ceremony.

If Lizzy were herself that day, she would have replied with a cynical zinger, but she was so shocked by the loss of her son, she did not respond to much that day, not to the minister's readings, not to the many condolences at a reception after, not to Thomas' whispered, "I am so sorry, Lizzy. Andy should not have let him go."

Throughout that day, Andrew avoided his brother, since Thomas would be sure to bring up Andrew's life-altering error. But Thomas' opportunity came soon enough after the reception. Thomas and Rhonda were to stay overnight. Rhonda excused herself for a "long, hot bath after such a sad day as this," while Lizzy and teenage Janey said goodbye to the church ladies who had organized the reception.

Andrew sat in his burgundy wingback chair while Thomas stood by the fireplace and smoked a pipe. Andrew pretended to read a *National Geographic*, but Thomas was not fooled. He was poised to interject, but Andrew simply stared at the pages to avoid the sermon.

Thomas pounced. "Andy, I've thought carefully about this. Mother detailed the facts of Billy's death. How he'd wanted to drive his friends to a game, but Lizzy didn't want him to go because of her gut instinct, and you interceded. I don't suppose one can hold an individual responsible for an accident that happened miles away — in fact, it would be technically inaccurate to do so — but I question your judgment. I would not have let my child go out in a storm, especially in a car full of teenagers. Just what kind of reasoning did they teach you in those liberal-arts courses?"

Andrew shook his head in disdain.

"Did you hear me, Andy?"

Andrew tried to control his resentment, but how dare his brother challenge him today? He took a breath and began slowly. "Can't you let go? On this, of all days?"

"Your childish need to be right enabled this tragedy."

"Tommy, I do not intend to argue about the right, the wrong, the anything regarding my son's death. Not ever. My son died. Billy died. Now, for the love of God, let us grieve for him in peace." Andrew shuddered into his lap, and tears dripped on the creases of his black pants. Thomas moved to put a hand on his brother's shoulder, but Andrew jerked away. He choked out, "Tommy, you and Rhonda can stay the night. But in the morning, you two fly back to Silicon Wherever. And never darken my door again."

Thomas gasped. "We came all this way for you. With Father gone and Mother, well, not in good health, I'm the head of the family. This event affected all of us, not just you. But then, you've always held your own interests. Even as a boy. Everything was always about you, your whimpering, your constant complaints to Mother, 'I wanna, wah, wah, wah.'"

Andrew's anger simmered in a way he knew would come to a rolling boil if he uttered another word. Yes, he resented Thomas for his many putdowns, but also for his intellectual, physical, and financial superiority. Andrew, the professor, was an underachiever compared to a petty older brother. If this latest encounter had been simply another of Thomas' little digs, Andrew might have been able to shake it, but this was no little dig. Thomas blamed Andrew for Billy's death, and now he was pouring it on. Thomas was right, of course, but the Andy inside could not ask forgiveness, especially from the Captain.

So, Andrew silently walked down the hall and vowed not to say another word to Thomas, even to bid him goodbye the next morning.

Over the years, Andrew felt a righteous ache for losing what little brotherhood the two had, especially when their mother Noreen died one year after Billy. Again, Andrew was devastated. His mother had been his comfort, his solace, his hope as he grew up, the only parent Andrew felt cared about him. He attended her memorial service to honor her, but he avoided any interaction with Thomas and refused to attend the reception after because of his vow not to spend one more moment in the company of Thomas Ward.

"Andrew still grieves over Billy," Lizzy murmured to Thomas as an excuse.

"But you're here. Aren't you grieving too?" Thomas had replied.

THIRTY YEARS LATER, when Thomas walked into the hospital room, Andrew blurted loudly with a crooked grin, "Goddamn horse manure, it's Tommy!"

Four years older than Andrew, but twenty years younger in appearance, Thomas was tan and lean in faded jeans and a red long-sleeved polo, with white sweater sleeves sportily tied across his chest. His sunglasses were poised atop his close-cut gray hair, and a leather eyeglass guard dangled around his neck.

"I'm surprised you recognized me. How are you, little brother?" Thomas asked as he came to Andrew's right side and reached for his hand. Andrew tried to extend his left hand, so Thomas moved around the bed to grasp it. Each was overcome with tears, but Andrew's were of amazement, not reconciliation, since the last thing he remembered about Tommy was playing under the canoe.

"Whuhhhhh hair?" Andrew stared at Tommy's gray cut.

Jane sighed and muttered, "He sees his estranged brother and cries in glee, but he can't remember who in the hell his daughter is."

"Janey, today is not about you."

"Think how you would feel if he did not remember you."

Lizzy got Jane's point, but was weary of her neediness, especially on a monumental day like this. Thomas and Andrew were together after three decades.

Tears streamed down Thomas's cheeks. He grabbed a tissue from Lizzy's outstretched hand. "Rhonda sends her best. She would be here, but with her back problems, she cannot get comfortable in an airplane, even in first class. I didn't have time to charter."

After a silence, Lizzy tried to be conversational. "I hear that the security lines are terrible. Last time I flew to Chicago to see my brother, I felt like a sardine. Remember when all the seats were spacious, and the food was free?"

"I wish I had the same memories, Momma. I travel coach once a month for meetings, and it is like riding in a sheep transport."

"Thankfully, I never travel coach."

Andrew wildly flails with his left hand. "Horse manure. Horse manure!"

"Thomas, pay no attention. *Aphasia* is what the doctor calls it. A side effect of strokes."

Lizzy covered for Andrew, but she knew he had hit his target. She gave him a private wink. He tried to wink back, but his right eye didn't cooperate, and he had no clue how to wink with his left.

THOMAS HAD SETTLED in at the house by the time Sarah arrived at the hospital by taxi that evening. Six years younger than Andrew and ten years younger than Thomas, she was nervous about seeing her older brothers after so many years. Would they even remember her? Thomas had left for college by the time she finished elementary school, and he was in grad school by the time she finished high school. But then, Thomas did ask his wife to write recommendation letters for Sarah to attend Smith College, which gave her a full scholarship. And Sarah graduated *cum laude*, a finance major, no less. But like Lizzy, Sarah did not have a career after marrying an Amherst grad. His family owned a chain of high-end department stores throughout the Northeast. Now a wealthy widow, Sarah used her finance degree to oversee her late husband's estate.

Still lithe but gray-blond, Sarah had held her two older brothers in awe throughout childhood, especially Thomas for his early success. But she felt a closer bond with Andrew because he was the only one who had paid attention to "Sarah Little Shit" during their youth.

At the lake cottage, Andy would play marbles with her for hours, the only game invented without Tommy's rules. He simply refused to play and deemed Andy's version "girlie."

Seated at opposite ends of the long room, Andy and Sarah rolled marbles the length of the long, dark green floorboards. These were inch-wide painted planks with grooves between. Each child would place a marble as a target. Then the other had to hit the target with the shooter to "take it." Andy had a yellow and green cat's eye marble for his shooter, while Sarah had a gigantic sapphire-blue marble. As simple as the game was, playing marbles occupied many rainy afternoons. To this day, Sarah could still hear the sound each marble made rolling across those long green boards.

As the sixtyish Sarah rushed to hug Andrew, she was saddened to see he had no clue who she was. "Oh, Andy, I'm Sarah. Remember me? I haven't seen you in so many years, but I wanted to let you know how much I care. You always stood up for me when I was a little girl, like those times at the lake when, what was his name, Normie? Remember Danny Kaak's cousin from Chicago? Normie teased me constantly for being so thin. Now, that was the pot calling the kettle black. Skinny Normie making fun of me. Remember those days, Andy?"

"Goddamn horse manure." Andrew kicked his left leg and jerked his left hand.

Sarah gasped in shock.

Lizzy waved vigorously at Sarah as if to erase the swearwords. "Andrew, your sister *Sarah* came from Boston to see you."

Andrew looked about wildly. Then from a lightning synapse, he gleefully blurted, "Sarah goddamn Shit!"

Sarah shrieked. "I always hated that nickname, but now I'm happy to hear it."

"Sarah is staying with me, and I'm delighted to have her company. Thomas's too." Indeed, Lizzy was rosy with the duties of wondrous meals to prepare, beds to make, sheets to wash, and people to transport. "The back seat of the Jag will come in handy at last."

"Horse manure." Andrew's lopsided grin lit up the room.

FOR THE NEXT TWO DAYS, Lizzy shuffled Thomas and Sarah between the house and hospital, two visits each day sandwiched between Andrew's therapy sessions or medical tests. Afternoons, the group toured parts of the new Atlanta that Lizzy thought would impress them. Then she cooked dinner, or they went out to eat before the entourage headed back to the hospital.

For her first meal, Lizzy cooked veal *piccata* and fettuccini. Although she suggested a glass of wine, no one took her up on it. So, she also declined, for fear she could not control her tongue if Thomas irritated her. But she yearned for a nipper in a way no one else knew, or at least Lizzy hoped they didn't.

Late that night, when she listened at Jane's and Billy's bedroom doors and heard the snores of her guests, she tiptoed to the utility room, where she discovered she had to uncork another bottle of merlot. *That prig Alan finished it without even telling me.* She poured herself a full eight-ounce plastic cup, re-corked the bottle, then tiptoed to her bedroom, where she closed her door with a sigh.

"Spirit of Life, thank you for your gift of fermentation."

~

THE NEXT EVENING, Alan and Jane took everyone out for gourmet Southern cooking, a high-end spot featuring a gourmet chef's take on old-fashioned fried chicken and trimmings. Again, Lizzy refused a glass of wine, although Alan ordered a *pinot blanc* for the table.

"I appreciate the offer, but I don't think wine goes well with fried chicken."

Jane gave Lizzy a look of disbelief.

"Neither do I, Lizzy. A beer might taste better. I so miss Southern cooking. Some Boston restaurants advertise 'down home' food, but I think you have to *be* from here to know how to cook like here." Sarah's comment revealed a bit of what had been her Georgia accent.

Thomas left most of his meal on the plate. "I'm accustomed to less heavy foods. California cuisine is so fresh and light, you don't need all this grease."

Jane glanced to see if her mother shared her dismay. Her long-lost Uncle Thomas was a constant downer, and Jane would be relieved when he went back to California.

Back at the house, Lizzy brought out scrapbooks with hundreds of photos from summers at the lake. In one, the boys stood on shore and held the canoe above their heads like strongmen. Dressed in a fairy costume, tow-headed Sarah posed in front of the boys. She held out a wand as though her magic had elevated the canoe above their heads.

"What a treasure. Lizzy, I'd love a copy. Do you have a scanner?"

"I'll have to ask Janey. She knows about such things."

"We really were thin, weren't we, Tommy?"

"You still are, in a good way," Lizzy said.

"I think our family was blessed. Even to this day, I cannot put on a pound."

"Running does the trick for me. I don't know whether Andy told you, Lizzy, but he and I used to spend most of our summers under that canoe, not in it. We played World War II submarine for hours.

This boy here. What was his name? Danny, yes, Danny. He had 'heebie-jeebies,' we used to say. Panic attacks from claustrophobia under the canoe. I always wondered how that boy turned out. He was a baker's son. Last name was Kaak, pronounced like 'cake.'" Thomas smiled, but then his lips drew a determined line. "In the canoe, I was the oldest, so I always took the role of captain. I know that made Andy angry. Still is mad at me, I suppose, if he could remember anything."

"He seemed so pleased to see you," Lizzy said.

"Swore at me when I walked in!"

"Thomas, I've explained the profanity. Andrew has aphasia."

"Aphasia or Freudian slip. Lizzy, you know Andy never forgave me for taking him to task about Billy's death."

"Andrew was as heartbroken as I was on the night Billy — "

"But surely you blamed him in your own heart."

Lizzy shook her head. "Thomas, I think we should treasure the time we have together."

"Lizzy's right. I barely knew my brothers, and we have lived apart for so long. Here we are, in our so-called 'senior years.' We have a chance to reconnect."

Thomas ignored Sarah and pressed. "Tell me, Lizzy, did he ever admit he was wrong?"

Tears welled, and Lizzy felt she had to escape. She excused herself for the bathroom, where she dabbed her damp lashes. In the mirror, she whispered, "Damn you, Thomas. Andrew is an imperfect man. Stubborn to the point I was ready to divorce him. But he's a good man at heart. And he's right about one thing. You grab the jugular and refuse to let go. Maybe that's why you're rich as horse manure."

She spoke to the mirror as though Andrew's image was staring back at her. "That's the first thing you've said since your stroke that made any sense."

Chapter Fifteen

NOVEMBER 12 - FEBRUARY 2

Thomas and Sarah left the same morning that Dr. Fitzgerald transferred Andrew to a different building on the medical campus, the Emory Center for Rehabilitation Medicine. There, he would receive inpatient physical rehabilitation and speech therapy.

Although his right side displayed little improvement and remained limp from his right eyebrow and eyelid down to the tip of his right toes, improvement came slowly, as Dr. Fitzgerald had predicted. Andrew soon spoke in broken sentences, sometimes punctuated by cusswords or angry outbursts. He jumbled words and letters because he could not remember which word to say for which object, or which word went with each idea he wanted to convey. His comprehension of what others said was unpredictable. Sometimes he understood but could not form words to reply. Instead, he would shake his head and give a thumbs-up with his unstrapped left hand. If anyone pressed him for a cogent reply, he let loose with a profane stream that Lizzy had no clue he knew.

The rehab hospital had a daybed, so Lizzy slept there as many nights as she could. Having Lizzy near calmed Andrew greatly, calmed both of them. She became a woman with renewed purpose and took on as many chores as the rehab staff would allow. To be more comfortable, she bought blue scrubs at a hospital supply

store and wore those each day. She changed sheets. She held the
bedpan. She fetched ice, water, and straws. She fed him pureed
spaghetti in zero-fat tomato sauce, along with fat-free yogurt, and
green Jell-O.

Andrew could not take in the food, chew it, or swallow it easily
because the right half of his mouth remained lifeless. With each
spoonful, he grimaced, spat, and hollered something that sounded
like, "horseshit ghettie."

"I know. This spa-ghet-tie *is* awful," Lizzy enunciated to teach
him. "When you come home, I'll fix you some real spa-ghet-tie."

Times came when Lizzy needed more rest, so Jane stayed
overnight with Andrew. He still didn't know her as his daughter,
even though Lizzy insisted that's who she was. At least this woman
was pleasant and pretty, although a little sarcastic. Best of all, she
knew how to operate the TV, something Lizzy could not manage.
Andrew liked the *National Geographic* channel and hoped to see
more shows with naked tribal women. He also enjoyed PBS
Masterpiece Mysteries. When that came on, he smiled and nodded at
the lady who knew how to operate all sorts of technical equipment,
like her laptop computer and smartphone.

Meanwhile, Lizzy at home was a woman without enough to do.
Although she was an avid reader, a volunteer on the membership
committee at her church, and a sometime pianist, much of Lizzy's
life had revolved around Andrew's needs. With him gone, there was
too little to do, so she decided to have lunch with Ouisie every
Wednesday to break up her week.

This Wednesday, Lizzy was determined to stretch both of their
boundaries and chose a Vietnamese restaurant, although Ouisie
protested the ethnic choice. "You want me to eat roadkill?"

But determined Lizzy was. As she and Ouisie clumsily poised
chopsticks above huge white porcelain bowls of *phở tái bò viên*, or as
the menu described it, "Beef broth with rare beef and meatballs," a
Vietnamese server nervously interrupted to demonstrate how to add
the bountiful condiments of basil, cilantro, lime, jalapeño slices,
bean sprouts, and *hoi sin* or red pepper sauces.

"My goodness, thank you. We had no idea what to do. Everything looks so fresh, and this broth is delightful."

After Ouisie took a sip of the *pho*, she added more hot chili oil and another slice of jalapeño pepper, then nodded with surprised approval. But just as soon as the server left, she glanced to see if anyone else could hear. "Lizzy, how are *things*? Any news?"

"Andrew's improving, but slowly. A stroke is not something you get over in a week."

"I don't mean Andrew. I mean you. Your plans."

"He had a stroke. I'm not going anywhere. Deep inside, I have enough Christian guilt to wonder if my plans caused God's wrath, and all that."

"Lizzy, God would never blame you for wanting happiness, not after you've given so much to your marriage. You even gave a son. That's the same thing God did."

"Goodness, I can't live up to that comparison. And I wouldn't blame God for punishing me. When we married, I promised, 'for better or worse.' That's a vow. Now that Andrew is ill, I can't leave. Besides, there's no one at home to leave."

Ouisie patted Lizzy's hand. "Not to worry. After he gets home, you can leave him then."

"Ouisie — "

"I'm just joking, but I confess I wish Guy would go away now and then, for a week. No, make that a *month*. I tell you, that man does not have enough to do anymore, so he hangs around me all the time. That means I've got more to cook and clean. Of course, my cleaning service does the job now. I still don't understand why you won't get help. All that to do by yourself?"

"They never really clean things as well as I keep our home. I may move more slowly these days, but I have a plan and a list. Janey calls it a 'matrix.' I guess that's high-tech for 'plan.' There are a few tasks each day."

"Did you muck out Andrew's rocket barn yet?"

Lizzy looked down at her soup. "Why would I take that on? It's probably a landfill."

She didn't want to reveal that she had been to the workshop. She had slept at home to get more rest after a frustrated Andrew had uttered epithets right and left — or "reft and light, shit," as he would express it, telling her to "set some gleep, damn it." But once at home, she rummaged about like a woman who had lost a pair of shoes. There was no matrix to her movements. Room to room she wandered, opening drawers, exploring closets, looking for nothing really, just taking inventory.

Later, she fed Walter dinner in the kitchen, which was customary now that he was *her* dog and a much *cleaner* pet. She leaned to give the old guy a kiss and a few pats. "Your master will be home soon. I promise you that."

Out the kitchen windows, Lizzy saw the unlit workshop in the December moonlight. Dear, efficient Jane had the wits to lock the door on the chaotic night of Andrew's stroke, when ambulance lights flashed, and neighbors came to gawk at EMS workers as they invaded Andrew's refuge. They lifted him like a rag doll, strapped him on a gurney, wheeled him to the front, and drove away with him inside, as sirens blared, and Lizzy and Jane stood helpless.

Lizzy shook off the memory as she retrieved the key from a Toby jug beside the kitchen phone. With Walter at her side, she marched across the back porch, then down the path.

Despite his age, Walter eagerly leapt up the workshop steps.

"Now, Walter, don't get your hopes up. Andrew is not here."

The sunrise had not yet cleared the pines, so the workshop interior was shadowy when Lizzy opened the door. When she flipped on the light, a garish fluorescence illuminated the room. Although Lizzy had been there the night of Andrew's stroke, she'd paid no attention to the disarray. Oh, she knew Andrew was a packrat. The man still had his Little League bat, gloves, and ball, and when Lizzy suggested that an underprivileged child might benefit from a donation, Andrew refused, proffering, "My grandsons might play with that equipment someday."

"Andrew, you won't even have breakfast with those boys, much less play catch with them," Lizzy had replied with a smirk.

No, the man would not let a thing go. He even kept every research note and draft of his textbooks, which Lizzy saw stacked in file boxes that teetered with the weight.

"There she is, his 'other woman.'"

Lizzy circled the desk and rolled back Andrew's leather chair. When she sat, her feet dangled two inches above the floor. Walter curled around her ankles.

"So, this is what you do. You snuggle close to Andrew."

Unlike Ouisie's expectations, mucking out Andrew's cave was the furthest thing from Lizzy's mind. Instead, she wanted to understand why this place enticed him. Did that self-help book ever explain why Mars required a cave? And why Venus wasn't welcome there?

She fumbled through the clutter on Andrew's desk and found the "Georgia Family Tree" folder and the pages of Andrew's manuscript. She shook her head. "I'll read it when he asks me to." She peered at the page rolled into the typewriter and saw several paragraphs followed by the line, "*Not paying one bit of attention to his unhappy concubine who bumped along behind him — *"

After the last word, Lizzy saw a new paragraph begin with the letter "W," but it continued in a repetitive line of letters, "Wawawawawawawawaw," that ended with a hole in the paper. She touched the hole. "Over and over. He must have hit the 'W' and 'A' keys over and over."

Her misty eyes glanced out the workshop's window. The sunrise had cleared the pines and cast a beam toward her sunroom. So, this was Andrew's view each morning while he worked. A bright reflection shone from the sunroom window toward the workshop, which reflected a glow back at the house.

"He can't even see me in there, just a reflective glow, like light bouncing between mirrors." Lizzy sighed. "At least he needs me now. Ouisie may think I should go my way, but I can't. God and I made sure of that."

~

EACH SUNDAY during Andrew's stay in rehab, Guy Joseph came to visit after church, while Lizzy and Ouisie went to brunch. The moment Guy came in, Andrew's face lit up with a crooked smile. Guy brought the Sunday *New York Times* and several *National Geographic* magazines, and read articles aloud, line by line. Although Andrew did not understand every word, he nodded to Guy's oral accounts of the latest political scams.

Likewise, Guy enjoyed the renewed friendship with his colleague, even if Guy and Andrew's relationship had always been guarded. As a professor, Guy had gained a reputation for demanding thick papers with lengthy bibliographies from his students, papers that he checked cite by cite. Not one false reference slipped by his red pen. On the other hand, Andrew was a highly entertaining instructor who lectured to hundreds in spacious auditoriums. Over his career, he developed a large following of graduate students who hung on every word uttered by the exalted professor.

So, when Guy came to visit the now debilitated Andrew, Guy smiled with a bit of triumph, tempered by a dose of Unitarian Universalist benevolence.

Guy told Ouisie later that afternoon, "I hope I can help Andrew's mind come alive again. He and I certainly had our differences, but I'd hate to see that brilliant light go out."

He choked up, unable to say more.

Ouisie responded with a hug. "Andrew may have gotten the glory, but you were the silent hero of that department, the one who taught the truth of American history, not a glorified version of it."

HOLIDAYS WERE hell for Lizzy while Andrew was in rehab. First, there was Thanksgiving, several weeks after the stroke. Jane and Alan usually alternated Thanksgiving dinners each year between their parents' houses, and this was Lizzy's designated year to cook the big family meal.

"Now I'll have to wait two more years," she said with a sigh.

"Maybe we can switch with Alan's parents."

"But then, I'll be alone."

"You'll be with Poppa. The rehab will have some sort of Turkey Day meal."

"Horrid, processed turkey and canned peas."

"How about Alan and I host dinner for the whole family at our house? You could avoid the canned peas."

"But you wouldn't be at *our* house."

"Neither will Poppa. I thought it was about being together, not the house."

"Our house echoes without people in it. I can hear myself breathe."

"Momma — " Jane began, but instead, she silently patted her mother's shoulder.

So, Thanksgiving dinner was at Jane and Alan's, a grand catered affair with Alan's parents in attendance. Lizzy did not know them well because they lived in Sandy Springs, up the road from Atlanta. Besides, they were far more affluent than Lizzy and Andrew. She always felt like a frump around Alan's stylish mother, whose very name, Cherí, annoyed the hell out of Lizzy. Meanwhile, she had always thought Alan's father a bit of a sleaze. He was a trial lawyer who specialized in suing airlines and airplane manufacturers after crashes. Still, Lizzy thought he was quite handsome, but he had overdressed that day in a tailored charcoal windowpane suit, pink shirt, and silver paisley tie.

"No wonder Alan always dresses to the nines," Lizzy muttered.

But despite her negative preconceptions, Lizzy had a good time with Alan's parents and shared stories about Jane and the grandchildren.

The catered meal Alan's secretary had arranged was what Lizzy would call "perfunctory food," not the innovative recipes she always prepared. And she was appalled that anybody had to work on a holiday, so she slipped each server a five-dollar bill when Jane and Alan were in another room. When she realized the grandchildren were watching, she gave them a "hush-hush" sign.

"But Gizzy, Daddy already gave everybody a hundred-dollar bill and his business card," Billy Jay said with a shrug.

"As if waiters would need a high-dollar tax attorney," Lizzy snapped back.

"Gizzy's irritated again," Elizabeth called toward the dining room.

Mouths of babes, Lizzy thought to herself. "Now, Elizabeth, I'm not irritated, just frustrated. Let's all go finish that damn puzzle."

"Gizzy! No swearing on Thanksgiving!"

Worried that Jane might have heard, Lizzy nervously gives Elizabeth another hush-hush sign.

FAR TOO SOON AFTER Thanksgiving came Christmas. Although many UUs did not celebrate the divine birth of Jesus, Lizzy enjoyed the spirit of the season. At a Sunday brunch before Christmas, she and Ouisie had another of their rambling discussions about Jesus.

"I like to follow the teachings of Jesus, but I don't think He intended for us to think he is some almighty God," Lizzy said.

"I wonder if God feels displaced. Some of these TV evangelists have turned Jesus into God, not just the Son of God. Like we are not supposed to pray to God anymore, just Jesus." Ouisie's eyes glowed with conviction. She loved to talk about religion with Lizzy, because so many of Ouisie's neighbors had become dogmatic in their beliefs. In fact, Ouisie found it impossible to express any religious or political views to anyone beyond her congregation.

"I understand what you mean, Ouisie. My interpretation of the *New Testament* is that Jesus pointed the way to God. 'I am the light,' He said, which I took to mean, 'I illuminate the way to God.'"

"But how do you know if the *New Testament* is what Jesus said and did? It was written so many years later by followers of His followers, then interpreted and rewritten by monks and popes to suit their agendas. Who knows what's true? My goodness, white

Christian churches even have pictures of Jesus as a white man, but we all know he had dark skin. Most Middle Eastern people do."

"Wouldn't it be incredible to go back in time and see what Jesus looked like, follow Him, hear what He said, and see for yourself if He actually performed miracles?"

"You believe in miracles, Lizzy?"

"Ouisie, don't tell our new minister, but if I lived in that time, I'd be a Jesus groupie."

"Would you? That sounds more like something I would do. You've always had the sensible head between us."

"We've all got some quirks."

"Your Andrew sure does. Talk about a Jesus complex," Ouisie murmured mindlessly as she wiped her peach-colored lipstick on a napkin.

"What do you mean by that? What Jesus complex?"

"Lordy, I didn't mean to say that out loud. I'm sorry, what with Andrew in rehab, bless your heart. All your plans gone awry. How are you coping?"

"Don't change the subject. What did you mean?"

Ouisie stalled for time. She had not intended to blurt such a caustic remark, but she and Guy had spoken about Andrew that very morning on the way to church, and their conversation must have stuck in her mind.

At a stoplight, Guy had confided, "It's sadly ironic that the Jesus-like guru of our department is now so quirky he cannot put four words of a sentence together without a swearword."

Ouisie nodded. "Life slaps us in place when we need it."

Guy reached out his hand, and Ouisie held it, two underachievers feeling victorious now that the golden-haired professor emeritus struggled to say the word "spaghetti."

"Ouisie?" Lizzy prodded.

"Oh, Lizzy, you've caught me with my — Well, you know full well that Andrew and Guy didn't always see eye-to-eye about course assignments when Andrew was department chair. And Guy has told me things that you probably don't need to hear."

"And that would be?"

"Stuff from long ago, racial politics. You know I'm your best friend on this planet, but Andrew, well, he hasn't always been fair to Guy. I mean, I cannot imagine Andrew coming to Guy's aid if their situations were reversed. I mean, Andrew was Guy's boss, and I don't think he would stoop to read to him." Ouisie took a sip of water to cool her embarrassed flushing. She wiped her peach lips again with her napkin.

"You're getting that horrid lipstick all over that napkin."

"Oh, Lizzy, why must you always attack?"

"Attack! You essentially called Andrew a racist."

Ouisie did not answer. She was as angry with herself as she had always been with Andrew.

Lizzy could see tears in Ouisie's eyes. "Yes, I know all about Andrew, but any choices he made were definitely not about Guy's race. There's a hierarchy in academics."

"And you've always rubbed that in. Guy and I always felt less-than around you two."

"Lizzy, I regret opening my mouth."

"Ouisie, I never considered you or Guy less-than. And I can't help it that Guy's career was stymied."

The two women fell silent except for sniffles. Each felt a wound from a different blade. Lizzy thought Ouisie had affronted her unfairly for what was Andrew's failure to be a mentor to Guy. Meanwhile, Ouisie again felt the unfairness of Guy's inability to rise in the very White academic world, even if Guy was now president of the very White UU church board, and Andrew lay disabled in the hospital.

This was not the first time the women had argued, but the tiff came unexpectedly on this Sunday. Beyond the breakfast that Lizzy enjoyed the day before with Jane and the grandchildren, this brunch was her only holiday cheer. She had no other plans, since Jane and Alan were headed to his parents' for Christmas Day.

Still, Lizzy had too much pride to show any tears. Her friendship with Ouisie had always reflected Lucy Ricardo and Ethel Mertz on the 1950s *I Love Lucy!* shows, with Ouisie in the role of Ethel, the pudgy underdog who married an average guy, but worshipped the beautiful Lucy, whose husband was a star.

Ouisie dabbed her eyes with her lipstick-stained napkin. "I'm sorry, Lizzy. I didn't mean to bring up negative things today. It was a mindless comment. Something Guy said earlier. I don't know what got into me."

Lizzy took a long time to respond, and when she did, her words were not so much an apology as a velvet hammer.

"I'm sorry too. I'm sorry you and Guy resent Andrew and, evidently, me. I don't know if Andrew ever understood how Guy felt when Andrew was named department chair and received *emeritus* status. We all know those titles were political. Not to excuse my husband, but he grew up with an abusive father who favored Andrew's brother, Thomas, who later made money like Bill Gates. And Andrew's sister is brilliant in her own right. She married a multimillionaire who died and left her department stores to manage up and down the East Coast. To Andrew's siblings, we are the chumps who didn't have the smarts to leave Atlanta. Maybe Andrew made the wrong choice to stay at Emory. Why not Harvard or Stanford? Surely Guy felt that way too. And then, midway into our lives, we lost our — Oh, there I go again with tragic memories. Regretfully, they never leave. After that, Andrew simply shut down. Shut himself off. Still, we must try to make the best of our journey because there's no way to turn around. I've tried, but look what it got me. I just wish I could change the arrogant way Andrew must have behaved toward Guy, and evidently, you think I have behaved toward you, my dearest friend. I am so sad you think we are racists."

Overwhelmed by gushing tears, Ouisie bolted for the restroom, her overly round rump rolling like apples under her Christmas-red wool pants.

Ordinarily, Lizzy would have run to console her, and the two would have had a big hug and crying session, with many paper towels wiping Ouisie's smudged mascara and lipstick. Instead, Lizzy sat at the table and let her emotions flow, let the inevitable tears fall, despite her attempts to quell them. So what if other diners stared? She was more angry than sad. Oh, her apology had sounded sincere, but in Lizzy's eyes, Andrew's success was not at Guy's expense. Yes, Guy was stereotyped as a Black professor, capable of teaching only Black history. And perhaps Andrew could have done something as department chair to help Guy's academic star rise, but Guy's lack of achievement was not entirely Andrew's fault. For years, Ouisie had mentioned her concerns that Guy was not publishing enough, not politicking enough.

Funny how perspectives differ through another's eyes, Lizzy thought. She left her merlot unfinished, put a twenty on the table, and headed to the rehab. She did not remember that she had left Ouisie without a ride.

At least Andrew needed her. "Luuuuuzzzzzzy," he shouted when she walked in.

∼

THE NEXT DAY, Lizzy woke with an ache in her gut. She felt the need to talk to someone about her argument with Ouisie, and wanted to feel that she was right to stand her ground. But her only confidantes were Ouisie and Walter, and neither would speak to her. She thought about calling Jane but imagined that her daughter would deliver another edict about what Lizzy should do or not do, putting Lizzy on the defensive. Oh dear, she had so few options.

Ouisie had urged her to see a counselor, and maybe she was right. As Lizzy ate her cereal, she whimsically flipped through Yellow Pages ads and pondered whether to call a telephone psychologist. Just dial 1-800, and she could stay anonymous. But how could she be sure who was on the other end of the line? Or where they really were. China? India? And what about credit card fraud?

Perhaps the church had a list of recommended therapists. The office was usually closed on Mondays, but this Monday was Christmas Eve. There was a service that night, so Lizzy impulsively dialed the office, thinking she'd hear a volunteer's voice, but was startled when the minister himself answered the phone.

"Mrs. Ward, I'm pleased to hear from you. You are on my list of key people to meet."

"I'm surprised that you answered, Reverend Chester. I was calling to find out — " Lizzy cleared her throat, trying to gather courage before she continued. "Well, I wondered if our church has a list of recommended counselors. I have a friend who needs help."

"I do a bit of counseling myself. Is your friend a member?"

Lizzy was stunned. The new minister had volunteered to counsel her "friend." Should she take him up on his offer? If so, she would have to admit that she was the friend.

To her silence, the minister repeated, "My services are no charge to pledged members. In fact, I have an opening at two this afternoon."

"This afternoon?"

"Good as any. Can your friend come on such short notice?"

"I'll ask her, Reverend Chester. Thank you."

Lizzy went into a state of nervous shock. She had agreed to see the renegade minister. She was going to a psychological counselor. Should she do this? Or should she simply not show up and blame the friend? If she went, what should she say? How much should she tell him? Should she trust this man that Ouisie and Guy distrusted so? What had she gotten herself into? She desperately wanted to call Ouisie to ask her advice, but Ouisie was the reason she had called the minister.

For hours, she fretted and fussed. Her hair, clothes, shoes, nose hairs, and chin hairs must be perfect. She wanted to make a good impression and not appear vulnerable, even if she was. So, she chose a bright red blouse for the season, a black skirt to slim her hips, a pair of black pumps, charcoal hose, and a gray tweed jacket with red speckles to pick up the red in the blouse.

As she surveyed the results in Little Grandma's mirror, she heaved a sigh. "Old, but maybe he'll see a glimmer of the real me from my younger days."

At the church, the minister extended a plump hand when she walked in. "Welcome. I've heard you are one of our founding members. Please sit anywhere that's comfortable."

"Thank you."

"Goodness, please call me Byron. And may I call you Lizzy?"

"Of course," Lizzy said, but she was uncomfortable being on first-name terms.

"While we wait for your friend, I thought I might invite you and your husband to services this evening. We'll have a wonderful children's pageant and a potluck buffet after."

Lizzy's tone was more caustic than she had intended. "Reverend Chester, no friend is coming, and potluck is not what I need."

"Well, then. Don't be embarrassed. Lots of my clients make appointments for 'friends' who don't seem to show up either."

He chuckled, and Lizzy tried to smile.

"I've never been to counseling. I'm nervous about it."

"That's natural. If I can ease your mind, I'll tell you a bit about me. Besides being your church minister, I'm a licensed counselor. So, we don't have to focus on religion. Instead, you and I will talk, but you'll do most of the talking. And don't hold back. Nothing you say will ever leave this room. I promise."

Lizzy nervously smoothed her skirt. "That's good to know."

"And so, Lizzy, what's troubling you?"

"Well, uh, Byron, I argued with my best friend yesterday. After church, she made a disparaging remark about my husband, as much said he was a racist. It's a long story, but my husband had a severe stroke and is in rehab — he's not a member here, so you don't know him. But when my friend insulted him, I was so angry, I let her have it. Verbally, of course."

"Do I know this friend?"

"Ouisie Joseph, you know, Guy's wife. He's board president."

"Of course, I've met Guy and Ouisie. He might be one stern taskmaster. Ouisie too."

"She will tell you where you stand, that's for sure. Although I still think I was right to let her have it, I woke up with a terrible ache this morning. I felt very guilty, but I am so weary of Ouisie's jealousy. You see, my husband and Guy were academic colleagues at Emory. There was competition for key spots, and Guy struggled, perhaps because of his race. Academia has always been a white man's club, although I hope that is changing."

"Me too. I imagine your friend Ouisie is as upset about your argument as you are. Have you called her to talk things over?"

"No. Ouisie needs to stew. We've been friends since elementary school. She's got one heck of a temper, and each time we argue, she takes a while to get over her 'mad.' If I called her today, we'd have an even bigger argument."

"I think this time of year puts too much pressure on us to be merry and bright. With your husband's stroke, you probably have an overwhelming amount on your plate. You've had a spat with your friend, your husband is ill, and you may feel lonesome. If I might encourage you again, I think you might enjoy tonight's festivities."

"I must be at the rehab with Andrew. He needs me, now."

"Now? Did he need you before his stroke?"

"Not really. Except for meals and laundry, and so forth."

"Has this been a good marriage?"

"It was. We were happy for years, except for the usual trials." Lizzy paused, then said quietly, "But then our son died."

"I'm sorry to hear that. When did he die?"

Lizzy did not want to talk about this. "Thirty years ago, this year. A car accident. That's not the problem."

"You said his death had an impact on your marriage?"

"I don't want to talk about that — " Lizzy stopped short and her voice broke. "The problem is — " She suddenly shuddered into uncontrollable tears. The minister gently positioned a box of tissues on her lap, and despite Lizzy's determination not to be vulnerable, she wept like a baby for about five minutes.

"Lizzy, I'm so sorry. Why don't you take a moment to recover? I'll go make some tea."

After Lizzy had cried all the tears she could cry, she went to the restroom and washed off what was left of her makeup. In the mirror, she saw her swollen eyes and was mortified that she had collapsed in front of someone she barely knew, especially a minister Ouisie and Guy had ridiculed.

"Get hold of yourself," she said to her reflection. She didn't even know if she could trust this man. Maybe she should have stuck with a 1-800 counselor.

"Now then, I've made some chamomile," the minister said after Lizzy returned.

"I think I'll head home now. This is not at all what I expected."

"But Lizzy, we've made progress. You've gotten in touch with your feelings, and it's clear that you need to talk to someone about all this, your son, your husband's illness."

"But I feel terrible going on this way. Especially after what Ouisie said."

"About your husband?"

"Oh dear, no. I shouldn't bring that up."

"But *you* are the one who is here, not Ouisie. So, with your permission, let's focus on what brought you to tears. You said your marriage was happy until your son died. What happened after that?"

Lizzy reluctantly perched on the leather couch. "Well, you might say my husband pulled away. Plunged into his work. I barely saw him. And when he retired two years ago, I still didn't. He spent most days in his backyard workshop. Writing a novel, he said, but who knows what he did out there, other than hide out with his precious dog, Walter. He rarely talked to me or paid any attention to his daughter or grandchildren."

"Does he blame you for your son's death?"

"No, no. This is such a long story, and that's not why I came today. I wanted to talk about my argument with Ouisie!"

She started to get up, but the minister patted her arm firmly. Lizzy felt trapped.

"Lizzy, in my experience, the reason people seek counseling often turns out much different from what they expected. It's Christmas Eve. I've got nothing to do until 4:00 p.m., so let's get back to your long story."

Between many deep breaths, Lizzy methodically chronicled the night of her vision when Billy was a newborn, the afternoon years later when she saw Billy's letter jacket for the first time, the stormy day of Billy's death, her weak protests to Andrew's bravado, Andrew's self-blame, her own righteousness, Jane's pressure to heal her parents' marriage, Lizzy's decision to leave Andrew, and the guilt she felt over his stroke. Had she caused it? Her litany left Lizzy emotionally spent, and the box of tissues empty.

"The story of your vision is phenomenal. Sometimes we cannot question the inexplicable, which is probably why Calvin dreamed up his theory of predestination."

"My grandmother had premonitions too. One came true. Her sister killed herself."

"My goodness. This mystical stuff, well, I'm not one who buys into the supernatural, and yet something occurred in your life beyond earthly understanding. No wonder you feel guilty about a spat with your best friend. Your stress level has been over the roof for thirty years. You should give yourself a break."

Lizzy shuddered. "I try. I take long baths. I drink wine, too much. I have breakfast with my daughter Jane and the grandkids every Saturday. I have brunch with Ouisie every Sunday and lunch with her each Wednesday, or at least I did. I know in my mind that I didn't cause Andrew's stroke, but my stomach feels that I did. Just like when Billy died. I felt like my premonition caused it. I should have known, should have stopped it."

"You probably know our denomination does not preach a doctrine of predestination or damnation. We leave that stuff to the Presbyterians and the Baptists."

Lizzy smiled, relieved.

"You also may know that even the very early UU doctrine preached universal forgiveness. A loving God does not cast blame upon you or your husband for your son's death. Or blame you for your husband's illness, your desperate decision to leave him, or your spat with your friend. A loving God forgives unconditionally. All you must do is try to live a moral life. If that means apologizing to your friend, then you should do so. But I don't think you owe your husband an apology."

"So, why do I feel so guilty?"

"Sometimes what our internal sensor identifies as guilt — that ache in the gut — is actually our drive to set things right. Even if you were right, you have an urge to heal the rift. In your family's case, I suspect the guilt you and your husband feel over your son's death is more your urge to change history. Your family experienced a terrible event. So, you live life in regret. And your guilt about leaving him is your gut instinct to work things out. After all, you love him, right?"

"Yes. Always." Lizzy sniffed.

"That's your answer. Your daughter Jane — meddling as she may seem — is right about a bunch of things. You've waited thirty years for your husband to make the big move. Obviously, he can't. So, you've got to meet him more than halfway. Not run away. Do your best to stay in the present and focus on the joy of today. Just that moment. That hour. Take it one step at a time and don't look back."

"Easier said than done."

"Oh, I know. The term is called 'grounding.' You make conscious mental choices to stay in the here and now."

"Again, easier said — "

"Well, some tools you might use are deep breathing, relaxation, like your hot baths, and a conscious focus on present-day activities and plans. Try it."

"That may help with Andrew, but what should I do about Ouisie?"

"I imagine your lifelong pal feels as much anguish as you. Give her a break. She's human."

"Thank you, Byron. I must say, I'm surprised that you are such a good counselor."

"I don't know what Ouisie's told you, but I hold a master's in psychology and had a private practice before returning to earn my doctorate in theology. The psychology part helps with the ministry part, especially with a congregation that does not put all faith in

God. Now, if only I could do as well with my contentious board of directors, led by a very determined Guy Joseph."

Byron shook his head with a wry smile.

Lizzy patted his hand. "I'll put in a good word for you with the president's wife."

~

EACH WEEKDAY MORNING of Andrew's rehab, a burly physical therapist came to help him into a wheelchair. Lizzy could not provide much help, so she nervously coached and urged Andrew to plant his foot, lift his thigh. The struggle was intense for all, but at least Andrew could get out of his room for a while.

Andrew called the therapist "Mack," a word he could say. He did not know what the therapist's real name was, so he said, "Hi, Mack!" every morning when the therapist came in.

Dr. Fitzgerald's name was simply "Doc." She usually arrived mid-morning to listen to Andrew's heart, peer into his eyes, ask him to lift his right hand or right foot, which he could not do, praise him for left-sided movements and improvements, check various reports, talk with the nurses, and give Andrew a wink when she left.

"Doc, tanks," Andrew managed, his left thumb up in reply.

About two months into rehab, Andrew managed to stand on his own in the physical therapy room, or "PT" as it was called. Andrew called it "TP," which made Lizzy smile because "TP" was her abbreviation on grocery lists for toilet paper.

When Andrew stood with both arms on twin support rails, Mack shouted, "Atta boy, Professor Ward!"

Andrew winced with effort, then smiled like a baby who had stood for the first time. "Up stand, goddamn!"

Mack applauded. "Professor, you'll be walking around Woodruff track in no time."

Andrew wasn't sure he understood what Mack had said, but he smiled, chest puffed, until his body suddenly quivered and collapsed into the safety net of Mack's arms. He gently guided Andrew's limp body into his wheelchair.

"TP" was hell in Andrew's mind, but the toughest part of rehab was the aphasia therapy. Every day, an aide took him to see a speech therapist named Victoria. Her bundle of red curls reminded Andrew of Orphan Annie, so he called Victoria "Red."

She worked with him for an hour each day to help him recognize words and match them to images, with the goal of understanding others and improving his recollection and pronunciation. Red held up colored cards with illustrated images and diligently pronounced a line she wanted Andrew to repeat. "I want some watermelon, spaghetti, and noodle soup."

Her statement ended like a question, since she wanted Andrew to recite the words back.

He took a breath and blurted, "Water goup ghetti, shit." He slurred so badly, Red could not understand more than "ghetti shit." But in Andrew's mind, he had repeated the phrase exactly as Red had spoken it. He waited expectantly for praise.

"Good try. But let's do this again. Be sure to look at these pictures as you say the words to me. 'I want some watermelon, spaghetti, and noodle soup.'"

With each attempt, Andrew grew more frustrated, if not downright angry. He shouted and enunciated as best he could. "Wan' cannaloupe, macaroni cheese, damn it."

Red had tape-recorded this effort and played Andrew's words back. He was chagrined. He knew the melon was a watermelon but had uttered a slurred version of "cantaloupe." He knew the next picture was spaghetti, the long noodle with red sauce, but he had shouted, "macaroni." And he knew there was a bowl of soup on that third card, but he had not mentioned "soup" and even threw in the word "cheese" and another word he did not understand.

This is torture. I'll never get it, Andrew shouted internally as he slammed the table with his left fist, his eyes enraged with tears. Red patted his shoulder to calm him, handed him a Kleenex, and held up her image cards again.

This fucking goddamn bitch is too damn persistent, Andrew thought to himself, but realized for the first time that he was swearing like a sailor. *My goodness.* Lizzy was right about his profanity. He took a moment to think that through, then looked at Red with renewed determination. *I've got to try harder on this therapy shit. Speech therapy.*

As Doc HAD PREDICTED, Andrew eventually made solid progress. About two months into rehab, he pulled himself out of bed and walked with a walker. Mack whistled a cheer. Lizzy's eyes brimmed with joyous tears.

"What cha tink, Mack?" Although Andrew still slurred, his speech was understandable if you spent time with him daily.

Lizzy understood almost everything Andrew said and was delighted to hear him use fewer swear words to punctuate each sentence.

Jane and Alan came for a visit later that next week and saw Andrew use his walker to get down the hallway. Jane applauded with a big grin, and Alan gave Andrew the okay sign.

"Thanks, Janey," Andrew said as naturally as rain. No major realizations or regretful admissions. Andrew simply said his daughter's name and knew who she was.

"Okay, Poppa." Jane's lip trembled as her eyes brimmed with joyous tears.

Yes, Andrew knew who Jane was. But he wasn't clear about this Alan fellow. Was this Janey's latest beau from college?

After four months in rehab, Dr. Fitzgerald told Lizzy that Andrew could go home in a few days, but he would have to continue rehab on an outpatient basis. To celebrate, the family dined together in the center's cafeteria so Andrew could have his nutritious diet and practice his social skills. He had worked hard with the occupational and recreational therapists to relearn how to feed himself and be sociable in the company of others.

"Jane tells me you'll be back to work on that manuscript soon, Andrew," Alan said.

Andrew nodded politely at his son-in-law. He would get a glimmer that he knew this Alan fellow, or those three bratty kids who were always around, but the memory quickly faded. Yes, Lizzy had told him who these people were, but he did not feel that he knew them. Not really.

"Dr. Fitzgerald says you should not be alone in that workshop. So, I'll set up a workshop inside for you. Maybe in Momma's sunroom, if that's okay. There's plenty of space for a second desk."

"I guess that's okay." Lizzy was perturbed that Jane would enable Andrew to have another escape zone. But at least it would be in Lizzy's sunroom.

"Wha' 'bout Walter?" Andrew could recite his best buddy's name, that's for sure.

"It will be good to have the old boy around the house. Walter, I mean, not you!" Lizzy waved away her words, flustered. "Oh, you know what I'm trying to say!"

"Poppa, I'll set up your iMac in the sunroom."

"Key puncher," Andrew blurted.

"Momma, does he mean that old typewriter?"

"Computers are easy, Grand Pop. Even Weenie Girl uses one," Billy Jay said.

Elizabeth's grin lacked two teeth. "Yeah, Grand Pop. Even a weenie girl like me!"

"Good for you — " Andrew wondered if this girl's name was "Weenie Girl."

"Elizabeth," Lizzy prompted.

"Zizabeth."

"And my name is?" Billy Jay said.

"You're — " Andrew looked at Lizzy for help, but she shrugged as if to say, "You're on your own, dear."

"My name's Billy Jay. Actually, I have four names: William Montague Ward Cates. I'm named after my Uncle Billy, but my Mom calls me 'Billy Jay' after some bird she saw, 'day I was born."

"But whuurrs Billy?" Andrew scanned the table until his eyes landed on young David's face, Billy's look-alike.

Alan whispered to Jane, "Uh-oh. He thinks David is Billy."

Jane jumped to put a protective arm around David's shoulder. "This is David. My son, Poppa. Remember?"

"I do, 'course," Andrew said, although it was clear to the adults that he did not.

Jane tried to change the subject. "And you know my name, Poppa, don't you?"

"Janey." Andrew gave her a crooked grin.

"And me? Who am I, dear?"

Andrew pretended he could not remember. He fretted, fussed, and wildly looked at the ceiling tiles for the answer.

Lizzy took the bait and seemed crestfallen, until Andrew blurted, "Luuuuuzzzzzzzy!"

Everybody laughed in relief. But Jane and Alan exchanged glances that said Andrew was still miles from complete recovery.

ON THE WAY HOME, Jane mused aloud. "I wonder if Poppa will suddenly realize that Billy is dead. Or does he have to feel the pain all over again?"

"We all must feel that pain. You women will not let any of us forget."

Jane was teed off by Alan's sarcastic remark. But she said nothing in return because the kids were in the back seat. She would get her revenge later. There would be some small thing she would not do or a touch he would not feel or an affectionate word he would not hear, and Alan would know that he should not have said what he did.

But for now, she let him have the last word.

Chapter Sixteen

FEBRUARY 3 - MAY 13

B ecause of the heavy winter rains and warm trade winds that swept across the South, an early spring had sprung at Atlanta's Piedmont Park. Dogwood trees and azalea bushes bloomed in pinks and whites. Tulips and irises of every hue nodded greetings from the lush beds that surrounded the jogging path.

Alan and Jane ran side by side and chatted in brief bursts. The kids had gone to visit Alan's parents for the day. Jane was on sabbatical from her job since Andrew's stroke. Alan thought she seemed relaxed for a change. Her perpetual frown had lightened. She could finally enjoy a Sunday away from parenting, visits with Andrew, and time spent at Lizzy's house.

"It's good to be outdoors again, just you and me." Alan glanced over at Jane, but she kept her eyes straight ahead. He'd meant his comment as a first step. He knew he'd done something wrong, but who knew what?

Jane could tell he wanted to make up, but she did her best not to reveal her emotions. She answered back somewhat cynically. "I'll bet you're relieved to escape the drama."

Alan decided to stick to the facts. Jane would come around if she didn't feel she was being played. "What time do you pick up your Dad tomorrow?"

"The nurse said after Dr. Fitzgerald releases him. Probably mid-morning."

"Lizzy on high alert?"

That made Jane smile. "She makes daily trips to the grocery. Low sodium this, zero fat that. Says the kids can't have bacon or doughnuts anymore at their Saturday breakfasts."

"Grease is the culprit?"

"Yes, grease is the reason lives throughout the world do not turn out as planned. Eat salami and your husband will have a stroke. Eat bacon and your son will die in a wreck. Eat doughnuts and your only daughter will become a forgotten child."

"Aw, Jane, please. After all, Andrew remembered who you are, but he still doesn't know my name."

"He remembered my name, but that old man does not know who I am."

"I realize you think I don't understand, but this situation — and I sympathize — affects your mother and Andrew the most. You're a secondary victim. Maybe it's time for you to let go of your wounded inner child."

Darn it, there he goes again. Jane did not want an argument. She gritted her teeth and burst into a silent run, furious with Alan's litany of advice. Her angry tears blended into the drops of sweat that ran down her cheeks as she ran to the point of exhaustion.

Alan ran after, and his longer legs easily caught up. He glanced over. Jane's arms were in a tense pump as she stretched to outrun him. That was Jane. Competitive to a fault, although Alan was much taller, with longer, hairier legs, who could outrun his wife at will. But he held back. Slowly jogged at her side, trying to understand the emotions roiling in the female of his world. He desperately wanted Jane to get off her soapbox about her father. How could Alan achieve that without pissing her off more?

As he paced his stride to Jane's, he reached and put a hand on her shoulder. As soon as he touched her, Jane bolted and ran even faster. *Oh, God. This is just going to get worse unless I break through.* As he ran after, he suddenly called loudly between urgent breaths, "Jane,

Jane. Stop. I know you think I'm an argumentative schmuck, but there's one thing you may not know. Not at this moment anyway."

Jane slowed slightly, enough so that Alan knew he had gotten her attention. But what was the one thing he could say that would put an end to this argument, at least for today?

"I love you. Do you know that? I love you, Jane Cates. Did you hear me? Do all you other joggers hear me? I love this woman terribly. Completely. Yes, I love you, Jane Cates. Even when you go on and on about Billy, your parents' marriage, your loss, and yaddah, yaddah. I love you. Call me selfish, but I also want you to love me. Get unstuck. Be with me. Can't we try that for a while? Be 'us' in our world?"

Jane jogged farther. She had heard every word, but did not quite know how to respond. Her usually pretentious husband had shouted, "I love you!" in the middle of Piedmont Park as hip runners all around stared and whispered. Should she trust this shift? Did he truly understand, or was this a manipulation?

Jane slowed to a halt.

Alan caught up quickly and reached for her. He held her closely while runners passed by. Some glared, some giggled, but for once, Alan did not care.

Jane burst into laughter and tears. "I hate you, Alan Cates. I hate you for being so damn manipulative. But you always know how to get to me. And I do love you back."

Alan laughed and spilled a few tears too. He had surprised himself when his feelings gushed out in front of the world. He wanted his marriage back. His wife. Her joy. Her love. Her smile. Her happiness.

Jane pulled away. "Alan, there are times you are my best friend, who says things I need to hear. Maybe it's time for my wounded inner child to grow up."

"That's the spirit. Take this less personally, and you can be a helpmate to your parents. Help Lizzy plan and fuss over his meals, but don't try to solve their marital problems."

"For gosh sakes, I don't want to cook for the man. That's

Momma's world. I'm just happy she's still healthy and can take care of him."

"Yes, that's a plus for our side."

"Dr. Fitzgerald told me that his right-side motor skills should get even better with PT. Still, I worry about the 'aftershocks' that might happen. The doctor called them 'TIAs.' Little strokes that cause more damage until another CVA happens and all hell breaks loose." Jane tensed up again. "God. I don't want to go through another family death."

Alan pulled her closer. "How about I go in late so I can help you get Andrew home?"

Jane let her shoulders relax with a quiet sigh. "You don't need to miss work, especially this tax season. I'll simply drive Poppa home and be a 'helpmate,' as you said. The staff can load Poppa in the minivan, and he's got his walker to support him. Uncle Guy will be there too. I've missed enough work for both of us, remember?"

"This sabbatical is not what we planned for your days off."

"When Poppa's out of danger, you and I can send the kids to your parents' house for a week. We'll go somewhere so remote that when we make beasty noises, no one will hear a sound."

"Schweetheart, I like the sound of that."

Jane smiled the best she could at Alan's Groucho-esque leer. She loved him, yes, she did, but secretly wished he would update his routine.

AFTER CHURCH, Lizzy drove to meet Ouisie for brunch at the Georgian Terrace Hotel. The two were at least speaking. The friends' pre-Christmas tiff had been months before. The first week after the spat, they did not speak by phone or have their Wednesday luncheon. Lizzy wondered if she should call Ouisie, as Byron suggested, but let Ouisie simmer some more. But when the first Sunday rolled around, Lizzy came early and sat in her usual pew. Moments later, Ouisie and Guy joined her, like always. The two women chatted politely after the service. But at Lizzy's invitation, they met for brunch, each going in separate cars.

At brunch, the women were cordial, yet neither spoke words of apology or forgiveness. Neither seemed to have the courage. Not that Sunday or the next Wednesday lunch or the next Sunday brunch, although they kept up their meeting dates as usual.

But now, months had passed, and with Andrew on his way home, Lizzy felt the time was ripe to clear the air. She suggested a quiet restaurant, "where we can talk," and gave Ouisie's curious black eyes a meaningful look.

This Sunday was gloriously sunny, so they sat outside. Shaded by a broad, white umbrella at a wrought-iron table, they had a sidewalk view, lined by lush gardens dotted in reds and yellows. As the waiter poured their San Pellegrino water, Lizzy began.

"Dr. Fitzgerald told me that Andrew has improved so much, he might just run out of rehab tomorrow. Of course, the doctor was joking. His right side is still weak, but he gets around with a walker."

"Good thing your house doesn't have two stories."

"But we've got those porch steps in front and back. Janey's Alan had a contractor build ramps so Andrew can navigate."

"She seems to have lucked out with Alan. You know the troubles couples have in today's permissive culture. At least that's what I read in *People* magazine."

Lizzy smiled. "No marriage is perfect. I imagine Alan can be difficult. He's an attorney, after all, but Janey doesn't talk about their relationship. She just wants to talk about mine."

Ouisie chuckled. "Maybe Janey keeps working to earn Alan's respect. Modern husbands seem to want Super Women who are beautiful, brainy, and career stars."

"Thankfully, our husbands didn't. Andrew simply wanted a career and family. He hired a contractor to add the wrap-around porches to our home, with the idea that we could watch the children play in front or back. That was until he found out what small children were like, so he put that darn rocket barn in place. As the kids grew, we added that right wing for my sunroom."

"That's why your property rambles so. I mean, in a good way." Ouisie's eyes looked away, for fear she had insulted Lizzy again.

"Oh, Ouisie, don't worry. Our house is a conglomeration. Kind of like our imperfect lives." Lizzy paused and gave her friend a meaningful glance.

Ouisie sensed the opening and put down her fork. "Andrew should count his lucky pennies to have a woman like you for his wife." Tearing up with emotion, Ouisie dabbed her eyes with her napkin. "And I'm sorry for what I said. Your Andrew was a top professor, far more famous than my Guy. I admit that it bothered both of us. Sometimes, it's easier to blame others. Even Guy admits that he could have done more, published, politicked, pressured, but he didn't. He wasn't lazy. He was angry. That was his bag to carry, not Andrew's. He was a genuine star at Emory, what with his looks, books, articles, and speaking engagements. He needed a wife with a solid head on her shoulders. I'm lucky to have you as my best friend, if you still are." She blew into a tissue.

Lizzy's eyes overflowed too. "Thank you, Ouisie. I'm also sorry for our argument over the holidays. You and Guy have been our friends for so long, race has never entered my thoughts. I was so upset I even went to see a counselor."

"You did not."

"Yes. And you'll never believe who it was. Reverend Byron Chester."

"The lecher?"

"Ouisie, I don't know a thing about his personal life, but he was very helpful. I think the board should focus on church business, not his romantic pursuits."

"Girl, I am floored. May I tell Guy about this?"

"Yes, please do. Byron helped me understand why I let loose at you. The problem wasn't that you called Andrew, well, you know what you said, but that I'd decided to leave him. But I love him, Ouisie. He's had a stroke and needs me now. Byron told me that the ache I felt in my gut over our argument was my urge to set things right. I was running away, not facing my side of the equation. The talk-therapy process was a revelation. I can't believe I went to see him, especially after all the bad things you said about him, but I'm happy I did."

"I'm glad too. Truly. I only wanted you to leave Andrew because I didn't want you to be hurt anymore."

"I know. I also want you to know how much your and Guy's friendship means to me and Andrew."

"Thank you. Guy is so pleased to be Andrew's friend again."

"So, are we all made up?"

"All made up. But woman, if you ever get mad at me again, please don't leave me without a ride."

"Oh, my goodness. I did, didn't I?"

Ouisie nodded.

"But that gave you a chance to get a ride with some hot guy."

"Funny thing, the guy's name was Guy."

The two women giggled into their tissues, relieved that their sisterhood had mended.

El Niño's rains returned the next day as Jane's minivan pulled into her parents' driveway to deliver Andrew from rehab. As she slid to a stop, she shouted, "Let's get inside before a storm lets loose!" She jumped out and opened a small umbrella, then pulled open the van door.

Lizzy stepped down and stood under the umbrella beside Jane. Lizzy sucked in her tummy to make herself as thin as possible so that Andrew and Guy could fit there too.

Jane sighed in frustration. "Momma, I'll walk you inside first."

"I need to help you with Andrew."

"Guy and I will take care of Poppa. Let's get you inside."

A clap of thunder startled the two women as they hunched under the small umbrella. Step by step, Jane escorted Lizzy to the covered front porch. Then Jane sloshed back in the deepening water and held the umbrella over her damp curls. With her free hand, she pulled Andrew's walker from the back, then brought it around to the open door.

"Screw this rain," Jane screamed. "Why today, of all days?"

Jane watched as her Uncle Guy attempted to help Andrew out. As soon as he reached to support Andrew, she could see that Guy was almost as weak as her stricken father. She cringed at what might happen if Guy dropped Andrew in the rocky driveway, or if Guy fell himself, but she could only hold her breath and the useless umbrella in the hope that these two elderly men could muster enough strength to get her father out of the car.

As Andrew peered at the gravel, the distance seemed unfathomable. He tentatively extended his stronger left leg while Guy held him by his right armpit.

Jane could see Guy's frail forearms quiver, and his face flush and sweaty from the effort. Or maybe the moisture was splatter from the rain that pummeled the van's roof. Abruptly, Jane gave the men a halt sign and shouted toward the porch. "Momma, get Poppa's golf umbrella!"

Like a shot, Lizzy rocketed into the house. She was at her best when needed, and Jane surely needed her today.

"Golf umbrella, where in the world is Andrew's golf umbrella?" Lizzy asked the question as if the answer would appear. Magically, it did. She zoomed into the utility room, where she spied the blue and white umbrella behind a dusty golf bag. Without a thought, she opened the umbrella and locked it, then sprinted out, only to have the umbrella catch on the doorway. Lizzy shrieked, then tried to release the umbrella's metal close button but wasn't strong enough. So, she angled the umbrella on its side and squeezed it through the doorway, then went through the kitchen, down the hall, and then angled it out the front door.

"Just call me Lucy Ricardo," she muttered as she ran out to the van.

Jane climbed inside to help offload Andrew. Silently, she hoped the men had regained some strength while they waited, or at least developed a plan.

But their helpless looks revealed the immense challenge at hand.

"Guy, I'll take Poppa's right side, and you take the left. I know the angle from up there is tricky. I don't think Alan could have done it alone, either."

"Aww, don't worry about us, Janey. We've got it covered. Don't we, Andrew?"

"Cake of piece."

Jane could not tell if her father's words were sarcastic or simply aphasic, but she desperately wished she had not sent Alan to work that day. When another deep clap of thunder struck, and a lightning bolt hit not one second after, she looked to the heavens as if she could see God through the headliner. "Why do you always have to storm on this family?"

Startled, Guy whispered in Andrew's ear. "Is she talking to me, or to you?"

Andrew tried to muster a fatherly reprimand. "Now, Janey — "

Lizzy proved a diversion as she splashed through puddles in the uneven gravel.

Andrew cringed in guilt over his long refusal to finish bricking the driveway.

Lizzy stood on tiptoe in ankle-deep water and held the umbrella over the van door.

Inside the van, Jane held Andrew's weak right side as Guy gripped Andrew's stronger left side. The two stabilized Andrew well enough that he could lower himself and stand beside the walker.

Steadfast, Lizzy centered the umbrella over the two men and Jane, then waded alongside on her tiptoes as the three inched toward the new ramp.

Andrew advanced with his left and dragged his right foot until he and his helpers mounted the porch. Except for their footwear and the hems of their pants, the men had kept dry, but Jane's back and hair were soaked, and Lizzy's body was a river.

As soon as Jane realized how drenched her mother was, she shouted at the heavens, "And you can't even let up on my mother, today of all days, can you?"

"Janey, hush your venting. We're just wet. We're fine. Andrew's home, and nobody got hit by God's lightning bolts."

"Momma, promise me you'll take a hot bath to warm yourself."

"I'll take a bath, if you'll take a bath."

The two women looked at each other, then dissolved in giggles.

Guy watched in worried disbelief. Since he and Ouisie had three sons, he didn't understand this banter between a mother and daughter, especially the younger one, who ordered men around, shouted at the heavens, told her parents what to do, and later dissolved in laughter and tears.

Andrew gave Guy the okay sign. "Women. Baths."

MUCH LATER THAT NIGHT, after Lizzy's gourmet, zero-cholesterol meal, Andrew rested in his bed for the first time in six months. As he surveyed the room, he remembered little about this room, except the green floral bedspread. As he touched it, he recalled how Lizzy's figure had curved under the flowers beside him each night. A crooked smile fluttered across his lips.

Across the room, a huge flatscreen TV awaited, and Andrew had remote controls within reach, thanks to Jane's insistence that her parents live in the twenty-first century. She also made sure the house was wired for high-speed Internet.

Meanwhile, Lizzy stacked past issues of *National Geographic* on the nightstand and asked Andrew several times if he needed anything before she took her overdue bath. Within a minute after she climbed into the tub, Lizzy shouted, "Are you all right?"

That annoyed Andrew, but he answered "Uh-huh" with a sigh and brashly turned a page in his magazine. He could not figure out how to turn on the TV.

After her bath, Lizzy scurried into the bedroom, her yellow terry-cloth robe cinched tightly. Andrew followed her movements with renewed delight and a lopsided grin.

Lizzy caught a glimpse and wondered if Andrew's smile was his goofy stroke expression or a downright leer. For decades, she had received little attention from him and did not expect this first night to be any different. She turned off the overhead light and took off her robe, revealing an aqua nylon gown with pink flowers appliquéd across a low-cut neckline.

She noticed that Andrew's nightstand lamp was still on. "Shall I get that light, Andrew?"

"Don't 'member dark."

"Does that mean you'd rather leave the light on?"

"Tonight."

"I usually sleep while you read, anyway." Lizzy got under the sheets on his left side and curled with her back to Andrew. She paused before she began her prayers. "Does it feel good to be home?"

"New, all new."

"It may take a while before this feels like home again, but I'm glad you're here. And I'm glad I'm here too." She paused. "I love you, Andrew."

"Uh-huh."

Was that an "I love you" back? Lizzy waited. There was more. Andrew reached with his able left hand and patted Lizzy on her behind. Amazed by his touch, she told herself not to make much of it but felt comforted that he had curled close enough to touch lightly.

Andrew's gaze traced Lizzy's figure under the floral spread, then he glanced down his torso in amazement. A door had opened. A modest erection had created a tent of delight under the covers. Andrew patted Lizzy again and felt like a teen who felt desire for the first time.

Lizzy patiently hoped for another move, but before long, Andrew's hand slipped off her hip, and a sharp snore answered her question.

∼

LIZZY WAS RELIEVED to see the sunlight sparkle through the draperies she opened the next morning. She rose early to prepare breakfast, which she brought to Andrew on a tray: zero-fat yogurt with sugar-free Mandarin orange slices, Eggbeaters zapped in the microwave in a blue silicone gadget Lizzy had discovered at a kitchen store, orange juice in a packet with a straw, and a cup of zero-fat oat cereal with fat-free milk.

While Andrew ate with his left hand, Lizzy interrupted him every thirty seconds to ask if she could help.

"Do self!" Andrew sounded more like a child than a man.

Lizzy sighed. At least he could feed himself and seemed interested in the TV documentary about Franklin Roosevelt that Lizzy had managed to turn on. Jane had tuned it to the PBS channel and showed Lizzy how to push the "on" button. So, with Andrew occupied, she went to the utility room. There, she gathered a bucket of sudsy water, a long-handled brush, and a stack of towels, then headed to the living room, where she crouched to scrub the carpet free of the muck tramped in the day before. A woman with purpose, Lizzy had no idea Andrew had turned off the TV.

"Horse manure," he deemed the Roosevelt program as soon as she left. He slid the tray onto the bed, got up with the help of his walker, and shuffled down the hall to the kitchen door. The moment he opened it, a mud-coated Walter bolted up the ramp and barked with glee. The big dog almost toppled his master, but Andrew gripped his walker and stayed upright.

"Whoa, Walter. Me miss?"

The dog barked urgently, then loped down the ramp and up the path to the workshop.

Andrew steadied himself and used his weaker right hand to wave Walter back to the house. Suddenly called into duty for such a familiar task as signaling his dog, Andrew's right hand performed better than it had since his stroke.

"Walter, come. Short leash. You, me, lap dogs." With that, the dog bounded past Andrew and stormed into the kitchen. Mud smudged Lizzy's linoleum floor.

Lizzy called from the living room. "Is that you, Andrew?"

In response to Lizzy's voice, the dog ran to the front, where he found his mistress on her hands and knees. Walter jumped to greet her and flattened her on the carpet. In response to her shrieks, he licked Lizzy all over, his muddy front paws planted on her back.

"No, Walter, no! How did you get in? Andrew! Get Walter out."

Walter gave a mighty shake of his fur, then licked the back of Lizzy's neck. Her anguished squeals eventually turned to giggles.

Andrew heard Lizzy's shouts but played deaf. He turned back inside and shuffled his walker twice as fast as he ever did in rehab.

"Andrew! Did you let this dog in? He's coated with mud!" Lizzy reached for a leg of the piano and used it for leverage to stand. With a dismayed sigh, she surveyed the mess Walter had made, then took the dog by the collar to the utility room, where she penned him with a baby gate used long ago to keep the grandchildren in check. "Stay. You are going to have a bath."

By that time, Andrew had made his way to the bedroom, where he wiggled inside the covers, muddy pajamas, and all. He turned the TV back on and pretended to watch when Lizzy came in.

She stood at the door, aghast at his pretense. "Why are you breathing so hard?"

"Show exciting."

"Well, let me tell you why I'm breathing so hard. You let the muddy dog in. Look at me. I'm a disaster. Now I have to clean the carpet, mop the kitchen and utility room, not to mention wash your pajamas and our bed sheets, and give the dog *and* you a bath."

Andrew's low whisper attempted contrition. "Walter miss me."

"Andrew, I care about Walter too. He's been a pleasant companion while you've been away. But when the dog is wet, he must stay outside until he's dry and we can brush him."

"Inside dogs muddy not."

Lizzy sighed. "You make a good point. Our weather seems to have turned Atlanta into a rainforest. So, I'll get the dog bathed, the carpet cleaned, the linoleum mopped, you bathed, your PJs washed, the bed sheets clean, and Walter can be an inside dog. But you will have to take him out to do his business. In the past five minutes, you've shown far more agility than you ever did at the rehab hospital, so I'm on to you."

Andrew saluted her with his right hand. "Orders march."

Lizzy noticed he had used his primary hand, but she caught herself. Better not to mention it. One of the "Mack" therapists had said not to make a big deal when Andrew's automatic movements returned.

"When a task becomes automatic, the brain becomes more efficient. So, it spends less energy processing movements. When things happen naturally, they will happen with a lot less effort," Mack had said.

Lizzy silently returned Andrew's salute, then went to call Jane, who came over about ten to help clean.

About noon, Jane put Walter in her minivan and took him to a pet salon. Next was another stop at the grocery to buy more items at Lizzy's request. As Jane pushed her cart down the aisle, her cell phone rang. Her neighbor Meryl.

"Did everything go okay yesterday, Jane?"

"It was a cyclone! Rained in sheets. If you can picture Poppa, he's half-paralyzed, and his buddy — I call him 'Uncle Guy.' He may be even older than Poppa. So, Guy and I hoist my father out of the van in a friggin' downpour, while my seventy-two-year-old mother holds a golf umbrella over us. I was well drenched by that time, but Momma kept Poppa and Guy dry all the way to the house. She looked like a drowned cat by the time we got inside."

Meryl laughed. "Oh, you should write a blog about this."

"Wait, the plot continues. This morning, my father — remember he is half-paralyzed — got out of bed and let the mud-caked red setter in. The old dog even flattened Momma on the living room floor!"

"Your father couldn't think things through. The stroke — "

"You can't blame this on Poppa's stroke. The man is a brat. I do not understand my mother's devotion. Right now, I'm shopping for her latest list of exotic spices and fat-free items to heal Poppa's paralysis, clear his mind, and prevent strokes forever."

"You are so funny. Is there anything I can do to help?"

"You've done so much, but if you could keep Elizabeth for a couple of hours after school this afternoon, that would be great. I need to set up the iMac I bought Poppa so he can write."

"You seem as devoted to the brat as your mother is."

"Maybe I'll win the 'favorite child award' after all."

After Jane finished shopping, she drove back to Andrew and Lizzy's, where she lugged in four bags and helped Lizzy stock the utility room cupboards, since the pantry was overstocked already. There were cans, boxes, tins, plastic containers, bottles, and cartons everywhere, every conceivable type of healthy, wholesome item one could buy.

"Momma, you can't cook him into good health. There's no recipe for that."

"I can darn well try, young lady."

Lizzy's eyes expressed such determination that Jane knew better than to press.

While her mother started lunch, Jane went to the sunroom, where she surveyed the space and electrical outlets for Andrew's new "writer's office."

Just outside the doorway, Andrew leaned on his walker and silently watched his daughter make notes on her smartphone. He grinned in fatherly admiration at her determined frown and feminine physique, much like Lizzy's when she was younger.

Jane turned to head out and almost ran over her father. "Gosh, you scared me!"

Andrew pretended he had just shuffled by. "Women amok."

"Don't tell me you are a sexist pig." Like a girl, Jane impulsively kissed Andrew on his cheek and headed into the kitchen.

"Going where?"

"Your workshop. You don't have a harem chained to the ceiling, do you?"

"Not yet."

"Is the door still locked?"

"Ask boss." Then Andrew remembered and shouted with all the vocal power he could manage, which wasn't much more than an old man's hoot. "Manuscript. Get!"

"Okay, Poppa!" Then Jane asked Lizzy, "Momma, is the workshop door still locked?"

"Why do you want to know?" Lizzy had not told Jane that she had been out there.

"I'm going to get Poppa's stuff. Remember? I'm turning the sunroom into his workshop." Jane got the key from the Toby jug. "You want to come?"

"No, thank you. I'm making lunch."

"But you always wanted to go out there."

Lizzy's reply was a dodge. "I've been there. The night your father had his stroke."

Jane looked to see if her mother's eyes revealed more, but Lizzy had turned to coat fish fillets in fat-free yogurt with garlic, then gluten-free, unsalted rice-cracker crumbs.

Jane felt Lizzy was evading her. She watched for a clue. "I'll keep the door open."

"Fine, dear." Not for anything would Lizzy admit she had snooped in Andrew's cave.

JANE WAS AMAZED by the workshop's disarray. "Gosh, Poppa. What a mess."

She measured Andrew's immense desk and realized it would never fit in the sunroom. Then she saw the iMac she had given Andrew two Christmases before. "Stinker didn't even open the box. But I'll fix him. He will learn to use a computer even if he doesn't want to."

She reached to grab the box but noticed the stacks of files, folders, and papers on Andrew's desk and decided she would have to get boxes and a dolly from the garage to handle the load. She started to leave but saw Andrew's typewriter with a page of his novel still there. She gently fingered the hole in the paper and put two-and-two together.

"He was writing, and here the stroke hit and then I guess — " Jane's voice trailed off. Her mind elsewhere, she bumped Andrew's manuscript near the edge of the desk. The papers slid under her touch and scattered over the floor. She leaned to pick them up, then sat in Andrew's chair and reconstructed the work. *Goofy guy didn't even number.* She found the title page, "*To Leave a Memory, A Novel and Apologia*, by Andrew Comstock Ward." Next, she located what appeared to be the first page, but she would have to read every page to sequence the manuscript correctly.

Jane snickered. "Well, here we go!" She had the perfect excuse to read her father's novel.

ANDREW SAT at the round table and tapped his left fingers.

Lizzy put fish fillets into a metal pan. "Oven-baked orange roughy with lemongrass."

"Sick o' fish."

"Just be glad I haven't turned us into vegans. The hospital dietician told me, 'If what you eat has a liver, it has cholesterol and fat.' And, she said your body makes cholesterol in response to fat. So, you need to reduce your intake of high-fat meats. Be grateful we have this amazing protein from the sea that is almost fat-free."

"Flavor free."

"Shame on you, Andrew Ward. I've made a gourmet, fat-free fish dish with a delicious gluten-free, crunchy, lemongrass topping, and you will love it." With that, Lizzy slammed the metal baking pan on the countertop and went to the pantry.

Andrew puffed out a sigh.

Armed with a can of canola oil spray, Lizzy exaggeratedly sprayed the fish topping, then sprinkled each fillet with lemongrass and several shakes of various salt-free seasonings.

Andrew shrugged off Lizzy's dish of guilt. He peered out back. "Wha's Janey to?"

"She went to get your computer. Wants to renovate my sunroom with 'cutting edge technology,' whatever that means."

"Just wan' key puncher. I go self." He started to get up.

"You will not. Dr. Fitzgerald says I must keep a close eye on you in case of a TIA. But that won't happen. Not if I have anything to say about it." Lizzy put the metal pan in the oven and slammed the door.

Andrew felt like his jail door had just slammed. The kitchen soon grew steamy with aromas of fish and spices. He desperately needed fresh air. He peered out back. *What is Jane doing out there?* He should simply go outside — to heck with Lizzy and her edicts — but he did not want any grief. *Damn this stroke. I'm trapped,* he thought, but instead he stammered, "Might her back hurt stuff." He had tried to say, "Janey might strain her back by lifting that stuff."

"Janey's a big girl. Smart too. She'll find a way." Just then, the oven timer went ding. Lizzy rushed to the oven and pulled out the steaming fish dish.

Intense aromas swirled into Andrew's universe, and he felt faint. *Where was Janey with his manuscript and typewriter? Where was his escape and fresh air?*

~

By the time Jane had sequenced the typed pages, she had tilted back in Andrew's leather-padded chair with her ankles crossed on his desk. She noted his many red-penned corrections and the comical [NOTE TO SELF] comments he had made for follow-up research. She laughed aloud at some of Andrew's less artful lines. "Colorful work, Poppa. Are these preposterous people supposed to be my ancestors?"

~

LIZZY CLEANED UP AFTER LUNCH. Andrew had grimaced through the meal. Although it was actually delicious, he did not say so. She knew that was simply Andrew's way, especially since his stroke, but she had worked hard to cook this dish. First, she found the recipe in the *New York Times,* then went to several stores for the ingredients.

She could retreat in disappointment or follow Byron Chester's advice. She attempted to break the silence. "The fish was so fresh. The butcher said they flew it in yesterday."

Andrew did not reply.

"I went to an Asian food store near Doraville to buy the lemongrass and bought a bottle of Asian fish sauce for another recipe that calls for just one-fourth teaspoon. At that rate, the bottle will last us centuries, if we live that long."

Andrew did not reply, but wanted to. Problem was, he could not find the words to say the fish was wonderful. He had been such a lout before the meal, but did not know how to navigate the neural path to normalcy. He, too, wanted their life back, not the one he and Lizzy had lived so distantly, but life when they were younger, when there was promise, when they were Lizzy and Andrew and Jane and Billy. Not a life staring out back windows and grunting ill-formed phrases to the woman he loved so much, but could not reach out to for the life of him.

Lizzy sighed and cleared the dishes. Well, at least she had tried.

Andrew checked the kitchen clock and peered out for Jane. "She's there hour."

"I'll go check on her if you want me to."

Andrew weighed the evils: two women in his workshop or one woman. He shook his head. "Janey's big girl."

"I believe I said that a moment ago."

Andrew sneered a mimic and whispered, "Told so."

"You got that right."

Andrew peered out again, but this time he saw Jane rolling a dolly with several boxes stacked on it. "Key puncher coming."

Lizzy chuckled. "Typewriter."

Andrew snapped back in defense. "What I said."

∽

WITH THE SAME focus that drove her at her office, Jane took two days to set up Andrew's office. First, she found a small desk stored in the attic. She sanded and repainted it one day, then placed it by the sunroom's back window and plopped Andrew's iMac on top. Then she placed Andrew's "Family Tree" binder beside the computer. Finally, she and Billy Jay brought in Andrew's desk chair from the workshop. The only thing missing was his manuscript, which Jane had taken home to re-read but forgot to return.

When Andrew saw the set up, he demanded his "goddamn key puncher."

"Poppa, stop swearing. Today, you are coming into the present."

Jane's smart-aleck determination irritated the devil out of Andrew. He had always resisted computers. Even when Emory's administration set up electronic grading, Andrew attended mandatory training, but none of the instruction penetrated his resistant hide. So, his graduate assistants had handled computer operations, even answered his e-mails, and completed his grade reports. His excuse was that he did not have the time. In reality, he felt an overwhelming fear that one computer keystroke would propel him into an incomprehensible universe. He realized this was irrational, but each time his finger poised above the keyboard, he was afraid to push a button for fear he could not find his way back.

Although the sun had set hours before, Jane thought she should get in one lesson before she went home. She booted up the iMac, which then required a photo of Andrew for the very first function.

"Poppa, you've got to sit in this chair for a moment."

With a smirk planted on his already crooked smile, Andrew shuffled to his desk chair. Jane aimed the iMac display at her father's head. She clicked the track pad and, bingo, the iMac beeped three-two-one and took Andrew's photo. Thanks to his lopsided grin, scraggly beard, uncombed hair, and half-belted robe, the resulting image resembled a villain from a chain saw massacre film.

Jane was unstoppable. "We'll do another when you're spiffed up a little better."

Andrew barely tolerated this exercise. He did not intend to use this device. As soon as Jane left, he would ask Lizzy to retrieve his typewriter. If she could lift a cast-iron skillet, she could lift a damn typewriter. Andrew was not about to write without his red Selectric.

Jane took Andrew through the iMac basics, then went through the steps to install word processing software. Next, she put her arms around her father's shoulders and guided his fingers to the keyboard and track pad.

"Using a word processor is like typing, Poppa, only you can change things, save things, delete things, and move things. See?" She showed how to type, backspace, delete, copy, cut and paste, save, and name a file.

Andrew felt claustrophobic again. "Gibberish," he growled. He did not like the newfangled keys that barely went down. He liked to press a typewriter key and see the type ball jump and hear it go "thunk." This iMac contraption operated with quiet clicks and scary beeps whenever he did something wrong. And the track pad. He could not get the hang of that at all.

"If I can't teach you, I'll get a professional trainer in here. I am on a mission. This is the only way you're going to write from now on. The typewriter is dead."

"Poop needs puncher."

"I know you're nervous about this, but once you learn word processing, you'll never go back. And this weekend I'll teach you to use the Internet for research. There are many genealogy sites, public records, you name it."

"Okay, Miss Analyst Systems."

"Systems Analyst. But I will ignore your sarcasm." Jane pointed at the screen. "Now, take this and click on that blue 'W' icon."

Andrew clumsily took over the trackpad but could not get it to do anything right.

Jane realized Andrew had positioned the pad upside down. "No wonder." She laughed as she turned the pad around, guided his hand, and pressed his finger. She heard a click, and a blank page appeared on the screen. "Bingo, Poppa. See, it works."

"Blank," Andrew said.

"What did you expect?"

"Novel."

"Poppa, your novel can't magically appear. You need to enter the data."

"Whurr's it?"

"What?"

"Data."

"What data?" Jane turned away to stall for time. She realized he wanted his manuscript, but it was still in her bedroom.

"Manuscript. Novel. Go get," Andrew stammered.

"I'll get it for you tomorrow. Besides, you've got a lot to learn. Let's do a few more tricks."

"I'm dog old."

Jane mimicked that she would wring Andrew's neck. "Walter is an old dog. You are a resistant poop."

Andrew smiled. This was kind of fun. He liked it when his daughter gave him shit.

LATER, after Jane returned home, she and Alan read in bed. The antithesis of Lizzy and Andrew's bedroom, Jane and Alan's had expansive walk-in closets and dressing areas that were more like rooms than closets. Each had carpeted benches and sliding ladders that reached the top shelves. The bathroom was larger than Lizzy's entire bedroom and had a tile shower with so many faucets and sprays it looked like a Roman bath. The bedroom décor was contemporary, with furnishings Alan picked out, exotic woods with burl inlays. The bed frame and nightstands matched, as did the dresser. Alan liked things to match. An eighty-five-inch TV hid behind an elaborate media center. The couple rarely watched TV in bed, but Alan had wanted a media center in the master to show off during the Druid Hills homes tour.

While Jane read Andrew's manuscript, Alan looked over the *Georgia Bar Journal*. He glanced over and saw the typed pages. "Your nerdy boss sent work home?"

"Don't tell anybody, but this is Poppa's manuscript. His novel."

"The one nobody's ever seen?"

"I found it in his workshop. Just fifteen pages so far. There's one still half-written sheet in the typewriter. There's a hole where Poppa kept hitting the keys."

"Why did you leave it?"

"I didn't want him to think I was snooping."

"But Jane, you've got his manuscript."

"He doesn't know I do."

"For all intents and purposes, you are snooping."

"Alan, please take off your powdered wig. I want to read my father's novel. He calls it an *apologia*. I think it's a way to atone for Billy's accident."

Alan sensed he was headed into another discussion about Jane's relationship with her father, and this would lead to a sob-filled vent about Billy, then to her parents' estrangement — my God, the woman was indefatigable — so Alan lightened his tone. With grand gestures, he mimed pulling off his British lawyer's wig. "So, what's his story about?"

"So far, it's like a 'B' western, but he mentions the color of everything, which must be some sort of symbolism or imagery. The plot is a corny adventure about a cavalry officer who buys a gold mine, marries a French prostitute, then sets out to find gold."

"Kind of like most young couples starting out?"

"I guess so."

"Maybe it's an allegory about your father and mother?"

"An allegory. That would be what Poppa would write to avoid being direct."

∾

THE NEXT MORNING AFTER BREAKFAST, Andrew aimed his walker to the sunroom, where he sat at his new desk and fumbled with the new-fangled track pad and iMac keyboard. "Damn! Wan' my puncher," he shouted just as grandson Billy Jay walked in. School was on break for parent-teacher conferences, so Jane had brought him to visit.

Walter rose from Andrew's feet, but the dog slipped on the sunroom's wooden floors.

Billy Jay reached to help the old dog. "Hey, Walter, are you a house dog now?"

"Jailbird like me." In Andrew's peripheral vision, he saw Jane walk by. "Janey!"

She kept going for fear an embarrassed blush might reveal she had read his manuscript.

"Grand Pop, Mom said this is yours." Billy Jay handed Andrew the pages.

"Wha's mine?"

"These papers here. Mom said to give 'em to you."

"Ah, hah! She read it?"

"I dunnoh. Hey, you learned to use the iMac! I told you it's easy, didn't I?"

"Easy not."

"I do book reports and essays on my computer at home. I'm thirteen now, you know."

"How 'bout help Grand Pop?"

"Help you what?"

Andrew called loudly so that Jane would hear. "Punch data, says Miss Analyst."

Jane heard him hoot and stuck her head in the door. "Are you practicing?"

"Fingers don't punch damn keyboard, see?" Andrew put on an act to look helpless.

"Don't buy it, Billy Jay. He can do it himself."

"How much you gonna pay me, Grand Pop?"

"Chip off block."

"What does that mean? Mom calls me that too."

"You like dad. Tax shyster."

"Are you making fun of my dad?"

"Dare not, Billy Jay. How 'bout twenty cents page?"

"Make it fifty cents a page and you've got a deal."

"Shyster. Chip off block."

From the doorway, Jane smiled as the boy and old man shook hands and shared a grin. Probably the first time the two had been together alone since, well, ever.

LIZZY PREPARED ANOTHER ELABORATE LUNCH. Pots, pans, seasonings, vegetables, fish, bread, and herbs covered every inch of the counters.

Bemused, Jane sat on her usual stool. "Billy Jay is helping Poppa with his novel."

"You're kidding."

"No. Billy Jay is inputting Poppa's manuscript."

"All these years I held out for a game of catch."

"What?"

"Oh, never mind. Just an old baseball fantasy."

"So, what's on the menu at Lizzy's Gourmet Health Café today?"

"Steamed snapper with a white wine sauce, green beans with chives and sliced almonds, new potatoes with dill, and French bread brushed with olive oil and topped with truffles."

"My gosh! This is lunch?"

"Andrew complains about having fish all the time, so I doctor it up. He growls and grumbles, but I can tell he likes it. He cleans his plate anyway."

"You are spoiling him."

"Maybe I should."

"This is a new strategy. If I fixed Alan a lunch like this, he'd think I wanted something.

"Well, I do."

"Dare I ask?"

"You're not mature enough for me to discuss my romantic life with you."

"Momma, I know you and Poppa 'did it.' Where else did I come from?"

"Darn if I know. Besides, it's not sex I want."

"Are we back to that? How long does Poppa have to stay in his self-imposed doghouse?"

"I need to keep the door open. That way, maybe he can — " Lizzy stammered, frustrated.

"Can what?"

"Forgive himself," Lizzy whispered so that Andrew would not hear.

Jane was amazed that her mother had confided in her, so she whispered back. "Have you? Forgiven him?"

"He didn't ask me to."

"So, that's it. He has to say, 'Please forgive me.'"

"No. I never once said, 'I told you so.' Never." Tears welled in Lizzy's eyes.

"But Poppa never said, 'I'm sorry.'" Jane's tone was more an admonition than a question.

"He doesn't have to. God and the rest of us have forgiven him, haven't we?"

Jane wondered if she knew the answer.

IN THE SUNROOM, Andrew watched with a grandfather's pride as Billy Jay keyed in the first page. Walter had shifted allegiances and was nestled at Billy Jay's feet as he typed. The boy saved the file in a document folder titled "Grand Pop's Novel." Then Billy Jay made sure Andrew knew how to locate the icon on the computer and open it up.

"Hey, Grand Pop, this is like some old Western on TV. I figure the dude Ward fights in the saloon is the bad guy, right? Will he try to steal Ward's mine?"

"Write that down. You chip my block too." He tapped his own shoulder.

Billy Jay got the joke and grinned.

ANDREW WAS STILL full from lunch when summoned to consume dinner, but he knew that Lizzy's feelings would be hurt if he did not finish every bite. So, he poked down the meal, then used his walker to pull himself from the table. He nodded a silent "thank you," then scooted across the linoleum and down the carpeted hallway for another few hours of work before bed.

Lizzy could tell where Andrew was by the sounds his walker made. She listened as he thumped into the wood-floored sunroom. "Another night of writing," she whispered to herself. "Why did I think having Andrew inside the house would be better than having him out in that rocket barn?"

Andrew could see through the open drapes that a full moon illuminated the backyard. As he passed the mirror above Lizzy's desk, he glimpsed his workshop's reflection in the moonlight. He saw what Lizzy often saw, the workshop's aluminum siding aglow. Andrew chuckled to Walter, who had padded in after him. "Barn space glow."

At his desk, Andrew struggled to find the file icon Billy Jay had saved earlier. Andrew's left hand trembled on the trackpad. He clicked the contraption and, lo and behold, the document appeared.

"Go bingo, Walter."

Andrew clumsily scrolled to the last line and murmured as if alone in his workshop, "Whurr was I?" He reread his previous scene that described his hero Ward and wife Charlotte as they trekked up a winding road. They stopped for Ward to survey the deep purple ridges and dark green valleys ahead.

Andrew's voice rose louder. "Ah, the ridge. Ward lost."

From the kitchen, Lizzy heard Andrew's voice. "What did you say?" She aimed her question in a shout down the hallway.

"Talking self," Andrew hooted back. "Damn," he swore under his breath. No longer could he ramble to himself without a human in earshot.

"Please mumble loudly enough that I can hear you. Your voice keeps me company."

Andrew did not answer.

"Or say nothing at all," Lizzy called out. She reached for the last sip of her second glass of merlot. The wine gave her the courage to tiptoe down the hall and peek through the crack in the door. In the corner, Andrew arduously pecked one key at a time with his left index finger and hit the space bar with his right knuckle, his brow so intense with effort, Lizzy realized she should not disrupt the forces that drove him. This was Andrew's quest. After fifty-something years of marriage, Lizzy knew when to back off.

~

On a gloriously crisp and sun-dappled spring day in the purple-hued mountains of northern Georgia, Ward and Charlotte rode on a rocky, brown, dusty, narrow trail toward their destination, Findley Ridge. Trouble was, Ward suddenly realized he was downright lost, but he stubbornly refused to admit it, not to himself and especially not to his common law bordello wife.

Pretending that he needed to take a whiz, Ward called out for Charlotte to stop her horse for a break from their arduous ride. They both dismounted. Charlotte arched her back and indiscreetly scratched her lovely derriere, sighing loudly in relief, while Ward headed to the woods. After urinating a yellow stream on the white bark of a scrubby, white oak tree, Ward came back by the horses and made a grand display out of checking the angle of the midday sun. He aimed his compass this way and that to find this direction or that, then marked giant XX's on his map as destinations. Then he laboriously drew connecting lines to mark the routes that would take him to the various XXs on his map.

Trouble was, Ward did not have the right XXs. He had marked the wrong intersections where his mine was supposed to be, as well as the X that marked Findley Ridge. In fact, he did not know where in the world he was.

Meanwhile, Charlotte shivered in the crisp air. A smart and sassy cookie, even if she was an immoral tart, she began to wonder if this Ward Comstock she had married was much of a mountain man. His Cavalry post had been in Fort Stockton, Kansas, he had told her, but perhaps Kansas was not the best place to learn how to navigate mountain passes and forests.

"Sure is a wonder how anyone ever got where we're going," Charlotte said in a tease, doing a bit of baiting to see if Ward really knew where he was. What she would have done if he admitted he was lost, she did not know. She had spent most of this journey one mental step away from turning her horse back to Atlanta.

"Only a fool couldn't find his way with a good map and a fine instrument like this compass," Ward said in reply, trying to convince both of them he knew the way.

After putting his instruments away in a saddle pack, he lifted Charlotte back on top of her ruby mare, then remounted his tan gelding. "Giddy-up," he said, kicking his heels into the horse's flanks. Dust flew in a sandy white cloud as the gelding bolted forward. Off the two-person, four-animal caravan went, with Ward leading the fretful, shivering Charlotte up a barely used trail where the horses picked their way and the mules dragged behind amid patches of midnight green trees and shadowy grey rocks that loomed like religious monuments.

"I've never been up this high. Très froid, even on a spring day! Are you sure you know where you're going?" Charlotte asked, her voice quivering with each word.

"Never fear. Findley Ridge isn't far. We'll camp one more night on this trail before reaching my gold mine," Ward said resolutely.

"Our gold mine," Charlotte reminded him curtly.

"Yes, of course. Our gold mine," Ward sighed with resignation. How he was going to get out of this arrangement was a plague that had entered and reentered his mind throughout most of the day. Here he had

impulsively brought a bordello wench with him, wanting access to her loins as much as he wanted to discover gold, but now that the fever of desire had been assuaged, he found himself ensnared. What had he done? Just to get inside that honey pot, he was now committed to her for the rest of his life.

"Marriage," she had insisted.

Was this legal? Would a judge deem her his common-law wife?

[NOTE TO SELF: RESEARCH COMMON LAW MARRIAGE IN GEORGIA DURING THIS PERIOD. HOW LONG COUPLE MUST BE TOGETHER, ETC.]

Although Charlotte had funded this expedition with the greenbacks she had earned on her back, satisfying the likes of bank clerks, gruesome rail workers, and who-knew-else, was there a way Ward could find a justification to send her packing back to her father?

～

WHILE ANDREW METHODICALLY PECKED, Lizzy headed to the living room. She was weary from her efforts to cook three meals and clean for a man who expressed little enjoyment or gratitude other than a polite nod.

She sorted the mail Jane had brought in earlier. Ordinarily, Lizzy would do this chore at her sunroom desk, but Andrew was in her sunroom. So, she used the piano top as a desk and carefully ripped up credit card offers and stacked to-do items in a separate pile. She went to the kitchen for a third glass of merlot, then wandered back. As she sighed in wine-infused *ennui*, she rummaged through the bookcase and hesitated at the college yearbook. She decided, no. *Yesterday was yesterday. "Stay in the present."*

Relaxation. Maybe something on TV. Jane had made sure the vintage floor model could play cable channels. But Lizzy had no desire to decipher the remote control, not after three glasses of wine, so she picked up a novel she'd never finished, *One Hundred Years of Solitude*. She sat to read in Andrew's burgundy chair, but her memories drifted, despite Byron's admonitions. She caressed the chair's upholstery and recalled when it was gold. That was during her harvest gold and burnt orange period. Soon her thoughts sailed to a night before Billy died.

BILLY WAS on the phone in his room. Janey was on a sleepover. Andrew had smoked a pipe and read his magazine, or that's what he told Lizzy later.

"I put my magazine on the end table and snuffed out my pipe. I know I dumped the ashes in the metal ashtray, not in the wastebasket, and I remember I put the pipe on the stand. But somehow the stand tipped over. Maybe when I stood up, my robe caught it."

Andrew and Lizzy were both in bed by the time the stand fell over. The two snuggled into a pair of human spoons and drifted soundly to sleep before Lizzy could finish her prayers. While they slept, cinders from Andrew's pipe ignited threads of the chair's upholstery. The cloth smoldered at first, then thread after thread curled back in flames. Insidiously, smoke billowed as the seat cushion caught fire.

Lizzy stirred. "Andrew, I smell smoke."

Andrew's eyes opened, bewildered.

Moments later, the two rushed down the hall and discovered the wingback chair was ablaze.

"I'll get water!" Andrew dashed to the kitchen, but did not know where a bucket might be. "Lizzy, where's the bucket?"

"On the shelf in the utility room!"

Lizzy ran to the hall linen closet and yanked out the first thing she saw, a lacy tablecloth. She took a wild swing and flailed at the fire. The filmy lace ignited in a whoosh and flashed Lizzy's face. Flames singed her eyebrows. She dropped the cloth onto the chair, but that only made the flames soar higher.

"Andrew, the fire is getting bigger!" Lizzy did not want to admit she had added fuel. She dashed back to the hall closet and grabbed a heavier tablecloth this time.

Andrew ran into the room with a full bucket, just as Lizzy ran toward the chair. The pair collided with such a bump, Andrew dropped the bucket. Water splashed all over the carpet and Andrew.

"Damn it, Lizzy!" he shouted in a rare tirade.

"Sorry! I didn't see you." Flustered, Lizzy soaked her tablecloth in the spilled water and beat at the chair seat. Smoke and steam fogged the living room.

Andrew grabbed his bucket again. He intended to go for more water, but Lizzy's tablecloth tangled between his legs during one of her mighty swings. He tripped and fell on the soggy carpet.

"You're some help!"

Lizzy refused to apologize for Andrew's clumsiness.

He struggled upright and ran down the hall.

She flailed at the flames, but the smoke and steam choked her. Her eyes stung. "Call the fire department!"

After a minute, Andrew reappeared with a second bucket. "Lizzy! Back away."

She refused. "I've almost got it out!"

"We're going up in flames if you don't move!"

Just as Andrew swung, Lizzy took another mighty swat with her wet tablecloth. Andrew's bucket smashed into her arm, but the water splattered over the chair. The fire breathed out with a sizzle.

Lizzy's arm stung. Aghast at being hit, she glared in silence at what she could see of Andrew through the smoke. He had never hit her, never threatened to, not even when they roughhoused in their youth or had their most intense, heated "discussions."

Andrew did not realize that his bucket had hurt her. He grabbed her cloth and continued to beat the hot spots into submission. Smoke and steam still rose, so Andrew layered the cloth over the seat, then climbed on it and stamped out any live ash. By that time, he was as irritated with Lizzy as she was with him, but through the vapor, his blue eyes locked onto her green eyes.

In that moment, their anger melted to relief.

Andrew coughed and laughed. "Boy, we are a pair."

"We? Who started the fire?" Lizzy coughed back, her eyes alight with laughter.

"I think it was Ricky Ricardo. But Lucy did everything she could to fan the flames!"

"Ricky, you hit me pretty hard with the bucket!" Lizzy said in her Lucy voice.

"*Aiyiyieeeee*, I'm sorry, Lucy, I'm an *ideeeot. Plizz* forgive me."

"Aw, Ricky, I forgive you." Lizzy reached to help Andrew down.

Billy trundled in, still on the phone. The curly cord stretched all the way to his bedroom. "What the heck happened?"

Andrew and Lizzy looked at each other. "You 'splain, Lucy." Then each broke into laughter and could not stop.

Billy rolled his eyes. "You should see this. The chair's all burned up!"

Andrew and Lizzy simply laughed.

"You won't believe my parents," Billy had said into the phone as he shuffled to his room.

ALTHOUGH THE WINGBACK chair's harvest gold upholstery was now burned toast, the frame was only singed. So, Lizzy had reupholstered it in burgundy. Seated now in that same chair, she thought maybe a soft blue would freshen things up. She patted the arm and felt comforted. Yes, she had looked back, but this time she relived a happier time. Whole, normal, confident in life and love. With renewed commitment, Lizzy vowed not to give up until she recovered that joy.

BACK IN THE SUNROOM, Andrew was in his creative universe.

After camping for the night, but still nowhere near Findley Ridge, the newlyweds were awakened by blazing strokes of lightning that shot in angular bolts across a green-black daybreak sky. Deafening thunder rumbled all about, then cracked and exploded as a burst of white-yellow lightning hit a nearby pine tree. Grabbing their dew-damp blankets about them, the youthful couple led their frightened animals to the protection of a nearby ledge. The entire caravan was soaked to the skin as they watched the lightning send fireballs dancing across sinister grey clouds and then flare into the ground all around them.

"God is taunting us. He will murder us with his shots of gold!" Charlotte cried, feeling guilty for the greed that had compelled her to abscond from her saloon home and marry a man she did not really know and certainly did not love.

"The sky's golden burst is an omen, Charlotte. Just think of all the gold I'm going to find once we get to Dahlonega," Ward shouted above the storm, as if his pledge of gold was all he and Charlotte needed to be happy and satisfied.

Unfortunately for both, that was what each needed. Charlotte's bright green eyes calmed, and she huddled into Ward for warmth and assurance that all would be well once they were knee-deep in golden nuggets. He, too, was reassured, thinking that if he just gave this tart some gold, perhaps she would go back to Atlanta.

∽

"FOOLISH WARD. SO SELFISH." Andrew whispered, so Lizzy would not intrude.

With ears that could hear an azalea bloom, Lizzy heard him anyway and came in to say good night. "Talking to yourself or Walter this time?"

Startled, Andrew snapped, "Both."

"Shall I put the dog outside for tonight? It's clear and dry. Did you see the moonlight?"

"Walter, go doghouse. I'm mine."

"Your doghouse comes complete with servants."

"Joking."

"There are two sides to funny, Andrew. One who tells the joke and one who laughs or doesn't." Although Lizzy had drunk too much wine, she realized her comment sounded too harsh. But she was exhausted to have Andrew about full-time. Before his stroke and during the months he spent in rehab, she had gone about her business without demands from another who now occupied her territory. Andrew's workshop had come inside to taunt her.

"Walter, go outside. Lizzy us not like."

Lizzy gave up and went to the bathroom for a long, hot soak.

After she left, Andrew felt guilty. He thought to himself, "*I know how Ward feels. Lost, afraid to admit he's made a mistake, and he has a wife with the smarts to know.*"

He resumed his one-handed description of the pair's soggy ride toward another mist-shrouded summit. After their ascent, they again headed downhill as Charlotte complained loudly about her sore buttocks and the "ever bumping beast" she rode.

❧

"*My feminine intuition says we are lost. We should head back to Atlanta before we catch pneumonia or starve to death,*" *Charlotte said.*

"*Phooey to your woman's intuition. Don't be such a mother hen,*" *Ward said with disdain. From Charlotte's angry look, he could tell that he had said the wrong thing.*

❧

Andrew sat back and mulled Ward's dialogue, words that echoed Andrew's arrogant dismissal of Lizzy's premonition long ago, the same bravado that had cost them their son.

I hope Lizzy will understand from this scene what I want to say about genetic footprints, Andrew said to himself, except for the last words, "genetic footprints." He realized he had sounded the two words aloud. Had Lizzy heard him? "Genetic footprints" came out correctly for a change. He waited silently. Maybe Lizzy would ask again what he had said. *This* time, he might tell her. Do his best with his imperfect speech to absolve the agony between them.

For too many years, he had teetered on the edge. If he moved in any direction, he feared he would rip apart. Could he let Lizzy see his pain? If he did not speak now, would his *apologia* be enough? More than that, was he a good enough writer that Lizzy could read between the lines of his tale?

He heard Lizzy draw her bath. *Guess she couldn't hear me over the rush of water.*

Resigned, he wrote until midnight, then called it a day.

Chapter Seventeen

MOTHER'S DAY

Andrew walked slowly onto the outdoor deck of a bistro in Atlanta's historic Highlands district, aided only by a cane in his left hand and the support of his son-in-law at his right arm. The walker had been left at home.

"Professor Ward, I think you can consider yourself about eighty percent back. And the way you've improved, you might find yourself near to your old, rather, your former self," Dr. Fitzgerald had said with a smile during his most recent appointment.

Lizzy, Jane, Ouisie, and Guy held court at the long table. As usual, Andrew had not been to church that morning. Neither had Jane, Alan, or the kids, but Andrew made the effort to put on a sports jacket, dress shirt, and tie, with help from Jane. She had suggested the jacket, telling Andrew the restaurant required them, although that was a lie. Jane knew Lizzy would expect the males to spiff up. So even Jane's boys and Alan had donned jackets, and Elizabeth a frilly pink dress.

Andrew took his assigned seat between David and Elizabeth, directly across from Billy Jay. He had no choice. Lizzy had gone so far as to put place cards at each seat to ensure this arrangement.

Near the end of the table beside Guy, Ouisie was gussied up in a pink floral sundress with cap sleeves that did little to hide her plump upper arms. "Andrew, I must say, it's a wonderful treat to see you walk in here on your own two feet."

Elizabeth shouted, "Aunt Ouisie, Grand Pop still talks like he's drunk sometimes!"

"Elizabeth Jane!" Jane tried to hush her precocious daughter.

"Aww, Janey. Zizabeth's right. I still slur sometimes, but at least the words now come to me. I'd lost them. Couldn't reach them."

Billy Jay didn't want Elizabeth to get all the attention. "Uncle Guy, I helped Grand Pop use a computer to write his novel."

"Writing fiction on a computer, Andrew?"

"Janey's turned me into a technocrat. Billy Jay typed in the 'data' from what I wrote on the typewriter, and Janey taught me word processing. I bumble along. The whirligig is a great contraption, but I like the touch and feel of paper. The story is stuck inside."

"You can print it, Poppa. I bought you a printer and paper too."

Andrew shrugged.

"Looks like that's our afternoon lesson. Printing."

Andrew faked a sarcastic lack of enthusiasm. "Oh boy, I can't wait."

"Lizzy says your novel is a family saga," Ouisie said.

"An allegory. My version of history."

"He won't even let his wife of fifty years read it."

"When it's finished, Lizzy," Andrew shot back.

"It's like a Western. This Cavalry guy and a prostitute hunt for gold, but a bad guy causes them trouble," Billy Jay said.

"How come your grandson gets to read it before your wife?"

"How come you Unitarians celebrate Easter when you don't believe the plot?"

Ouisie quickly countered. "Today is *Mother's Day*, not Easter. And just how did we get on this topic?"

"Poppa has a discombobulated way of dodging bullets."

Alan jumped to defend another male. "Andrew, I thought your *segue* was a smooth move, even if you got the holiday wrong."

"The only smooth move I can make at this age is to land right side up in my coffin."

"Andrew, I don't feel one step nearer death, even after fifty years of marriage to you."

"Poppa, sixty-six is the new seventy-six. You have many years to be active."

"My dear daughter, I do not want to take a spin class."

"Poppa, you could at least take walks. The doctor said you should walk daily."

"Oh, yes, the doctor, the daughter, and the wife — all females, I might add — they've always got a plan for what I should do, and they're always right. Especially Lizzy, who never lets me forget."

Ouisie shook her head at the family's perpetual debate. "Goodness, I didn't mean to stir the pot with my silly comments."

"Don't worry a bit. This is our family at its best," Jane said.

"Ouisie, if you'll forgive an old friend for making another smooth move, Lizzy tells me your new minister has stirred things up at the UU church."

Ouisie was grateful for the subject change. "I know Lizzy doesn't agree with this, but I think he's a gosh-darn lecher. He's single, you know. Right after he arrived last fall, he replaced the longtime office manager with a floozy he hired for his own sexual gratification."

David's eyes lit up. "What's 'sexual gratification'?"

Alan put his fingers over his lips to hush David. "I'll tell you when you're forty."

"The board and I will keep a sharp eye," Guy said with a firm knock on the table.

"I think the board should stay out of Reverend Chester's personal life. There's more to this minister than rumors," Lizzy said.

"I've always wondered why we need ministers. If there's really a God, He'd show up."

"This proves again that religion is not a topic to discuss at the dinner table," Lizzy said.

"How about sexual gratification?" Andrew said.

With a dare, Elizabeth chimed in. "Grand Pop, what's 'sexual gratification'?"

Jane glared at Andrew. "Poppa, there are children here."

"I want to talk about sexual gratification," David grinned.

For a flash moment, Andrew thought the boy was his son Billy. But he caught himself and wondered if anyone else noticed. He toyed with the utensils. No, this boy was Janey's David, the one who pinged his heart each time Andrew saw his face. And across the table was Billy Jay, his helper, the one whose very name brought memories of his own little Billy. And little Elizabeth on his left reminded him of Janey, how innocent and happy she had been.

"There's sex in Grand Pop's novel. I got to type all sorts of stuff," Billy Jay said.

"Billy Jay — " Alan's voice carried a stern caution.

With a dare gleaming in his eyes, Andrew grabbed a roll from a breadbasket and leaned across the table. He clumsily tried to stuff the roll in Billy Jay's mouth. "Put a roll in it."

Billy Jay dodged Andrew's thrust, but then the boy laughed. With a swift left hook that no one could have anticipated, Andrew poked the roll solidly between Billy Jay's front teeth.

The boy hammed it up. With the roll stuck halfway out of his mouth, he loudly mumbled the details of Andrew's sex scene, but his revelations were unintelligible.

Everybody giggled, even Lizzy. Sure, Andrew was his contentious self and stole her Mother's Day show, but he had walked in on his own power and socialized with family and friends. What a miraculous turnaround from his lifeless state months before. Besides, Lizzy was used to her role as second banana to a showoff.

LATER THAT NIGHT, Andrew and Lizzy got into bed. His right-sided motor skills had improved so much, he could reach and turn off the lamp on his nightstand.

As Lizzy curled with her back to him, she recalled the morning's fun at brunch. She waited a beat, then took a risk. Reached out. She wriggled in Andrew's direction and pressed lightly against him.

His eyes lit up. This time, Andrew reached over and patted Lizzy's hips.

She thought he had patted her to say goodnight. "Goodnight, Andrew. Thank you for going to my brunch today."

"I wasn't saying, 'goodnight.'"

Lizzy rolled to face him. "What do you mean?"

"I think my meds have stirred things up." Andrew motioned with a nod toward the pointed rise under the floral spread. "We have a visitor."

"Are you sure you're up to it?"

"Lizzy, this is no time for a pun."

She blushed. "I didn't mean it that way."

"I'm afraid if I move, our visitor will go away."

Lizzy gently slipped back the covers and whispered seductively, "Then don't move."

Chapter Eighteen
MAY 15

While Lizzy washed dishes after Monday's breakfast of homemade turkey and tofu sausage, scrambled Egg Beaters, decaf coffee, and low-sodium, gluten-free toast with sugar-free marmalade, Andrew sat at his desk in the sunroom's back corner, as Walter curled at his feet. Andrew massaged the dog's neck and ears.

"Don't tell that Cocker Spaniel next door, but this old dog got laid last night. Although it wasn't what I'd call the heated passion of youth, it surely was a pleasant sort of heaven."

Lizzy called from down the hall. "Did you say something, dear?"

"My darling wife can hear a pine needle drop," Andrew whispered. Then he shouted toward the kitchen. "I was talking to Walter. Dear."

Curious to know what Andrew had muttered, Lizzy tiptoed nearer. "I thought you might need me for another romp, dear," Lizzy said, but she held her hand over her mouth to make her voice sound like she was still in the kitchen.

Andrew whispered to Walter. "She took care of me pretty well last night, that is, for an old bitch. No new tricks, but then Lizzy didn't even know what sex was until I came along. I was a professor *emeritus*, you know."

Lizzy silently tiptoed into the sunroom and stood right behind Andrew. She leaned over and whispered. "Old bitch?"

Andrew jumped. "Oh golly. That was a metaphor. You know, man to dog."

"Your relationship with that animal is not normal."

"Would you rather I call Guy and say, 'Hey, Lizzy and I made out last night'? Or would you prefer I call Alan? Or, how about my brother? He'd think I wanted to one-up him, since his wife's osteoporotic bones might fracture in a strong wind."

"I expect you to keep our intimate relations to yourself. A gentleman would."

Andrew patted the dog. "I never told her I was a gentleman." Walter scrambled from under the desk. "Down, boy. I'll take you out later."

"Oh, I give up. You and your dog have a wonderful morning. I will go for a walk with Ouisie. She and I are going to exercise twice a week and regain our hard bodies."

"That'll be a treat for the men in your congregation. Most of those UU women look like they've never been near a fitness center."

"The pot calls the kettle. And while we're on the topic, please don't insult people of my faith just because you don't have any. Faith, that is. I've never insisted you 'get religion,' but if you are not supportive of my pursuits, you won't get to play with this hard body anymore." Lizzy headed out, quite proud of her comeback.

"Walter, we are both in and out of the doghouse at the same time. Let's see if we can get this darn chapter written before somebody tells me I can't do that anymore, either."

Off Andrew went with his hero Ward and the ever-complaining Charlotte, who had arrived at a small mountain lake, ready for a meal and a night's rest. In Andrew's scene, Ward did not have any bait, so he used his last bit of jerky to lure a fish.

∾

WARD WAS weary of Charlotte's constant whining. "Build us a good fire, Charlotte. I'll rig up the fishing line." He rummaged through his packs for the hook he had packed and then went to a nearby birch tree to cut a long branch to serve as a rod.

In the meantime, Charlotte gathered wood scraps and built a fire in the center of a clearing near the lake, adding more branches that she had hacked off smaller trees with Ward's knife. While she worked, Ward sat on a big white rock beside the fire and fastened the fishing hook to a line he had tied to the tip of the rod.

"Thank goodness you brought that hook," Charlotte said, amazed that Ward had done anything right on this so-far disastrous journey. Five days out of Atlanta, and there was still no view of Dahlonega in sight. The small town was only sixty-six miles from Atlanta, and the horses and mules had made a good twenty-five miles a day carrying humans and supplies.

"A good soldier plans ahead," Ward said, baiting the hook with a bit of dried jerky. "Let's see what these mountain fish like to eat." He walked toward the lake.

Shivering from the chill and having spent most of the day wet or damp, Charlotte huddled beside the orange flames of her well-built fire. Beyond her, Ward threw his line into the forest-green water. Out of Ward's earshot, Charlotte muttered, "On my father's drunken soul, Ward planned ahead. I've had jerky and biscuits for days now. What I wouldn't give for a real meal. Some chicken or fish, with potatoes and butter, and some fresh greens. Mère de Dieu."

Oblivious to Charlotte's whispered rant, Ward stood at the lake's edge, staring into the deep emerald pool. The water was so still and clear, he could see down about fifteen feet. He fantasized that a big crappie was circling his hook. Ward leaned further to see if he could spot a fish. He stared into the dark waters, all but willing a fish to bite, but saw only his reflection in the bottle green mirror of the pool. He was startled at the vision, how he looked more like his father than the young Cavalry officer Ward still imagined himself being.

Charlotte stoked the fire and added more wood. As the bright flames rose, so did her hunger. "If this man does not catch a fish, I am going to *make a bed and sleep for days. Only after my sweet derriere is rested, will I get back on that atrocious horse, and only then so I can ride back to Atlanta and my warm bed. I miss my bed. I even miss my drunken Pa-Pa!" She cried softly to herself, with the drizzle from her tears painting her flushed cheeks as she dropped another load of branches onto the growing fire.*

Ward had become so entranced with his image in the reflective pool, he did not see the fat crappie that was circling his lure. He also missed seeing the fish attack the jerky bait. But Ward felt the tug on his line and jumped back from the water's edge. He tested and tugged, then yanked the pole backward and above his head. Set firmly on the hook and as surprised as Ward, out came a fat, silver-green crappie. The fish swung in wide circles around Ward's head.

[NOTE TO SELF: DO MOUNTAIN STREAMS HAVE CRAPPIE?]

"Charlotte! I caught me a fish."

"You caught me a fish!" Charlotte said.

Ward stood with the fish still circling on the line. "Come help me! I can't get this beautiful thing to stop flapping round my head!"

WITH LIZZY GONE, Andrew was relieved that he could relish his work aloud.

"Memories *are* like gold dust, Walter. I remember the origin of this scene like yesterday. I got up before everybody and fetched a piece of bacon, then cut it into strips. Then I stole out front, ran down the twenty-two steps, and struggled to open the heavy wood garage doors.

"Inside, the space was more like a barn, with high wooden crossbeams. All around were stacks of fishing poles, boxes of tools, our aluminum canoe, an ancient rowboat balanced on two sawhorses, and a sailboat hull in one corner that Daddy and Uncle Luke always said they'd make into a real sailboat someday, but we all knew they never would.

"I picked out the longest cane pole. Must have been twelve feet. My mind equated the length of the pole with the size of the fish I hoped to catch. No short pole for me, *no-sir-e*, except this pole was so unwieldy, I couldn't get it out of the garage door. So, I pointed it like a spear out to the end of the dock, where I unraveled the line like I'd seen Otto and Danny do.

"I speared bacon with the hook, then tossed it in the water and waited. Lucky for me, the line was set at the right depth with a red and white bobber. More suddenly than I expected, that little ball plunged under like a tiny depth charge.

"Was it a fish? I felt a sustained tug. I yanked the pole back hard. The long tip whipped straight back at me, with a silver-green crappie on the end of the line. Round and round my head, the fish flapped beyond my reach. I held tight and turned to keep the fish in rotation, for fear the dang thing would slap me in the face.

"Help me, somebody! I caught a fish!" I shouted uphill, but never took my eyes off the crappie that shimmered green and silver in the sunlight.

"Momma came down and saved me. Then she cooked the fish for my breakfast. Served it on good China, with fried potatoes and fresh tomatoes. Made a big deal so Tommy could see. She used to do that. Take my side, so Tommy wasn't always the big cheese.

"'See this beautiful fish Andy caught?' Momma said, eyes alight.

"Tommy glowered a bit in jealousy.

"I'll never forget how proud I felt that day."

Andrew patted Walter's head and resumed his tale. But before he could make progress, another recollection soared into his mind's eye as if a bird had hit a window. He wondered if he should create a scene about it in his *apologia* to help Lizzy understand the whys, the reasons beyond simple genetics. Why Andrew was Andrew.

Snow rarely made an appearance in Atlanta on Christmas Day. So rarely, his father often included that fact in a corny joke. *"It'll snow on Christmas Day in Atlanta when — "* Then Comstock would fill in the blank, such as *"When I win a million dollars,"* or *"When Noreen stops dyeing her hair."*

But this Christmas, his brother Tommy had turned twelve. For a special present, he got an olive-green English bike with narrow racing tires and three gears.

Just eight, Andy only had a chain-driven tricycle that surely would not keep up with Tommy now.

As soon as breakfast was over, Tommy got dressed to go out.

"Not today. The weather report says there's a chance of snow."

"Noreen, you can't keep the boy off a Christmas bike because there's a chance of snow."

"Come on, Momma!" Tommy cried.

Andy silently prayed Tommy could not go, not out of concern for Tommy's safety, but out of gut-wrenching envy.

"Noreen, I'll be promoted to bank president before it will snow on Christmas in Atlanta."

"But Comstock, I've got a feeling, an odd feeling. And you know what that means."

"Oh, phooey to your woman's intuition. Don't be such a mother hen."

Tommy took this as a green light and rocketed to the garage.

Andy ran after, and so did Comstock. The two watched Tommy climb aboard his sleek bike, although it was a used bike. Comstock never paid retail and had picked it out at a pawnshop downtown that specialized in sporting goods.

Tommy's feet barely reached the pedals, so Comstock lowered the seat a few notches.

When Andy played with the gears, Tommy hollered for him to stop. Andy got so angry, he screamed, "I hope you fall and scrape your face!" But he immediately felt a knot in his stomach. Should he take that back?

Before Andy knew it, Tommy took off down the driveway.

Comstock called to him, "Be back in thirty minutes. You hear?"

Tommy was too preoccupied to respond.

Andy could see the bike was too much for his brother. The wheels wobbled as he peddled and tried to figure out the gears. He turned the corner on Juniper Street and disappeared from view.

Andy and his father watched and waited, but eventually, Comstock motioned Andy inside, where they both endured the guilt Noreen served up in the kitchen.

Dolled up in her red sheath and a green apron, Noreen furiously stuffed the turkey. She was a tall but hippy woman, who had been blond as a girl and kept her hair light by "toning" it, she said. She did not want to admit that she bleached it. Her blue eyes darted with anger above her high, angular cheekbones. "Comstock, if anything happens to our boy — "

"Nothing will happen, Noreen. You are overdramatizing."

Comstock and Andy went to the living room to play with the electric train Santa had brought for Andy. The train was a snazzy gift, except Comstock was the only one who knew how to operate it. He lined up the cars, then Andy made the engine go too fast, so the locomotive and cars flipped off on the curves. Comstock went beet red every time he put the cars and engine back on track, then gave Andy a look that dared the boy not to run them off again.

Andy knew his father did not like him very much, an ache that never stopped. Even so, today was Christmas, so Comstock played train with Andy for about half an hour. Then, just as he put the locomotive and cars back on track again, Noreen shrieked from the kitchen as if a cockroach had run across her feet.

"Snow! Comstock, it's snowing! I'm worried about Tommy."

"Tommy can walk the bike home, Noreen. He knows the neighborhood."

Just after Comstock said that, Andy heard a distant screech like a wild animal that the elderly Andrew could still hear today. Comstock and Andy bolted toward the front door, but Noreen ran past them in a blur of red and green. She was a long-legged woman who could outrun most, especially if her child was in danger.

Andy tried to keep up, watching Noreen's derriere bounce like Jell-O under her red sheath, and her green apron flew like an angel's wing as she ran toward the screams.

When Andy got to the corner, he saw a red Oldsmobile 98 in the middle of the street with the driver's door open, and a man in an overcoat bent over something ten feet away. Then Andy saw Tommy's olive-green English bike, crumpled. And when the man stood up again, Andy saw Tommy writhing on the slick pavement.

Noreen screamed, "Tommy," but her tone was muffled by what had become a sopping snowfall with huge white flakes. She would have swooped Tommy in her arms except for Comstock's shouts as he caught up.

"Noreen, don't pick him up! Might hurt his neck or back!"

"Oh, my baby. Where does it hurt, Tommy?"

"My leg," Tommy screamed. "My leg."

"I didn't see him, ma'am. This crazy snow blinded me."

"Are you all right, son?"

Andy was frozen in shock. Tommy's shinbone stuck out through his blood-purple jeans. Blood stained the snow beside him.

Comstock asked the driver for his overcoat and threw that over Tommy. Then, Comstock ran in a blur to call an ambulance.

The driver apologized over and over, but Noreen turned her back and tried to soothe Tommy. She tucked the overcoat tightly and smoothed his hair to distract him from the pain.

Andy was astonished to see that his mother really loved his brother. Since Andy hated Tommy almost every minute of each day, he could not fathom how Noreen, or anybody, could love the arrogant brat. But she clearly did.

Forever seemed to pass before sirens blared and police cars, an ambulance, and even a red fire truck came. Andy was not sure why the fire truck showed, but it sure gave the moon-faced neighbors something to gape at when they came out from their dinners.

"A bike ride in this snow?" one neighbor asked.

Comstock shrugged. "My son's first bike."

After that, all anyone could hear were Tommy's cries, Noreen's coos, and the driver's apologies for not seeing Tommy.

By that time, Andy was ready for Tommy to shut up.

Comstock knew his goose was cooked, even if his Christmas turkey wasn't. Noreen did not say so in front of Andy, but she said it behind closed bedroom doors that night, after the family spent

Christmas at the hospital and came home exhausted to find Noreen's half-stuffed turkey still on the counter with bloody juice all around.

Without a word, Comstock threw it in the trash out back.

After a bath, Andy's mother kissed him goodnight with an extra, "I love you, both of my sons, so much." But a bit later, Andy heard angry voices muffled through the bedroom walls.

"I warned you, Comstock. I knew something would happen."

After a series of loud protestations and more accusations, Andy eventually heard his father say, "Noreen, I'm sorry."

"EVEN HE SAID IT. A horse's rump like my father. You would have thought I'd learned a lesson, but history repeats." Andrew slammed his hand on his desk and sighed. "There I go again with the memories, Walter. If Lizzy were here, she'd think I was a fool. I'm pleased that the memories have come back, but like always, they are too loud. Maybe you and I should get out of here. Sneak up to Sonic and get a burger."

LIZZY AND OUISIE chatted excitedly as they walked in their bright warm-up suits on a sunlit path at Piedmont Park, just west of Druid Hills near downtown Atlanta.

Ouisie suddenly stopped in the middle of the trail. "I cannot believe you did it."

"Well, we did!" Lizzy said, then giggled and blushed as deeply pink as the azaleas on either side of the trail.

Ouisie was breathless. "Do you think you should have?"

"We're married, for gosh sakes."

"But sex must be stressful on Andrew's vital organs."

"His penis is not where the problem lies. Anyway, he suspects that his medications have stirred things up. He said he's, well, re-energized."

"Maybe it's like that old movie, *Cocoon*. Remember how the geezers swam in the magic pool where aliens laid their mysterious eggs, and then the men ran home horny? We could use some of that at my house. Guy hasn't, well, the stories about Black males are truly a myth. We haven't done the do in years!"

"Neither has Andrew, until last night."

"Was it, as they say, good for you?"

"I refuse to provide graphic details, but everything was quite pleasant."

"Com'on, Lizzy. Say something exciting. Something that sizzles. Something, oh, I don't know, what would I tell you if Guy and I —" Ouisie's voice wandered off, wistfully. "Was it as passionate as when you made love for the first time? Remember how full of wonder, even a bit shameful, we thought sex was?"

Lizzy snickered. "I'm amazed you can remember anything from so long ago."

Ouisie swiped at Lizzy, but she darted away. Ouisie tried to catch her, but Lizzy was faster. After fifty yards, the women were both so out of breath, they gave up and succumbed to giggles. Younger runners dodged by as the two women hugged and laughed.

Their eyes expressed what their voices did not say. *Even old girlfriends still share secrets.*

∽

ANDREW MADE a solid effort to rummage through the kitchen for a mid-morning snack but could find only vegetables, yogurt, raw fish, and zero-fat, zero-cholesterol, zero-salt canned goods to eat. "She's got us in zero-taste prison."

He shuffled to the bedroom and struggled to dress. He even took a moment to comb his hair and brush his teeth before he headed to get the car keys.

"Com'on, Walter. You and I are Butch and Sundance."

In the garage, Andrew retracted the black top of his red MINI Cooper convertible, a prize he had bought two years before with his textbook royalties. Then he urged Walter to leap into the right front seat. The big dog could barely fit, but Andrew wanted him there because that violated another of Lizzy's commandments: no dog in any car.

"Let's get something greasy." Andrew slammed the convertible into reverse.

Once on the paved street, the MINI Cooper peeled out. Walter seemed to relish the freedom of being on the lam with his master. At an ATM, Andrew got cash, then pulled into a Sonic Drive-In. Since it was still early, there were many slots, so he chose one in the shade of a giant pine. He fumbled with the speaker button but vocalized his order well enough to be understood.

Ten minutes later, a cute brunette on roller skates zigzagged out with two double-bacon cheeseburgers with chili, jalapeños, and guacamole, two orders of chili-cheese tater tots with onions, and two double-cherry chocolate shakes.

"Is this for you or the dog?"

"It's escape and survival." Andrew tipped her two dollars.

As she skated away, he opened the MINI's glove box to use as Walter's "tray." He unwrapped one burger, broke it onto the wrapping paper, and gingerly balanced the mess on the tray.

Walter gobbled his meal in two bites, including the paper.

Andrew laughed without a care for who might take notice. "Atta boy!" When he took a big bite of his own burger, guacamole and chili ran down his chin. Walter eagerly stretched to lick the juices. "Okay, boy. That's enough. Enough!" Andrew reached for a napkin and one of the shakes. "Here, boy. You thirsty?" Andrew popped off the lid and held the cup while Walter's long tongue lapped the cherry-chocolate heaven.

"If Lizzy would serve this stuff, she'd have to fend me off every night." Andrew knew that was a boast. He would be lucky to have another erection ever. "Ah, but life is good today. We need to focus on what's right with our universe. Yes, I messed up. God, I can never forget it, but for today, right now, life is good beyond my self-inflicted tragedies."

Andrew tossed the dog a final chili-cheese tater tot. Walter gulped it down without chewing. "Atta boy. We both still got it."

Andrew's watch said eleven, so he worried that Lizzy's walk would be over. After all, she might bring Ouisie back to the house to see what Andrew was up to. He trashed the evidence, then went to the drive-in window for more napkins and water to clean up the car.

All finished, he cranked up the MINI and headed home. Walter hung two-thirds out and panted in the breeze. When Andrew pulled into the garage, he sighed in relief to see Lizzy's car was not there. He let Walter out, then dusted the telltale red hair off the seat, and double-checked the dashboard and glove box for any signs of grease.

"Walter, you go do your business. I'll save you from the doghouse later."

Back at work in the sunroom, Andrew wrote several pages in spirited language about Ward and Charlotte's sexual pursuits after their fish dinner. For Charlotte, the sex was her reward to Ward because Ward had caught a fish. The next morning, the couple mounted their horses and headed toward Findley Ridge, at least according to Ward's miscalculations.

～

"WE CAN MAKE DAHLONEGA TONIGHT," Ward called out above the clunk of horse hooves.

"Is there a hotel? What I'd give for a hot bath, a real toilet, and a bed," Charlotte cried.

Before Ward could answer, both horses lurched in a frightening display of power. "The horses sensed something the humans could not. Hold your filly, Charlotte!" Ward commanded.

Charlotte's ruby mare bolted forward. "Whooooaaaaa, Whooooaaaaa," she cried as the horse ran downhill and away with her.

"Hold her!" Ward yelled after her.

"I'm tryiiiiinnnnng. Whooooaaaaa, Whooooaaaaa," she screamed as her mare bolted in a sharp downward angle, with Charlotte pulling hard as she could on the reins.

Ward gave his gelding the lead to follow. "Hold on, Charlotte!" he encouraged his bordello bride, but her horse continued a wild descent until Charlotte fell off, tumble-bumble, hitting the rocky ground with a sharp cry. Ward pulled back on his horse's reins, but the tan steed reared and pitched Ward onto the hard rock trail. Dazed, he called out for Charlotte.

"Over here!" Charlotte's wan voice came from beyond a brushy evergreen. She moaned, "Mere de Dieu, mere de Dieu," while Ward followed her pathetic call to where she had fallen on her back, and was covered in dirt, dust, and brush.

"I think I broke my entire body," she moaned. "Did you catch my horse?" she asked expectantly.

"I jumped off mine to take care of you," Ward lied. He did not want her to know that he, the great horseman, had also fallen.

"A fine cavalry officer you are. You should have stayed with the horses. Now all I've got to travel upon are these aching feet," Charlotte cried.

Feeling even more like a failure, Ward gingerly helped her regain her footing. The two dusted themselves off and started walking. After a while, Charlotte stopped to rest and sat down on a rock. Ward retrieved his compass from his pocket. "Let's head this way. My compass says this is the right direction," he said confidently.

"This way, that way, do you know where you are going?" Charlotte asked, not expecting an answer because the two had to go in some direction, right or wrong. So off they walked toward Ward's newest course, but that trail ended at a precipice above a distant valley that was surrounded by a deep forest that gave off a violet hue.

"You haven't a clue where you're going, do you?" Charlotte said aghast, more a statement than a question.

Ignoring her, Ward silently checked his compass, but Charlotte interrupted him. She had seen something far below. She pointed and screamed, "There, there! Do you see them?"

Ward took a while, but eventually he saw dust flying downhill in the distance, two riderless horses running, and then far beyond the horses, a *clearing with a settlement of stone buildings. From this distance, Ward could even see steam rising from chimneys.*

There it was, far below, the gold mining town of Dahlonega. Their new home.

~

AN HOUR LATER, Jane dropped by. The front door was open, so she came in. "Momma? You home? Poppa?" There was no answer. She peered into the sunroom and saw her father at work. She was about to interrupt, but peeked through the door crack, just as her mother had done. She watched Andrew peck at his keys but noticed that he sometimes typed with both hands. His right hand had regained more function. Jane nodded a silent *thank heavens*, then left Andrew to his story.

~

AS SOON AS the couple had located a place to live in Dahlonega, Ward found work three days a week as a blacksmith's assistant. On the remaining days, Ward went to work at the mine. Unfortunately for him, the mine he had bought turned out to be nothing more than a huge hunk of mountain for Ward to chop up by himself. There was no mining infrastructure in place, no prior dig, no ditches, no tunnels, no equipment other than what he could buy or borrow and tote with him each day. If he left any tools at the mine, other miners nearby would steal them, or so he found out the first day when he left a shovel and pick, only to find both missing when he came back two days later.

Months passed, and it was winter. Although snow fell thickly at this elevation, Ward labored to clear the snow each day and bashed the ground with a pick, separating rocks from Mother Earth. He awkwardly hauled the rocks by wheelbarrow to the nearest cold creek, a good hour's trek, where he dumped his rocky harvest on the banks and smashed stones to bits. He shoveled the resulting gravel into a sluice box he had set in the steam's powerful flow. The purpose of the water was to whoosh away the lighter-weight gravel and leave behind the heavier gold nuggets. This was a rudimentary process and nothing like the hydraulic mining that the large companies were now using in that area.

[NOTE TO SELF: GOOGLE DATE HYDRAULIC MINING BEGAN.]

But alas, there were no nuggets. Still, Ward remained a stalwart and optimistic miner.

Only a mile away in a rudimentary shack next door to the saloon, Charlotte posed before a cracked mirror adorned at the top corner with a scraggly Christmas wreath. As she turned to one side, she caressed her swollen belly. Her pregnancy was showing.

~

LIZZY PADDED down the hall in her robe and slippers. She investigated the sunroom and ventured, "Still at it?" Because Andrew did not respond, Lizzy let him have time alone and headed to take a bath. In the tub, she fondly recalled the Mother's Day lovemaking session but hoped Andrew would not want sexual relations every night, just now and then.

"A girl needs her beauty rest," she whispered as she soaked. Lizzy had decided to cut back on the wine, so a glass of iced chamomile tea perched on the soap dish.

~

WARD WAS a dark silhouette against the backdrop of rock and ice-white melting snow when he emerged from his mine with a rickety wheelbarrow full of red rock. Although March was half over, the warming suns of springtime had not yet lifted the cold, hard winter. Ward remained discouraged, although not broken.

Struggling to find both the inner emotional fortitude and outer muscular strength he needed to carry on, Ward pushed and pulled his heavy load to the frosty stream nearby, where he chipped at the larger pieces of rock with a hammer and washed the resulting gravel through a sluicing box. Again and again, Ward washed rock and found not one bit of gold nugget. His hands were raw and blue from the cold. When his wheelbarrow was empty, Ward cried out in anguish, throwing a shovel as far as he could heave, until it careened off a rock twenty feet away.

Back in town, a midwife examined Charlotte's gigantic stomach.

Charlotte yelled, "Ouch! Be gentle. I'm not made of stone."

Day after day, month after month, Ward chopped rock and then hauled out more wheelbarrows of the recalcitrant stone. But one icy day, he was surprised to see a grisly man standing not thirty feet away. The shadowy character was bundled in a filthy sheepskin jacket and furry cap, and he wore buckskin boots. Ward had a gut feeling, then eventually recollected that this fellow was the angry rail worker from Gerard's saloon in Atlanta, the one who had tangled with Ward and spat phlegm at his boot.

"What brings you here?" Ward asked suspiciously.

"Did you think you could brag about your mine, but keep all the gold for yourself, Cavalry Boy? You made it too easy to find you," the rail worker growled.

He grabbed one of Ward's mallets and lunged at him, but Ward scrambled away and picked up his Winchester lever-action shotgun. He aimed it at the rail worker. "Get away from here or I'll shoot."

[NOTE TO SELF: SEE WIKIPEDIA FOR DATE REPEATING RIFLES WERE PRODUCED.]

The rail worker grinned and swatted the mallet at Ward's gun. "You can't get off a shot before I can kill you," the rail worker said as he charged at Ward again.

Ward turned and ran as fast as he could, all the while pumping his shotgun. He heard the intruder's steps coming fast, so he spun wild-eyed and pulled the trigger, relieved that his little-used shotgun actually fired.

A blast of pellets stung the rail worker on his buckskin britches. He shrugged it off and jumped menacingly at Ward, swinging the mallet.

With a smack, Ward felt a glancing blow on his head. He fell, but pumped his shotgun and let another round fly.

This time, pieces of shot lodged in the intruder's shoulder. He shrugged off the pain and was about to pounce again, but held back when he heard a voice advancing.

"Hey there. What's the trouble?" another miner called as he rounded a ledge.

The rail worker hesitated, then ran downhill, disappearing into the woods. Ward resisted the temptation to fire at his back.

"A Cavalry officer would never shoot a man in the back, no-sir-e," Ward said to himself as he greeted the other miner who came to help.

THE NEXT MORNING ABOUT TEN, Andrew's hired hand, Billy Jay, fetched the stack of papers from the printer. As Billy Jay read through the work, Andrew pointed to the section about the rail worker. Billy Jay gave Grand Pop a high-five for including the boy's suggestion to make the rail worker the novel's troublemaker. But Billy Jay grew upset when he read that Ward had been hurt in the battle but had not killed the rail worker.

"That guy's not gonna kill Ward, is he?"

"Life doesn't always come out hunky-dory, Billy Jay."

"Don't let him kill Ward. He's got to find the gold for his wife and baby!"

The boy shouted with so much innocent sincerity, Andrew felt guilty. He had not planned a happy ending for this work. That was the point. Ward's foolishness and untimely death were Andrew's allegorical metaphors for his failings. But from Billy Jay's reaction, Andrew wondered if he should keep Ward alive. Maybe use Ward to convey to Charlotte a metaphorical apology — the one Andrew wanted to express to his own wife.

Andrew nodded at the boy and patted Billy Jay's shoulder. "Good ideas, although I haven't decided on the ending."

Billy Jay arranged the pages and manually numbered each. "Did you know you can number the pages in the computer?"

"I feel another lesson coming. Show me how, Smarty Pants."

~

THE NIGHT after Ward had fought the evil rail worker, Ward and Charlotte lay in bed in their shanty. In a deep sleep, he was weary from mining and his battle with the intruder, but Charlotte sat up, still awake. She was hugely pregnant under what covers she had scrounged from a church charity, there not being enough money for the couple to set up housekeeping properly. Getting out of bed, Charlotte struggled to put on her tattered coat and leather boots. She lit an oil lamp that hung by the door, and when she opened it, the freezing air whisked whirls of snow inside that stirred Ward from his sleep.

"Where are you going?" he asked sleepily.

"To the outhouse. Must have been all those beans. Or maybe the jerky." Charlotte held a hand across her belly.

"If I wasn't so dizzy, I'd walk you," Ward said, touching the heavy bandage on his head.

"If you had found gold instead of getting into a fight, I would have a house with an indoor toilet," Charlotte snapped back.

[NOTE TO SELF: RESEARCH INDOOR PLUMBING IN THIS ERA.]

As Ward watched his expectant wife head into the chilly night, he lay limp, feeling like the failure he was. But his feelings were short-lived as he drifted again to sleep.

Shivering against the bone-chilling cold, Charlotte walked three hundred feet to the community outhouse, shared by twenty shanties in the area. She held her lantern in front to guide her. Once inside the unheated space, she held her nose to avoid the stench and strained to relieve herself of the day's meals.

"Mère de Dieu, what did I eat to feel this way?" Charlotte cried as her face glistened with sweat. She strained and contorted. Her face became more anguished with each grunt. "Jésus et mère de Dieu!" As she strived and grunted, she heard a rush of water splashing into the dark space below that smelled of ground lime and a full day's stink. Wondering if she had urinated, she peered underneath, then felt the

compelling urge to give a mighty grunt, as though the fecal matter inside was a watermelon she desperately needed to pass. She screamed with the effort but felt the pain of pressure in her forward parts. She strained and strained until suddenly there was a release and a relief, and she heard a squishy plop as a sweet pink baby landed in the foul slush beneath.

Stunned, Charlotte held her lantern high and peered between her loins at the bloody mess of a ghostly blue umbilical cord stretched fully, still attached to a squirming infant that screamed for all he was worth, face up in the ooze below. Only then did she realize she had given birth.

"Help me! Ward, help me! Come save our baby!" Charlotte screamed into the night.

From Ward's deep slumber, he didn't hear his wife's cries.

Luckily, nearby neighbors came running to save her and the baby.

                                             ❧

AFTER ANDREW PUSHED the print button, Billy Jay read the latest page and grimaced. "Grand Pop, that's gross."

"It's a metaphor, Billy Jay."

"What does that mean?"

"One thing stands for another. The true meaning can be interpreted in several ways."

"No baby should be born in a pile of poop."

"Is it better to have been born in an outhouse, or never to have been born at all?"

Billy Jay shrugged.

Andrew shook his head and turned away. "Why would I expect a boy to understand things at this intellectual level?"

"Grand Pop, you better not act like the stinker you used to be. I'm just here because Mom made me help. I don't like you or anything like that." With that, the boy reached for his jacket.

Andrew realized he had a choice. Be an ornery, isolated man, or reach out to the grandson whose very name had caused him to avoid the child most of his thirteen years. He stood slowly and extended his left arm to keep Billy Jay from leaving. Then Andrew reached with both arms to hug the boy for the first time.

Billy Jay held back at first, but Andrew knew how to sell an idea, slurred speech, and all. "I'm sorry for being a smart ass. I got carried away. And it's okay if you don't like parts of my story or if you don't like me. But I like you a lot. And I can't write without your help. You've been a helpful son, er, grandson to me, and I hope you will help me some more."

Astonished that Grand Pop seemed to care, Billy Jay leaned tentatively toward Andrew and the two managed a clumsy hug.

Andrew's eyes misted. "That's my boy. Janey's boy. Now, where were we, son?"

Billy Jay peered over Andrew's shoulder and pointed at the computer screen. His other hand propped fondly on Andrew's shoulder as the boy read aloud the old man's typed words.

≈

As soon as Ward was healthy, he went back to work at his mine but finished each arduous day weary, filthy, and, most importantly to his wife's mind, empty-handed. Not wanting to face her whining another day, he stared off at the fading sunlight and watched as it painted the surrounding ridges with a shadowy violet hue. Defeated, Ward wiped tears from his eyes.

Later that night, with the baby at her breast, Charlotte served the glum Ward a meager meal of beans, hardtack, and wild onions. "We can't live on your part-time pay as a smithy's assistant. This is the last of the supplies. If you can't find gold tomorrow, we'll have to go to Atlanta and borrow money from my father," Charlotte snapped.

"My dear Charlotte, I can see the gold in there, deep inside the rock. The color tempts me, blazing like the lightning you and I saw from that ledge during the storm. But I can't get far enough inside the rock to reach the gold that's there," Ward said as anguish tinged his voice.

"All I see is this golden-haired baby who needs a full breast of healthy milk. I'm tired of begging at the church for handouts."

"*Charlotte, I'm one man with a whole ridge to chop. After working my hands to the bone all frigid winter, I'm only two feet into that rock face. I need better equipment and workers, like the hydraulic mining companies have. I can't do it alone,*" Ward pleaded.

"*You need to try harder,*" Charlotte said without sympathy.

"*There's a time when a man must admit he has made a mistake. Tomorrow, I'm going to post the deed for sale at the courthouse,*" Ward said dejectedly.

"*And if the new owner finds gold? Our future will be lost because you've made another poor decision,*" Charlotte said.

"*A man can only try, best he can, with whatever wits God gave him. The baby needs nourishment. I'm going to sell the mine,*" Ward affirmed with firm conviction.

"*And my hopes with it,*" Charlotte glowered.

"*My dear, for all the false hopes and empty promises I gave you, I humbly offer the only thing a gentleman can: my apology,*" Ward said with genuine sincerity.

~

BY THE TIME Billy Jay finished reading what was for Andrew the lengthy task of writing those few allegorical paragraphs, Jane beeped out front to take Billy Jay home.

After the boy left, Andrew reread his work and leaned back with finality. "There. Lizzy will read this someday and understand what I meant. She's a smart girl."

Lizzy called from the kitchen. "Dare I ask if you are addressing me?"

Andrew shouted back harshly. "Why can't a man simply talk to his dog?"

"I'm sorry, dear. I thought you needed me."

Although Andrew resented Lizzy's interruptions, his frustration melted into sentimentality when he imagined her reading his story.

"I didn't mean to sound so harsh."

Lizzy was shocked. *Andrew apologizing?* "Let me know when you are ready for me to read it."

"I need to gather more research. I don't have enough material to complete a novel-length story, but soon enough you will read it, soon enough."

Chapter Nineteen

JUNE 22

Another Saturday brought Jane and her kids to Andrew and Lizzy's front porch on a humid summer morning. The kids rang the doorbell in their annoying ring-a-ding, but no one answered. Jane tried the door, but it was locked. *Highly unusual.* Worried, she rummaged in the overgrown flowerbed and found Lizzy's bronze "hide-a-key" frog.

"Momma? Poppa? Anybody home?" Jane tentatively went down the hall to an empty kitchen. Other than the kids' footsteps, the only sound was Walter scratching at the back door.

David let the dog in while Jane dialed Lizzy's cellphone.

Lizzy answered with a cheery hello.

"Is there anything wrong? We're here for Saturday breakfast. Where are you?"

"Oh, my goodness. I completely forgot. Andrew had a makeup PT session this morning. His therapist was ill last week, so they called us yesterday to see if Andrew could come today. In the hubbub, I didn't call you."

"That's not like you."

"I know. How about tomorrow after church? I'll invite Ouisie and Guy too."

"We're going to see Alan's parents tomorrow."

"Well, next Saturday, for sure."

"Everything else all right, Momma?"

"Everything's fine, dear. And don't you dare accuse me of having a 'senior moment.'"

"If I were to accuse you of anything, it would be too much merlot last night."

"For your information, I drank chamomile tea last night. Aren't I allowed a human error without being accused of alcoholism?"

"All right, Mother. Do you mind if I make breakfast here? Alan is playing racquetball, and my cupboard is bare."

"Go right ahead. My kitchen is yours."

"Tell Poppa to work hard at his PT. We'll see you both when you get back."

After eggs, toast, and juice, Jane cleaned up, then spread a black and white zebra puzzle on the round table for the kids to solve. She had an ulterior motive and went down the hall. As she sat in front of Andrew's iMac, she put her finger on the trackpad but hesitated. Should she wait until he gave her his blessing?

Billy Jay came in before she could decide. "Mom, David's taking over the puzzle."

"Well, go watch TV in the living room, but keep it quiet. I need to concentrate."

"Are you reading Grand Pop's novel?"

"Mind reader," Jane said. She was embarrassed he had caught her snooping.

"It's in this folder," Billy Jay said slyly. He enjoyed knowing his mother's secret.

As soon as Jane found where she had left off reading before, Billy Jay headed back to the kitchen. Jane could hear him and David resume their argument in loud whispers. She sighed, exasperated. Those two were always at each other. When could she enjoy a moment of peace? She closed the door. Better to ignore the boys and simply plunge in.

Perplexed by the scope of what she read, Jane suddenly guffawed loudly when she got to the scenes of Charlotte giving birth. "Oh,

Poppa. A bloody baby born in an outhouse? Is that supposed to mean life is shit?"

She leaned back in a laugh, but as she did, her eyes caught a flash in Lizzy's oval mirror. Jane got up and looked into it. She had to move around to find the right position, but eventually she could see the sunlight beaming from the mirror out the window to the metal workshop, and then reflecting back at the house.

"No wonder Momma calls that thing a rocket barn. It's like a reflection of a reflection. Good Lord. Now I'm using imagery. This literary bent must be genetic."

Back at Andrew's desk, she skimmed his last paragraphs. While she read, the boys' argument grew to shouts and then a bloody screech from Elizabeth.

"Mommy! David is killing Billy Jay."

Jane bolted for the kitchen and found David trying to choke his brother, but Billy Jay, older and stronger, held David's hands away.

Jane pulled David up by his shirt collar. "Young man, control your temper. Go outside and play with Walter. As for you, Billy Jay, stop taunting your brother and go watch TV as I asked you to do."

"What should I do, Mommy?"

"Elizabeth, you and I will finish the zebra puzzle."

Elizabeth grinned victoriously as David sulked out, and Billy Jay shrugged down the hall.

"Okay, show me a piece you think will fit." Jane realized she had rewarded her daughter for snitching, but the boys deserved it.

Out the window, Jane could see the old red setter lope toward David, but suddenly the dog bolted to the garage as Lizzy's Jag honked in the rhythm, "Shave and a haircut, two bits."

"Saved by the Jag!"

"What does that mean, Mommy?"

"I forgot to take care of something." Jane rushed to the sunroom and nervously closed the computer file. She surveyed the screen and desk to ensure she had left no telltale signs, then rushed back and sat beside Elizabeth at the kitchen table.

Out the window, Jane saw Andrew walk over to David and give the boy a hug.

"Amazing," Jane said.

"What's amazing, Momma?"

"Your Grand Pop just hugged David."

Billy Jay strolled into the kitchen. "Why is that amazing?"

Jane tried to gather the right words. "Grand Pop's feelings were hurt when your Uncle Billy died, you know, my brother who looks like David."

"David doesn't want to look like that guy," Elizabeth said.

"I know, but he is Billy's spittin' image. That's amazing too. And I suspect Grand Pop has avoided David, maybe both of you boys, because you remind him of Billy in some ways."

"That's not our fault."

"No. And it looks like Grand Pop has come around to that same conclusion."

Jane watched as Billy Jay walked down the ramp to join his brother. Walter routed in a pile of leaves and retrieved a long-lost tennis ball that he brought solicitously to Andrew. With his right hand, Andrew threw it long, and Walter went to fetch. The dog brought the ball back to Billy Jay for a throw, then to David on the next turn.

Moments later, Lizzy flew in. Her face was flushed with a delighted smile. "Andrew is playing fetch with Walter and the boys."

"I can see." Jane reached out to pat Lizzy, but that turned into a fond hug.

Now a news watcher, Andrew clicked off the late evening repeat of the PBS news report. He reached for his *National Geographic* and read for a while. Beside him in bed, Lizzy was amazed at Andrew's wizardry with the TV remote, but she was more thrilled to see him use both hands with almost equal agility. She abruptly kissed him on the cheek.

"What was that for?"

"I'm not supposed to mention this, but your right hand seems to have come back."

"Coming along. What should I do with it?"

Lizzy giggled and curled with her back nestled against Andrew's side. She waited.

He put his magazine on the nightstand and turned out the light. Then he curled and snuggled into her.

Lizzy knew better than to say, "I love you," since it would seem like a question.

As the two cuddled, Andrew's visage was perplexed. Although he had written Ward's apology in that day's chapter, Andrew realized that his Great American Novel was a short story at best. He was chagrined that all his research and pretense of writing a grand work had come up short and probably were not worth the cost of the printer ink.

All this effort to leave a legacy, his grand *apologia*, why couldn't he simply say, even just in a whisper, "I was wrong not to listen to your warnings. I was wrong to let Billy go."

"Just say it," he whispered aloud, but did not realize his words were loud enough for anyone to hear.

"Say what, dear?"

Chagrined, Andrew did not say more. If Lizzy had turned to see his eyes, she would have seen a man dismayed at his persistent inability to articulate his tragic mistake.

L izzy's eyes popped open as the first sparkle flittered through the blinds. She awoke in the same position as she had lain down, with Andrew nestled around her. As she quietly unwrapped herself from his arms, he appeared to be in a deep sleep. She nestled her pillow under his arm so he would not feel her absence. She moved cautiously so as not to awaken him, donned her robe, and headed to the kitchen. Habitually, she pulled out ingredients for breakfast.

Walter had spent the night in the utility room, so Lizzy let him out. Thankfully, the sky was clear again today. Absentmindedly, she called down the hall, "Andrew! Do you want an Eggbeater omelet? I'm also making tofu sausage and my world-famous oat bran and cranberry muffins." She listened, but heard no answer. "Oh dear, I should have waited. He's still asleep."

Andrew's eyes opened as the morning sun shimmered hotly on his eyelids like they did so long ago on the sun porch at the lake.

Lizzy put her muffins in the oven and marked the time, a good half hour since she last called out to Andrew. She let Walter back in, then went down the hall with the dog at her heels. "Andrew, should I start the eggs?" Again, there was no answer. At the bedroom door, he saw Andrew curled in the same snuggle she had left him in. "Sleepyhead, it's time to get up. Almost nine."

Walter jumped on the bed and licked Andrew's face.

"Walter, down!" Lizzy reached to tap Andrew's shoulder. "Walter and I are lonesome." When there was no response, Lizzy shook him gently.

Andrew rolled limply on his back, his open eyes frozen in a stare, and his mouth ajar in a drool. Walter jumped on the bed again and licked Andrew's face as though the dog's rough tongue could wake the dead.

"Walter, down!" Lizzy leaned nearer. No expression, no recognition, mouth slack, drooling. "Andrew!"

His glazed eyes stared at the ceiling with no glimmer of awareness.

"Oh God, this can't happen again. Not now! Damn it!"

Lizzy jumped off the bed and called 911.

Chapter Twenty-One

ANDY

I tune the big radio in the living room, next to where Grandpa Ward sits in his old brown chair. He's almost bald, except for a long white piece that he combs over the top of his pink head. His black cane hooks over one arm of the chair, but Grandpa Ward doesn't get up much since his stroke. Mostly he sits, smokes a pipe, and listens to the radio.

Two of my giggly girl cousins from Texas climb onto Grandpa Ward's lap to play beauty shop. They comb his long piece and braid it, then tie the braid off with a red rubber band. Grandpa Ward looks stupid with a braid, and my cousins laugh a lot, but Grandpa doesn't seem to mind. I think he likes having little girls fuss with his hair.

When they're done, he lights his pipe. The aroma of cherry tobacco fills the room.

"And now, ladies and gentlemen, it's time for a new edition of 'You Bet Your Life,' starring Groucho Marx," a radio announcer says.

Grandpa Ward grimaces and motions for me to tune to another station.

"We're pleased to bring you an encore presentation of 'Gun Smoke,' brought to you by Chesterfield Cigarettes," the next announcer says.

Grandpa Ward frowns as sweet smoke rises after a puff.

I tune the dial again.

"It's the seventh-inning stretch, and most of the lucky fans here in Yankee Stadium are enjoying a break in this intense pitchers' duel. If you just tuned in, welcome to an all-New York World Series between the New York Yankees and Brooklyn Dodgers," the announcer says.

Grandpa Ward nods and settles back to listen.

I spy a *National Geographic* in the rack beside Grandpa's chair. I leaf through and secretly look for pictures of naked native women.

The announcer goes on, "I was astounded when Casey Stengel started Eddie Lopat against Joe Black. Lopat had shoulder problems all year and only won ten games for the Yanks, this after going twenty-one to nine last year. But Lopat's shoulder didn't seem to bother him today, and the Yankees have tied it up in the fifth, courtesy of a Gene Woodling homer."

Daddy strides in. "Who you pickin', boy?"

"Whoever Grandpa's pickin'." That's the easy way out. I really don't care.

"You gotta pick one team or the other, Andy. Be a man. Take a stance."

"I don't like either. They're all Yankees."

"Son, here's how we'll do it. I'll take the Yankees, even though I despise their very existence, and you and Grandpa can have the Dodgers. You got a nickel on you?"

I reluctantly reach into my pocket. "That's all I've got, Daddy. I'm saving for extra hot fudge sauce at Matt's."

Tommy comes in. "I'll take *your* side, Daddy."

"Tommy boy, you've got an eye for income. Andy, you'd do well to follow in your brother's footsteps. Shall we make it a nickel per inning?"

"I've only got *one* nickel, Daddy."

"I've got you covered, Andy," Grandpa says.

He is a lot nicer to me than Daddy, and I'm relieved I don't have to lose even more money to my brother. Tommy glares at me like he's gonna win, and he probably will, but I vow then to get back at Tommy somehow, someday, some way.

ME, Tommy, and Sarah Little Shit are squeezed together in the backseat of Daddy's boss's car, a shiny turquoise Cadillac Eldorado with a wrap-around windshield, air conditioning and electric windows. This is an amazing car, except I'm also smashed beside the boss's son Artie Weismann, Jr., and his sister Megan Marie. Mind you, my baby sister is in a plastic car seat, but that's five of us kids, even if Megan Marie is just a baby.

Daddy and Momma are in front with Mr. Weismann. Mrs. Weismann is not there, and I don't know where we are headed or why, but the Cadillac's air conditioner sure cools us off. Frigid air blows out two wide plastic tubes that stick out of the back deck.

"Artie, it's ninety-nine outside, but it's a cool breeze in here," Daddy says.

But about ten miles down the road, the air conditioner freezes up. Ice crystals spew out of the air tubes and land on us kids' faces and the adults' hair and necks. Tommy and I try to catch the ice with our tongues.

"Boys, nice as this Cadillac is, we don't know what that ice is made of," Momma says.

Embarrassed, Mr. Weismann adjusts the thermostat.

We drive along until Mr. Weismann's daughter Megan Marie cries out, "Daddy, I'm gonna be sick." This is just one second before the little pip vomits a stream on the back of Mr. Weismann's seat, and the splatter goes all over Megan Marie's aqua sundress and the floorboard.

Mr. Weismann's neck and face turn red and puffy. He pulls over, opens the back door, and cleans the vomit as best he can. Daddy urges Momma to help. She makes flustered motions, but I can tell she doesn't want to put her hands in Megan Marie's barf.

"Artie, let's take off her dress. We can use that to wipe her off, then put it in the trunk."

Mr. Weismann ignores Momma's suggestion. "Megan Marie gets car sick in the back. Would you please switch with her? I'd greatly appreciate it." This is not a question, but an order.

Momma's jaw drops and her eyes get big, but she manages a fake smile.

Daddy gets out and holds my sister's plastic seat while Momma squeezes beside us three boys. She takes the infant seat into her lap.

With Momma there, the back seat seems even tighter. I get a stuffy feeling and elbow Tommy to move over. Tommy elbows me back.

Mr. Weismann pulls back on the highway, with Megan Marie and her vomit-soaked sundress in the front seat beside Daddy. The smell is awful. Daddy clears his throat, and Momma sighs in a gasp.

I feel like I might vomit too, so I heave in a choke, but nothing comes out.

Momma pats me. "Breathe through your mouth, Andy."

After I heave two more times, Momma gets desperate and pushes the button on the Cadillac's back window. The glass goes down halfway and fills the car with clammy air.

A stack of Mr. Weismann's papers on the back deck scatters, so he says in his boss's voice, "Noreen, honey, you'll have to roll up that window."

Momma pushes the button, but the window doesn't budge. Mr. Weismann pushes his driver's side button too, but the window stays half down.

Again, Mr. Weismann gets red, but without a word, he pulls over. Thankfully, he leaves the engine running, so we still have air conditioning. He gets out and pulls the window glass upward, while Momma pushes the "up" button.

"Noreen, are you sure you're pushing in the right direction?"

"Yes, Artie. Up is up."

Mr. Weismann doesn't believe her, so he reaches inside and pushes the button himself. At the same time, Daddy stretches his left leg past Megan Marie in front and revs the engine to give things more juice, but that doesn't help, either.

Mr. Weismann gets back in the car. "Damn window. I told that dealer."

"Artie, if I had known the window was broken, I never would have opened it."

"Noreen would screw up a ball bearing," Daddy says.

The two men chuckle and scoff.

"Gentlemen, I simply pushed the button."

Tommy smirks. "But Momma, it was *you* who pushed the button."

The men chuckle again, and Tommy guffaws.

Momma gives Tommy a look like she's going to kill him, but she doesn't say anything out loud. That way, she won't have to hear more backtalk from Mr. Weismann and Daddy.

I feel sorry for Momma and holler, "It isn't Momma's fault."

"Sorry, Artie. My youngest boy is still on the sugar tit."

The two men laugh while I seethe in silence. I turn to see that Momma is pissed off too.

Chapter Twenty-Two

JUNE 23

Beyond the memories Andrew's mind replayed like lightning bolts between long stretches of blackness, his body was back in the intensive care unit at Emory University Hospital. His eyelids fluttered as he rode down a highway, then suffered from vomit stench, claustrophobia, and now anger.

He had no idea his wife stood beside his bed. Nor did he see the tall South African nurse named Elani, who checked this monitor, noted that IV line, dialed this button, and injected that medicine.

He quivered in agitation in response to the realistic scenes inside his head.

Chapter Twenty-Three

ANDY

Momma's on the phone with Grandma Ward. "I'll drive the bed down. It'll fit on top."

Daddy overhears. "Noreen, you will not drive that bed to the lake cottage by yourself. I'll borrow a pickup and bring it when I come for the weekend."

"But we need the bed. The boys and I can handle it."

"Noreen, you cannot drive a hundred and fifty miles with a double bed on top of the car."

Momma doesn't say a word, so technically, she never agrees.

School is out for the summer. Daddy takes Momma's black Chevy to work so she'll have the "better" car for our trip to the lake, his yellow and black Buick Roadmaster. Little does Daddy know, but Momma has a secret mission to deliver a double bed to the cottage's new back bedroom Uncle Luke built last winter.

After Daddy leaves, Momma calls Tommy and me to the garage, where we find the bed that her brother Yates slept on during law school. We three struggle to lift the box springs onto the Roadmaster's black roof, then hoist the mattress on top of the box springs. I watch Momma's arms tense as she strains to tie everything down with the clothesline. Just the tip of the bed peeks over the car's front window, but some of the bed hangs over the back window.

"I'll have to use the outside mirror. You boys can play scout. We'll make it a game."

She runs to get more clothesline, then strings it over the bed, down through the car windows, and 'round the vertical bar between the front and back seats. Then she ties off the line.

"This is a bowline, my daddy taught me. He was in the Navy."

I marvel at Momma's flexed muscles when she tightens her knots. I didn't think ladies had muscles, but there they are, taut beneath her fair skin.

"That should hold us. The windows can't go up all the way, but we should be fine."

Suitcases loaded, we head out with Tommy and me in the back. Sarah Little Shit is in her infant seat in front. The drive is supposed to take about two and a half hours, but as soon as the Buick Roadmaster gets going fast, the front half of the mattress lifts off the car and bends backward, so the box spring lifts too and pounds the top of the car.

Tommy rolls down his window and leans out. "Momma, the bed is going to take off."

I lean out like Tommy and look up. The powder blue box springs bounce on the black roof, and the blue flowery mattress bends back like a giant flap.

"Hush now. I have a good feeling about this," Momma says. But I can see her worried eyes in the rearview mirror. She slows down so the mattress settles on the box springs and the whole mess stops pounding. "Now there, we'll just go slowly."

By the time the Roadmaster gets south of Macon, Tommy is asleep. Momma tunes in Vaughn Monroe. He croons something about a "Ballerina," and Momma sings along.

I drift off too, but suddenly comes a "Pow!" that scares the sleep out of me, then another "Pow! Bang!" that wakes Tommy. He shoots up, and both of us look out back as the mattress flies off the car with a "Shuuuuusssssshhhhh" sound. Then we hear a "Thunk!" when the box springs hit the asphalt and cartwheel onto the shoulder.

"Oh, no!" She shakes her head. "Now I'll really hear it."

"Daddy warned you."

"Tommy, hush your tattletale mouth." Momma pulls off the road. "You boys stay put and watch your baby sister." She gets out and walks back to where the mattress and box springs sprawl.

I holler from the window. "Momma, a car might come."

"I swear, I'm gonna tell Daddy," Tommy whispers. He's too chicken to say that so Momma can hear.

I holler at him, "Don't you dare say a word, Tommy Ward."

Sarah Little Shit stirs and starts crying.

Momma tries to drag the mattress off the highway to the shoulder. She struggles with the bulk and weight, so I get out to help. Just then, I hear a car engine pull up behind us.

A man shouts from the driver's side of a wood-sided station wagon, "Y'all need some help?" Then he gets out. He's in a uniform with eagle wings.

Momma's voice quivers. "I guess so."

"I'm Colonel Keith Lumas, U.S. Air Force." The driver extends his hand. Momma darn near collapses in his arms and tells him her troubles, complete with sobs and tears. "Now, now. You settle down. I understand. I've got a wife and family too."

Within a few minutes, the Colonel lifts the mattress and box springs back on top of the Roadmaster and locks the car, while Momma loads us three kids in the back of the Colonel's station wagon. She rides in front with him and chatters along, as he drives over some bumpy roads to Warner Robbins. Momma says the town used to be called "Wellston" before the military put Robins Air Force Base there.

The Colonel parks in front of an old cotton-farmers' store. We go inside and see a jumble of pickles in barrels, nails in crates beside the pickles, all sorts of rope and chain sold by the length, and a smudged glass case with red peanut patties and golden peanut brittle. The Colonel buys one of each for us at two cents apiece.

"I cannot tell you how much your help means. If you wouldn't be offended, I would like to offer a gratuity."

I thought Momma might even curtsy.

"No, ma'am. I'm just happy to help. But I can't understand why your husband would let you drive alone with a bed on the car."

"He didn't know. I tied it down properly. My father was in the Navy and taught me a few tricks."

"Ma'am, a knot is only as good as the rope. Your clothesline wasn't thick enough for that amount of stress."

When we get back to the Roadmaster, the Colonel lashes the bed with thick rope. Then Momma gets us back inside, starts up the engine, and heads back down the road. The Colonel even follows us for a good ten miles to make sure we're all right. Then he toots his horn, waves goodbye, and turns around to head back to the air base.

When we reach the cottage at sunset, it takes all my uncles and aunts to unleash that rope and get the bed off the car. Grandma Ward bustles about and cleans everything with a canister vacuum. Then Momma takes us outside to bathe under the pump.

The water is so cold I shiver and shake until Momma dries me with a rough towel and slips on my pajamas.

Back in the room, I watch Aunt Sally put fresh sheets on the bed. They are crisp and smell like Ivory soap flakes and summer sunshine.

Momma tucks us in. Tommy on the right, baby Sarah in the middle, and me on the left.

After Momma closes the door, Tommy whispers. "I'm still gonna tell Daddy."

"I'll kill you if you do." I get so mad at Tommy, I can't sleep.

About midnight, I hear the distant "Hoooooooo-hooooooo."

As the locomotive comes near, it roars so loud, Sarah Little Shit screams. The force of the passing cars rattles the walls.

Momma comes to get the baby. "Goodness, that train is the loudest thing."

Tommy wriggles and whines. "The walls shake, Momma. Do I have to sleep in here?"

He's pitiful. I think the locomotive roar in this new room is the most amazing thing I'll ever hear, and I can't wait to hear it again. The power of its engine, the roar of the following railcars, and the clack of wheels, until the little caboose rocks past, and the sounds fade into distant clicks and clacks.

I listen for more. Minutes later, I am rewarded by a distant, lonely-sounding "Hoooooooo-hooooooo" as the locomotive approaches the next crossing down the line.

Chapter Twenty-Four

JUNE 23

I n the ICU, Andrew's body shuddered, his eyelids trembled, and his voice called, "Hoooooooo-hooooooo" in a drool and smile.

Lizzy patted him and whispered, "Are you having a dream?"

The nurse Elani overheard. In her Afrikaans accent, she murmured, "After some of my stroke patients got better, they told me they couldn't tell the difference between the past and present. Sometimes they saw just black. Sometimes they saw things that weren't there. Hallucinations. Other times, they relived the past. They could remember things that happened long, long ago, but couldn't remember what happened the day before."

Lizzy's eyes never left Andrew. "I wish I could see into his mind. See what he's remembering."

≈

LATER ON, when Lizzy called Jane's mobile to tell her about Andrew's stroke, Jane interrupted Lizzy's matter-of-fact overview of Andrew's situation. "Why didn't you call me before now? I'm stuck on Northeast Expressway!"

"I'm sorry, dear, but things have been so hectic."

"The last time this happened, you called me first, and then I called EMS and came over and — " Jane trailed off. "Momma, I'll get there somehow, but I'm not able to move an inch in this traffic." Jane put on her flashers and honked her horn. "Move over, you selfish jackass."

"Janey, settle down. Some redneck might shoot you. Just drive safely."

"I can't believe this happened. We were talking and being together and — Why didn't you call me, Momma?" Tears dripped down Jane's blouse.

"Jane, pull off the road. I'll call the highway patrol to come help."

"Don't do that. I'll see you when I get to the hospital." Without a goodbye, Jane clicked to end the call.

Trouble was, her minivan was in the middle lane behind a hulking red Dodge Ram pickup with double-axle back wheels. To her right was a gigantic black Suburban, and to her left a silver Porsche Cayenne.

"I'm surrounded by monsters!" Jane launched an attack with her horn, which beeped in a nasal tone. "God, what a wimpy horn." She held the instrument down until the Dodge Ram driver peered back at her from his rearview mirror. Jane motioned for him to move forward. If he did, she could maneuver to the right, in front of the Suburban, then get to the shoulder and find an exit. That is, if the Suburban would grant her enough space. Jane honked and waved at him, to no avail. The Suburban driver stared straight ahead and mouthed into his mobile headset.

The Dodge Ram driver gave her the finger.

"Redneck!" Jane turned off her car and got out. She could see the Dodge Ram driver's eyes in his outside mirror as she walked up and knocked on his window. Inside, the obese redhead, with a too-large head and auburn beard, was clearly pretending he did not hear her knock. So Jane knocked again. Again, the driver did not flinch. Jane shouted through the glass, "Look, fella, I have a family emergency. My father's in the hospital. Will you please move forward so I can pull over in front of the Suburban?"

The driver lifted his empty palms to show he could do nothing.

Jane walked to the front of his truck, where she saw he had three feet between his bumper and the car in front. She motioned with her outstretched hands. "You've got three feet. I could move over if you pull up. My father is in the hospital. I just got the call."

Again, the driver gave her the "I can't help you" signal with his empty hands.

Jane seethed as she walked back to her car. "Macho Bubba. Probably has an AK-47 that he got at Cabela's for Father's Day. I'm lucky he didn't use it on me. Yet." She slammed her door, cranked up the minivan, and pressed both hands on her horn. She held it down so long, the nasal tone faded into a choked "bleep," then stopped working entirely.

Jane screamed to the heavens. "You know what you can do with this wimpy horn?"

To her right, the Suburban driver still yakked on his mobile headset, which reminded Jane, "My God, I need to call Alan."

The male receptionist answered in a lilt. "Cates and Harris, this is Rob, may I help you?"

"Rob, it's Jane Cates. I need to speak with Alan."

"Oh, Mrs. Cates. Long time no! How've you been?"

"Rob, there's a family emergency. Not the kids, my father. I need to speak to Alan."

"Oh, Mrs. Cates. So sorry your father is having problems again. I'll see if Mr. Cates is in. But I have to put you through to Posey first. Protocol thing-ee, hang on!"

"Mr. Cates' office," Alan's secretary Posey said.

"Posey, it's Jane Cates. Is Alan there? I need to speak with him."

"No, Mrs. Cates. He's at a meeting. I don't expect him until the afternoon."

"I'll try him on his cell phone."

"Mrs. Cates, you can't. I just tried to reach him myself, but — this is so funny — a phone rang in his office every time I called. I eventually figured out that it was Mr. Cates' cell phone. Can you believe that? He left his mobile on his desk!"

"Posey, it's a family emergency."

"I remember when Billy Jay broke his arm a few years ago."

"My father's had another stroke."

"Oh, that again. Well, let me call the client and try to reach Mr. Cates."

"Oh, that again?"

"Yes, ma'am," Posey said as she jumped to attention. "I'll have Mr. Cates call you."

"Thank you. I didn't mean to be brash. I'm stuck in traffic."

"Yes, Mrs. Cates. I understand completely."

Posey's voice had a wee hint of sarcasm, but Jane held her temper. "I'll await his call," Jane said as she hung up. "Darn it. Now, Posey will have more evil things to say about me to her petty, uncultured, uneducated, uncooperative office pals who sit in the break room and eat pie every afternoon." Jane pressed hard again on her minivan's horn, but it gave out one final, feeble bleep, then died again. "Now even you fail me."

Just then, Jane's phone rang. "Alan?"

"No, Mrs. Cates, Posey again. You didn't give me your cell number, so I had to use caller ID to call you back. Anyway, I could not reach Mr. Cates. He's at Delta, and the receptionist said she could not disturb meetings unless something like a bomb went off. They have really strict rules. So I told her to give Mr. Cates a message to call you the moment he gets out of the meeting."

"Posey, what's the number at Delta? I'll call her myself."

"Yes, ma'am," Posey said with a bite as she gave Jane the number.

Jane hung up without a thank-you. Pushing buttons was one way Jane knew how to solve problems. That is, when stuck on the freeway. She urgently dialed the number Posey had given her. A Delta receptionist answered.

"My name is Jane Cates, and my husband Alan Cates is there for a meeting today. I need to reach him because of a family emergency."

"Mr. Cates' secretary wanted me to do the same thing, but corporate policy is — "

"Do you understand this is a family emergency?"

"Yes, ma'am, but it doesn't involve anyone from Delta."

"You don't care about emergencies that happen to other people? May I speak to your supervisor?"

"She's at a conference in Denver."

"Then may I speak to your supervisor's supervisor?"

"He's in the meeting with your husband."

"Then give me his cell phone number or his e-mail address."

"I don't know if I should do that."

"You should do that."

"I really don't think so," the receptionist trailed off.

"Let's try this. If I wanted to do business with Delta, you would give me a direct line or e-mail address, wouldn't you?"

"Probably."

"Then, just pretend I want to buy a planeload of tickets."

"In that case, you'd want reservations. I'll put you through."

"Nooooooo," Jane screamed when she heard the hold music.

Then she heard another voice, "Delta Airlines reservations. May I help you?"

"Hello. The corporate office receptionist put me through to your number. My name is Jane Cates. My husband is in a meeting with Delta executives today, and I need to speak to him."

"But this is Reservations," the voice said.

"I realize that. But we have a family emergency, and I need to speak with my husband, Alan Cates of the Cates and Harris law firm. He's in the executive conference room at Delta corporate headquarters. You are my only hope. Will you please take my name and number, then get someone to give a message to my husband?"

"But we're in Augusta."

"You have phones. You can call."

"I'll try, ma'am," the voice said, trailing off.

"I'll expect a callback within ten minutes. If I do not hear from my husband by then, I will call you back. What is your name and direct line?"

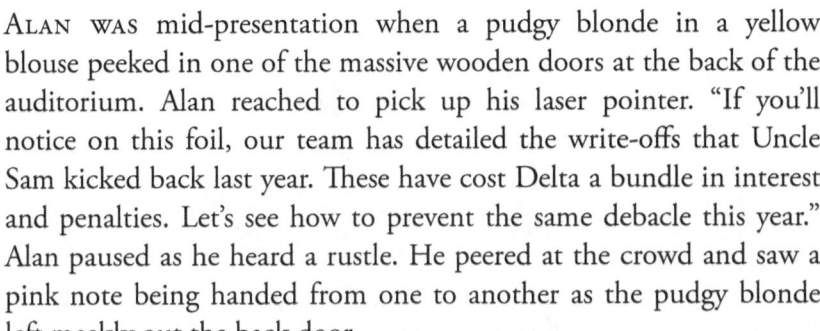

ALAN WAS mid-presentation when a pudgy blonde in a yellow blouse peeked in one of the massive wooden doors at the back of the auditorium. Alan reached to pick up his laser pointer. "If you'll notice on this foil, our team has detailed the write-offs that Uncle Sam kicked back last year. These have cost Delta a bundle in interest and penalties. Let's see how to prevent the same debacle this year." Alan paused as he heard a rustle. He peered at the crowd and saw a pink note being handed from one to another as the pudgy blonde left meekly out the back door.

Alan was dismayed at the disturbance. "As I was saying — "

Hand-to-hand, the pink note continued its journey forward until it reached the front marketing VP, who looked at the note, then handed it to Alan. "Sorry, Alan, but it's for you."

A room full of chuckles followed.

"Great. There's an administrative assistant who will get a lecture this afternoon."

As Alan glanced at the note, more chuckles ruffled through the crowd. "I apologize for that delay. Let's see what write-offs won't offend our dear Uncle Sam this year."

TRAFFIC WAS STILL at a dead stop twenty minutes after the Delta reservations operator called back to ensure Jane that her message had been delivered. But Alan still had not responded. Jane's emotions quickly devolved from frantic agitation at the surrounding drivers to anger at Alan for not calling her back.

"What client's taxes are more important than the fact your wife's father is seriously ill?" As if Alan were there to respond, Jane immediately rebutted, "Okay, so I can see how an emergency involving the kids or your own parents might seem more important to you than one involving my aging father who has been barely cordial to you, much less friendly, over our twenty years of marriage, but this is my emergency, damn it, Alan, and I need you."

The pickup driver in front furtively stared back at her from his rearview mirror.

"Yes, I'm talking to myself because you will not move two feet forward, so I can convince the driver on my right to let me squeeze in front toward the shoulder."

As her voice echoed, Jane sensed movement. She could not see movement, since enormous cars surrounded her, but she could hear engines. She rolled down her window. Yes, engines. Then she saw the Porsche to her left inch forward. And in front, Big Daddy revved his Dodge Ram.

"Oh, thank God, whoever you are," Jane said as she put her car in drive. But her lane did not move. Jane tried her horn again, but found it mute. She rolled down her window. "Get your redneck ass out of the way!"

The Dodge Ram driver flipped her off again, but he inched forward.

"See? All it took was a little camaraderie!" Jane screamed before she rolled up her window. "You Bambi killer!" she screamed until her throat became sore. She took a sip of bottled water. "Please move. I've got a sick father who needs to see his daughter. Or, maybe it's the other way around. I'm a daughter who needs to see her father before he dies." Jane stepped on the gas pedal as the Dodge Ram roared away.

BY THE TIME she arrived at Emory University Hospital, Jane had to wait until 11:00 a.m. to be admitted to the ICU. Visitation was restricted to two visitors at a time, and the doctor was there, along with Lizzy. Once Jane had been buzzed inside the locked double doors, she walked down a wide aisle of glassed-in rooms with wide sliding panels. On either side, people lay propped in beds, each in various states of dying or living. Jane could not tell which. A woman

— or was it a man? — seemed all but dissolved in one room with filmy drapes drawn about the bed, but not tightly enough to hide the patient's condition as Jane glanced in to see if that was her father's room.

To her left, a five-year-old girl with a shaved head sat in a bed, surrounded by her parents. The three chattered and laughed, unlike the terminally ill patient across the hall.

Emotionally overcome, Jane said a silent prayer, "Please meet these people at their point of need." Then she vowed internally to take the children to church more often.

In the far back row of ICU rooms, Jane eventually found Andrew. She walked in and stood at the foot of his bed, wondering why her mother wasn't there.

Andrew lay still, the only peaceful part of a room that buzzed with beeps and clicks.

Jane patted her father's toes, which peeked from under a white blanket. "I'm here, Poppa."

Eyes open, Andrew did not appear to know she was there, but his heart-rate monitor showed a rise of twenty beats per minute. There were so many tubes and cords taped to the IVs in his hands, Jane did not know whether to come hold his hand or simply maintain position at the foot of the bed.

Suddenly, nurse Elani came in. "Ah, you must be our 'Janey.' Your mother told us to look for 'Janey,' and to tell you she went home to get some things."

Jane hoped Lizzy would take her time. After Jane's harrowing morning, she wanted some time alone with her father. Whenever Lizzy was there, the focus was on Lizzy and Andrew, and Jane felt it was her role to support that. But she also felt she had no corner of her own in the family rectangle. There was Andrew and Lizzy, and Billy's death. Jane constantly jumped from one to the other and could not seem to land on her own.

As soon as the nurse left, Jane sat beside her father and cleared her throat in preparation. A confession was on her mind, her way, her hope of breaking through.

"Poppa, I read your story. Last Saturday, when you were at PT. I came over with Billy Jay. He was so proud to help you and showed me where your novel was. I hope you don't mind that I read your work. You know me, I couldn't resist hacking. I always wondered if you called me 'Miss Systems Analyst' because you were making fun of me, or you were proud of me."

Andrew did not respond. The nurse came back to inject something into the IV line.

"Here's your nurse with more joy juice."

Andrew stared at nothing.

"Can you hear me, Poppa?"

"He might be able to hear you, but he cannot answer. Just talk. It's good for him to hear voices he knows."

"Thanks. But he probably doesn't know who I am. Last time, he didn't. Took him forever."

"They have trouble remembering."

"Oh, I know. Sorry. I hope I'm not in your way."

"Don't worry. You have some things to say to your father."

"What do you mean?"

"Your 'pa' has had a critical event, and with his history — "

"Damn it. I knew this was serious." Jane walked to the window.

"Can I get something for you? A soda?"

"Thank you, no. I'm just fine. Thank you." She pulled a chair beside Andrew's bed and sat quietly until the nurse left. Then Jane leaned close and spoke in a fervent whisper. "Poppa, I know you're trying to tell us something with this '*apologia*,' but why all the colors and metaphors? Wouldn't it be better just to tell Momma — "

In a flash, Jane recalled Billy as he got ready to go, dressed in his pressed black jeans and starched white shirt. He donned his letter jacket and insisted there would be no problems, while Andrew scoffed at Lizzy's worry.

"Can't you just say you're sorry? I know that's the problem between you, between you and all of us. That's why you need to say it, Poppa." Jane grabbed Andrew's hand, needles, tubes, and all, and gripped tightly. "Tell her, Poppa. Tell us."

In Jane's mind, she saw her brother dissolve into a vapor of white and black and navy blue as he headed out, his blond hair cut close in neat trim. And she remembered a loud rush of wind just before the front door banged shut with finality.

"All you have to do is say, 'I'm sorry I let Billy go.'" Jane's body tensed. Her eyes streamed. "Poppa, damn it. You let my brother go out in a terrible storm with a bunch of teenage boys. Momma tried to warn you. And he died!"

Andrew stared unresponsively.

The nurse came back. Her empathetic eyes saw Jane's anguish. She silently handed Jane a box of tissues, then slipped out.

Jane blew her nose and patted Andrew's hand. "Oh, Poppa. I didn't mean to lambaste you. Here you are, sick. I suppose I've blamed you all along. I was just a girl, and I was so angry. I realize that now. You made a mistake, a human error, and things turned out so badly. But I shouldn't blame you. That was terribly wrong of me. All of us. Momma, me, Uncle Thomas, who else? We have all been blaming you, expecting some big apology, as if that could bring Billy back. Instead, it is I who owes you an apology, don't I? Will you please forgive me for blaming you, Poppa?"

With no response from Andrew, Jane looked up at where her father's eyes were staring. Both peered at the white, dotted ceiling squares as if they might be God or whoever had the answers to Jane's questions.

Chapter Twenty-Five

ANDY

Every exhibit at the Georgia State Fair smells like poop. Cow poop, pig poop, chicken poop, goat poop and horse poop. We get to the pony rides, and Momma buys us western outfits. Then Tommy wants to ride a pony. Momma says okay but watches with worry from behind a rail as Tommy and I mount gray Shetland ponies with the help of a rodeo cowboy. Sarah Little Shit pouts on a bench. She's way too young to ride. Besides, she's dolled up in white boots and a pink cowgirl dress with fringe.

Tommy's ridden a pony before, but I haven't. As soon as he mounts, he takes off in a trot and shouts back, "Catch me if you can, Greenhorn."

I hold the reins high like cowboys do in Western movies and kick the pony's sides with my boot heels. "Giddyaaaaapppp! Giddyaaaaapppp!"

The horse jolts. I hear the cowboy shout, "Whoa, boy."

That little pony has more power and speed than I figured. My hat flies off. I pull upward on the reins. "Whoooooaaaaaaa! Whoooooaaaaaaa!" I holler.

The pony rears on its hind legs. I fall off and land face down in a pile of horse poop. It's gooey and smells of shit. Green straw pokes out of the poop. I scream until the rodeo cowboy comes to help. Momma and Sarah Little Shit trail after.

Momma hovers. "Does anything hurt, Andy?"

"He smells like poo-poo," Sarah says.

All I can muster is a howl.

Chapter Twenty-Six

JUNE 23, LATE MORNING

Lizzy bustled in about half an hour after Jane's confessional with Andrew. The two women hugged silently. Lizzy could see that Jane had been crying, but Lizzy decided not to say anything. She knew the reason, anyway. Not exactly why, not *the* reason that day, but Lizzy knew Jane was angry. Hurt. Jane needed more than Andrew could give. Lizzy had felt the same way for too long herself.

Lizzy unloaded a bag she had stuffed with pajamas, red robe, slippers, boxers, t-shirts, toiletries, several of Andrew's favorite poetry books, low-calorie, low-sugar, low-fat snack bars, and *National Geographic* magazines. Only after she had organized everything did Lizzy sit beside his bed, opposite Jane. Each woman held one of Andrew's limp, IV-bruised hands.

"If I can just get him home again. Just get us back." Lizzy trailed off.

"We'll get him home. I'll do everything in my power."

"We both will. That's for sure."

Jane stayed until four that afternoon but left to pick up groceries and tend to her family.

The ICU administrator came in after Jane left and explained to Lizzy with great sympathy why she could not stay overnight, because it was against the rules.

～

JANE DROVE to the Briarcliff Whole Foods. From her car, she phoned Alan again but got his voicemail. She left another message tinged with weary frustration. She did not say in so many words, but her tone conveyed her frustration that Alan had not called by now. Next, she called her kids. Billy Jay answered the phone.

"I'm afraid I have some sad news. Your Grand Pop has had another stroke and is in the hospital. I was there all day. He's in the intensive care unit."

"Like, you mean it happened again?" Billy Jay said.

"Yes, I mean again. And don't start sentences with 'Like.'"

"Is he gonna be okay?"

"If I have anything to say about it."

"But you don't."

"Don't smart off, young man. I've had a rotten day. I only called to let you know I'll be home soon. We can talk then."

"Well, okay, Mom," Billy Jay said in sarcastic frustration.

"Well, okay, yourself!" Jane said, then hung up. She immediately realized that she was being more childish than her son and called him back. "I'm sorry, honey. I'm just upset."

"Okay, Mom. I'm upset too." Billy Jay's tone was softer and had the hint of tears.

"I'll be home in a bit. I've picked up dinner. I love you."

"Love you too, Mom."

As Jane pulled into the Whole Foods parking lot, she realized she had not yet called her boss to tell him where she had been all that day.

"My gosh, the weasel probably fired me." She dialed her boss's direct line.

～

ALL EVENING, Andrew remained expressionless. Lizzy held his hand and read poems from Coleridge and E. E. Cummings. Even if he could not respond, she imagined his mind could hear her voice. At seven o'clock, she was exhausted and called Jane to let her know she was headed home.

"Let me know if you need anything, Momma. I'd invite you over, but I've got to help the kids download their lists for school supplies. Can you believe it? School starts in early August this year." The excuse was a lie, but Jane did not want Lizzy to be there when one hell of a row festered between her and Alan.

THE DRIVE home that evening was the loneliest Lizzy had ever felt. She had been independent and strong that morning, but wilted under the realities of Andrew's illness. She thought about phoning Ouisie and Guy, but they usually ate dinner by five-thirty and headed back to church for a committee meeting. Besides, Ouisie's emotions might overflow, and Lizzy did not want to deal with more angst. She thought about calling her minister, Byron, and made a note to do so the following morning.

As she approached the turn to Jane and Alan's mansion, Lizzy considered dropping in. But something seemed awry in her daughter's world. She had been quiet and removed at the hospital and appeared exhausted. Certainly not the usual "take charge" Jane Cates, full of bravado to protect the inner wounded little girl.

"Janey doesn't need to spend her life living mine," Lizzy whispered to herself with a sigh.

As soon as she got home, she microwaved a frozen Indian dinner, then sat at the round pine table. She scratched Walter's head with one hand and fed herself with the other. After she cleaned up, she took the dog out for his business, then made sure all doors were locked before she went to the bedroom.

"You can stay inside with me tonight, Walter."

Head cocked, the old boy looked confused as Lizzy closed the blinds and the bedroom door. When she undressed and headed for a hot bath, Walter paced beside the tub. He whined and licked water drops that splashed from Lizzy's bath sponge.

"It's okay, boy." Lizzy leaned back and relaxed as the warm water caressed her weary body. The temperature did not seem hot enough, so she turned on the hot faucet only and ran for a while.

Walter leaned over the rim to taste the steamy downpour.

"No, boy! Shoo. That's hot!" Lizzy turned off the spout and reclined again. Only then did she collapse in tears that streamed into the water.

Walter whimpered and tried to climb into the tub to help, but Lizzy shooed him away with a hand.

As she soaked and cried softly, she could not manage even words for a prayer. She was exhausted and defeated that her life with Andrew had been so unfairly affected by tragedy.

"Oh, Andrew," she whispered, then succumbed to a deep grief, until no more tears would flow.

As Walter panted beside the tub on a bathmat, Lizzy soaked silently until the water grew cold. "I'd better get out before I freeze and shrivel." As she toweled off, the red setter started licking her legs from ankles to thighs. "No, no, Walter. Down boy. If anyone saw us, they'd think we were a bit queer."

Lizzy donned her pajamas and robe. "Let's go have a nightcap," she said as she urged Walter out of the bathroom. Lizzy slid her feet into her open-toed slippers and headed down the hall as Walter trailed behind.

"I can see how people who live alone talk to themselves and sometimes turn into drunks."

JANE UNPACKED six grocery bags of quick-fix items that the kids and Alan could survive on while she commuted to the hospital. Earlier that day, she told her boss she needed a three-month family leave. She figured her father's rehab would take longer than before, and she was determined to take a stronger role to ensure progress.

Although Jane's watch said seven, Alan was still not home. That was not unusual, but he was rarely so late without notice. Jane dialed his cell phone again, but again got his voicemail.

"That stinker is dodging me," she muttered.

She took out three bags of frozen pasta meals and read the cooking instructions. But just then, she heard the garage door open. She called out to the kids to get washed up, but kept her back to the inside garage door and pretended to read the instructions when Alan came in.

Wordlessly, he walked past Jane and went to the bedroom.

"The asshole is angry with *me?*" Jane muttered. She put the pasta in the microwave and slammed the door. Dinner would be short and sweet. After that, Jane and Alan would have an unavoidable and unpleasant conversation.

～

AFTER LIZZY'S NIGHTCAP, she felt high enough to want conversation, but with whom? She counted the people active in her life: Ouisie, Guy, Jane, her grandchildren. Okay, so she added one person, her minister, Byron. And there was the chair of the membership committee at church, a woman Lizzy did not even like. "Wow, that's stretching it to think of calling her. Looks like you're it for the night, Walter. Com'on. Time for your final nighttime business."

Lizzy grabbed another glass of wine before she headed out back.

Walter obliged quickly, but then sauntered down the path and up the workshop steps. He sat and whined at the door.

"No, Walter. Andrew isn't in there. I'm sorry."

Walter whined again.

"Oh, you poor boy. Here, let me show you." She went back for the key, then unlocked the door and flipped on the lights. The room flashed fluorescent. Walter sniffed around and headed for Andrew's desk. Lizzy felt less discomfort this time. After all, this was her property too. Her fingers lightly skimmed the dusty books and papers. "I should have come out here by now to clean, although that might require a special team from NASA."

She sat at Andrew's desk, poised her hands above the typewriter, and imagined herself writing. She took another sip. Then her words flowed as freely as her tears had streamed earlier into the bath waters.

"Oh, Andrew. We've been together all our lives. But our time seems rushing to a close. I don't feel like I'm finished, or we're finished. You accomplished enough, made a good living, and a name, but now I wonder why I didn't aspire to accomplish something too. Beyond the house and children. Maybe I could have been a professor or a lawyer like my brother, or a politician, maybe a senator or congresswoman. Of course, that's silly to think about at this age, especially now that Georgia has turned so right-wing. I'd have been voted out of office. But even with your success, we've always swum upstream. Ever since Billy. Even before that. Your life was always a competition. First with Thomas, then with Guy. Who knows, maybe with everyone. Maybe that's the way it is with male egos. That Mars and Venus book I read went on and on about giving men space and not criticizing or offering advice. Even when I tried my hardest, your ego seemed to take up so much of our world. Your efforts to be successful. Your need to show Thomas, Guy, your father, or me that you were the best.

"I didn't want to compete with you, so I shied away. And I was always proud of your achievements. Most wives root for their husbands, that is, any good wife. I've always pulled for you. Even after Billy. Even when I knew how much you blamed yourself, knew how painful it would be for you to admit that mistake. I always hoped you could work through that. And forgive me for being so damn right. My minister figured that out. I've felt guilty too. How could I have known? How could I have had a vision about my son's death eighteen years before it happened? That's a life mystery I wish had not visited me. But that was long ago, and now you're off to visions of your own that I cannot see. I don't know if I can reach you again. But I hope so. Oh, I hope so, Andrew."

Lizzy wept again. As her eyes and nose gushed, she frantically looked for a tissue. She rummaged in a drawer and found parchment paper Andrew used for carbon copies. She blew her nose into several pages and slipped the crumpled packet into an overstuffed wastebasket. She vowed again to clean this place while Andrew rehabbed.

Walter jumped and licked Lizzy's face to taste her body salts.

"Walter, thank you. What will we do if Andrew doesn't come home?"

THROUGHOUT DINNER, Alan and Jane avoided each other's eyes.

"When will Grand Pop be able to come home?" Billy Jay asked.

"Probably never," David said.

"David, why would you say a thing like that?"

"Because Grand Pop is old, and it's time for him to die."

"Don't hurt Mom's feelings. Grand Pop will get better so he can finish his novel and pay me what he owes me."

"Billy Jay, wouldn't it be better to hope your Grand Pop gets better for his own sake? Not because you want his money."

Billy Jay considered his mother's words. "Yes, ma'am."

"Even if he gets better, he'll still be about to die."

Alan frowned. "David, what bothers you so much about Grand Pop?"

"Old people like him don't like me very much."

"He hugged you boys just the other day, remember? That was a first, but I guarantee your Grand Pop loves you a whole lot. All of you kids," Jane said.

Elizabeth chimed in. "Grand Pop loves me better than anybody!"

Billy Jay shouted, "Does not, Weenie Girl!"

"Now hear this, kiddos: your Grand Pop will get better. He will finish his novel, and he will pay you what he owes you, Billy Jay. He loves you, David. He loves you, Elizabeth, and Billy Jay too. He loves us all very much." Jane's voice broke. "He just can't show it." She lowered her eyes and expected Alan to reply in sympathy.

Instead, he excused himself and told the kids to help their mother with the dishes.

Jane seethed in silent tears.

By the time the kids had bathed and were in bed, the kitchen clock showed ten thirty p.m. on what had been a long day. Jane dreaded the coming confrontation, although she thought she had more cause to be angry than her husband did. She went to the primary wing, well out of earshot of the children's rooms. This floor plan was a 'must-have' the couple had sought when they bought the place. A haven for romance, but tonight it would be a courtroom.

Jane tested the closed bedroom door handle to see if Alan had locked her out, but the door opened. Relieved, she heard the shower in full force. She yearned for a soak in their jetted tub, so she undressed quickly. But the bathroom door was locked.

She yelled at the locked door, "Why are you pissed at me? My father had a stroke. I tried to reach you, but you didn't call me back." She figured she could get away with her tirade because Alan could not hear her from the shower.

Jane sat on the bed and thumped her foot on the carpet. Alan took his sweet time and finally came out about ten-thirty.

"What's with the locked door? And the silent treatment. Seems to me it should be the other way around."

Alan wiped the back of his neck with a towel and glared sarcastically. "What cause do you have to be angry with me?"

Jane noticed he had a second towel wrapped around his lower half, a bit of modesty that she saw as a sign of emotional distance. "You didn't call me back. Not all day."

"My cell phone was at my office. I only got your one thousand voice mails and texts as I drove home."

"I sent you a message at Delta."

"Yes, you did, didn't you?" He glared at her steadily.

"So that's it. You're pissed because I contacted you at Delta?"

Alan did not reply.

"Here, my father might be dying, but you're angry because I tried to contact you?"

"You embarrassed me in front of a major client."

"I embarrassed you? How did I do that while I was stuck between pickups on the freeway?"

"You pestered some admin to interrupt my presentation."

"I thought you'd want to know about Poppa."

"Andrew's been ill for months."

"'Oh, that again.' That's the same attitude your beloved Posey gave me when I called your office, as if my father's condition did not matter."

"Cut the melodrama. Delta has strict policies. But rules, protocol, these things don't matter to Jane Cates. After the meeting, the receptionist was upset because 'that lady,' who happened to be my wife, had sent a message to me through reservations. How do you think that made me look?"

"Always thinking about appearances, aren't you?"

"My appearance is three-fourths of our combined income. You embarrassed me. Can't you even apologize for that? I know what you're like when you are on a tear. Good luck to anybody who stands in your way. The problem is, you don't care about repercussions."

"Oh, 'my problem' again. Even when you say you love me out on the running track, you tell me I have a 'problem.'"

The two fell angrily silent. Alan donned his robe and headed upstairs. Jane soon heard the media room's expensive sound system blaring through the ceiling.

"Another replay of *Master and Commander*. I might as well grab a glass of wine and take a hot bath." She headed toward the kitchen but stopped short and went instead to her closet.

TEARS EXHAUSTED, Lizzy rose from Andrew's desk and called to Walter, who leapt out of the workshop door. The sky had darkened to a bluish gray with a hint of deep burgundy. Lizzy encouraged the dog "to do his nighttime business," one final time. As the dog lifted a leg in the tall grass, he jumped to alert and barked. Lizzy saw a reflection of headlights and heard tires on gravel. With another bark, Walter bolted to the front.

"Come back here!" Lizzy was afraid a car would hit Walter, so she followed, but stopped short when she heard a car door open and close. "Who's there?" Lizzy called. She heard footsteps on the gravel. Walter barked again.

Jane walked around the corner, carrying a suitcase. "Got a spare room?"

"You scared the devil out of me. What are you doing?"

"I thought I'd keep you company for the night."

"What about Alan and the kids?"

"Alan's pissed at me, and I'm pissed at him. Long story about my trying to reach him at Delta. I 'embarrassed him,' or so Alan says."

"Probably a miscommunication, dear. Come inside and soothe your nerves." Lizzy was relieved, even happy, to have a guest. Especially one who needed her.

Once inside, Lizzy brought out a Chardonnay. She knew Jane preferred white. The two sat at the round table as Walter curled beneath. His fur touched each of their toes.

Jane looked more closely at her mother. "You look puffy. Have you been crying?"

"My dear, you don't look so hot, either."

"Touché. I cried all the way over. Tell me, how are we supposed to make it through married life?"

"I've tried to answer that question for fifty years."

"Sometimes I just want to run away from home."

Lizzy patted Jane's hand and gave her a wry smile. "But honey, you haven't run away. You are home."

Chapter Twenty-Seven

JUNE 24

T homas Ward arrived at the ICU in the late afternoon, although Lizzy had not heard one peep from him after she left a voicemail the day before. The unseasonal rains had returned, this time in sheets, but Thomas breezed in like a model for a cruise to Los Cabos, wearing pressed khaki slacks, a light green polo, tan cotton sweater tied around his shoulders, and designer sunglasses perched atop his silver hair.

Lizzy and Jane were startled when they heard Thomas' "hello."

He barely acknowledged the two women as he rushed to Andrew's side and shouted, "Andy, I'm here. How are you?"

Unlike months before, Andrew did not acknowledge his brother's presence.

"Uncle Thomas, the nurse tells me he can hear you, but he cannot respond or react."

"Can you hear me, Andy?" Thomas shouted again.

"There's no need to yell. He's not deaf." Lizzy's tone was uncharacteristically harsh. She walked to the opposite side of Andrew's bed and hovered protectively. If Thomas had looked her way, he would have seen a stern glare.

"Not to worry, Uncle Thomas. Yesterday, I found myself shouting at Poppa too."

Thomas ignored Jane's remark, just as he had ignored the visitation rules sign posted on the outer door to the ICU.

"Only two visitors per room. Contact an ICU nurse before entering."

He silently stared at his brother, chin propped on one hand, as though he planned to invent new circuitry. After a long silence, he asked Lizzy, "Is our sister on her way?"

"I left her a voicemail. No one answered. I've tried several times."

"I'll try myself." Thomas reached for his cell phone. "But then, do you have Sarah's number? I've never called her. Rhonda keeps all those details."

Lizzy walked to the window seat to retrieve her purse. Out of the drizzly glass, a trash truck pulled in. "Thank heavens. I couldn't bear to look at that soggy pile of garbage another day. All this rain cannot last forever, can it? The news said that airplanes have been delayed all day. So, how in the world did you get here, Thomas?" Her tone was tinged with regret.

Thomas did not appear to have heard her.

Lizzy pulled out her address book and fumbled for Sarah's number.

Just then, Guy and Ouisie walked in. They, too, had paid no attention to the ICU visitation rules and had tailgated in after other visitors. Ouisie gave Lizzy a hug. "We got your voicemail and rushed right over."

"Oh, my goodness!" Lizzy was so surprised to see her friends, she bobbled her address book. It cartwheeled out of her hands to the center of the room.

Both Guy and Thomas stepped to pick it up, but the two men's heads collided. Guy reeled back, landed on his left hip, and gave out a rousing "Owwww!"

Guy's fall tripped Thomas, who grabbed Andrew's bed rail, but slid on the floor beside the bed.

Ouisie rushed over. "Oh, Honey! Did you break anything?"

Guy was more embarrassed by his pratfall than injured. "I imagine I'll have a very unwelcome lump on my *gluteus maximus*, but other than that, I seem to have survived with only embarrassment. And you, sir, I hope you are uninjured?"

Thomas fumed in silent unrest.

Jane crouched beside Thomas and offered to help, but he silently shook his head.

Ouisie reached out to help Guy. He took her hand and attempted to pull up, but Ouisie was not strong enough to provide resistance. She slid on the slick floor and fell on her knees on top of Guy. The skirt of her pink patio dress flew up to reveal bright red bikini panties stretched over her plump buttocks.

Lizzy rushed to straighten Ouisie's dress. "My goodness. Are you all right?"

"I'm so embarrassed, I could just die."

"This certainly is a slapstick moment," Guy said from the floor.

"Aunt Ouisie, let me help you up." Jane thought she could use her relative youth and strength to set things right. But neither she nor Ouisie could get enough leverage on the polished linoleum floor. She tried to lift Guy with the same result. "We'll have to get someone to help."

Jane pushed the call button and rolled Andrew's bed as far as she could to give Thomas room to rise. Still on the floor, he did not speak or move.

"Thomas, I hope you're not hurt. I'm sure Guy had no intention, but as for Ouisie, well, we've known about *her* issues for some time." Lizzy giggled, but no one else did. She tried to control her laughter, but it escalated to a guffaw, and then a case of what Lizzy's mother had called "the shallers." She used this word to describe moments when people cannot stop laughing, and tears run from their eyes.

Her laughter became contagious to Ouisie, who giggled so hard she squealed. "I think I just wet my panties!"

Even Guy chuckled as he tried to angle his thin legs and launch an ascent. "Thomas, these two have gone round the bend. And I apologize for my contribution to what appears to be a case of communal chaos."

Ouisie stuttered, "Thomas, we're just like family, except I'm going to kill Lizzy."

Thomas's continued silence annoyed the others except Andrew, who lay bizarrely undisturbed.

Jane tried again to engage her Uncle Thomas, but he refused to reply. His rudeness made Jane angry enough to yank the asshole up. She moved behind him and was about to put her hands under his armpits when a burly male nurse with a gold earring came into the room.

So did Jane's husband, Alan, to Jane and Lizzy's astonishment.

"What in the world? Is anyone hurt?" the nurse said.

"Just our pride," Guy said.

"Oh, goodie! Two powerful men!" Ouisie giggled.

Lizzy took a breath to control her shallers.

"What are all these people doing in here?"

"We seem to have gone overboard. I'm sorry," Lizzy said.

The nurse shook his head. "I turn my back and World War Three breaks out!"

He and Alan pulled Ouisie upright. She rose in a flurry and hastily smoothed the ruffles of her patio dress. "I should have worn petti-pants!"

Lizzy extended a hug. "My dear, I had no clue you still wore dating underwear."

After Alan pulled Guy upright, the nurse moved to help Thomas. "Sir, are you in any pain?"

Thomas silently shook his head but refused the nurse's outstretched hands. Instead, Thomas pushed himself up like a warrior rising after battle. He said nothing but smoothed his clothing as if he had been in a schoolyard tussle.

"Now that everybody's upright, please pick the two who will stay. You can take turns every fifteen minutes. The rest of you march *slowly* and carefully down the hall to the visitors' room."

"Thomas, you should be one of the first two. You've come so far," Lizzy said.

"Guy and I will go down the hall. As I said, we're like family." Ouisie said the last phrase in Thomas' direction.

Alan avoided Jane's eyes. "Lizzy, I'll head to the office and come visit this weekend."

"Alan, it was wonderful to see you, wasn't it, Janey?"

Jane avoided her husband's eyes, but she was pleased he had made the effort.

"I don't know what we would have done without Alan, do you, Janey?"

Alan pursed his lips and nodded to Lizzy before he walked down the hall.

Jane gathered her purse and briefcase. "I'll head to the visitors' room, Momma."

"Are you sure? Maybe you should go home and tend to Alan and the kids."

"Alan can cool his heels another night," Jane shot back as she headed out.

The nurse grinned and shook his finger at Lizzy. "Mrs. Ward, you're under orders to make sure everybody behaves from now on."

All that remained were Lizzy and Thomas, but because Thomas kept up his moody silence, Lizzy did not want to stay. "Thomas, I'll let you be alone with your brother." Again, Thomas did not reply. Lizzy reached for her things, then stood beside her brother-in-law at the foot of Andrew's bed. She reached up to put her arm around his shoulder. "Thomas, perhaps you'll be able to get some reaction from Andrew. The last time, he didn't remember many people, but he sure remembered his big brother Tommy."

Thomas did not respond.

Lizzy stamped her foot. "Thomas Ward, you answer me."

Thomas turned to her with tears in his eyes. "I heard you, Lizzy."

"Then why give me the silent treatment?"

"Lizzy, stop your everlasting needling! I simply do not operate at this *level*."

"What *level?*" Lizzy trilled back.

"This!" Thomas shouted as he waved his arms about the ICU. As though the room, the bed, the equipment, Lizzy, and even his brother were a third-world country to him.

"None of us wants to operate at this *level*. But we've got to pull together for Andrew's sake."

When Lizzy walked out, she hoped Thomas had enough sense to check into a hotel that night. The man's condescension was more than she intended to bear any further that day.

IN THE VISITORS' room, Lizzy sat beside Ouisie and Guy, as Jane checked her smartphone across from them.

"No wonder Andrew calls Thomas a horse's ass," Ouisie said.

"Poppa and Uncle Thomas never got along, did they, Mom?"

As Lizzy shook her head, she saw a human-shaped blur go by the open doorway. "Was that Thomas?" She went to the door and watched her brother-in-law stride down the hallway, shoulders hunched. "Thomas! Thomas," Lizzy called after him, but he had rounded the corner to the elevators.

She turned to Jane. "I guess he's gone. And maybe for good."

Jane scoffed. "What a terrible day for Uncle Thomas to visit from sunny Silicon Valley. More of our torrential rain. And then the slapstick in Poppa's room. He'll have some stories to tell Aunt Rhonda about this side of the clan."

"I think Guy and I messed things up for your family."

"For gosh sakes, the man cannot blame us for slipping on that slick floor. Maybe he's got something else against us," Guy said with a bite.

"Now, Guy, you two *are* our family. Andrew and Thomas were never close, and I've been shocked both times that he flew out to visit. Must be guilt or something. From what Andrew has told me, their father openly favored Thomas, at least in Andrew's eyes. You know what that does to children, when they feel they are 'less than' the other sibling."

Jane nodded. "Yes, I do."

The urge to issue a hundred admonishments darted through Lizzy's mind, but she did her best to ignore Jane's insecurities. "If anybody ran off Thomas today, I did. I lost it in the ICU room after you all left."

Jane's voice cracked. "He deserved it. I feel sorry for Aunt Rhonda. Loving a self-absorbed jerk is heartbreaking."

"Uh-oh. Are you and Alan having problems?" Ouisie leaned across to offer a consoling auntie's tissue to Jane.

As Guy's eyes darted from woman to woman, he could tell that a female sharing session was about to ensue. So, he quietly excused himself to go to the cafeteria.

Jane sniffed into the tissue that Ouisie offered. "We're both a bit weary. That's all."

"Too much work and not enough time *together*," Lizzy said.

"That's certainly a problem with two-career couples. Back in our day, Lizzy and I were not supposed to work. We stayed home to care for the children, the house, the groceries, the repairs, took care of everything, really, and spent our free time with our husbands."

"I think today's couples are torn between work and home, but home is what really counts. Family," Lizzy said.

Jane sighed heavily. "Okay, ladies, I've enjoyed your last-century mantra. I love you both dearly, but I also love my career and my family. By hook and crook, we manage. But I will take your advice and go home. I'm exhausted. I hardly slept last night in that pink taffeta twin bed."

Lizzy smiled and nodded silently, as if to say, "Good girl."

When Guy returned a half hour later, Lizzy motioned for him and Ouisie to take their turn to visit Andrew. Lizzy could wait. She had that afternoon, the next, and the next.

JANE DROVE through the downpour to Lizzy's house, then ran in long enough to retrieve her things from the night before. She did not have to rush home. Alan was at work, and their neighbor Meryl had taken the kids that day, first to the aquarium and, better still, for dinner and a sleepover with Meryl's children, who were about the same age. Although there were no children to manage, Jane dreaded the fact that there was another confrontation with Alan headed her way. She detoured onto North Decatur Road to buy a bottle of her favorite dry Riesling. As she headed back, her automatic wipers pounded away, and she could barely see.

"I just want to sit in the tub, sip some wine and listen to this damned rain," she muttered.

When Jane opened the garage door, Alan's car was not there. Although she had not expected him to be home, she felt disappointed when the jerk wasn't. He probably would stay late at his office, his *modus operandi* when the two had a spat. Alan was not the kind to go out for cocktails and hustle women, like so many middle-aged attorneys in his firm. Instead, he was a workaholic like Jane, who found solace in his workspace.

Jane slipped the wine into the chiller, then checked her voicemail and e-mail to see if Alan had left messages. She found none.

She mentally prepared her argument. She had to be ready. After all, her husband's profession was the argumentation of opposing facts. Alan could make a case, right or wrong. Even if he agreed with Jane, he sometimes maintained the opposite position just to challenge her, while Jane exerted interminable energy trying to balance the value of his points. Jane's career was to explain a system's pros and cons matter-of-factly. So, she drove herself crazy to weigh Alan's ever-changing positions. Neither gave an inch until the two would simply go silent for a day or two, until some late night when Alan could not stand it anymore. He would reach out to Jane, and she would melt into his body, a nonverbal sexual encounter that brought out the frustrated animal in both. Beasty sex.

Jane uncorked the chilled Riesling and took the bottle and a wineglass to the bedroom. From there, she set the security alarm so she would hear when Alan entered — if he came home. In the bathroom, she undressed and wrapped her frizzy curls in a pink Turbie Towel that Alan called her 'Lana Turner Towel.' She settled the wine glass beside the huge, jetted garden tub and ran steamy water. "Bubbles. I need bubbles." She squirted liquid and turned on the jets, which quickly produced a mountain so high the bubbles oozed over the rim. She shut off the jets, got in, and held the wine glass in a self-toast as bubbles dripped from her hands.

"Now, this is a scene from a Hollywood movie." She drank deeply and leaned into the slope. But just as she relaxed, the alarm went off. She heard the codes beep, then the alarm silenced. Alan was home.

Shit. I do not want to go through this. If he comes in right now, I am trapped. I should have locked him out.

In the kitchen, Alan poured a Scotch and Pellegrino. He was still pissed that Jane had left the night before, not to mention that she had downright ignored him at the hospital when he came to show his support. Glass in hand, he headed straight for the bedroom, at his limit with the perpetual divide. Where had their life gone? First, Jane's work, and the kids took every other moment of her time, but these past months everything was about Andrew, Lizzy, Billy, and some apology Andrew needed to utter to absolve him of Billy's tragic death, a death that Lizzy swears she had a premonition about when he was a baby. My God, he had married into a *Twilight Zone* plot of guilt, blame, and regret.

Since the bathroom door was closed, he coached himself in the dresser mirror. *She's stuck in melancholy. Be firm, but sympathetic. Remember how she responded to your meltdown at the jogging track? Love her, yes, but persuade her to realize that her obsession negatively affects the life she has with you.*

He took a deep breath and strode in with a feigned but handsome smile. "Monumental bubbles" was his line.

Jane wanted to bolt, but then Alan was smiling. That was different. After a moment, Jane said with a lighthearted tone, "The jets made the bubble bath go crazy."

Alan put a towel on the edge and sat. "I'm sorry you left last night. I don't think running away solves anything."

"You locked me out of my own bathroom."

"I didn't want Elizabeth to bust in on me. She's tried to do that lately. Catch me."

"You should have warned me. She's just curious."

"I don't want her to see my amazing schlong."

"I'll talk to her. She needs to respect your privacy. Little girls see their brother's but always wonder what Daddy looks like. I know from experience that she doesn't want to see her father's dick."

"Uh-oh. Something you'd rather forget?"

Jane laughed and quickly recounted a time when she was about eight. She had gone into the bathroom while Andrew was in the shower. Seated on the potty, she pulled back the curtain and peeked while her father shampooed his hair. She was amazed at the size of his genitalia, the colors, and the hairiness.

"All I'd ever seen of Billy was a little boy's pink dick. I couldn't stop staring at Poppa's equipment until he started rinsing his hair, and I realized he might see me. So, I tucked the curtain back. But, dumb me, I flushed the toilet before I ran out, and he heard me in there. But did he know I peeked? I was so scared, I ran into my room and hid the rest of the night. I couldn't get the sight of him out of my mind. I just wanted to be his little girl again."

"I'm amazed at the wonderful stories you remember from your childhood." Alan was in trial lawyer mode as he plied his witness.

"So now you are an understanding husband?"

"Let's not be adversarial. You ran away last night. That hurt my feelings. I was angry too, but the kids are gone tonight. We're alone. Let's be together for a change."

"I'm sorry, Alan, but I cannot forget that my father may be dying. And when I tried to reach you, you didn't seem to care."

"That's not true. I care, but you beat the dead horse. Let's look at the facts. Thirty years ago, your family experienced a tragic loss from which none of you has recovered. You relive Billy's death every time a mention comes up. Meanwhile, your parents have done their parts to propagate this gloom. Your father is a defensive, arrogant recluse who does not have much use for his wife of fifty years, his daughter, his grandchildren, his brother or sister, his former colleagues, or anybody except his dog. Like yourself, your mother is mired in masochism. She more than likely drinks to dull the pain, and you two feed off one another to a degree I call psycho-symbiotic. Although Andrew's illness has brought you and your parents closer, you continually push away from me. By trying to save your birth family, you ignore your responsibility to the kids and me. We are your family now."

"I know, Alan. Truly, I do. But I must reach him. Why can't you understand?"

"Honey, I know you love him, but he's never been the father you needed. Why extend all this emotional effort? To keep Billy alive somehow? Do you think you could have prevented his death?"

"You are a better lawyer than a psychologist, Alan. I didn't get to say goodbye. I've told you that a million times."

"What does that have to do with your father?"

"He never apologized. He knows he screwed up, but he has not atoned for it. Yesterday, when I was at the hospital, I realized something I didn't know. I've also been blaming him for Billy's death all these years. His hokey attempt to write a 'novel' is his way of asking for forgiveness. He's trying to tell Mom, me, maybe all of us, that he's sorry."

"Most people simply say, 'I'm sorry.' Why does Andrew have to write a novel?"

"He's a professor. A teacher. Maybe he wants his *apologia* to be a work that lives on. He's also a male of a different generation. Maybe he can't admit that he made a mistake that cost his son's life. This is his way of doing what he's got to do before he dies."

Alan wanted to understand, but couldn't.

Jane gathered her thoughts for a few moments and then spoke softly. Her words formed awkwardly as her feelings jelled. "Alan, I didn't get to say goodbye to my brother. I didn't get to tell him I kept his secret and always would."

Alan perked up. "What secret?"

"A childhood thing. Billy got a bad grade, but the principal changed it so he could play football. Billy made me swear never to tell. Momma and Poppa never would have allowed that grade to be changed. Out of guilt, Billy confessed to me, and I swore I'd never tell, and I never did. I kept my promise. That's why I want to help my father keep *his* promise, to say what *he* needs to say before he dies. I guess that's my way to forgive him, but also my penance for blaming him." Jane fell silent at her revelation, then shuddered into tears again.

Alan sensed the moment that sometimes arrived during mediations when he realized the gut human truth of the litigants' issues, not the legal concerns that had brought his clients and their opponents to a misunderstanding. "So, what's troubling you is that you don't want your dad to feel the same regret you still feel. Why didn't you tell me this before?"

Jane blubbered. "I didn't know what I thought until now."

"Bubble therapy." Alan climbed into the tub, Armani suit, dress shirt, Prada tie, tassel-toed loafers, silk socks, and all. He sat across from Jane in the bubbles, curled his legs and arms around her, and enveloped her while she cried exhausted tears.

The displaced water and mounds of bubbles flooded over the sides of the tub.

When Jane finally stopped sobbing and pulled away to take off her soaked hair towel, Alan brought her close again and kissed her sweetly. "I'll help you any way I can, sweetheart." This time, his voice more closely resembled himself than a game show host.

"And here I thought you were a jerk."

"A jerk is what I have to be eight hours a day. As you say, I should change wigs when I get home."

"Wigs, nothing. You're going to need a whole new suit."

As THE NURSE puttered about Andrew's ICU, Lizzy sat beside the bed and read him excerpts from *National Geographic*. When she looked up from a page, she noticed his left leg trembling under the covers. "He must be dreaming. Maybe he's running."

The nurse noticed too. "If he's dreaming, that's a good sign. Some brains are so damaged after a stroke, the patient loses the ability to dream. Some others see only hallucinations. If he's dreaming, he may find a way back."

"All I can do is hope he comes back to a real life soon."

Chapter Twenty-Eight

ANDY

Danny, Tommy, and I can't wait to find our pennies smashed by the locomotive the night before. We hunt down the railroad ties, but we don't find a thing.

I turn over cinder rocks. "Somebody must've stole 'em."

Tommy glares. "Stole 'em? Who knew about the pennies except you, me, and Danny?"

I shrug. "Well, they ain't here this morning."

Danny tries to stop the argument. "You sure that was how those pennies got flattened at the State Fair?"

"They got a machine at the State Fair. But this should've worked," Tommy says. "A train would've smashed those pennies the length of my little finger."

I turn over more rocks. "Maybe the pennies got vibrated off."

Tommy glares again. "Or maybe somebody snuck out in the middle of the night."

"You accusing me?"

"You were the one who slept in the back bedroom. You could have snuck out."

"Tommy, you're a jerk and I hate your chicken poop guts. I didn't steal the pennies."

"For all I know, you've got 'em stuck in your girlie pink piggy bank. And I'm gonna tell Daddy when he comes this weekend."

"Don't you dare! That's a lie!" I bolt toward Tommy, put my head down, and aim for his gut. I run hard, but he sidesteps at the last second. I can't stop in time, so my face smashes the fence. It hit my nose hard. My blood runs like a splash of paint. Covers my t-shirt and jeans.

Danny rushes over. "Holy cow, Andy!"

Tommy saunters off. "Serves him right."

"Serves who right?" More blood spews out of my nose.

"You're the one who got your face smashed," Tommy says.

"Andy's right, Tommy, you *are* a jerk!" Danny pulls off his white cotton t-shirt and wads it around my nose. "Hold your head back. That's what Momma makes me do."

Tommy stands his ground. "You look like a pig with that shirt curled on your nose."

"I hate your guts, Tommy Ward!" That only makes the blood gush worse. A huge clot runs over my mouth. I try to breathe.

"That's what you get for stealing the pennies," Tommy yells.

"I didn't steal 'em, you jerk!" Another bloody glob squirts out.

Danny hushes me in his motherly tone. "Tommy will get his someday, you can count on that. Now, lean back and let me pinch your nose."

After the blood stalls to a trickle, I get up, but I'm wobbly. So, Danny puts his arm around me and guides me toward the house.

I'm still pissed. "Not yet, Danny. Let's find those pennies." I hunt and hunt until I see something peek from under a big cinder rock between two crossties. "Looky here!"

"Maybe some wolf came along and pushed 'em off the rails."

The copper shimmers in my hand. "Looks like the pennies vibrated off when the train got here. We learned about vibration last year in school."

Danny's dejected. "We didn't have that subject yet."

We search the other side for the second penny and find it near the track. I hold the penny high. "Momma says, 'Always pick up a penny and put it in your pocket for luck.'" I put both coins in my pocket, give Danny a wink, and run down the railroad ties toward the house.

"Hey, those are *my* pennies!"

"I'll give your dang pennies back, but I gotta get this blood off before Momma sees it. Last one in the lake is a piece of crappie poop."

We bound down the tracks to the opening in the fence. Our tennis shoes are a blur as we run down the twenty-two steps, then across the gravel road and lawn, and run thump, thump, thump to the end of the wooden dock.

We hold our t-shirts like bloody war flags and jump in, "Bonsaaaaiiiiiiiii!"

Chapter Twenty-Nine

JUNE 25

With worry evident in her brow, Dr. Fitzgerald greeted Lizzy, Jane, Alan, and the three grandkids in the hospital ICU visitors' room.

"I'm sorry to report that Professor Ward has experienced a very severe stroke. But there is some good news. He can breathe on his own, and he can swallow, so we did not have to tube him. But results from the tests we've run show that he probably will have some sort of permanent physical and cognitive disabilities."

Lizzy's mind was in denial. Surely this was not true.

Billy Jay blurted, "Won't Grand Pop's brain get better?"

Dr. Fitzgerald put a hand on the boy's shoulder. "The brain is a mystery. Are you into computers?"

Billy Jay nodded.

"Well, the brain is somewhat like a computer. Sometimes you can fix the hard drive with programming or memory cards. But sometimes the drive is damaged beyond repair. You might be able to recover some data, but not all. There are missing connections. Fragmentations. Our tests show your Grand Pop's brain has more severe damage than after his first stroke. That's why I'm not sure how many of his injured brain cells can come back online. He recovered almost ninety percent last time, but I don't expect as much recovery this time. I'm sorry."

Jane sighed in dismay. "Oh, no. Poppa's novel. He's writing a novel, or at least trying to."

"I doubt he can complete something that long, but writing a poem or diary would be excellent therapy if we can get him to the point he can try. His words might be reversed, or the phrasing may seem unusual or disjointed. But somehow the meaning still comes off the page, like in a poem."

"Andrew's no poet. He'd be frustrated with that style of writing."

"He won't be happy doing nothing, Momma."

"As you can tell, his cognitive state is in disarray. So, writing an entire novel or even walking without a cane or walker, well, I question if those things will be possible. The fewer expectations you put on him, the better. Right now, our goal is to give him meds to prevent further damage, blockages, and loss of brain cells. Then get him back to rehab," the doctor said.

Lizzy sat silently and absorbed this news. She did not know what to think. Andrew had gotten well before. Now this young woman — just how long had Dr. Fitzgerald been out of med school, anyway? — had pronounced that her husband would not get better.

Jane noticed her mother's emotional retreat. "Momma, we'll help him find a way."

Two days later, Andrew was moved to the rehab. Eyes frozen on the ceiling, he appeared unaware that his family surrounded him.

Lizzy patted his shoulder while the rest of the family attempted to be encouraging.

"Poppa, I can get you an assistive technology system where you can write your novel with just one finger or a blink of your eye."

Alan jumped in. "I saw something about that on *60 Minutes*. Isn't that how Stephen Hawking wrote his novels?"

"Hawking used a computerized system with a speech synthesizer. Remember that British-accented voice? We'll have Poppa talking like Anthony Hopkins."

"I'll come help. You don't even have to pay me," Billy Jay said.

The other kids nodded with naïve sincerity, then looked to their parents for what to say next. Jane and Alan were as bewildered.

Andrew lay unresponsive, his eyes a frightened void of expression. Lizzy wondered if she would ever see his eyes shine the way they did when they were young, the way they had reignited this summer. Opalescent.

Alan ahemmed. "Well, kids, we'd better not tire Grand Pop."

"Momma, you are welcome to spend the night at our house."

Lizzy silently shook her head. She was not about to budge.

One by one, the kids, Alan, and Jane hugged her goodbye, then filed out.

Lizzy sat at Andrew's side and waited until she was sure no one would interrupt. Then she took a breath of courage and leaned close to Andrew's ear. "Andrew, can you understand me? Please wiggle a finger if you can."

Lizzy watched and waited until, amazingly, Andrew's left index finger quivered. Was that simply a tremor? Or a signal? Lizzy's heart raced. She tucked her finger inside the curve of his. "Andrew, squeeze my finger if you understand."

Andrew's hand trembled, but Lizzy felt the slightest pressure.

"Oh, Andrew, you're really in there, aren't you?" Lizzy laid her head on his chest and stretched her arms around his body. "You're not the only one who has something to say. Please know that I love you, and I know you love me. We could go on and on about Billy, and the rights or wrongs, the way you punished yourself, the way you punished me, the time lost between us. You pushed me so far away, I was going to leave. But none of that matters now. 'I love you' is all that needs to be said. Squeeze my finger if you understand."

When she lifted her head to see if there was a reaction in Andrew's eyes, a tear fell onto his cheek. Lizzy gently wiped it away.

Andrew's eyes revealed just the faintest glimmer of understanding. His finger trembled and lightly squeezed hers — at least that's what Lizzy felt. Again, she nestled her head on Andrew's chest for the last minutes of her visit.

Chapter Thirty

JULY - OCTOBER

T hroughout the summer, Lizzy cursed the humidity each morning as she made her way to the rehab and cursed the humidity each evening as she arrived home to a muggy house that the air conditioner could not seem to cool. "We'll have to upgrade the air conditioner if this tropical weather keeps up," she told Andrew during one of her many visits.

He barely nodded a reply.

Progress was slow. Andrew had so little muscle strength, a burly staffer had to hoist him from his bed to the wheelchair. A month passed before any therapists attempted to see if Andrew could stand alone, but he fell backwards, unable to support his weight. When he regained vocal skills, he often swore in frustration, lashed out with his left hand, and wept occasionally when he could not comprehend what someone had said, or if he realized he was expected to reply but had no clue how. At night, straps restrained him, not because he might run away, but because he flailed at the stream of nurses and aides who came and went.

But he always knew Lizzy. He grinned crookedly when she walked in, but he could not speak her name except an utterance like a calf hollering for its mother. Other times, a slew of swearwords came as he thrust his left hand to emphasize whatever unintelligible point he was trying to make. Frustration spewed from his reddened, angry eyes.

When meals arrived, he attempted to feed himself with his tremulous left hand, but he bobbled the fork or spoon, missed his mouth, and spilled the food. Flustered, Lizzy fed him, which teed Andrew off. He grunted and swore, pushed Lizzy's hand away, spat out offending morsels, then grunted and swore again.

Lizzy almost swore too, dismayed at the entire situation.

"I do not operate at this *level*," Thomas had shouted. Lizzy now understood what he meant. Devoted as she was to Andrew, she did not want to spend each day at the rehab. Although the journey was not long, and she had little else to do, the hospital setting was a drain on her spirit. She wanted Andrew home with her and Walter, who whimpered each time she left him alone, no matter how many treats, toys, or back rubs Lizzy gave him.

Although she still lunched and brunched with Ouisie on Wednesdays and Sundays, Ouisie was usually full of church gossip, always the church. Although Lizzy loved Ouisie like a sister, the gossip Lizzy once enjoyed bantering with her about now seemed silly, if not annoying, compared to the daunting obstacles Lizzy faced at the rehab each day.

At the women's most recent luncheon, Lizzy found herself unable to feign interest in Ouisie's latest news and even murmured in dismay, "Oh, Ouisie, let's talk about something other than the church." To Ouisie's hurt eyes, Lizzy quickly apologized. She did not want to alienate her best and only friend.

Lizzy realized she needed to see Byron again. She had nowhere else to turn. And when she called for an appointment, his voice sounded eager to see her. Lizzy hoped that was not because he relied on her to overcome his problems with the board.

She chose an emerald jacket this time.

"Such vivid green eyes. I didn't notice the last time you were here," Byron said as Lizzy sat across from him.

"Oh, thank you. It's the jacket, I think."

"Yes, indeed. Please make yourself comfortable. I had hoped to see you again."

Lizzy demurred and told him about "things getting better." That is, until Andrew had another stroke. Byron again probed for the reasons for Lizzy's visit, beyond her annoyance at Ouisie. As Lizzy told him about Ouisie and her church gossip and Lizzy's recent impatient response to her friend's conversation, the discussion led to the way Lizzy felt when she arrived home after their visit.

"Drained, I expect," Byron said.

"Empty."

"Yes. And rightly so, Lizzy. You've given all day. To your friend, to your daughter, to your very ill husband, and when you get home, there is nothing to give you the energy you've expended. I'm sure you've heard about the book *Women Who Love Too Much*."

Lizzy nodded. "I also read that book about Mars and Venus. Can't remember the title."

"Ah, that one. Written by a man for men. As for women who love too much, I would say you are one. Except you are wise enough to know when you are empty. You have a need. You came here."

"I guess so," Lizzy sniffed.

"You did the right thing. And I want you to come see me whenever you need to vent, cry, complain, whatever. But there's a price. What interests you? What do you enjoy?"

"Oh dear, I've been so busy. But I do read. And I putter at the piano. It's been too long since my lessons."

"Ah-ha. Two excellent activities. Let's do this. I realize you are busy right now, but you can take a break now and then, right?"

"I don't know about that."

"You have lunch with Ouisie, and you come to church. So, let's add two more breaks each month. One is the church book club. It meets on the third Thursday at noon. We read one book and have a luncheon discussion. I'll sign you up for that."

"I don't want to become a 'church lady' like Ouisie. But don't you dare tell her I called her that."

Byron patted her hand. "Not a word, promise. And here's the second thing. Our music director, Brent Walker, is one heck of a piano teacher. He holds one class each month for people who want to brush up on their skills. That's at Brent's house. It's not a church deal, but I'll talk to him and enroll you for that too."

Lizzy felt overwhelmed. Classes. New people. "I don't want to get too busy."

"Two activities a month? You can handle that. Right?"

Lizzy nodded, although she wondered.

"I guarantee that some new activities will help fill your energy bucket. But I still want to see you once a week for three months. That way, I can keep tabs. You are far saner than most people I know, but you need to nurture your soul. Don't tell anybody I said this, but even my amazing Sunday services cannot provide all the nurture you need." He finished with a wink.

As THE SUMMER yielded to cooler but rainy October weather, the grandkids came to the rehab. They had not visited in some time because Jane wanted to limit their exposure to Andrew's violent outbursts.

The kids timidly approached the bed and offered Andrew a giant box that held a lush red terry robe, a new version of the faded robe Andrew had worn for so many years. Only this robe had "Professor Grand Pop" monogrammed in gold on the left breast. As the kids watched Lizzy unwrap the box, they were unaware that their grandfather didn't know who in the hell they were. He clumsily caressed the terry pile and smiled a lopsided grin.

The kids waited for an expression of gratitude from an old man who could not say his name, much less recall theirs.

Jane tried to save the day. "Your grandchildren bought this handsome new robe with the money you paid Billy to help you with your novel."

Andrew did not know what this woman had said or who she

was, either. His smile turned to frustration. He grunted, "Suck this fit. Goddamn it." He burst into tears and flailed. The box fell off the bed.

"Uh-oh, Mommy."

"Elizabeth, we talked about this, remember? Just ignore it."

Lizzy quickly picked up the robe and box. Then displayed it a good arm's distance from Andrew. "Isn't this robe a thoughtful gift that your grandchildren and your daughter Janey bought for you?" Lizzy recited the words like an elementary school teacher, so Andrew would have time to comprehend.

He did not know if Lizzy had asked a question or stated an opinion, but her words explained who these people were. He did his best to sit up and grinned one of his goofy smiles.

Jane and Lizzy mustered smiles back and nodded in response. Elizabeth hid her face on her mother's thigh, and the two boys stood, eyes down, clearly disappointed.

Andrew realized he should say something, so he grunted, "Tough shit." He thought he had said, "Thank you."

Elizabeth squirmed. "Mommy, I want to go home now."

LATER THAT NIGHT, Jane tucked her boys in bed. She reminded them to be sympathetic. "I'm sure that your Grand Pop loved your gift. He just couldn't say so."

"I gave up my salary for that darn robe," Billy Jay said.

"So that's why Grand Pop will probably put you in his will instead of me."

"David! What a thing to say."

"Well, Billy Jay is named after, you know, the 'saint up in heaven.'"

"What saint are you talking about?"

"Uncle Billy. The one everybody treats like some saint, and everybody is all upset about."

Jane pulled the bedcovers around David's ears. "Little pitchers have big ears."

"What does that mean?"

"You are wiser than your years. Go to sleep now and don't worry about who will get what in Grand Pop's will. He loves all of you, and I'm sure he didn't leave Billy Jay something instead of you or Elizabeth. In fact, he probably will leave everything to Gizzy, if we must talk about wills. I, myself, prefer to think my father will get better."

LIZZY FOLLOWED Byron's advice and attended the church book club and took piano lessons. She also visited Byron once a week to keep him posted on her progress. He insisted that was his only fee for counseling, but Lizzy tucked an extra check in the plate each Sunday. She found her sessions with him a tremendous comfort, and their conversations stimulating. She never had a male friend before, only her girlfriend Ouisie, but Lizzy was surprised to be communicating on a close emotional level with a man who was not her husband.

"I do my best to stay grounded, but with Andrew so ill, I have a hard time wanting to interact. Conversations seem so meaningless when there's so much worry about Andrew."

"That's normal, Lizzy, but the only way to make connections is to try. Promise me you will. I'll bet that six months from now you'll have a better opinion of your extra activities and have some new friends too."

Lizzy did not tell Ouisie about her sessions with Byron because she would want details. But Lizzy did tell Ouisie at brunch about her new book club and piano lessons. Perhaps Lizzy should have held her tongue because she quickly realized Ouisie was jealous.

"Who's in this book club? Maybe I should join too, unless it's a bunch of — Well, I can't believe you didn't tell me about this. Or did you think I don't read books?"

Lizzy counted to ten rather than counter Ouisie's defensive reply. "I went without thinking. Of course, you'd be welcome to join the book club. You're the board president's wife, and I'm sure the others would be delighted to have someone as important as you in their mix."

Ouisie's dark eyes sparkled after that.

Although Ouisie could be petty at times, Lizzy had learned long before, as a Brownie in Troop 261, to "Make new friends but keep the old. One is silver, and the other gold."

NOT UNTIL LATE October did Andrew grow more alert. Improvement came in blips, especially one Sunday morning when frost chilled a fog on his rehab window. His colleague Guy had come to visit after church and brought a *National Geographic* and a box of Cracker Jack, which Andrew eagerly crunched while Guy pulled up a chair. This was the first time after Andrew's recent stroke that he realized who Guy was. Before this morning, some man he didn't know came to read to him. But this Sunday, Andrew said, "Hi, Guy!"

With a big grin, Guy balanced the magazine on Andrew's chest so he could see the four-page pullout photo of five lovely young women from a still-primitive tribe in New Guinea.

"I thought you'd get a kick out of this month's issue. These are from the Korowai tribe in New Guinea. Remember how pictures like these could stir the boyish hormones?"

Andrew nodded and grinned.

Guy flushed, remembering. "The moment my father's issue came in the mail, I put it in my back pocket and sneaked out to the shed. There wasn't a light in there, but sunlight peeked in, and I spent hours in arousal over women from exotic locales."

Andrew grunted a "Damn it" in agreement.

"Can't say times have changed. Just the ability to do much about it." Guy sighed.

Andrew grinned. "Self speak." He meant, "Speak for yourself." He indeed could do something about it. The two old men exchanged wide smiles.

Andrew was buoyant that he had responded appropriately to Guy's conversation with a two-word sentence. He lopsidedly beamed and exhaled in relief. There was hope.

Chapter Thirty-One

OCTOBER 14

J ane had learned a lesson from her first misadventure when she brought her father home. This time, she asked Alan to manage the transfer so Jane could be at her parents' house and oversee the delivery of a rented hospital bed.

Proudly dressed in his "Professor Grand Pop" robe, Andrew sat in a wheelchair pushed by a rehab staffer. Andrew called him Mack. This wasn't the same Mack as before, but every male staffer was "Mack" to Andrew.

At the hospital's entry, Guy, Ouisie, and Lizzy hovered close beside Andrew, while Alan went to retrieve Jane's minivan. Lizzy fluttered about, tightened Andrew's robe against the cool air, double-checked the brake on his wheelchair, smoothed wisps of his silver hair, and did anything else she could fuss over while she awaited Alan's return with the car.

"Sunshine, Atlantans. Yes, Mr. Sun has chased El Niño away," the radio announcer said as Alan drove the minivan into the half-circle drive, where he parked by the entrance and got out.

"Thank God for clear skies," he said as he helped the orderly lift Andrew into the second seat.

Eager to help, Guy wheeled Andrew's chair to the back of the van, where he clumsily attempted to collapse the heavy metal contraption. Luckily, the orderly came to help, then assisted the ladies and Guy into the van.

∽

WHEN "MACK" leaned in to say goodbye, Andrew abruptly kissed him on the cheek.

"Thank you, Professor Ward, but I'm straight."

"Thank you for everything, Mack," Lizzy said with a laugh.

"Norm. My name is Norm," the orderly said with a grin.

"Norm!" Andrew mimicked the line from the old TV show "Cheers!" that he had seen on the hospital's TV.

∽

AT ANDREW and Lizzy's house, Jane supervised as a delivery man positioned the hospital bed on the bare wall opposite Andrew's desk.

"I'm sorry, but could you move the bed nearer to that desk in the right corner?"

The deliveryman looked confused.

"Please, just put it as close as you can to the desk."

"In the middle of the room?" the deliveryman said.

"This doesn't have to make sense to you, just to us."

The delivery man rolled dubious eyes but pushed the bed beside Andrew's desk. When he left, he muttered, "Liberal feminist," under his breath.

Luckily for him, Jane did not hear his comment. She had sat at Andrew's computer to research software and peripherals for the disabled. "Aha! Surely, he can manage this," she said to no one but Walter, who had sauntered in as soon as the hospital bed was in place. The dog curled under the bed as though he knew Andrew would soon be there.

The moment Jane heard the van drive in, she rushed out, eyes alight with technical discoveries that could help Andrew complete his novel. Before Alan could get Andrew out of the car, Jane announced, "I've got the solution. I had it FedExed to your house overnight. Momma, be sure to sign for it. I can come by this weekend to set it up."

Andrew gave Jane a twisted smile. "Shit Analyst."

She knew he had meant to say, "Miss Systems Analyst." She grinned back. Her father suddenly knew who she was. Again.

"That's our Janey. Always solving puzzles."

"Block chips."

As Alan pushed Andrew up the ramp built after his first stroke, Lizzy looked at it sadly. Just this past spring, she had hoped to take the ramp down.

In the sunroom, Alan, Guy, and Jane hoisted Andrew onto his new hospital bed. Jane did most of the lifting for Guy.

Andrew looked quizzically at Lizzy, who was his designated interpreter. "Room gong!"

"We put your bed in here so you can work on your novel in bed, just as soon as Janey gets things hooked up. Your buddy Walter can be in here too."

"In fact, Walter is already under your bed, Poppa."

That comment brought another misshapen grin from Andrew. "Dog shit."

"Now remember, Mom. Sign for the delivery that comes tomorrow."

Andrew gave Jane a dubious look and struggled to wiggle the fingers of his left hand.

"Just give me until next weekend, Poppa. This won't take much dexterity on your part. After I install this system, you'll be in business."

Chapter Thirty-Two

OCTOBER 18

Ouisie and Guy met Lizzy at church, while Jane stayed with Andrew at the house. Along with Byron and the congregation, the three old friends in their third-row pew recited verses of a Maya Angelou poem.

"Late October," the program said, "#539 from *Singing the Living Tradition*." Ouisie liked it so much, she penciled a star on the program, determined to reread it later.

Lizzy quickly found her eyes misting to the melodious, but sad little poem about autumn leaves and gray-black skies and life winding down.

When Ouisie glanced over, she saw Lizzy's tears and put her arm around her friend.

Guy sniffed, but did his best to remain stalwart for Andrew.

After the service, Lizzy and Ouisie went for a quick bite.

"I can't stay long. Jane is with Andrew, but she has to work this afternoon."

"On a Sunday?"

"She says she's lost rank from her leave of absence."

"You are lucky to have such a devoted daughter."

"I suspect Janey is more devoted than Billy would've been. Those Saturday breakfasts were her determination to hold us together."

"And you still are together. Just think, last fall you were going to leave him."

"Don't remind me. I still feel guilty, even if Byron says I shouldn't. But now, Andrew is, well, not making much progress. Jane arranged for a caretaker to come weekday mornings to help Andrew bathe, dress, and eat. His name is Jefferson. He's a big African American fellow, or should I say, "Black," although his race doesn't matter, and I don't know why I mention it, except, of course, Andrew calls him 'Black Mack' and I cannot get him to stop."

Ouisie giggled.

"I hope you were not offended. After breakfast, Jefferson loads Andrew into my Jag and drives him to therapy. This is a relief for me, but after Jefferson brings Andrew home and then leaves, Andrew just dozes off in his bed. Jane bought some step-stairs so Walter can jump up there. The two take a nap until I wake them for dinner. Then I help Andrew eat. I worry he is giving up. He zones off into 'stroke world.' Doesn't watch TV or read magazines like he did in rehab. Your Guy is so dear to visit. That ought to perk Andrew up."

"Guy says Andrew got a card from that stinker, Thomas?"

"Cards, plural. A new version arrives each week, signed, 'Love, Thomas and Rhonda.' When I show Andrew the cards, he says, 'Horse Shit.' We both know that Rhonda is the one sending them."

"Oh, dear."

"I just hope Andrew can get interested in something to keep him motivated. Janey bought some whiz-bang electronic stuff to help him write. Janey and her computers."

WHEN LIZZY ARRIVED HOME, Guy had left, but Jane was there to install the assistive technology software and peripherals Lizzy had signed for earlier that week.

"Lucky I already bought Poppa that iMac. He can see the monitor from his bed, so all I needed was an iPad and some apps to connect him with his Microsoft Word."

Lizzy nodded and smiled, although she had no idea what the terms "apps" or "iPad" meant. "Has Andrew had lunch?"

"Oh yes, I fed him your gourmet leftover fare, didn't I, Poppa?"

"Taste low."

While Jane bent over the electronics, Lizzy shooed Walter off Andrew's bed. She dusted a place for herself, then wriggled beside Andrew's feet. She glanced at the back wall, where the oval mirror hung. She could see the workshop reflecting in the afternoon sunlight. She wondered if Andrew could see it from his point of view. Lizzy glanced at him and saw that he had followed her gaze into the mirror. The light glinted in his eyes like fire in an opal.

"Space ball."

Lizzy laughed. "Rocket barn. Now you can see why I call it that."

Andrew grinned crookedly, and the two shared a long gaze.

"By the way, I've been out there since you went to the hospital, and I can show you a thing or two about clean up, once you're on your feet."

Andrew managed another lopsided smile, then glanced again at the mirror. His eyes darted from it to Lizzy's desk to the window, and he could see how the light grew stronger as the sun headed toward its apex in the afternoon sky. As the beams streamed in, and then reflected off her mirror and out the window again, he realized that rays of light were passing or colliding — only a physicist would know what to call this phenomenon — but Andrew knew what it meant metaphorically. This was an image he wanted to capture in his novel. But how could he describe this scene when language eluded him? Suddenly, he burst into a crying jag, overwhelmed by his inability to communicate.

Lizzy silently patted him as he wept, and Jane tried to reassure them both that technology could solve all of Andrew's communication problems.

∾

AFTER JANE REBOOTED Andrew's iMac with the installed software, she placed the iPad on her father's lap and positioned a stylus between his fingers. "Poppa, this screen is like a computer, but it's also your keyboard and your track pad, all inside this small contraption. It communicates to your iMac wirelessly — no cords — so you can access the same programs and files you have on your iMac. There's no keyboard except the keys that appear on this screen when you touch it. See? It's perfect for your hunt-and-peck style. Just poke the stylus at the letters. Then, after you type, your iMac monitor displays what you've done. That's why I put your bed right next to your desk. You can see your iMac fine, can't you?"

Andrew jabbed at the iPad screen as his left hand quivered.

"Poppa, you don't need to push the keys down. This is different. Just touch each key with the stylus. It's more precise than your finger. You can also touch icons to open your software and documents."

Andrew stared at Jane with his mouth curled in a sneer.

"I know, Poppa. This is a lot to absorb. But this iPad is an excellent tool. The assistive app I've installed can hear even you. Just touch this icon."

When Jane poked the speech assistant, the computerized voice said in a British accent, "Where do you want to go?"

Lizzy was amazed that her daughter knew how to do all this.

"Open Microsoft Word," Jane said. "Poppa, you can say that when you get your speech back."

Andrew watched as the software booted up on the wide iMac display next to his bed.

Lizzy clapped her hands. "Wonderful! Janey's got you all fixed up to write."

Andrew shook his head. "Write shit."

"Dr. Fitzgerald said you might not be able to remember every word, so this fiction writing tool I installed has menus for when you want to find what word to say."

As Jane helped Andrew aim the stylus, he was frightened by this newfangled equipment, but curious too. He shouted, "Fuck this self," although he wanted to say, "Let me do it myself."

"Poppa!"

"Shit, do self," Andrew grunted in such an angry tone, Jane and Lizzy backed away to let him operate the contraption. He struggled to press the stylus to the keyboard, but his fingers shook. He touched the wrong letters and clicked on the wrong applications.

Jane tried to assist, but Andrew flailed her away. "Shit, do self!"

"Okay. You wanna do it yourself," Jane mimicked, as though he were a child. Like a proud parent, she backed off with arms folded. After a few minutes, she saw on Andrew's iMac that he had opened a chapter in his novel. "My God, you got it going."

Andrew managed a crooked smile. Jane's eyes glistened.

Lizzy slipped off the bed and smoothed Andrew's covers. "Now he can get back to writing his novel."

Andrew steadied his aim, pointed, and touched one icon or another app, and experimented with this and that. Although his illness had taken away his ability to walk and speak, other neurological pathways must have opened. With just a bit of guidance from Jane, who had spent an entire day learning the new software so that she could teach it to her father, Professor Grand Pop had suddenly become a computer whiz.

Jane laughed. "A tech *savant*."

Two weeks after Jane installed the technology, Andrew's left hand still fumbled, but he could write with the stylus. His right hand remained useless. In fact, his entire right side was paralyzed. But there was a wee bit of progress on left-sided activities each day.

His after-school and weekend helpers, Billy Jay, David, and Elizabeth, had developed an elaborate system to retrieve printouts for Andrew's review. Billy Jay, now an official teenager and self-designated boss, read each printed page like a proclamation. With Andrew's nod of "approval," Billy Jay then handed the page to his assistant David, who put it in a clipboard and gave that to David's assistant Elizabeth, whose job was to sit on Andrew's bed and grip the clipboard so that he could review the printed page.

Elizabeth had to stretch her arms to balance the clipboard on Andrew's chest. "Hurry up, Grand Pop. My arms get tired."

"Weenie girls won't be paid a dime if they can't do the job," Billy Jay said.

Lizzy came to see what the ruckus was about. "Billy Jay, I'm the Grand Weenie in this family and in charge of paying you when you're finished. So, I'd suggest you be nice to your little sister. Let me get a bed tray. She can set the clipboard on that."

With that, Lizzy left to retrieve a tray, thrilled to take part. While she was gone, David whispered loudly, "Hush your smart mouth, Billy, or you'll get us fired."

"Yeah, Billy Jay, fuck it!" Elizabeth hollered just as Lizzy walked back in.

"Elizabeth Jane!"

"Grand Pop says 'fuck' all the time."

"Elizabeth, we've talked about this. Andrew, please do not swear around these children. If they get out of line, simply let me know." Lizzy winked.

Andrew gave her a drooling grin.

"We've got a system, Gizzy. Grand Pop figures out what to do. Then he types instructions for me and hits print. When the page comes out, I read it aloud because I'm going to be an attorney."

Lizzy and Andrew exchanged smiles. "Sounds like you've got a great system."

"Loookkkk, Luuuuuzzzzzzy," Andrew managed. He laboriously poked his stylus at the iPad then nodded to Billy Jay. The printer whirled and spat out a page. Billy Jay read aloud, "This one says, 'Notes for Chapter One. Is a fool born or made? If Ward and Charlotte were my great-grandparents, my terrible mistake must have been *gentic ... gentic*'?"

Lizzy reached for the paper. "'Genetic.' That's the word."

"What does that mean?" Elizabeth asked.

"Might mean that being a fool is an inherited trait," Lizzy said.

"Is he saying we're all fools?" Billy Jay asked.

"I guess we'll find out," Lizzy said. She handed the clipboard back, then headed out, thinking to herself, *I think he's trying to explain himself to us, some sort of metaphor.*

After she left, the kids and Andrew stepped up their momentum as he alternated between the speech assistant, fiction software, word processor, and pushing print.

Lizzy peeked back through the doorway and promised to remember this vision of the three grandchildren and Andrew busily working together.

~

IN ANDREW'S NOVEL, Ward nailed a "Deed For Sale" notice on a wall outside the federal courthouse in downtown Atlanta.

While Ward posted his deed, Charlotte sat wearily in the dusty wagon seat. Her eight-month-old baby boy slept in the back, curled in a burlap-covered, crude wooden cradle. Dressed in britches and boots, despite the summer heat, Charlotte stoically stared ahead, angry with Ward for not being all to her he had promised, and angrier with herself for being a fool.

After Ward posted the deed, he steered his wagon to the rail yard area and pulled up in front of Gerard's Inn.

Charlotte felt a blue chill as a drop of sweat rolled down her back. Ward stoically leaned to kiss his common-law wife on the cheek, then got out of the wagon and retrieved her luggage and the baby's cradle from the back.

Frantic to try one more time, although she knew in her core that this gold-struck idea of a marriage would never bear fruit beyond the babe she had delivered from her loins in an outhouse, Charlotte cried, "What kind of life is this for your wife and son?"

"Charlotte, I'm not leaving forever. I'll be back as soon as I sell the mine. I need to work it so that it will look profitable to potential buyers. Perhaps I'll find gold while I'm waiting. Either way, I'll have money to spare when I return for you and the child. In the meantime, I'll know that you and the baby will be well fed. Even your father wouldn't turn his back on you with a child in your arms. Just promise me you won't resort to prostitution," Ward said in earnest.

"You may come for us only if you have pockets full of gold," Charlotte said, her face flushed with despair.

She felt abandoned, although Ward in his own heart thoroughly intended to return. Anguished, he watched Charlotte walk into the saloon with their son.

A week later, Ward was back at the mine, aimlessly kicking worthless rocks. He was discouraged and lonely, to boot. Although he and Charlotte were not a love match, she was at least a bit of company, and a decent cook, while the boy, his son, gave him a joy he had never known before. The two of them had borne a child together, and that tied them as family for eternity.

Footsteps suddenly woke Ward from his musings, footsteps that echoed around the ridge. Ward wondered at first if the steps might be Charlotte's sweet, tiny feet returning to him. Such was his lonely state, he would joyously welcome her back.

"Halloo, Charlotte, is that you?" he called, peering down the trail. But instead, Ward saw a shadowy figure that was somehow familiar. "You come to see the mine that's for sale?" Ward called out with a hint of fear in his voice.

Before Ward could comprehend what was happening, the figure raised a gun. After seeing a flash, Ward heard a loud, delayed bang. He grabbed his left arm, which stung like a nest of wasps had attacked him. Seconds later, another loud flash-bang came, and Ward grabbed his chest. This time, the wound felt like a pickaxe driven through his lungs. He felt out of breath and inhaled deeply, but found himself choking on blood. With thick red liquid gushing from his mouth, Ward fell into a ball of pain, knowing he was a dead man. He heard the stranger's footsteps draw nearer and saw a pair of boots. He strained to see the owner's face. His murderer glared sadistically, vengeance in his eyes. Oh, no! It was the evil rail worker from Gerard's Inn.

"I saw your mine is for sale. But with you dead, it'll be sold at auction for peanuts, and I'll be there to pick up the deed," the rail worker said.

In his agony, Ward exhaled a choked-out "Hah!" before dying. His face contorted in an ironic smile. He had been killed for the deed to a mine that was as worthless as the rocks lying beneath him.

❧

BILLY JAY READ the last action aloud. "Aw, Grand Pop. Why did you have to kill him?"

Andrew managed a nod in reply. "Crap. Huuuuuhhhh?"

"Darn it, I wanted Ward to find the gold," David said.

"Toooooooo, meeeeeeee."

"Why don't you let him? You can make your story turn out how you want!"

"David, it's a metaphor, isn't it, Grand Pop?" Billy Jay said.

Andrew nodded and grinned as if to say, "You got it right this time, son."

"Grand Pop is so old, he knows everything!" Elizabeth said.

Andrew laughed in a goofy stutter that the kids thought was funny. They giggled so hard and long, they couldn't catch their breath.

Even Andrew was caught up in the laughter. *What a wonderful invention grandchildren are. Three bright, beautiful, loving beings that emit such energy and life force — all descended from my loins,* he thought to himself. And then it hit him. *My line didn't stop with Billy's death. Janey's brood carries it forward.*

As the late afternoon sunlight glowed through the window, he felt its warmth and relished its radiance. He had been so blindsided by the loss of his son, he had not seen the others who would carry his life force into the next generation — each a child of water, sunlight, air, and memories.

Chapter Thirty-Four

ANDY

S unday after Otto's fish fry, everybody's so full, we're about to go to sleep. Even the adults are having a hard time stayin' awake.

Daddy yawns and says, "Hey, let's play some football to work off all this food."

Everybody groans, but the men and boys get up slow. Uncle Luke heads up the twenty-two steps to get a football and, before you know it, two teams face off on the wide stretch of grass beside the shoreline.

Daddy, Tommy, Uncle Luke, and me are on one team, and Danny, Otto, Normie, and Danny's sister Elle are on the other. She's the only girl, but she's grown up and tall, a big girl like her mother Anna. Even more, Elle's name fits the family joke. I never found out why Howie didn't get one of the forward-backward names.

We line up and play for fun at first. But the game gets rough after both teams score. We've got the ball back, but our running game is lousy. Elle turns out to be a real maniac and tackles everybody, even us younger boys.

Daddy says in the huddle, "Com'on, boys. We can't let that girlie team beat us."

Tommy laughs. "I'll get free, Daddy. Throw a long one and I'll take it home."

"You go down the right side, Tommy. I'll run down the left. That way, Daddy will have two shots at a touchdown."

Uncle Luke hikes the ball, and I run down the left side as Elle passes me. On the right side, Normie and Danny double-team Tommy.

I holler, "Here, Daddy. Here I am!" and hold up my hands.

Daddy throws long, and I see the tan oval spiral my way. A high pass, way too high. I leap best I can, but the ball barely tips my hands. I still try to catch it as it flies by, but I fall squish into Mr. Ground's septic tank grass. Damn.

Behind me, Elle intercepts Daddy's pass and pivots on her long legs to run back for a touchdown. The other team hoots and hollers, and my gut feels like I might heave my fried fish.

Daddy starts a long "boo" that lasts about a minute. At first, I think his jeers are for Elle, but then I realize they are for me. Downfield, I see his glare.

I holler, "The pass was too high, Daddy," but he just glares. *Not fair*, my gut says. *Not fair.*

That night, I can't sleep. My mind replays Daddy's pass. I imagine myself leaping high enough to catch it and win the game. Daddy would be so proud of me then.

Chapter Thirty-Five

NOVEMBER 2

When Lizzy came into the sunroom the next morning, she opened the drapes with a flourish. "Good morning, dear. The weather's sunny and cool. Lovely, for a change."

Andrew silently flailed the air with his left hand, his eyes full of anguish as Lizzy hovered, knowing this was another major TIA, or worse, feeling that Andrew's spirit had drifted too far for her to reach him the way she could so long ago.

"Oh, Andrew. I'm not ready to let you go."

Chapter Thirty-Six

NOVEMBER 11

After another two-day stay in the ICU, followed by a brief assessment in rehab, Andrew came home for good on a sunny November afternoon, just two weeks before Thanksgiving. He would be home for the holidays this time, Lizzy had told Ouisie earlier that morning.

As Alan drove the minivan from the hospital, Lizzy admired the glorious display of fall colors from the sugar maples and black walnut trees that dotted her street. "What a glorious homecoming, Andrew," she said in a cheery attempt.

Earlier, Dr. Fitzgerald had signed Andrew's release papers and told Lizzy, "We'll see him twice weekly for PT, but Mrs. Ward, I don't think you should expect a full recovery. Again, the good news is that he can breathe on his own. He can swallow, he can use a urinal, and a bedpan. These are major things, believe me. And your daughter has hired Jefferson full-time. Otherwise, I would place Andrew in assisted living."

"I will never allow that," Lizzy huffed.

"If things get too much, I will help you find a facility."

"We will let you know, Doctor," Jane said as Lizzy shook her head no.

The doctor gave Lizzy a pat that as much as said *I'm very sorry.*

As soon as the family was back at the house, Jefferson settled Andrew in the sunroom bed, then went to gather ice, towels, straws, and washcloths.

Andrew's left hand struggled to reach the iPad that Jane had positioned nearby before she and Alan left for work.

Lizzy noticed. "Do you want me to help you?"

Andrew struggled to issue an affirmative, "Damn it."

Lizzy took that as a yes. She stepped on the lever that elevated Andrew's bed to an upright position. Then Lizzy placed the iPad on his chest. His left hand shuddered with the effort. Lizzy did not have a clue how to operate the contraption and did not realize that Andrew needed the stylus pointer.

Lizzy called down the hallway, "Jefferson, do you know how to operate this?"

Andrew tried to say, "stylus," but said, "Stinker, damn it."

Lizzy thought he had called her a name, so she got in a fluster and pushed the iPad nearer Andrew's left hand.

"Stinker, bitch!"

She tried not to get angry. "No need to swear. Billy Jay will come after school to help."

When Jefferson returned, Lizzy quickly escaped as if all were well. But as she went down the hall, she felt tears sting her eyes. *Andrew may not be able to get better.*

Later, from the kitchen, Lizzy heard the front door open.

"Gizzy? Mom said you needed to hire me." Billy Jay went to the sunroom and heaved out a prepared statement. "Mom says you can't talk much except swear, but maybe you can point your stylus."

Walter shuffled from under Andrew's bed to greet Billy Jay.

Andrew perked up. His left hand trembled.

"Okay, Grand Pop. I'll get things going." Billy Jay put the stylus in Andrew's left hand and guided it to turn on the iMac.

Andrew managed an "Uhhhhhhhh" as the iMac came on.

"Bingo!" Billy Jay slapped Andrew a bit too hard on the shoulder.

"Goddamn."

"Sorry, Grand Pop. Let's open Word."

"Shit fire!" Andrew let Billy take the stylus.

"Word says you were on Chapter Six."

Andrew angrily shook his head. "Damn no."

"That was the most recent chapter."

Andrew grunted and swore as he struggled to aim the stylus at the "New Document" icon.

Billy Jay was confused. "You wanna start a new chapter?"

"Damn, no!" Tears brimmed in Andrew's eyes.

"I can't understand you, Grand Pop. Just do what you want and make a loud noise when you need me." Billy Jay sank sullenly into Lizzy's desk chair.

Walter headed back under the bed.

"Tank shit," Andrew growled.

Billy Jay grinned in relief. He understood his grandfather meant "thank you." After that, Billy Jay's philosophy was to let the old guy go for it. Grand Pop would figure things out. "Hey, how much are you paying me?"

Andrew managed a garbled "Zulch" and a grin. Then he focused on the intense effort required to position his stylus where he wanted it to point.

Billy Jay slid under the bed to play with Walter.

Andrew arduously pointed the stylus letter to letter. On the iMac display, a bit of lower case text appeared, "to lizzy wife, lizzy".

Although this was a simple phrase, Andrew took an hour to complete it. In fact, sunset had transformed his workshop outside from a flare of afternoon brilliance to a golden orange and then a deep silver-blue by the time Lizzy walked in with a dinner tray of applesauce, yogurt, and broth.

"Time for dinner. I know you won't like it, but you need it."

She put the tray beside Andrew's bed, then leaned to peek under it, where she found Billy Jay curled up asleep. Walter was his pillow. "Some helper, eh? You can't see this from here, but the boy is sound asleep on Walter."

Andrew became flustered. He did not want Lizzy to see the text on the iMac screen. He jabbed the stylus but could not turn off the computer. He stared at Lizzy and wondered if he should swear at her to distract her.

"Billy Jay, it's dinner time. Do you want something to eat?"

"Mom said she'd come get me," the boy answered sleepily.

As if on cue, Lizzy heard Jane's minivan pull into the drive and the door slam.

"There she is now!" Billy Jay rushed to greet his mother.

When Lizzy followed, Andrew heaved a sigh of relief.

"How is he today?" Jane whispered to Lizzy as she let her in the front door.

"He can barely move a finger, but seems able to work on something."

"I thought Billy Jay could help."

"He got the machines started, but Andrew's pretty frustrated."

Jane was dismayed. Lizzy gave her daughter the look of a woman who had accepted the future but wanted to protect the daughter who had not. Lizzy put her arm around Jane's shoulder as the two women walked to the sunroom. She thought perhaps she would suggest a mother-daughter talk, but then Lizzy suddenly remembered that she needed a spoon for Andrew's dinner.

"The spoons, the spoons are calling me to the kitchen!" With dramatic flair, Lizzy danced sideways down the hall and warbled a spot-on imitation of Ethel Thayer, played by Katherine Hepburn in the film version of *On Golden Pond*.

"Momma should have been an actress."

"Joan," Andrew said, but he wanted to say, "Joanne."

"No, she was doing Katherine Hepburn."

"Joan Woodshit," Andrew stuttered, trying to say, "Joanne Woodward."

"Joan Woodshit?"

Andrew swore in frustration.

Billy Jay wanted to escape. "Mom, I'll be out in the car." But he had a guilty afterthought, "I'll see you tomorrow, Grand Pop."

"Shit right," Andrew blurted with a hint of a smile.

"How are you feeling, Poppa? Were you able to work on your novel?" Jane asked.

"Damn no."

"Momma said you got the computer going?"

"Damn right."

"Would you like me to help you?"

"Damn no!" Andrew shook in agitation. His daughter was the more likely one to peer at the iMac to see what he had written, so Andrew stabbed his stylus and struggled to scroll the text off the iMac screen. He sighed in relief and swore again.

Jane realized he had sworn *at* her this time. "I know you're struggling, Poppa, but I — " She methodically closed the door, then sat on the edge of Andrew's bed. She took his left hand in hers, stylus and all. "This is hard for me, Poppa, but I want to say something. Please try to understand."

Andrew kept his grip on the stylus until he realized Jane had no desire to see what he had written. Instead, she seemed intent on making eye contact with him. The touch of her soft hands was the touch of a mother, his daughter, surely, but a woman who had taken the hand of a diminished male. She held his hand in such a persistent way, he knew he had to stop and listen.

In a low voice, Jane recited the words she had practiced on her way over. "Poppa, I want you to know that I love you. And I hope you get well. But in case, well, sometimes it's important to say things to people you love, like you're trying to do for Momma. But what I've got to say is for my brother Billy, too. I hope you will understand."

Andrew nodded and grunted.

"My biggest regret when Billy died was that I didn't say goodbye. I know you also felt that way, but if you — I know you're not a religious man — but if you find a heaven-like place, a spirit land, or some electronic universe where you can interact with Billy's spirit, please tell him, Poppa, that I loved him and still do. He was my hero, my big brother, and shining star. And please tell him I kept my promise. He'll know what I'm talking about. I miss him so. And I love you both very much." Jane shuddered as she bent over Andrew's chest in tears. When she lifted to look in his eyes, Andrew's face displayed so much concern that Jane mistook it for confusion. She blubbered loudly, "Do you understand what I'm saying?"

Andrew gave her an affirmative nod and gripped her hand as best he could.

Both sets of eyes flooded with tears. Jane leaned again and hugged her father.

Just then, Lizzy opened the door and breezed in with the spoons. "The spoons are welcoming you home, Andrew."

"Oh, Momma!" Jane hid her tears as she rushed out.

Lizzy called out for her to come back, but Lizzy heard the front door close, and then Jane's car engine. "What in the world? Did you say something to hurt her feelings? Did you swear?"

Andrew avoided Lizzy's eyes, but she could see that his were full of tears.

"Oh dear, I must have interrupted something. I'm sorry. This situation is too much for Jane, and especially for you." She patted Andrew's shoulder and pecked him on his cheek, looking into his tearful eyes with the understanding only a wife can give.

THROUGH THE EVENING, Andrew struggled with the iPad. Instead of writing his novel, he wrote a note to Billy Jay.

On the iMac display, the text began, "Billy Jay room living get the".

The complete note took Andrew another exhausting hour. He fell to sleep with the stylus still in his hand.

Lizzy peeked in after her bath and saw Andrew asleep with his iPad and stylus still on his lap. She worried that moving the devices might ruin his work, but also feared the stylus might poke him, or Andrew might crack the iPad's screen if he turned over.

So, like a girl playing pick-up sticks, Lizzy plucked the pieces from Andrew's lap and put them on the desk. She glanced at the iMac display to see if she should turn that off. But, like Andrew, the iMac had gone to sleep. So, she tiptoed back and kissed her husband lightly. When she pulled away, his face seemed to glow with the joy of a child. She turned off the lamp and left Andrew to his rest.

Chapter Thirty-Seven

NOVEMBER 12

The following afternoon, when Billy Jay came over, Andrew pointed his stylus toward the printer.

Billy Jay picked up the page Andrew had printed the night before and read it to himself. "Okay, Grand Pop, I'll get it." The boy sauntered off to the living room.

Andrew sighed in relief and rested on the pillow. He closed his eyes and waited for Billy Jay. There was one more page to print. Billy Jay would take care of the rest. Andrew was weary, but he would stay alert until his work was done.

Chapter Thirty-Eight

ANDY

As I saw a piece of wood in the garage, Tommy's pissed 'cause I won't let him help. He hears Momma's voice coming and hollers, "Momma, you gotta *do* something about Andy."

Momma walks into the garage and sighs. "You, two boys. Oil and water. What's Andy up to now?"

"He's making a mess out of Daddy's tools."

"I'm building a boat," I say.

"I'm gonna tell Daddy," Tommy whines.

"Now, Tommy, this is just scrap wood that Andy's sawing. Why don't you help your brother? Make it a project for you boys to work on together?"

"I don't want Tommy to help. This is my boat."

"Andy, I understand, but you should let Tommy help."

"This is *my* boat." I start crying.

"That's fine, 'cause I don't want to make any stupid boat with a crybaby."

"Tommy, be nice to your little brother."

"I'll go fishin' with Danny. He's not a crybaby."

Tommy runs out.

My angry tears spew. I stare at my boat through pools of liquid. I hope Momma will leave too, 'cause I want to make the boat myself, sail it myself, and get the heck away from Tommy, Momma, Daddy, and everybody.

"What kind of boat are you making, Andy?"

"A ship. A sailing ship." I sniffle a bit.

"May I help? I put things together pretty well."

I don't want Momma to stay, but I figure I gotta say yes. After all, she is my main line of defense. "Okay," I say, but not like I really want her help.

"You've already got a hull, and you did a fine job sawing that. This dowel rod can be good for a mast. And we can use this old red rag for a sail."

"It's gotta have more sails than that."

"What kind of sailing ship did you have in mind?"

"An explorer ship."

"Oh, a big ship with lots of sails. I think my grandfather would call that a square-rigger. He was a lieutenant commander in the Navy. Served on the *U.S.S. Greenwood* in the Pacific during World War II. That's a destroyer escort. Anyway, his son, my father, also taught me a lot about ships and navy things like tying knots."

"Momma, you brag all the time about your daddy's knots." I rummage around the garage while Momma works. I don't want her to take over my project, but my pride in "my" boat grows as I see her build an actual ship before my eyes.

Momma cuts pieces of dowel for two masts and the "yards," she calls 'em, the crosspieces that hold the sails onto the masts. She drills holes in the board that I sawed and sticks the dowel rods in with some wood putty she finds. Then she nails the yards to the masts, cuts six rectangles out of the red rags, and attaches them to the yards with brass tacks and string. When she finishes, my ship has two tall masts and six red, rectangular sails.

"Let's see if your ship is seaworthy."

"Now?"

"Yes, if you want to, Andy. She's your ship."

"I want to put a message on it too. A message in a bottle."

"Well, it's got to be a little bottle. We don't want your ship to be top-heavy or unbalanced. Let's see what we can find." Momma rummages through some drawers and finds a small, corked vial that holds rusty screws. "Here, Andy. Let's clean this up and put your message in here."

"First, I gotta write it." With that, I run out of the garage, then up the twenty-two steps, then inside to the sunroom, where I write my secret note on a torn piece of yellow paper. I roll it tightly to fit in the vial, then head back down.

"May I read it?" Momma says after I get back.

Momma's always snooping. "It's a secret!"

"All right, Andy. Now, let's attach the bottle to the mainmast and send your ship on her maiden voyage." Momma tapes the vial to the dowel rod with thin strips of duct tape.

Then Momma and I march out and over the gravel road and lawn, then down the weathered dock where Tommy, Danny, and Normie are fishin' for crappie with cane poles.

Momma holds my ship for everyone to see.

"Pretty neat, Andy. Ya gonna launch her?" Danny says.

"If Andy made it, that dang thing will sink like a rock."

"I helped build this masterpiece, Tommy, so you better hope it sails like a dream. This ship is called a square-rigger," Momma says.

"Is that her name?" Danny says.

"Oh, we didn't think about that. What do you want to name your ship, Andy?"

I think for a moment. "*The Noreen*."

"Sugar tit," Tommy mutters, loud enough for everybody to hear.

Nobody but him laughs, and Momma glares at Tommy.

"I am honored, Andy," she says as she gives me a hug. "If we had champagne, we could sprinkle *The Noreen* when we launch her."

Danny holds up a half-full green bottle. "I've got some Coca-Cola left."

"Coke is perfect. I'll pour while Andy repeats after me. Say this, Andy: 'I, Andrew Ward, Admiral of the Lake Blackshear Fleet, hereby commission this vessel in the service of the state of Georgia and the United States of America. I name this ship, *The Noreen*. And God bless all who sail in her.'"

As Momma dribbles Coke over my ship and pauses between each phrase, I repeat each section. Then I squat to set *The Noreen* on the dirt-green water.

Within a few seconds, the breeze catches, and my ship tilts on her way. She bobbles on waves near shore. Then, as the breezes fill her red sails, she angles out toward the main lake. We four boys and Momma watch *The Noreen* weave her way between cypress tree stumps.

"Let's see if we can keep an eye on her," Danny says.

With that, we jog along the shore but stop now and then to spot *The Noreen*. Yes, there she is, my square-rigger with a secret message. She gets smaller in my vision as she bobbles further out. By the time the sunlight fades to gray shadows, and Momma calls a halt, all I can make out is *The Noreen's* tiny silhouette.

Suddenly, I realize I will never see *The Noreen* again. "She's too far out! Maybe Danny and I can take Otto's boat out to get her."

"You don't build a ship to keep her in dry dock. She's a fine vessel. And maybe another boy across the lake will find her and sail her back with another message when the winds shift. You keep your eyes peeled, Andy. You never know. You might see her again."

Chapter Thirty-Nine

DECEMBER 2

A t the Druid Hills Unitarian Universalist Church, Lizzy sat beside Ouisie and Guy, both dressed in black. Also for the event, Ouisie had dyed her hair fully black again, removing her blond and strawberry highlights.

When Lizzy noticed, Ouisie murmured, "This is a sober moment, and I wanted to honor my dear friends."

Dressed in a black robe, Byron led the congregation in reciting alternate lines of Reading #720, "We Remember Them," from *Singing the Living Tradition.*

"In the rising of the sun and in its going down, we remember them," the minister said.

"In the blowing of the wind and in the chill of winter, we remember them," the congregation recited back.

In front of the minister, a chalice was alight with flame.

"In the opening of buds and in the rebirth of spring, we remember them."

On a pedestal beside the chalice, an ornate wooden box with a bronze plaque read, "Andrew Comstock Ward, Professor Emeritus," along with the dates of his birth, his tenure at Emory University, and his death.

"In the blueness of the sky and in the warmth of summer, we remember them."

In Lizzy's memories, she recalled dancing in her aqua taffeta dress with Andrew.

Jane, Alan, and the kids sat beside Lizzy, dressed in their Sunday best. Andrew's brother Thomas, his wife Rhonda, sister Sarah, and her four adult sons sat in row four, as well as Lizzy's brothers Yates and Louis with their wives, scattered adult children, and grandchildren. Former colleagues from Emory, students from Andrew's teaching days, and members of Lizzy's book club and piano class had squeezed into the remaining pews and chairs.

"In the rustling of leaves and in the beauty of autumn, we remember them."

An image flashed through Lizzy's mind of Andrew as he walked with Walter to the workshop. Their feet rustled in the brilliant autumn leaves.

"In the beginning of the year and when it ends, we remember them," the voices read.

Lizzy imagined Andrew curled close, like spoons when they were young and even when they were old.

"When we are weary and in need of strength, we remember them."

"When we are lost and sick at heart, we remember them," all said together.

Lizzy recalled the night she and Andrew had held one another and sobbed in grief over Billy's death. Despite her determination not to cry at this service, Lizzy wept anew.

Ouisie handed her a Kleenex and patted her skirted thigh.

"When we have joys we yearn to share, we remember them."

Through her tears, Lizzy suddenly smiled as she recalled the night the wingback chair had caught fire, when she and Andrew laughed so hard they could not stop. They had hugged each other and laughed while Billy gawked with a teenager's incredulity.

"So long as we live, they too shall live, for they are now a part of us, as we remember them," the congregation read together.

Many sniffs and blows of noses filled the sanctuary. Byron instructed the congregation to light a candle at the railings beside the side windows. The pianist played Claude Debussy's *Claire de Lune* as Lizzy lit four candles, one for Andrew, Jane, Billy, and herself. She said a silent prayer and took a deep breath to keep her emotions in check.

When she returned to her pew, she cast her eyes on the bas-relief sculpture on the wall and took solace in the carving's lovely ovals that represented the interconnectivity of life, faith, and humanity. Who said that Unitarian Universalism meant one had no faith? At that moment, Lizzy felt an all-encompassing faith in the spiritual connectivity of humanity.

~

LIZZY WAS grateful for such a bright December afternoon.

Crowded into the family home for a reception, Guy, Ouisie, Byron, family, many colleagues, former students, and Lizzy's new friends mingled over hors d'oeuvres and drinks. Many exchanged memories with Jane and Lizzy.

In the backyard, Alan engaged the grandsons in a game of catch with Andrew's old baseball mitt and ball. Between throws, Alan sent Walter to fetch a frayed tennis ball.

Inside, little Elizabeth heaped olives and pickles onto a plate, but noticed that Gizzy had seen her. Afraid, Elizabeth put her plate down and shied away.

"Elizabeth, I'm not upset with you."

"Momma told me not to eat a lot of sweet pickles, but I just love them, Gizzy."

"Me too, Elizabeth. Don't tell your momma, but you have my permission to enjoy them all you want today."

"Oh, good. I got scared when you stared at me."

"I wasn't staring, or I didn't mean to. You see, when I look so closely at you, I'm remembering what it was like to be a young girl. I'm seeing through your eyes how it feels to be your age again. You might think it's great to be a grown-up, but not always."

Elizabeth nodded silently, although she did not understand.

"You're probably sad that your Grand Pop died, and confused or frightened by death. Or maybe you're a bit jealous, because the boys are playing ball outside."

"Yes, ma'am." Elizabeth looked down at her pickles.

"When I was your age, I had two older brothers too. They seemed to do grand things, while I was the youngest and only girl. Lots of times, I had to play by myself. My brothers seemed so much bigger and smarter. I used to sneak into their rooms while they were gone and play with their stuff. I'd get in trouble when they found out, but oh, how I loved to play army men."

"You did, Gizzy?"

"Yes, but my brothers didn't get to do everything. I loved to help my mother on holidays, making fancy cookies or stuffing the turkey. And there was one thing I loved that the boys hated: sweet midget gherkins like the ones on your plate. I also loved ripe olives, but not the ones with pits. So, every holiday, my mother and I put out a silver plate with olives and pickles, just like this platter today. I'd sneak as many as I could before dinner. And I promised always to remember what it was like to be a young girl. So, when I saw you with your pickles, I was a little girl again, sneaking treats."

"You were?"

"I was. Just like you."

"Oh, Gizzy. I love you lots and lots and lots." Elizabeth gave Gizzy a hug.

As Lizzy held her granddaughter close, she spotted Byron in a corner of the dining room, where he whispered intimately to the overdressed office manager that Ouisie had labeled "The Bimbo." The two were a couple, and Lizzy had to chuckle, since Byron didn't appear to be the type who would court such a floozy.

Aghast that this woman had shown up at Andrew's wake, Ouisie strode over to Lizzy and whispered in her ear, "She rode here with him in his car."

Lizzy acknowledged Ouisie's remark with a cursory nod and moved down the hallway. Today, of all days, Lizzy was not in the spirit for Ouisie's perpetual church gossip. After all, Byron had been there when Lizzy needed someone. If the man had a girlfriend, then he had a girlfriend, floozy or not, and the board could accept that and move on.

Lizzy cast her eyes down the hallway to the sunroom where she had found Andrew three mornings before, cold and stiff, with his eyes closed in peaceful relief. She did not call 911 but simply sat at her husband's side. She wept deeply and watched out the back window until the sun rose beyond the treetops. As the light beamed onto her mirror, then out to the workshop, Lizzy positioned herself inside the glow and felt its warmth radiate as she became one with the light and her husband's spirit.

After she eventually called 911, Lizzy found out how much bureaucratic chaos reigned when someone died at home. First, the police arrived to determine if the death appeared to be from natural causes, then a coroner took Andrew's body for an autopsy. All sorts of records had to be signed and filed with the county.

Then there was the visit with the funeral home to arrange cremation, and Lizzy became miffed at the funeral director, who pressured her to buy a sterling silver urn.

"Just a nice wooden box, please. After all, we're not serving him for high tea."

"Now, Momma." Jane patted her mother's shoulders.

"Mrs. Ward, I know you've been through a lot, especially with a home death. The bureaucratic paperwork is simpler when the beloved dies in the hospital," the funeral director had said.

"I'm pleased that Andrew died where he loved being, at home with me."

~

THROUGHOUT THE AFTERNOON of Andrew's reception, Lizzy found herself torn between the role of hostess and bereaved widow.

She wanted her guests to enjoy themselves and commemorate Andrew's life and work, but she was emotionally exhausted and could not wait until everyone left, except then she would be alone.

Thomas and Rhonda chatted in the living room with Sarah and her sons. As they went through scrapbooks, Thomas pointed to photos of himself and Andrew.

"You both were so skinny," Rhonda said.

"We swam and fished until we dropped. Those were the days. Kids today, well, they don't have the same opportunities. We didn't have smartphones, so we made up games, like hop, skip, and jump on the railroad tracks."

"Railroad tracks! If kids did that today, someone would sue!" Rhonda said.

"In those days, we knew when the trains came. The rest of the time, the rails were a great place. We hopped and skipped for miles. Got so hot we'd run and jump in the lake. I'll never forget those times. When my grandparents sold that ramshackle place to developers, my heart broke. There's a mansion there now. If it comes up for sale, I'll buy it. Buy all the houses on that cove, just for the memories."

Thomas' eyes filled with tears.

"Andrew used to tell me so many stories about the lake, I felt like I was there. I'm sorry you two never shared your memories. He treasured those times. Do you remember Andy's ship he made with Noreen, or the time he caught his first fish?"

"Ah, Andy's fish. Mother made such a big deal. He was just a little guy, maybe six. But somehow, he caught a fish and started hollering down by the shore. Mother ran down and rescued him and his little crappie, not six inches long. But Mother filleted that sorry fish, breaded it up, and fried it for Andy. She always made a big production over him. He was her baby boy, while I was expected to be the grown-up one, take the lead."

"Andy always thought your daddy favored you. And he regretted that you two were not closer," Lizzy said, although part of that was a white lie.

"Oil and water don't mix, no matter how hard you shake. Mother always favored Andy."

"I can't imagine a mother loving one child more than the others," Lizzy said.

Rhonda nodded, as did Sarah. "I had four boys and not one is my favorite, although one has caused a bit more of a stir than the others." She smiled and patted one son's knee.

Thomas shook his head. "That may be true for you ladies, but not for our mother."

"But Thomas, you and your father were close. Andrew always wanted your father's attention, but felt he only had time for you."

"Dad worked too hard. That's why I wanted more and wanted Andy to have more."

"Andrew did just fine. He may not have been a wealthy man like you, but he enjoyed being a professor. And his work will live on. He wrote a novel, you know." Lizzy looked as if she was about to invite Thomas to see it.

Jane interrupted. "Momma, I wouldn't —"

"Wouldn't what?"

"Well, I don't mean to interrupt, but your minister is leaving out the back door. Maybe you should see him off." Jane ushered Lizzy to the kitchen, where Jane discovered Elizabeth by the bay window with a pile of sweet pickles, ripe olives, and now brownies on her plate. "Elizabeth, you'll make yourself sick."

"But Mom, Gizzy said I could!"

"Jane, did you do the buffet?" Ouisie interrupted, eager for another peek at the minister before he left.

"Whole Foods Catering and the UU women's group did everything."

"A lovely banquet."

"Thank you, Aunt Ouisie. You and Uncle Guy have been such good friends to Momma and Poppa, and to our family."

Lizzy headed out the back door where the minister had parked in front of the garage. "Byron, before you go, please — " Lizzy rushed over and hugged him. "I want to thank you again for your counsel."

"It was my pleasure, Lizzy. Did you ever put in a good word with the president?"

"The First Lady, anyway."

"Looks like I may need it," Byron said with a sigh.

"I don't know if this would help your cause, but you might rehire the previous office manager. There was a lot of concern when you let her go and hired your, shall I say, 'lady friend'?"

"That's it? Does it matter that the woman I fired was stealing from the collection? I didn't want to send her to jail, so I let her go."

"Maybe it's time to clear the air, confidentially, of course."

"I gotcha, Lizzy. And thanks for *your* counsel," Byron said as he got in his car.

Alan took a breather from his game with the boys. He sat and watched them play catch. Ready for a rest himself, Walter sauntered over and lay down. "Had enough, old man?" Alan stroked the dog's head. Walter panted as if "yes" was his reply.

David called, "Come on, Walter! Here, boy."

"You boys give him a break. Remember, he's old," Lizzy said.

"Gizzy, if Walter keeled over and died today, that would be a metaphor," Billy Jay said.

Alan grinned. "Looks like Andrew taught his grandsons a thing or two."

Suddenly, Jane called in a frantic voice from the back door. "Momma, Thomas and Rhonda are leaving."

Lizzy rushed back into the living room, where she found the two in their overcoats. "Thomas, Rhonda, you're not leaving already."

"Well, I — " Thomas paused.

Rhonda whispered to Lizzy. "Thomas doesn't feel that Andrew would want him here."

"Thomas, you and I have had uncomfortable moments, but there's no reason for you to leave. You are Andrew's family."

"Lizzy, this is Andrew's house, and I know he does not want me in it. But I need to say something to you." Thomas inhaled as if gathering oxygen for courage. "I want to apologize to you for my behavior when Andy was in the hospital. I, well, I'm sorry if I caused you discomfort. Andrew, our estrangement. I wanted to set things right, but realized I could not. Too much water." He paused, unable to communicate the thoughts that rushed through his mind. Abruptly, he headed for the door.

"Thank you for everything, Lizzy," Rhonda stepped in to say. She grabbed Lizzy's hand and shook it limply. "We hope you will stay in touch."

Thomas rushed out in a blur, his silver-topped head bent forward. Rhonda hurried behind him as Lizzy waved to their backs. She could see Thomas was in tears and felt dismay at the futility of two brothers who had competed for their father's love, a father who did not deserve their lifelong struggle.

After Thomas drove away, Lizzy and Jane said goodbye to Andrew's sister and her sons. Then Jane headed down the hallway to the sunroom.

Curious, Lizzy followed.

"Makes me sad to look in here," Jane said.

"Me too, honey."

"I'll stay tonight to keep you company. First thing tomorrow, I'll take all this down, so you'll have your sunroom back."

AFTER ALL THE guests had said their goodbyes, a weary Alan loaded the kids into the minivan, looking like he was destined for another viewing of *Master and Commander* as soon as he got the kids bathed and in bed.

From the front porch, Jane and Lizzy waved as he drove away.

Back in the house, Lizzy headed to the kitchen. "The church ladies did a good job, but gosh, there's so much that still needs to be put away."

"Oh, leave it, Momma. I'll help you tomorrow. I just want a hot bath and a dish of chocolate ice cream."

"Maybe I'll join you after I tidy up. Byron told me I should reward myself after cooking and doing housework. Good medicine."

"I could use a dose of that. How about you tidy up the kitchen, and I'll take out the devices in the sunroom. Then we'll do our ice cream."

"What about Andrew's novel?"

"I'm no literary genius, but it's like a bad TV Western, hokey with imagery and metaphors. Maybe you can decipher what he tried to say."

"I'd cry all over the pages. In time, I'll take a look, a long time from now. I need to put one foot in front of the other. Forward motion. Don't look back. Stay busy, then reward myself."

"That's it! You're my next pupil. We'll keep the network and iMac in the sunroom, and I'll teach you the Internet for e-mail, banking, Facebook, oh my gosh. Breakfast and holiday recipes!"

"Wouldn't Andrew get a laugh out of that?"

While Jane took a long soak in the tub, Lizzy cleaned up the kitchen. To reward herself, she sat at the piano and picked out an improved rendition of "April Love," her voice rising in passion at the verse about love slipping through fingers. As usual, memories of the long-ago dance filtered through her reverie. She went to the bookcase and opened the yearbook to find her corsage once again, along with the dance invitation.

A folded piece of white paper slipped to the floor.

"What's this?" Lizzy picked it up. As she read, her lips quivered.

Moments later, Jane shuffled in with two dishes of ice cream. With her wet hair twisted in a towel, Jane was wrapped in Andrew's "Professor Grand Pop" robe, and she wore his tattered leather slippers.

"Here's your ice cream."

Lizzy was too choked up to answer.

Jane set the dishes on the piano. "What's the matter, Momma?"

Lizzy handed her the paper. Jane scanned it, confused by the disjointed phrases. Then she reread each one aloud, as Lizzy murmured what Andrew had told her about each word or line. By

Jane's third reading, Andrew's voice seemed to radiate through the aphasic prose, and both women felt his spirit enfolding them.

~

TO LIZZY WIFE, *lizzy I apology leave.*

Billy for, sorry am I. Never said. Could never. Darkest sorrow. You knew.

To you leave I memories gold dust velvet sky.

You, dancing Lizzy. Aqua shimmers, white corsage. Green eyes bright hope.

Our Billy. Hair sunlight. Eyes sky morning. Blue white jacket. Cheeks flush. Swirling green storm. Gone! Black despair.

Our Janey. Like Momma smart. Like Momma curvy. Puzzle solver. Walter beard doughnut dust. Workshop. Pal.

Workshop beam mirror. Reflections divided reunited.

Lake summers mossy cypress trees Daddy's chain saw fuming.

Sunlight flicker water. White caps shimmer. Chris Craft humming. 22 steps. Green lawn. Thump thump dock. Bonsai!

Silver canoe. Dive! Periscope! Danny sounds. Sparkle waves cool roll break.

First fish green silver flapping round sunlight flashes.

Momma bed driving. Pow! Splat mattress. Country store candies. Tommy tell. No!

Locomotive roar midnight shake walls click clack, click clack gone.

New Tommy bike. Christmas scream! Momma running red Jell-O wings angel green.

Momma explorer ship red sails message bottle: "Wish love Daddy me."

Bed, Lizzy, curves, green flowers delight. You for, deepest love give I.

Janey, Miss Analyst, love much. For help, progeny, thank you.

My bright pennies. Found.

Billy waits. I wait you. Remember love ours,

Andrew

A CONVERSATION WITH THE AUTHOR

1. Where did you get the idea for this novel?

In grad school at the University of Missouri, Kansas City, I was struggling in my first creative writing class. I'd taken it on a whim. My first short story received a "C," which was like a knife in my heart. I'm a competitive spirit and wanted to do this thing well: create characters who were alive with the joys and sorrows of life. My next assignment was to write opening paragraphs to four different novels, each with unique narrative voices.

I was so nervous I could barely type, so I loosened my inhibitions by having a beer. When I began writing the first-person segment, the character of Andrew spoke to me, saying, "I'm not concerned about getting old and bald and fat. I rather expected to be. But what concerns me are my memories. Who will have them when I'm gone? Not memories of me, mind you, but my own memories."

When I presented this paragraph to the class, a classmate shouted, "But that's Proust!" — as though I had plagiarized the famous author. But I had never read Proust. Regardless, the idea of communicating one's memories stuck with me. Over time, I wanted to help Andrew convey his. The story has changed along the way, with the addition of robust characters in wife Lizzy, daughter Jane, best friends, and Black Americans, Ouisie and Guy, and the grandkids. In the end, it has become a family story, with communication and forgiveness at its core.

2. Did you always want to become an author?

No, although people say you should do the first thing you try as a child. For me, that was trying to write a neighborhood newsletter on my parents' typewriter. Other than that, I had few aspirations. Mother simply told my sister and me, "Get a teaching degree, just in case." Later on, I thought I might like to be a hairstylist. I was known for cutting bobs in the dorm at Southern Methodist University. But I always excelled in English classes, and writing came easily. I used to bang out college papers moments before class and usually made good grades.

3. Did you major in creative writing?

I left SMU after one year. So, my first college major was in physical education at the University of Missouri, Kansas City. I thought I might coach high school swimming, but I kept taking English classes. One of my freshman comp teachers took me aside and persuaded me to look at an English major. So, I signed up for American Literature and Creative Writing classes, and that's where I met Professor James C. McKinley. He was brilliant, articulate, and funny as hell. I followed him from class to class, like some sort of academic groupie, not for romantic interest, but for his intellectual magnetism. The classes I took with Jim and the friends I made in the English department became my energy source. So, I changed my major.

4. Is this your first novel?

No. After I earned my bachelor's and master's degrees, I tried to publish a novel during the late 1980s, but it was an amateurish work based on my 17 years as the wife of an NFL (pro football) quarterback. Probably because of the commercial aspect, it was almost published. "Almost" was the key word. After a divorce, I had three children to support. So, I went into public relations and advertising, and sidelined the fiction until I retired.

5. Have you written other novels?

Out and In is a mystery-thriller with a female sleuth. The story has heavy doses of character development and romance, along with an exciting plot. I wanted it to be something to enjoy by the pool, but I also wanted it to have heart. It was fun to write, and I've recently completed the sequel, titled *Ice and Fire*. It's set on Hawaiʻi's Big Island and has a backdrop of the global astronomy community.

After *Out and In*, however, I wrote *Backstory*. It falls into "literary suspense." It's an emotional portrait of a Texas single mom's quest to find new love and success as a Hollywood screenwriter, but she doesn't realize a murderer is stalking her and her oldest daughter. It's a bit raunchy, but it's funny, poignant, scary, and romantic too. And it won an award: Honorable Mention in the Contemporary Fiction category for the *Writer's Digest* Self-Published E-book Awards, 2021.

7. Any screenplays?

Unless I land a Hollywood agent or get the attention of a studio film producer, authors like me find it tough to get a movie deal. But who knows? One can dream. Until then, I am honored whenever anyone reads my books.

8. How can readers get in touch?

For information about speaking engagements, book signings, or screen rights, please go to PatDunlapEvans.com, click on the "Contact Pat" icon, and provide your details.

ACKNOWLEDGMENTS

For the encouragement and support of my husband, William M. Evans, M.D., I am grateful. Many thanks also to developmental editor Jean Jenkins for her guidance and praise. I was very sad to learn that Jean has passed away.

My Dallas advertising buddy Pam Boyd Roberts and I sweated the book cover via many e-mails and phone calls, while the keyboard mastery of fellow author Tosh McIntosh handled the initial versions of interior formatting and e-book conversion.

For the support of family and friends, I am humbled. My children, Reed Livingston Bates, Stacy Livingston VanBecelaere, and Kelly Michael Livingston, have tolerated and cheered my writing most of their lives. I hope this novel proves Mom isn't completely crazy.

Decades ago, my UMKC collegiate pal Megan FitzGerald Edgington typed and re-typed drafts of this story, my first "work of length" for my post-grad degree. I still remember when James C. McKinley, my professor at the University of Missouri, K.C., scribbled an "A" on the submitted version. I was ecstatic. Emerging writers need affirmation, and I remain grateful for Megan's long-ago support and Jim's critical tutelage, along with our shared laughter at Kelly's Bar in Kansas City over too many Guinness beers.

PERMISSIONS

Pat Dunlap Evans was born in Michigan but at age two, her family moved to San Antonio and later Dallas, Texas, where she was an age-group swimming champ. At South Oak Cliff High School, Pat was a high-kicking officer in the renowned Golden Debs drill team. She also typed copy as co-editor of the school newspaper and won a scholarship to attend Southern Methodist University.

An early marriage and the birth of three children plunged Pat into the world of motherhood, until the kids were mature enough for her to complete her bachelor's and master's degrees in English at the University of Missouri, Kansas City. The master's degree program offered an emphasis in creative writing. Pat quickly fell in love with the craft of creating characters, predicaments, twists, and turns.

Pat's first husband was a quarterback with the Super Bowl-winning Kansas City Chiefs. She used her experiences as an NFL wife for background in the novel *Out and In*: a mystery-thriller. After the marriage ended, Pat stressed her way as a single mom through a career in advertising, PR, and marketing in Dallas and Austin. A second marriage to Dr. Bill Evans of Austin enabled Pat to focus on her true love of writing novels.

Pat has published three titles: *To Leave a Memory*: a warm coming together; *Out and In*: a mystery-thriller; and *Backstory*: behind the scenes of a famous film-thriller. A sequel to *Out and In* was released in 2025. Titled *Ice and Fire*, the mystery is set on the Big Island of Hawai'i, where Pat and Bill resided for three years. The pair eventually returned to the Mainland, choosing Las Vegas, Nevada, as their new home.

Please follow Pat on Amazon, BookBub, Goodreads, or her website blog, where you can keep up with Pat's raves and rants. If you enjoyed this novel, Pat requests your star ratings. No book report needed. Simply leave as many stars as you like.

To contact the author:
patdunlapevans.com

A.M. CHAI LITERARY NEWS

Out and In, a mystery-thriller by Pat Dunlap Evans, received a "recommended" rating from *Lone Star Literary Life*, a notable literary news magazine based in Texas.

"The **well-written** tale starts quickly and with a bang ... Evans has a fine ear for entertaining dialogue, and the use of short chapters helps her mystery-thriller move briskly, even though the plot includes several side angles." — *Lone Star Literary Life*

"*Out and In* hits the ground at a full gallop, brimming with murder, gossip, self-centered and entitled characters, and more than enough drama to go around ... *Out and In* is a tangled web of secrets that is incredibly fun to unravel. — *Ruthie Jones "Reading By Moonlight" Blog*

Not to be outdone, the literary-suspense *Backstory: Behind the Scenes of a Famous Film-Thriller* received a nod from *Writers Digest*.

"Telling part of the story with the script format was a very interesting concept. It was different and ... entertaining all around." — *Judge, 9th Annual Writer's Digest Self-Published E-Book Awards*

See the free first chapter of *Out and In: A Mystery-Thriller* on the next few pages. The sequel, titled *Ice and Fire,* is also available at your favorite retail site.

OUT AND IN: A MYSTERY-THRILLER

Chapter 1: Alone in My Cell

The worst part about being in jail is you can't leave. That may sound silly, but I've had claustrophobia since childhood. Being locked inside anything sends waves of panic through my soul. As I pace and try to relax, I stare up at a high window, where I can see the sky and watch for clouds and birds. That window is the only reason I've not gone loony. But my neck gets sore from the strain.

I refuse to lie down on that steel bed as I wait for Ryan Ingles to get me out on bail. How I wound up here astonishes me. This morning, Detective David Reed of the Dallas Police Department showed up at my house with a search warrant and asked me to come downtown to answer a few questions.

"What about?" I asked blindly.

"Well, you heard about the murder of Luca Scarlatti."

"It's all over the morning news on TV."

"You are a person of interest."

"A person of interest? I know nothing about Luca's murder. I only heard about it this morning."

"Mrs. Donovan, I can cuff you. Or you can walk to my car on your own two feet. Which would you prefer?"

I shouted down the hall to my twin sons, who staggered out to see what the ruckus was about. Both looked hungover.

"Boys, call Ryan Ingles. Tell him I need an attorney. Now."

"Mrs. Donovan, you may have your attorney present. I'll let you make a call as soon as we get downtown."

"Am I under arrest?"

"Not yet, but we have a search warrant and want to analyze a few things," Detective Reed replied.

Two other police officers then went inside and headed straight for my bedroom.

"Where are they going?"

"Ma'am, we have a search warrant."

"Then search the house. I'm fine with that. But why do I have to come with you?"

"Mrs. Donovan, if you prefer I arrest you, I will do so. But I'd rather we handle this the easy way. Less paperwork."

After a suffocating, anxiety-producing ride downtown in the back seat of the detective's car, I was led into a stark green interview room with a gray metal table, four metal chairs, and a gigantic mirror I presumed from seeing in so many crime shows was actually where the district attorney and whoever else peered at me — a person of interest.

I paced and paced. It seemed like an hour before Detective Reed returned. He motioned me to a seat and then sat across from me. I could smell stale coffee and a breakfast taco on his breath.

"Mrs. Donovan, your fingerprints are all over the gun that shot the Maestro."

"My gun shot Luca? Impossible. It's in the trunk of my car."

"Not anymore. It's in our lab. It was found at the scene."

"Then someone stole it. And how do you have my fingerprints?"

"We took them off your cello."

"You dusted my cello?" I was appalled. "That's a very expensive instrument. I hope you'll pay for cleaning."

"Sorry, not on our budget. Especially since our search revealed some clothes tested positive for GSR."

"You went through my laundry?"

"Part of the job."

"What does GSR stand for?"

"Gunshot residue."

"Well, of course. I shot my gun Saturday morning. I bought it recently because of the threats. You know. About Cole and the missing Odyssey funds. One wild-eyed man showed up at our house several weeks ago. I felt very sorry for him, but I couldn't get his money back. I don't have any myself. Not anymore."

"You've got enough to buy an expensive weapon."

"Yes, for protection. I'm alone now."

"Poor little you."

"Yes, poor little me. I bought a gun, but I didn't know how to shoot the thing. So I've been taking lessons at Dallas Gun Club. They'll tell you."

"We spoke to them. They said you left about noon on Saturday. But I want to know where you were at ten o'clock Saturday night."

"I've told you. I was at home. I practiced my cello and watched the news."

"Your twins. Let's see, Avery and Shawn, right?"

"Yes."

"Were they home too?"

"For dinner. Ask them."

"We did. Avery said the two left your house about eight-thirty to go partying on Lower Greenville. They didn't get home until after midnight. Can anyone else verify you were at home?"

"Maybe a neighbor. The old man who lives behind us complains when I play my cello late."

"We'll ask him. You can bet on that. Tell me again about Saturday night."

"I played my cello and watched the news. There was a story about an Addison restaurant that burned. Channel 8. Sally and Jonas. You know, the pretty blonde and handsome Hispanic guy?"

"Channel 8 replays the same newscast at midnight. You could have seen it then."

"I was sound asleep by midnight. Besides, why would I come home and watch the news if I had killed somebody?"

"Maybe to see if there was any news about the Maestro's murder."

"I was making a joke. I didn't kill anybody."

"Mrs. Donovan, I want to believe you, but you need to give me every detail."

"There aren't any details. After the news, I put my cello away. Then I took a bath and crawled into bed. I was exhausted. I started a new job last week at the Verano Highland Park Funeral Home. My best friend Lena Verano hired me. I have to work now."

"Welcome to reality."

"This doesn't feel much like it."

"Witty gal."

I didn't answer that one, just sighed in exasperation.

"Back to Saturday night. Did you call anybody? Send e-mails or do a little Facebook?"

"No. I don't like Facebook."

"So, tell me everything you did on Saturday."

"Again? Like I said, I took a gun class Saturday morning. We practiced until noon, and then I left for a League meeting at Rebecca Claridge's house. She'll tell you, anybody there will tell you. Call Doreen Ingles or Tina LeBlanc. Call Keith Warren at the Metroplex Opera office. He brought a baritone to the meeting. I can't recall his name. He was from Italy. One of Luca's pals."

"Is a baritone the high voice or the deep voice?"

"Deeper than tenor, higher than bass."

"You must know a lot about opera."

"Your question was pretty basic."

"Pardon my ignorance. I'm just a lowly public servant."

"Sorry, I'm just frustrated."

"So, Keith Warren and a baritone were at the League meeting?"

"Yes, Keith gave us an overview of rehearsals, and then the baritone sang for us. The meeting ended about five. I picked up dinner on the way home."

"What kind of dinner?"

"Chinese food. I paid with a credit card. Call Howard Wang's. They'll tell you."

"Now, what would your having Chinese food tell me?"

"That I ordered a lot of things, which means I had to lug in a big sack of three different soups, three egg rolls, a combo *lo mein*, General Tso's chicken, and Lake Ting Tung shrimp, not to mention rosy-fried bananas, three Diet Cokes, and my purse. That meant I left my gun bag in the trunk."

"You're implying someone broke into your trunk?"

"They must have. How else could my gun have killed Luca?"

"That's what I can't figure out. Moreover, Mrs. Donovan, I can't understand why one of your fancy hairpins was found at the scene."

I reached to see if my hairpin was in its usual place. It was. "My hairpin? Like this one?"

"Not exactly. It was fancier."

"You're saying one of my hairpins was found in Luca's condo?"

"That's right."

"But I've never been to Luca's condo. I have about twenty hairpins, most at home, and a few in my purse. Here's another one, see? And there was a hairpin in my gun bag. When I went to shoot, the earmuffs didn't fit over my up-do, so I had to take my hair down and pull it back in a George Washington."

"A George Washington?"

I let down my hair and pulled it back. "A low ponytail. See? Like this."

"Very pretty. So, you're saying someone stole your gun bag, and there was a hairpin inside that someone later stabbed into the Maestro's leg?"

"Stabbed Luca's leg? What do you mean?"

"Your hairpin was stuck in the Maestro's thigh. Our lab is analyzing the pin."

"I don't understand. I've never been to Luca's house, much less put a hairpin — "

"Funny how the evidence says you were there. Your new gun killed Luca Scarlatti. Your hairpin was found in his leg."

"You've got to be kidding me."

"Nope. I'm a serious kind of guy. That's why, Marie Harris Donovan, I have no choice but to place you under arrest for the murder of Luca Scarlatti."

"But you can't. I didn't kill him."

"Mrs. Donovan, you have the right to remain silent. Anything you say may be used against you in a court of law. You have the right to consult an attorney before speaking to the police, and to have an attorney present during questioning, now or in the future. Do you understand? If you cannot afford an attorney, one will be appointed for you."

"I cannot believe this. Call Ryan Ingles."

"That's a high-priced pair of tassel-toe shoes for poor little you."

I tried to control my angry, frightened tears. "He's a friend. Ryan and Cole played college football together."

Detective Reed punched an intercom button. "Ginger! Mrs. Donovan is lawyering up. Get that hunk Ryan Ingles in here. And get another box of Kleenex. We're out again."

"Yes, Boss," Ginger sighed back through the speaker.

"Mrs. Donovan, I realize you've had a hard time, what with your husband's suicide. But you're not the only one. My wife and I lost twenty-five thousand in Odyssey."

"I had nothing to do with Odyssey. That was Cole's doing."

"Pretty Mrs. Quarterback doesn't know a thing. But somehow, you've still got that big house in Highland Park, don't you?"

I blew my nose again. "It's for sale."

"How about you send me twenty-five K when you find a buyer? If your husband hadn't flown off that high-rise, I would have arrested the bastard and given him a piece of my mind."

"Detective Reed, Cole screwed all of us. You, me, our friends, people we didn't even know. You've got to believe me. I did not know a thing about Odyssey."

"Mrs. Donovan, I've been a detective a long time, and there's only one thing I trust. Evidence. Ballistics prove your gun killed the Maestro. Your fingerprints are all over the gun. The clothes you wore had GSR on them. Your flowery gold hairpin was stuck in the Maestro's leg, and I'll bet our forensics group will have more to say about what was on that pin, besides his DNA."

"But why would I want to kill Luca?"

"A whole lot of people say you and the Maestro had a big tiff about opera finances and his sexual advances. So, the means, motive, and opportunity add up to Y.O.U."

"But this is ridiculous. No one will believe you."

"I don't think there's a jury pool in Dallas that wasn't affected by Odyssey. Your chances are not great to squeak out of this one."

"I refuse to say another word until Ryan Ingles gets here."

"Stay mum if you want, but I'll bet Terrance Nichols will start salivating as soon as he hears about your arrest."

"Terrance Nichols is a gossip and a liar. He and the *Dallas Daily Herald* are always being sued for libel."

"But everybody reads his column, 'Out and In.' Even my wife, and she's not in your artsy-fartsy crowd. Terrance will have your arrest posted in his 'Preview' online edition by 6:00 p.m. tonight. 'Course, you'll be in the slammer."

"You mean I have to stay in jail? But I have claustrophobia. I can't stand to be trapped."

"Poor little you. You're a guest of Dallas County tonight. In Texas, you only have to see a judge within forty-eight hours." He poked the intercom button again. "Ginger! Take Mrs. Donovan to Booking. She can talk to her high-dollar attorney after we've taken her prints and pretty picture."

~

Want to read more of *Out and In*? See patdunlapevans.com, and click on the book cover.

NOTES

www.ingramcontent.com/pod-product-compliance
Lightning Source LLC
Chambersburg PA
CBHW021311250626
47155CB00002B/482